"Just take it easy there," said a voice Neil had come to know well. "Turn around, but take it slow and easy. In case you haven't figured it out, that's a gun pointed at your back. And another at your girlfriend."

Neil turned around very carefully. "That's Dr. Singer. Don't hurt her. She's young and brilliant and has a great career ahead of her. Just keep remembering that I'm the one you hate."

Chet laughed. "Touching, your trying to save her. But just keep remembering that I'll do what I want. How smart she is means nothing to me."

Neil stared deeply into Chet Hamilton's gray-blue eyes. He saw there only a cold, distant hatred. It would not be too dramatic, he thought, to call those eyes demonic.

Then he heard Julie Singer's soft voice behind him. "What are you going to do to us?" she asked, almost in a whisper. "Are you going to kill us, too?"

CODE BLUE

CHARLOTTE WHITE

PINNACLE BOOKS
WINDSOR PUBLISHING CORP.

To Larry and Todd with love

PINNACLE BOOKS

are published by

Windsor Publishing Corp.
475 Park Avenue South
New York, NY 10016

First printing: September, 1992

Printed in the United States of America

Prologue

On Saturday, September 23rd, not so very long after daybreak, it finally stopped raining in Bainbridge, New York. The rain had started at around 10 P.M. on Thursday the 21st, and had fallen steadily since.

For the first time in many hours, the doors of St. Paul's Hospital were unlocked and unguarded. Much of the crowd that had gathered had scattered, but some stragglers remained—those who were curious enough, perhaps even concerned enough, to want to see the very end of the ordeal. A few more disheveled figures appeared in the doorway to the emergency entrance, and those who waited outside pushed closer for a better look.

"Back," one of the remaining uniformed officers warned them. "Get on back now."

"How many were killed altogether?" called a reporter with an irritatingly shrill voice. Although his query brought no response from the shadowy figures emerging from St. Paul's, he seemed undissuaded and shrilled again, "Are both Hamiltons still alive? Can you tell us that?"

A man of medium height stepped through the doorway and shuddered involuntarily. He winced slightly, as if the daylight hurt his eyes. With one hand he rubbed the silver stubble on his chin. The other hand rested on the arm of the woman at his side.

Turning to the policeman, he asked, "Is it necessary to talk to them?"

"It's not necessary, Doctor, but I think it'd be helpful if you could make a brief statement. Nothing fancy. They've waited a long time. A word from you and maybe they'd be satisfied and go away, hey?"

Neil Dvorak looked dubious. Nevertheless, he advanced a few steps, then stopped. "It's over," he said to the few remaining sleep-deprived and dripping members of the press. "Hospital officials are preparing a formal statement, and I'm sure that will be released to you soon. It's been a terrible ordeal, something that will be with us always. But it's over now. We wanted to get through this without losing a life. We didn't make it. It was out of our hands. Those of us who survived are left to get on with our lives, see what sense we can make of things. Please, that's all I have to say now. You *will* get your official statement very soon, but no need to wait. The plan is to fax you the statement. Thanks for keeping the vigil with us. God bless you all."

With that, he was gone. His tone and demeanor had been such that no one who had heard him protested or tried to prevent his leaving.

"Who was that again?" someone in the small crowd wanted to know. Another reporter had the answer.

"Dr. Neil Dvorak. He's a psychiatrist. Very well thought of in the field, I hear. People come to Bainbridge, hole-in-the-wall that it is, just because he's here at St. Paul's."

"Really? Is he foreign, or what? I thought maybe he had a bit of an accent."

"According to my information, he's not foreign. He was born in the United States, but I think his parents were from Hungary or Czechoslovakia or something. And he did his residency in Europe, studied under the best. At least, I think that's the way it was. I'll have to research the details."

"Me, too. And I guess I'd better get out of here and do some homework before this statement is released. Say, any idea who that was with him? His wife, maybe?"

"I have no idea who it was. His wife died a year or two ago, though. With that coat and scarf and the way she didn't ever look up, it could have been anyone. Say, wanna go to that diner around the corner for a cup of coffee before we hit the road again?"

"Yeah, sure, why not?"

With the ceasing of the rain, the newly risen sun gained brightness, sending its beams down on old St. Paul's. Somehow, the three-story, red brick building looked refreshed after many hours in the rain. Some of the grime had been washed from its surface, and the brick was still wet enough to give off a soft glow. Even the gray statue of St. Paul looked better. The sculptor had depicted Paul, at the time when he was still Saul, kneeling on the road to Damascus, his head bowed. As the three-hundred-bed facility became more and more out of date, its fate uncertain in a place and time with modern, high-tech facilities only an hour or so away, there were those, even among the hospital's own, who were heard to crack that the statue was finally pertinent. "It helps not to look up at old St. Paul's."

But employees of St. Paul's who were now able, at long last, to leave its walls were not making that sort of joke. No doubt their irreverent levity would return. At this particular time, however, not a person passing by the statue failed to greet it with affection. There were, they knew, those who would never be able to mock St. Paul's again. How easily their fates could have been exchanged.

"It's over," Dvorak had said.

But there were those who wondered if, in some obscure way, it had really only just begun. Only when Saul was struck blind had he been truly able to see, and only then did he become Paul. Funny how things work sometimes.

As the two tired reporters sat drinking their coffee in the run-down cafe, a St. Paul's ambulance went by. The only sound it made was the noise any vehicle might make as it went splashing through the excess water in the street. No need for sirens or flashing lights this trip. The stretchers it carried bore those who were beyond anything old St. Paul's, or any other hospital, could do.

Over? Maybe. Maybe not. All the great truths are paradoxical, aren't they?

Chapter One

"Victim of a knifing on the way in," rasped the radio/intercom that was the link between the ambulance and the Emergency Room of St. Paul's, a small Catholic hospital located in Bainbridge, New York. Bainbridge was about fifty miles away from the hubbub of New York City—fifty miles in actual distance, but an eternity in philosophy and lifestyle. "White male in his early thirties," continued the information.

"Street fight?" asked Stephen Cates, one of the two RNs on duty at 9 P.M., evening shift, on Thursday, September 21st.

"Nope. Domestic disturbance. Wife went after him with a butcher knife."

"Bad?"

"Nah. Mostly superficial wounds to the chest and rib areas. She just hit fat and bone, missed going between the ribs to any organs. My guess is he'll get by with a suturing job and some antiseptic treatment, but what do I know? If—"

"I know, I know," Stephen interrupted with a weary laugh. "If you were a doctor, would you be riding around in an ambulance at this time of night, right?"

"Right," the EMT agreed. "I said that to you before, huh?"

"Only a few dozen times."

The EMT's answering wisecrack was half-lost in a burst of static. Stephen did not bother to ask him to repeat it. The guy wasn't known for his brilliance or originality, so why bother.

With a sigh he went off to set up a suture tray, and to alert Dr. David Rasmussen that a patient in need of his services was on the way in.

"How soon?" asked Rasmussen.

"Ten minutes, outside," Stephen answered.

The sigh on the other end of the line was deeper than Stephen's had been. How many such sighs had he heard in his five years as an ER nurse? He couldn't even venture a guess. Being disturbed from sleep, hobbies, meals, lovemaking, or showering was part of what it was all about in a busy, thriving hospital—even one like St. Paul's that was small, off the beaten path, and not the most modern facility in the world.

"I'll be there in twenty minutes or less. If the wounds look deep, get chest and rib films *stat* if he isn't bleeding too much. Use your own discretion. I'll back you up. Sounds like there isn't much chance of a pneumothorax, but it's best we rule it out completely. Anyway, handle it. I know you can do it. You always have."

"Sure," Stephen said, "see you in twenty minutes. He smiled to himself at Rasmussen's compliment. Dave Rasmussen was one of the few staff physicians of whom Stephen was not wary or skeptical. If Rasmussen said, "I'll back you up," then that was exactly what he would do.

Before Stephen had the suture tray completely set up, another radio call came in. He listened intently as Jennifer Weiller, the other RN on duty, took the details. Three eighteen- to nineteen-year-old males had lost control of their car and ended up in a ditch. All appeared somewhat inebriated but none seriously hurt.

"MVA," Jennifer told him in passing.

"Yeah, I heard. At least it doesn't sound like *they*'ll need stitches. No open wounds, just bruised up a bit."

"But you can bet they'll all come in strapped to backboards and wearing cervical collars—and that we'll have to do a bunch of X rays, most certainly trauma C-spines."

"Such is the world of L&L, my dear."

"L&L? In this business I'm used to a lot of initials and abbreviations, but that's a new one to me."

The corners of Stephen's mouth quirked as he looked at no-nonsense Jennie. She was great to work with, a real professional who was especially good in a crisis situation. Sometimes, though, he wished she had a sense of humor. Not only did she never make jokes, but she frowned at his—not disapproving frowns, just enough of a change in expression to indicate that she really did not understand. Tall, with straight blond hair and steel-blue eyes, Jennie was very Nordic-looking, and would have been quite pretty if she learned to smile a bit.

"Liability and litigation," he explained. "Don't worry about not knowing it. I just made it up."

As if to prove his silent observation, her regular features pulled into a slight frown. "I see. Well, I suppose you're right. It's terribly sad that so many people sue doctors and hospitals. It runs up bills so just to be on guard."

Stephen smiled, not at her words—which were all too true—but at the very soberness of her. He was getting ready to have one more go at trying to make a joke, when one of the ambulances pulled to a screeching halt in front of the plate-glass doors and windows of the ER. Now that the vehicle was at its destination, the siren that had split the otherwise calm night was silenced, but the blue lights continued to flash—as they would do until the patient was unloaded—in order to give warning to observers that critical care was under way.

As Stephen pushed the button to slide the doors open, he heard a raised male voice saying, "I can walk, dammit. Let me off of this thing so I can walk."

"No way, buddy," said a weary EMT, not the wisecracking one who had radioed in but his partner, a veteran who had been riding the ambulances for well over twenty years. He had seen it all and heard it all, and one more belligerent patient wasn't about to shake his complacency. "When you've been checked by a doctor and that doctor says you can walk,

11

then you'll walk. Until then, just keep your butt on the stretcher, okay? Just as a favor to all of us."

The patient, a young-looking male with short reddish-blond hair, muttered unpleasantly under his breath but did cease his struggling. He remained passive while the two EMTs deftly transferred him from the ambulance into the ER, and off the stretcher onto a gurney.

"Doctor alerted?" the older EMT asked Stephen.

"Rasmussen's on his way. Till he gets here, anything we should know?"

With a shrug, the man handed over a copy of the ambulance run record on the patient. Stephen's dark eyes scanned the sheet. BP 108/70, pulse 100, respirations 40 and unlabored, temperature 97.8. Nothing really out of the way. The blood pressure was slightly low for a male of this size, but nothing dramatic. The drop, if it was a drop and not normal for the patient, could be the result of blood loss and/or near shock.

"He pretty much soaked a couple of towels before we got there, but that seemed to be the extent of the bleeding," said the EMT. "By the time we arrived, the flow seemed to be clotting up okay."

"I applied some compressive dressings, but they've remained relatively dry," explained the other EMT.

"Great job," Stephen commented. "We'll take it from here."

They nodded and were on their way. Another call was already lined up for them to take. It had been quite a night, and the shift wasn't over yet.

Swiftly but carefully, Stephen took the patient's vital signs again and recorded the findings. Stable. BP climbing slightly. No problems thus far.

Debbie Malone, the young, chubby, red-haired ER secretary, walked up to them, clipboard and pen in hand.

"I'll have to ask you some questions, sir, so we can get a chart set up for you, but the nurses will be right here seeing to your needs. Did someone come with you who might answer the questions for you, or do you want to do it yourself?"

"If it's gotta be done, I'll do it," he said between clenched teeth. "God almighty! Can't the paperwork ever wait? What kind of outfit is this, anyway? What's the matter, so worried about whether there's insurance that the questions can't wait?"

"Hold on there," Stephen said, placing a hand gently on the injured man's shoulder. "We understand that you're upset, so no offense taken. But we *do* have to have a bare minimum of information. It's nice to have a name. It's also nice to know if you're on any medications, or if you are known to be allergic to anything, so yes, there will be questions. Just take your time in answering, okay? No one's pushing you."

The white man and the black man engaged in a stare-down. The mutual dislike was quite palpable. Recovering quickly, Stephen veiled his eyes and let professionalism take over. He might not like the guy, but he knew he could not let his antipathy get in the way of providing courteous medical treatment.

With a cold, sidelong glance at Debbie, the wounded man attempted a shrug, then said, "Ask away."

"Name?"

"Hamilton. Chester T. Hamilton. I go by Chet."

While Stephen inspected the multiple stab wounds to Chet Hamilton's chest and left side, Debbie slowly and carefully elicited the needed information from the patient.

"How many?" the man asked Stephen.

"Pardon?"

"How many times did she stick me? I was so busy wrapping towels around me to stop the bleeding that I didn't count 'em. Stupid bitch! I can't believe this. I was asleep when she landed the first couple, but even after I was awake and tryin' to hold her back, she kept on comin' at me."

Stephen nodded, looking back at the wound areas. "Six," he said, trying to keep his comments as brief as he could without being accused of being surly. "As you've already figured out, I'm sure, the bleeding is pretty much under control. Dr. Rasmussen will be here right away and see what needs stitches. You're a lucky man, know it?"

Chet Hamilton sneered, then said, "Depends on how you look at it."

From where he stood, Stephen gave another look. It was easy to tell which two blows Hamilton's wife had landed before he was awoken. Those were the ones that would require suturing. All the wounds were only an inch or so long, presumably the same size as the upper portion of the blade of the kitchen knife. One cut just below the left nipple extended into the soft tissues and adipose layers. The second deep cut, stabbing a less padded area, was between the fourth and fifth ribs. The other wounds, which, from Hamilton's description, had landed after he was trying to fight her off, were relatively superficial, two to the anterior portion of the left chest and two in the left rib area below the deeper one. These two shallow wounds intersected each other to form a curious, crooked T-shaped wound.

"Much deeper," Stephen said softly, pointing at the left nipple, "and that would have entered the heart and made a nice tear." His finger moved in the direction of the more laterally placed stab wound. "And that one, with a slightly more upward slant, would have pierced the left lung. The way *I* look at it, you're lucky."

Hamilton shook his head. "I can't get over how stupid that bitch is. She never does anything right. Anyone else attacks a sleeping guy with a butcher knife coulda put him out for good. Not Marianne. She can't even land a knife at a still target good enough to do any real harm."

Stephen struggled to keep his disbelief from showing. The bozo actually sounded disgusted that his wife hadn't managed to kill him. Just when he thought he'd met all kinds, a new variety of weirdo always showed up.

Mission completed, Debbie slipped away to enter the information she had gathered into the computer. Hamilton was thirty years old, a mechanic by occupation, had a group hospital insurance policy, and lived in a mobile home park in an old, run-down section of Bainbridge.

Stephen applied the antiseptic solution, and took a hidden pleasure in watching his patient wince.

"Goddammit, man, take it easy! That burns."

"Sorry," Stephen said, although he wasn't sorry in the least. "That's all, but it had to be done."

Before Hamilton could retort, Dave Rasmussen walked up, still working at fastening the tie ends of his green surgical smock.

"Bad?"

"Nah," Stephen told him. "We don't have X rays yet, but nothing's really deep. I just finished the Betadine scrub. It took a bit of doing to get off the dressings that had been applied en route. He'd soaked them up a bit, but there's no real bleeding now, just a little oozing."

As he talked, Stephen stepped back to let the older man in next to the patient. He took advantage of the fact that the patient's attention was riveted on the doctor to study Chet Hamilton.

Not a bad looking young man. Handsome, really, in an angular-faced, Kirk Douglas way. Piercing blue-gray eyes, hair blondish to red. From what Stephen could see of Hamilton as he lay on the gurney, he was both tall and well built. Okay in the looks department, but too bad he had to open his mouth and let his ignorance show. Stephen felt he had the guy sized up pretty accurately: hot-tempered, bigoted, close to illiterate, and proud of it. Without knowing any more of the details, Stephen was satisfied that good ol' Chet had deserved whatever "that stupid bitch" had in mind . . . and probably more.

"As usual, Cates, you did a great job cleaning him up."

"Hey, most of the credit belongs to the EMT in the ambulance. He's the one who got the bleeding stopped."

"So I'll give him credit when I run into him. In the meantime, just say, 'Thank you, Doctor.' "

"Thank you, Doctor," Stephen said with a laugh.

"Now, I'll just infiltrate a little Marcaine along the wound edges, do the soft tissues with 0-0 chromic and the skin with 4-0 silk. Not bad. We can get by with Steristrips on the others." Turning to address the patient, Rasmussen barked, "Know how lucky you are, young man?"

Hamilton gave a snort. "That's what the other guy was trying to tell me. How come I don't feel so lucky, huh?"

Rasmussen's reply was slow and even, the flow of conversation not causing him to pause in his skillful needle work. "I suspect that's because you are dwelling on the discomfort and inconvenience rather than on how much worse it could easily have been. What happened here, anyway, Chester? Which did you insult, her cooking or her mother?"

The patient's laugh was short and singularly unpleasant. "Chet," he corrected. "I go by Chet. We had a little spat. Like all couples do. She gets a wild hair and gets pretty bad out of line once in a while, and I have to let her see what's what. Just like its always been. Only this time she does this. Out of the clear blue sky. Jesus, I still can't believe it! I mean, this broad waits till I was asleep — this musta been a good hour-and-a-half after the spat — and she attacks me with a butcher knife. Talk about nutsy! I mean, that knife is so old and blunt it's all she can do to cut through the bologna with it. What did she think was gonna happen?"

"I have no idea, *Chet*," Rasmussen said, his eyes never wavering from the wounds on which he worked. "Maybe you could ask her when you both calm down a bit. Still, don't go putting ideas in her head. Just thank your lucky stars that knife *was* old and blunt. Date of last tetanus?"

"Huh?"

"Tetanus toxoid. Have any idea when you received your last booster?"

"I dunno. Maybe as much as ten years ago. A guy bit me in a fight when I was twenty or so. Had to have stitches then, too, and I got a shot in the rear to go with it. If I had one since, I can't think when it woulda been."

Standing back to give his work one last inspection, Rasmussen nodded approvingly. His face bore the dreamy, satisfied look of an artist contemplating his masterpiece. Once he had made the decision, years ago, to take a surgical residency, Dave Rasmussen had never had a regret-filled moment. He *liked* being a surgeon. He *liked* the cutting and the sewing and the putting things back together. Sometimes, in contemplative moments, he felt a little sad that so much need for his work existed. However, a positive person by nature, he didn't dwell on that aspect of his practice much. As long as the need existed, and was in no way of his making, he was merely glad he could do the job.

"Then you're definitely in need of one," he told Hamilton. "I'll write you a script for an antibiotic and some pain pills. You got a regular doctor, you go there in a week and get the stitches out. You don't have one, come back here. Anything gets infected or gives you a whole lot of pain, see someone pronto. That's it for now. Cates here will give you a tetanus booster before you leave."

"No X rays?" Stephen asked.

"Nope. You were right on the money again. Nothing is deep enough to be a problem." Turning to the patient, he said, "The odds are a million-to-one against it, but you have any chest pain or breathing problems, you get somewhere and get a chest X ray, hear?"

"I hear," Hamilton muttered.

After Hamilton had received his injection, and been allowed off the gurney to go make some phone calls to arrange a ride home, Rasmussen looked at Cates, pushed his glasses up slightly on his nose, and commented wryly, "I wonder what the odds are on that marriage staying together."

Stephen shook his head. "One never knows. Frankly, what I saw of the guy didn't exactly warm the cockles of my heart. Sight unseen, *she's* the one I feel sorry for."

"You think he deserved what he got?"

Now it was Stephen's turn to grin, knowing his feelings were just that—feelings. "Call it instinct. Call it a gut reaction. Hell, call it bigotry. I could be wrong, but I doubt it."

"Ah, well, another day, another dollar. At least we may get paid for this one. The insurance coverage was a nice surprise."

Their conversation was interrupted at that moment by Jennie walking up to them, her expression even more grave than usual.

"We just got a call from the police station, Stephen. They're bringing in a woman in police custody. Her name is Marianne Hamilton. She's the one who . . ."

Stephen nodded, taking a nervous glance out into the corridor just outside the Emergency Room. Hamilton was lurking there by the glass doors leading outside.

"He seems to be looking for his ride. With a little luck, he'll be gone by the time the police get here. Why are they bringing her here, Jennie? Did they say?"

"She's been beaten. They say the right side of her face is pretty much a mess. But that's not the big problem."

"Come on, out with it, lady. I can tell you're upset about this one."

"They want us to notify a psychiatrist to come here and do an emergency evaluation. The office explained that they need to know if she's a real danger to herself or anyone else, and they need to know if she's mostly a criminal case or a mental case. Get the picture?"

Stephen nodded.

"I get it."

Rasmussen clapped each of them on the shoulder and offered an impish smile. "I'll be running along, kiddies. You two have fun here. I'll let you get some other fool out now. No stitches required on this one, I gather, and psychiatry isn't my strong suit."

"Go ahead, stick around," Stephen said wryly. "We can give each other proverbs to interpret."

18

"No way. Keep your glass houses and spilled milk. I'm out of here."

Seconds after Rasmussen left, Stephen glanced toward the door again and breathed a sigh of relief to see Chet Hamilton climbing into a red and silver four-wheeler. The vehicle then sped out of the St. Paul parking lot with a lot of excess noise, the driver breaking traction the way teenage boys and drunks do on a Saturday night.

"Figures," Stephen murmured with a shake of his head.

"What figures?" Jennifer asked as she approached him.

"Just talking to myself, more or less. Good ol' Chet Hamilton is gone, so we won't have to worry about the two of them going at it tooth and nail here, anyway. Get in touch with Dvorak?"

Jennie nodded. "He was at home. Of all the doctors, he's generally the easiest to find. If he isn't at the hospital, he's home. Must not have much of a social life, but I'm not complaining. Too bad we don't have to call him out more often, though, since he's so accessible."

"Yeah, well, I figure that will change one of these days. He didn't used to be such a hermit. He's been different ever since his wife died — gosh, that must have been way over a year ago, maybe closer to two years. He's not such an old guy. I predict he'll rally and show some life one of these days."

"Poor guy. I'd about forgotten about that. I hope he does find someone. He's really quite nice. He didn't seem to mind at all that I interrupted him. He said be was going to call Dr. Singer and see if she wanted to be here also. He said she was really interested in abuse cases."

"Dr. Singer? Who — ? Never mind, I just remembered. She's the psychiatric resident working with Dvorak, right?"

"Right. But she isn't *that* new. She's probably been here six months, anyway."

"True, but since I always work ER, I have minimal contact with Psychiatry Service."

"Except for tonight."

"Right. Must be my lucky night. Is the moon full? Did anyone look?"

"I don't believe in that superstitious nonsense," Jennie said, with an almost audible sniff.

"You think the pull of the moon on the earth couldn't possibly have an effect on us?"

"Absolutely not. We are each in charge of governing our own emotions. We must be on guard at all times against letting ourselves get out of control, then blaming it on the mood, or other people, or hormones, or whatever excuse comes along."

"You think it's possible to be *always* in control?"

Her gaze was level and unblinking. "Why, yes, Stephen, that's exactly what I think."

"What about falling in love?"

"Yes . . . what about it?"

She seemed genuinely perplexed at his question.

"I take it that you believe falling in love is also 'governable.' "

"We can't help having feelings," she said, her manner almost prim, "but we can help what we do. If one is attracted to somebody wholly unsuited, then one should retreat. Think of the countless number of people who have mated because of some chemical reaction that didn't last. We are given minds to help us override such emotions."

Covering his mouth with a hand to hide an involuntary smile, Stephen searched for something to say. It wasn't often he was at a loss for words, but he was definitely stumped at the moment.

"Are you laughing at me?" she asked seriously, trying to peek between his fingers.

He was saved from trying to come up with an answer to placate Jennie when an ambulance arrived with the three teenage boys who were involved in the accident. The ER grew busy as Stephen and Jennie bustled about tending to the shaken-up young men. Debbie Malone had some difficulty obtaining the information she needed, since the boys were nervous that their parents would be notified, but in the end they were all persuaded to cooperate.

Their minor cuts and bruises patched up, the three youngsters were taken up to the X ray Department, to verify Stephen's opinion that no bones were broken. And he and Jennie hardly had time to take a breath before a black and white police car pulled up outside the ER. On this occasion there were no sirens, no flashing lights. The emergency was over. The culprit was in custody, and there was no reason to believe her escape was imminent.

Both of the policemen who got out of the car were fairly large men, making the woman who emerged from the vehicle to walk between them seem even more diminutive. Stephen took in the small figure, head downcast, long hair falling about her face, who was handcuffed to the taller of the officers. At his side, he heard Jennie's sharp intake of breath. As soon as the three entered the building, Jennie made a small sound and turned away.

Stephen placed a hand on her arm to steady her. "It's okay, Jen. Just take it easy. I feel the same way."

"That's no criminal," she said in a strangled voice.

"My reaction, too. But it doesn't matter what we think. Let's just be nice to her and do what we can . . . which probably won't be a whole heck of a lot."

"Officers Duncan and Sullivan," the taller one said. He did not look very happy about his task. As if to prove his discontent, his next words were, "As luck would have it there was no female officer on duty—or even on call tonight." With a nod toward Jennifer, he added, "I'm glad to see you, ma'am, and I imagine Ms. Hamilton here is, too."

Ms. Hamilton did not look up, keeping any "gladness" to herself.

Taking a tentative step toward her, Jennie placed two fingers under the woman's chin, gently tilting it up. "Let me take a look at you," she said softly.

"I . . . I'm . . . well, it's okay. This isn't the first time my face has looked like this. It always gets okay."

"Still, we need to have a look. That's why they brought you here."

"I thought it was because they didn't know what else to do with me."

There was a glint in her eye of near humor, making Stephen's heart turn over.

"Can we get her out of those things?" he asked, nodding toward the cuffs.

"I don't know," Duncan said, sounding as dubious as he looked.

"Where's she going to go? What's she going to do? You can both sit just a few feet away from her, okay?"

The officers looked at each other. Sullivan, who was apparently the senior of the two, gave a slight nod. Within moments, the cuffs were undone. Jennie put an arm about the young woman and led her toward an examining table.

"I'm Jennifer. He's Stephen. We just want to look you over and see what we can do to make you more comfortable, until the doctor gets here. You don't mind, do you?"

Marianne shook her head, not seeming sure she meant what she was agreeing to. Debbie Malone stepped forward to get information from the policemen to set up a working record for Marianne Hamilton, relieving the patient from asking questions.

"What happened here?" Stephen asked softly as he looked into the young woman's face. The left side of it was very swollen and bruised. The eye wasn't quite shut, but undoubtedly would be by morning.

"It's okay," Jennie assured her. "You can talk. We're just here to see what we can do to help. You don't have to justify anything to us."

"My husband hit me," she said dully. "He was . . . well, he was starting in on the kids and I tried to get him to ease up. When I did, he started on me."

"I see. How much does it hurt?"

22

"My face? Not a lot. It's been worse."

"Okay, then, just open your mouth. I want to see that your jaw works okay and that there is no dental injury."

Her hair was a soft brown, worn straight and long. Her eyes were grayish-blue. The record said she was twenty-eight, but looking so sad, disheveled, and broken, she appeared somewhat older. Maybe she was pretty, maybe not. It was hard to tell, her face as disfigured as it was, her manner so dejected, her hair and clothes so rumpled and disarrayed.

"Does it hurt anywhere else, Marianne, anywhere else at all?"

"My shoulder. The left one. He grabbed me hard and slung me. When I try to lift it, it hurts."

"Okay. The doctor will be here right away. We'll have him check it out, see if we need X rays. Any signs at all to make you think you might have concussion? Blurred or double vision, headache, nausea, dizziness, numbness, or loss of sensation anywhere?"

She shook her head. "I feel a little sick, I guess. But I think that's the strain. And worrying about my kids."

"How many children do you have?"

"Three. Two girls and a boy. Alix and Brie are eleven and nine. Jacob is only six. They all depend on each other so. At the police station, a social worker came by. They called her, I guess. She said they'd see to the kids right away. I know that means foster care. She said she'd try to keep them together, but I know it'll be hard with three of them. I . . ."

"Let's just concentrate on getting you better," Jennie said. "I'm sure the kids will make it okay for a few days, until things get straightened out."

Marianne gave a dull, flat laugh. "A few days? Chances are, I'm going to jail. I just felt I couldn't take it anymore. There was no way out. I thought it couldn't get any worse, but I see now I was wrong."

"Shhh," Jennie said, patting the patient's hand. "I see Dr. Dvorak's car out there now. He's a kind man, a good doctor.

23

You'll get on well with him. Just trust him."

For the first time, Marianne Hamilton looked her full in the face. Her expression said the word "trust" was foreign to her.

"You have to trust *someone* to help you out of this mess," Stephen said, offering her a grin. "Might as well start with us and Dr. Dvorak, right?"

"Did I hear my name taken in vain?"

Stephen turned to face Neil Dvorak.

"You may have heard your name, but never in vain, Doctor. Nice to see you. We don't get the privilege of your presence much, here in ER."

"Too much, though, it seems to me. And a fine night you picked."

"How's that?"

"Rain. It started raining on my way over."

Stephen and Jennie both looked toward the exit. Sure enough, the rain was coming down quite heavily. "Oh, well," Stephen commented, "let it rain. It has to happen sometime. It's been a lousy night anyway, so we might as well save the good weather for better times."

"We have a choice?"

Stephen grinned. "Not so's I ever noticed. Dr. Dvorak, this is Marianne Hamilton. Her husband beat her up earlier this evening. Eye grounds seem okay, no loose or missing teeth. He slung her around by the left shoulder and she says it hurts. You want to check and see if we need to get X rays, before you do the other evaluation?"

"The one to see if I'm crazy or not?" Marianne asked.

"We'll get to that in a bit," the doctor told her. "Come on now, look into my eyes, Marianne—and I'm not trying to hypnotize you, okay? I'm just checking for concussion."

"But they already—"

"So we do it twice. That's the way things are at St. Paul's—thorough to the point of redundancy."

From the corner of his eye, Stephen watched Marianne Hamilton's reaction to Neil Dvorak. Somehow he wasn't surprised to see a flicker of understanding in her eyes. She was not quite, he surmised, in the same intellectual category as her husband. With her obvious intelligence, what was she doing with a loser like Chet Hamilton? No way to figure these things.

Careful in every movement, every word, Dvorak gave the patient a cursory physical examination, all the while taking in every move and response of hers, every change in expression or inflection, no matter how slight. Jennie stood in attendance to give Marianne moral support, as well as the physical support of the touch of one hand on another.

Temporarily relieved of anything to do, Stephen glanced at his watch. 10:20. Another forty minutes and he was off duty. Then what? Home, he supposed. Home, where Elizabeth waited with her martyred air. Nothing about him pleased her anymore. She even took the hours he worked as a personal trial, as if he had deliberately set out to inconvenience her.

"Elizabeth, you don't have to wait up for me," he had said over and over again.

Her reply seldom varied. "I might as well. You know you always disturb me when you come in."

"I try to be quiet."

"Perhaps. But I'm such a light sleeper."

How many times had they had that conversation? He didn't want to think about it. He didn't want to think about his wife at all, right at the moment. His attention drifted back to Dr. Neil Dvorak. Medium height, somewhat stockily built, Dvorak had closely cropped hair that was silvery-white, and his eyes were a piercing light blue, the coloration in striking contrast to his dark-skinned complexion. Stephen knew the psychiatrist was pushing fifty, but he looked a decade younger despite the whiteness of his hair. It was the way he moved, the way he carried himself, Stephen decided . . . quick, jaunty, emanating an energy. Yes, perhaps that was it — that, and those eyes that saw, knew, and, most of all, cared.

Standing back slightly, Dvorak said, "I'm going to let these two good nurses here see to getting you to X ray and back, for pictures of your shoulder and head. They'll also fix you up with some cold compresses for your face, as well as some Tylenol, if you want it for the discomfort. While you're doing that, I'll see what I can do about keeping you here for a bit. I'll see you in my office as soon as they're done with you. Dr. Singer will be here by then. She's going to sit in, and assist some, while we talk. If that's okay with you?"

"Sure. Anything you say. It doesn't matter."

"Of course it matters. But we'll talk about that later."

He scribbled orders for the X rays and the medication on nearby pads, then tore off the sheets and handed them to Jennie. After receiving a murmured affirmation that she would like the Tylenol, Jennie gave the patient water and the tablets, while Stephen alerted the X ray Department that they were on their way over.

Doubt and fear both registered clearly in Marianne's eyes as she looked to where the psychiatrist stood, talking to the two uniformed men who had brought her to the hospital.

"I'm going to make arrangements right now for a ninety-six-hour hold," Dvorak could be heard saying. "I see no problems with getting it."

"That mean we're free to go?"

"As far as I'm concerned, gentlemen, you are as free as the birds in the sky."

Although they clearly did want to leave, the older one seemed slightly apprehensive. Dvorak gave him a reassuring pat on the shoulder. "With the case as it is, my friend, the order will go through immediately."

He spoke with such authority that they couldn't doubt him. And they had been through similar events before. Dvorak had never been unable to obtain a hold when he wanted one.

Shedding the last of their reservations, the two men moved out into the rainy night.

"What's a ninety-six-hour hold?" Marianne asked Jennifer.

"A legal term. It means you can be held here legally for

26

ninety-six hours, involuntarily. If you leave, it's the same as breaking out of jail. Understand?"

Marianne nodded mutely. In a way, she understood. In a way, she didn't. At the moment, she wasn't even sure it mattered.

Before leaving the ER for his office in the third-floor psychiatric unit, Neil Dvorak glanced out into the parking lot. His lips curved slightly into a smile as he saw the form of a tall, slender woman making her way through the curtain of rain. He moved to assist her, as she entered the corridor, with her dripping London Fog raincoat and collapsible umbrella.

"Glad you could make it," he told her.

"Wouldn't have missed it for the world," she replied in her slightly breathless voice. Surveying the puddle of water she had created on the shining tile floor, she added, "Dvorak, this had better be worth it."

Neil smiled into the dark eyes of Julie Singer, enjoying her youth and beauty in the same way he admired a work of art or a fine display of nature. From the tips of her long, slender feet to the near-black hair she wore about chin length, straight and smooth, she was pleasing to the eye. Not only that, she was sharp and competent. In the few months that she had been at St. Paul's for her residency, she had proved to be a tremendous help to him. That wasn't always the case. He could recall several instances when the residents had been hindrances and pains.

"Singer, it'll be worth it. Trust me. Come on up; I think we're done in here, and I'll fill you in."

To the casual onlooker, the adoration in Dr. Julie Singer's eyes would have been obvious. But if Neil Dvorak had ever noticed the sparkling, he assumed it was due to her enthusiasm for her work. Not even a man as trained and experienced as Dvorak was infallible. There were times when he could be just as naïve—or downright dumb—as any person on the street.

When Marianne Hamilton was safely in the hands of the

27

on-call X ray technologist, Stephen took another look at his watch.

"Just about time to go home, isn't it?" Jennie observed.

"So it is. Jennie, got time to go sit with me for a while over a Coke or a cup of coffee before we call it a night?"

She looked slightly startled at the casual invitation. Although she had worked with Stephen Cates off and on ever since she had started at St. Paul's, he had never before made such a request.

"Of course," he said mockingly, studying her grave face, "if you'd rather not be seen with a black man . . ."

"That isn't it, and you know it," she said, bristling quite involuntarily. "I just thought you were married, that's all."

Stephen grinned. "I am. It's just that my wife doesn't understand me."

He had hoped Marianne would laugh. Instead, she turned a dull red.

"I — I —," she stammered.

Stephen laughed out loud at her discomfiture. "Marianne, I suggested a chat and a snack, not an affair. Are we on or not?"

"Sure," she said at last. "I haven't had a break all evening. I could stand a bite and a moment to rest before I go out in the rain. Besides, I'd like to see how Marianne Hamilton's X rays turn out before I leave, wouldn't you?"

"That I would . . . poor girl."

"Our joyriding boys got by without any fractures. Maybe Marianne will too."

"I hope so, but it wasn't really the state of her bones I was thinking about."

"I know, Stephen. Believe me, I know."

They walked off side by side, totally unaware of what the next few hours would bring, to them and to all of St. Paul's. Stephen Cates wasn't in the mood to go home, and he wanted to have one more go at making Jennifer Weiller smile. He would come to regret his decision to stay.

28

Chapter Two

"Fait accompli," Neil Dvorak announced to Julie Singer as he hung up the receiver.

She looked at him and smiled. "You make it all sound so easy. Think it would have been a *fait accompli* if I had been the one on the phone?"

"Why should that have made a difference?" he challenged.

"It *shouldn't*. It's just that somehow I believe it would have. All in all, it's still a man's world, isn't it?"

"I can't believe you're saying that, Julie."

"You know, I can't believe it either. But I've tried cutting through red tape a few times, tried fighting City Hall. Sometimes I even won. But they were never easy wins. You sit there so casual, so assured, and make it look like nothing at all."

"You're how old, again?"

Flushing slightly, as if confessing to a great sin, she answered, "I'm twenty-eight, as you well know. So get to the point."

"I was twenty-eight once, also. At that age, I was at about the same point you are. I wanted things to happen for me that couldn't possibly happen. Twenty years ago—and that's just about how long it's been—I couldn't have gotten a ninety-six-hour hold order that quickly and effortlessly. Nor could I have firmed up and received verification of a restraining order. Maybe—or no maybe to it, sure thing—I couldn't even have done it a decade ago. But I've been in this county and at St. Paul's for over ten years, now. I've paid my dues. The judges and attorney generals and others of that ilk know I only ask for something when it is needed and when it is justified. I used to have to fight, struggle, prove, even beg to get what I needed. As I said, I've paid my dues. Until the system changes, I don't have to fight the system anymore. That," he said, pointing at the telephone, "did not happen because I am a man, or because I am *somebody*, or because I have someone in my pocket. It happened because time and time again I have proven my worth, stood behind what I asked for. In time, it will happen for you. But only in time. And even then, only if you have patience, and go about things persistently without being imperious or demanding."

Julie heaved a deep sigh. "Wow, talk about being put in my place."

"Sorry," he said, his mouth twitching slightly, disproving his spoken words. "I didn't mean to lecture. Came off a bit tutorial, didn't I?"

She shrugged. "I'm here to learn from you. For another six months, you are my mentor. I can't always agree with what you say, but I do listen, and think about it."

"And this case . . . is this a time when you agree, or a time when you require time to think about it?"

Julie pushed back a strand of hair that had fallen across her cheek. "Never run out of questions, do you?"

"Never," he agreed, quite firmly. "Have you run out of answers?"

"Never," she mimicked. "Oddly enough, I do agree. I *am* impatient. I want everything to happen *now* and *my* way. When I stop to think about it, I see how irrational that is. Trouble is, I don't often stop to think about it."

"You will, my dear. You will."

The smile he gave her then caused her heart to turn over inside her. She wasn't sure at exactly what point her feelings about Neil Dvorak had stopped being professional and objective. All she knew was that it *had* happened. He was, as he had just pointed out, a generation older than she was. His daughters were grown, both only a few years younger than Julie herself. He was obviously still grieving for his wife. Not even once had he given any indication that he saw her as a desirable woman. Those were the obstacles Julie faced, the obstacles that frustrated her on a daily basis.

Not exactly bashful, neither was she brash enough to declare an interest in someone so disinclined to reciprocate. A thousand times she had told herself that she was becoming obsessed and that she should clear her mind of him. And a thousand times she had tried, her fantasies betraying reason each and every time. Can't he tell? she often wondered. How could a man so perceptive, so intelligent, so experienced in gauging human emotions, fail to recognize a woman in love — especially when he saw that woman day after day?

"A penny for your thoughts," Neil offered.

Julie started, only then realizing that her reverie had created a long silence in the office. However, she was saved from answering when the telephone rang.

"Great," Neil said, having answered it. "Apply a clavicle strap, give her some cold packs for her face, and have someone bring her on up." Turning to Julie, he informed her, "The patient is through in X ray. Radiologist isn't out at this time of night, of course, but the technician, the ER doctor, and the intern on call all agree there are no obvious fractures. She'll be along up here in just a jiffy."

"You sure she won't mind there being two of us?"

"I asked. She didn't seem to. If she shows signs of being uncomfortable, one of us can slip out. I'm not really expecting her to open up a whole lot at this juncture anyway. Besides, it's late. I just have to have something to put in the record to justify my actions."

"In case she gets away."

"Exactly. And for other reasons we don't have time to get into right now."

And indeed they didn't, for at that moment an LPN ap-

31

peared at the door. At her side was Marianne Hamilton.

"Come on in, Marianne," he said, his manner as courteous as if he were inviting her to tea. Moving hesitantly, she entered the carpeted room and, even more hesitantly, sat down in the chair Neil indicated with a sweeping gesture of his hand.

"Thanks," he said to the nurse, thus dismissing her. "Marianne, this is Dr. Julie Singer. Earlier, I mentioned to you that she would be here with us. Is that still okay?"

"Yes," she said quietly.

Without seeming to stare, Julie took in the young woman's battered face and slumping form. This was a woman of approximately her own age. Dwelling on the differences between them, Julie felt twinges of guilt — guilt at her good clothes, her expensive haircut, her high level of education, guilt because she often felt sorry for herself. Face-to-face with Marianne Hamilton, a woman virtually stripped of hope, Julie saw the problems of her own troubled past, her uncertain future, dim in comparison.

"We won't keep you long tonight, Marianne. I know you're tired. So are we. This is just a formality we have to go through, all right?"

She shrugged slightly. "It isn't as if I have a choice. I'm being committed, aren't I?"

"Committed? I don't know that I would call it that."

"Then what would you call it? I'm not here because I want to be, you know, Doctor."

"Why are you so resistant to being here? Maybe you'll find some help. It's pretty obvious you need help, isn't it?"

The distraught young woman's hand moved involuntarily to cover the battered side of her face more fully with the ice pack. This was perhaps, thought Dvorak, to hide the ecchymosis and swelling, but perhaps also to acknowledge the presence of her injuries, which were a symbol of her need for help.

"I don't think anyone can help me. The way I see it, all you can do is make things worse."

"Worse? How could it get worse?"

"He'll do it again. Or he'll hurt the children. He might even kill us. He's threatened to do exactly that, and God knows, I have no reason to doubt that he's capable of it."

"I see. And is the life you live now so well worth living? Is the life in which you've placed and kept your children, the example you've let them have as parents, is *that* such a treasured thing, that it must be preserved at all costs?"

Julie frowned down at the pad in her hand. What was he doing? Didn't Marianne Hamilton, at this stage, need sympathy and support? Neil sounded as if he were holding her personally responsible for the entire mess. Not that she was without responsibility, but . . .

"Are you saying," Marianne began, her voice rising above a mumble for the first time that evening, "that I should just have let us all be killed, that we aren't worth preserving? I wouldn't argue for my own worthiness, but my children . . . my babies? God! How can you sit there so calmly and smugly and suggest those three would be better off dead? Don't they deserve a chance? Don't they—"

She broke off then, unable to find the words to go on. Julie felt her own frown relax. Now she saw. Now she knew. How could she have doubted the master? Neil's comments had drawn a flash of anger, just as he had intended they should. Expecting compassion, Marianne Hamilton had been drawn by the psychiatrist's seemingly judgmental words out of her depressive state enough to display sparks of irritation and defensiveness. It was his opinion — and he was right, of course — that any emotion was better than despair, that any action was better than lethargy.

"That isn't exactly what I said, Marianne. And I think you know that. I wouldn't be fit to practice medicine, would I, if I led my patients to think their lives weren't worth preserving. In truth, I think quite the opposite. I am just saying that nothing worthwhile is ever accomplished without a risk. We all think we want certain things, yet we don't dare to reach out. We wait for the right time, the right circumstance. Do you see what I mean?"

She nodded down at her hands, folded in her lap, not looking directly at either of the doctors.

"I suppose I see. I do want out. Even more, I want *them* out of it. Maybe you're right about waiting for a right time that isn't going to happen. Maybe that's why I lost it tonight, knowing there would never *be* a right time. It's all so hopeless. No one knows, no one would believe . . ."

Just then, the dejected woman raised her head just enough to find herself looking into Neil Dvorak's remarkably blue eyes. What she saw there caused her to stop mid-sentence. *He* knew, and he would believe — not because he liked her or knew about her life, not because he had lived such a life himself, but because day in and day out he dealt with people like herself, people with so much ugliness in their lives, in their hearts. He knew, and he believed, because that was his job.

He nodded encouragingly at her, causing a half smile to form at the undamaged corner of her mouth. But as quickly as it had formed, that half smile disappeared.

"My children . . . what becomes of my children?"

Tears filled her eyes and she fought them back, her blinking rapid and impatient; there wasn't time for that now.

"You know the answer," he said gently. "They're in the custody of Social Services. They'll be kept safe."

"Foster homes. And they probably won't even be kept together."

"Marianne, you know that's out of my hands. And yours. But I've had some dealings with these people, and I'm sure they'll do the best they can."

Marianne stared down again at her folded hands. "Out of my hands," she repeated numbly. "I suppose it is, Doctor. But it's still true that I'm here against my will."

"I know that. That's one reason we had to obtain the ninety-six-hour hold order. All of us understand that you don't want to be here in St. Paul's Stress Center, not even for a few days.

That's okay. You don't *have* to want to be here. We have it fixed so that legally and practically you are forced to be here. But there is no law in the world that can make you like it. So tell me, are you aware — *really* aware — of the alternative to being here?"

"Jail?"

"You tell me. What do you think?"

"Jail. You're right. But that's going to happen anyway, isn't it? Unless you or someone decide I'm crazy enough to be institutionalized for years. Either way, I end up without my kids, right? Or maybe I could be found temporarily insane, huh?"

For a long moment they regarded each other: the thin and disheveled young woman and the neat, trim man in his middle years. A challenge was given, then accepted, without a word being exchanged.

"How does it feel, Marianne, to talk about your options?"

She squirmed in her chair. "Funny, I guess," she admitted. "Like it's an advantage to be crazy. Anyone who watches TV or reads the papers knows about people getting off by pleading 'temporary insanity.' Looking at it that way, being crazy sounds pretty good."

"And you . . . do you think you're crazy?"

She squirmed some more, then shrugged.

"Come on." His eyes and voice were gentle, kind, yet quite firm enough to let her know she would not get off the hook too easily. "Take your time, but give me an answer. Any answer."

"And if it's the wrong answer?"

He granted her a most engaging smile. "You can always change your mind later, can't you? That's the neat thing about playing mind games; it's all so variable. It isn't like doing math, where two plus two must always be four."

"Since you put it that way . . . but I've forgotten the question, Doctor."

"Do you think you're 'crazy'?"

"No, I don't think I am," she said very slowly, choosing her words with obvious care. "It happened in a flash, those few minutes. I felt so trapped, so enraged. I took the only way out I could see at the moment. I see now it was wrong, totally stupid. What I *did* was crazy. Is *that* what's meant by 'temporary insanity?' "

"Could be," he said in an offhand way. "Hard to say exactly. 'Temporary insanity' is one of those terms that means different things to different people in different situations. But you do remember what you did, what happened that led to your being here?"

She looked startled, surprised that he could think she might have forgotten an incident of such magnitude. "Of course I remember. I remember all of it."

"And?"

"You want to hear about it?"

He grinned slightly. "Just the highlights."

"Chet had been drinking beer all day. He started in on the kids first. I could tell it was one of those times when he could turn real ugly in a flash. Just one wrong word, and . . . Well, anyway, I tried to get him stopped before he got started. Sometimes it works to do that. Usually not, but I felt I had to try. This time, I was too late. It didn't work. When I saw how he was headed, I got the kids out of the house. That made him really mad, and he turned it all on me. This was about the worst time. I honestly thought he was out to kill me . . . and there were moments when I wished he would, just to have it over once and for all. Then all of a sudden, he just stopped. He just pushed me aside and went back to the couch with a six-pack and started drinking again. When he passed out or went to sleep—I don't know which it was—I looked at him, and I felt such *rage*. I wanted to collect my kids and leave without looking back. But I didn't dare, you see. He's always said he'll find us if we do that, and I believe him. We're not people to him. We're things . . . *his* things, his possessions. And no one takes anything that belongs to Chet Hamilton. So I went to the kitchen and got the best knife in there, and went back to where he was on the couch and tried to kill him with it."

Her narrative was chillingly deadpan. Neil and Julie were

both careful not to react in any judgmental way, just to seem interested and supportive.

"Why did the attempt fail?" Neil asked. "Could it be that you really didn't try, that you didn't really want him dead?"

"I tried," she said, lifting from her lethargy slightly, her tone bitter, her manner weary. "In those few moments, I did try. But my best knife wasn't much . . . old, and on the dull side, I guess. And I didn't know the best places to stab him, so I botched it. I just hit fat and bone instead of vessels and organs. He was bleeding something awful, but he was plenty strong, and fought me off without any trouble. There was a lot of blood, but I don't think I did him any serious harm."

"And do you still wish you had?"

Her eyes grew even more clouded and dull. "I don't want to be a killer, Dr. Dvorak. My poor kids have enough to grow up under, without knowing their mommy killed their daddy. Still, they'll know — they probably already do — that their mommy *tried* to do just that. So, yes, I wish him dead. I really do. Because, you see, that's the only way out for me . . . for us. Even if by some miracle, the law let me off the hook and set me free, what then? He's waiting for me. You don't know what he's like. But you will. He'll be here soon. He'll have to see me. He'll never let me get away without his punishment. It'll start right away."

"He can't get in here, Marianne."

"How can you be so sure of that?"

"Because there is a restraining order against him. And you're under the ninety-six-hour hold we talked about. He won't be allowed to see you while you're at St. Paul's. And that's not just for your protection, it's for his, also."

Marianne flinched at the implication she was a violent person. "I have no butcher knife here," she said, her voice barely audible.

"True. But where there's a will, there's a way, right?"

He was trying for levity, and the patient knew that. However, the smile he had tried for did not happen. Marianne Hamilton

37

was tired, so very tired, and she told him so.

"I can see you are tired. I'll see that you get to go rest in just a moment. First, though, tell me your plans. No details. Just a sentence or two. Then you can rest. And so can Dr. Singer and I. Even doctors get weary."

She nodded her understanding, but said, "I have no plans."

"None at all?"

She sat with her hands still tidily folded in her lap. So young, he mused, and so robbed of hope. He did not really expect her to be able to relate plans to him. For the duration of her marriage, her only plan had been to survive as best she could by staying out of her husband's way, by sidestepping his wrath whenever possible. Still, as a doctor, he felt there was hope. There was always a grain of hope. And, if she was to survive, she had to start hunting for that grain. It was his belief that if one makes a plan, then one just might act on that plan . . . and slowly find the way to freedom.

"I suggest you make a plan, Marianne. I'll see that some writing materials are put in your room. Write down some things you'd like to see happen. Don't worry if they don't seem very realistic or possible. We'll get to that part later."

Again, she nodded, but without seeming too interested in his suggestion.

"So I can go now?"

"You may. I'll talk with you again tomorrow. Perhaps Dr. Singer might like a chance to visit with you, and one of the counselors will start giving you some psychological tests. But that's all tomorrow. For the rest of the night, you may go rest."

He buzzed for a nurse to take her to her room in the Stress Center, the short-term psychiatric unit that had been his realm for over ten years. When Marianne Hamilton was at the door, ready to go with the waiting nurse, she turned back around and looked at him — which pleased Neil, for she had rarely made eye contact with either doctor during the interview.

"It won't work, you know."

"Pardon? You mean making a list of plans? Well we'll see. What I want is—"

"Not that," was her almost impatient reply, "keeping Chet away from me, out of here. It won't work."

"What makes you think that?"

"Because, sir, I know him."

One hand reached up again to touch her bruised face before she slipped out of the door to allow herself to be led to bed.

Neil Dvorak was not in the least a superstitious man, but nor was he one who discounted hunches and intuition. In that particular moment, an eerie feeling possessed him. The way she had looked, the way she had sounded. *Because, sir, I know him.* That had made the small hairs on the nape of his neck prickle. *Because I know him.* Not a scientific explanation — not in the least. Yet it was an explanation in which he believed.

"You look . . ." Julie started, breaking into his reverie.

From across the room, he smiled at her. "I look what?"

"I don't know. I couldn't find the right adjective. Puzzled? Lost? Dreamy? Frightened? I'm not sure."

"Maybe all those adjectives are applicable," he said thoughtfully. "I just . . ."

"A goose walked over your grave? That's an expression my grandmother used to use."

"I've heard it. And I think it fits."

"You don't think she's right, that her husband can get to her here?"

"I know *she* believes he can."

"That's because," Julie said, "he's held a reign of terror over her for years and years. She sees him as a sort of omnipotent Satan. But in truth, he's only one man. Counting patients and staff, even at this time of night, there's at least three hundred people in-house. What can one man do against three hundred?"

Tongue-in-cheek, he reminded her, "Some of them are sick or injured."

"True, but still . . ."

39

"I'm sure you're right," he said gently. "I just had a bad moment, that's all. Now, overall, what do you think, as a first impression?"

"Pretty much typical, isn't it? Sad, but still typical. She's his superior in intellect and moral fiber, which he's all too well aware of. To boost his own self-image, to prove to the whole world that he's the man, the boss, he abuses her."

"That may be his reason. What is hers, for choosing someone like that, for staying?"

She smiled crookedly. "That gets a bit more complicated, doesn't it?" Bending toward him slightly, she went on. "You've heard of the Elizabeth Wiggins case, I assume. Perhaps this is . . ."

On and on they talked, mindless of the late hour. Neither of them had anyone waiting at home, and for both of them times like this were rare — the opportunity to match wits with someone their intellectual and educational equal.

In another part of Bainbridge, while Marianne Hamilton was having her body and mind tested, Chet Hamilton was not idle.

The trailer court in which the Hamilton family lived was a run-down eyesore. On a more or less routine basis, city authorities would threaten the owner of the crowded mobile home park with total closure. In response, the owner would chop down a few weeds, thin out the trailers a bit, move out some junk, and slap a little paint here and there. The battle had persisted for years. Ortman Trailer Park was not a pleasant place to live. Even so, it was always full — full because it was the cheapest place in the area.

Chet Hamilton made pretty good money as a mechanic for an auto dealership. Even so, he had a wife, three kids, and some expensive tastes, not the least among them being his drinking and smoking habits. A job for Marianne was out of the question. They had tried it a few times, but when she worked, the danger of her independence was much too possible. Accepting the dismal trailer and its surroundings as her lot, Marianne hadn't tried for independence lately.

"Man, this place is a dump," said Mick Hamilton, his now bloodshot eyes taking in the shabby interior of the trailer. It wasn't dirty, just crowded, old, and awful. The carpet was worn out, the walls stained, the furniture torn and mismatched, and every available corner and surface was stacked with clothes, toys, books, papers, and numerous miscellaneous items. With five people and their belongings in such a small area, there simply was not room to put everything away neatly.

Chet shrugged and took another drink of his beer. "Clean, ain't it?" he asked his younger brother.

"What I can see of it. But it's still a dump. No wonder Marianne knifed you. I might, too, you make me live here for long."

"You've lived worse places, Mickey-boy," Chet reminded him. "So have I."

"Yeah, well, don't remind me. I got a real nice place now."

"You gonna marry Pam?"

"I dunno. Not soon. Why?"

"Girl like that . . . got a good job, lets you move in her nice apartment with her, lets you use her car. Bet she even goes down on you whenever you want. Pretty cushy setup."

"Exactly," Mick said with a grin. "Why spoil it?"

"Married, it wouldn't be so easy for her to kick you out, you do something she don't like."

"No sweat," the younger Hamilton replied lazily. "Pam's okay. But she's not the only woman out there. She kicks me out, another one will take me in."

He wasn't bragging. It was fact. Both of the Hamilton brothers had been blessed with extremely good looks. When calm and sober, they could also be very charming. However, they were both hot-tempered, especially when drinking . . . and they both drank quite a lot.

Mick reached for another can of beer. "Speaking of women,"

he said, "what you going to do about that woman of yours, big brother?"

Chet's eyes narrowed. Mick was beginning to get on his nerves. He had a way of doing that. In some ways, he thought, the guy was the salt of the earth. One call, late at night, and he dropped whatever he was doing and drove all the way to St. Paul's to pick Chet up and see him back home. Now he was sitting here with him when he could be back at that fancy apartment with that skinny little blond chick ready to jump his body. Mick was all right. Chet kept reminding himself of that.

About the last thing he needed was to alienate Mick. Brought up by indifferent and troubled parents, the boys had learned to rely on each other. Throughout childhood, each had been the other's only constant. It was still that way.

"Guess right now, I don't do nothing," Chet said, after a long silence. "Cops told me I couldn't go near her. 'Restraining order,' they called it. Said it was to protect me as much as her. Only now I can't go near the kids either. Welfare office took 'em over. While I was at the hospital being patched, they just went and got 'em at Sue's place—Marianne had took 'em over there before me and her got into it so bad. I come back, and it's like, there's nothing. No wife, no kids. And the cops tellin' me I got no rights to them. Spooky feeling, you know."

Mellowed out by the beer, Mick nodded in agreement. He felt so sorry for his brother that he could have almost shed a tear.

"Hell, Chet, maybe it's all for the best. You can just walk away and start over. You can do better than that broad, anyway. I used to think she was good-looking, but I haven't thought that for a long time. A real drab, that's what she is. With what she did, they'll put her away a good long time. Brats are being taken care of, courtesy of the great state of New York. I can introduce you to some women who'll—"

"Hey, come on, who you think you're talkin' to, kid? *You* fix *me* up with women? Who needs the help? Who taught you most of what you know, huh? Being married ain't quite the same as

42

being dead. Dames come on to me all the time. And I don't always say no."

"Just enough to keep 'em guessing, huh?"

They both laughed uproariously, as if some great witticism had been shared. Still laughing, they looked at each other in appreciation. Not quite mirror images, but close enough. Mick was slightly shorter, a bit more stockily built, and his hair was a lighter red, with a tendency to wave, whereas his brother's was very straight. Still, for all those differences, their shared genes were clearly stated in their features, eyes, and mannerisms.

When they were through laughing, Chet drained the last of his beer, and took another. He popped the cap, took a deep swallow, sighed in appreciation, and said, "She won't get away with it, you know."

"Huh? Oh, you mean Marianne. Of course she won't get away with it. Like I said, they'll put her away good and proper."

"I wasn't thinking about what *they'd* do to her. I was thinking about me. Michael, my man, you asked the question yourself—what am I going to do about her? She'll pay. That's what she'll do. Pay, and pay dearly."

Wincing, he reached down and patted the compressive dressings over his stab wounds.

"But if you can't get near her, how you gonna make her pay, huh?"

"Don't know yet." With that, Chet got off the sagging couch, stumbled to the kitchen to find the telephone book, and began leafing through it. "Right now, I'll call her. That's what I'll do."

"Let me do it," Mick said, taking the directory from him. "You sound drunk. I'll make the call."

Using his charm, playing the role of concerned relative to the hilt, Mick was able to elicit the information from the Bainbridge Police Department that Marianne had been transferred from the city jail to St. Paul's Hospital.

When the information was relayed to Chet, he mouthed the word "hospital" in drunken disbelief. "I didn't hurt her much. A black eye, a few bruises on the face. But not bad enough for no *hospital.*"

Mick shrugged. "All I know is what the cop that answered the phone told me."

"Then we'll call there and I'll talk to her there. Look up the number. This time *I'll* do the calling. St. Paul's, huh? Damn, I was just there."

While Chet dialed the number and initiated his conversation, Mick sat and watched. He watched his older brother go through the nice manners and charm bit, then he watched his face and neck flood red with anger at what he heard.

"What do you mean, you can't give out that information?"

"Exactly what I said, sir," said the switchboard operator. "The information is confidential. I can't tell you anything at all."

"Not even her room number? You can't even connect me to her room and let me ask her myself if she wants to see me?"

"No, sir, I'm sorry, but I can't. No one is allowed to see her. She's to have no visitors. No one at all is allowed in."

"I'm her husband, dammit."

The girl swallowed hard, glad that this was only a telephone call instead of a visit in person. Gently, quietly, hoping to turn away his wrath—hadn't she heard somewhere that it worked?—she said, "I'm truly sorry, but family members aren't allowed in either. No one."

"You let me talk to the administrator. Right *now.* I'll hold."

"Mr. Hamilton," she said, trying again, "it's late. The shift is almost over. Administrators and people like that aren't here at these hours. Call or come by in the morning, and I'm sure someone can explain it to you. I just make a few bucks an hour. No one explains anything to me. I just do what I'm told."

"You haven't heard the last of me, sister," Chet replied, the words of warning followed by a string of obscenities.

"What now, Chet?" Mick asked, when the receiver had been replaced in its cradle.

"We go see her."

"Huh? But the broad just said—"

"What the broad said don't matter to me none. Marianne's my wife, and I got rights. No one anywhere tells me when I can see her. Not the law. Not the damned hospital. No one."

"So what you got in mind, man?"

Chet smiled, the lax and happy smile of a drunk. "I ever show you my special tool box, little brother?"

"I don't think so. What's so special about your tool box?"

"That's what I'm gonna show you right now. Come on out back."

As Mick removed himself from the chair, he reached for another beer.

"Take it easy on that stuff," his brother warned.

Mick reddened with anger. "Look who's talking! You had more—"

"Don't get upset, Mick. No lecture. It's just that we got a big job ahead of us. We better do what we can to sober up so we know what's goin' on."

The sullen Mick was not to be so easily pacified. "How do I even know I'm gonna be in on this? You haven't even told me what it is you got in mind."

"But I will. Just leave the beer and look at my tool box. After that, you wanna come back and just drink, I won't stop you."

"And you?"

"I'm going to see Marianne. I could use your help. But if I have to, I'll go it alone. No one—"

"Yeah, yeah, I know . . . so let's see this tool box."

Together they stumbled through the trailer and out of the ill-fitting back door into the dark September night. Chet fumbled around with the key ring until he found the right key to fit the lock to a small metal storage building that sat next to the trailer, almost abutting it. It blocked one of the windows so that when the three Hamilton children looked out the window of their bedroom, they saw the storage building, nothing more.

"Nice shed," Mick commented. "Been a while since I was out back like this. I'd forgotten all about it."

"This baby caused quite a little fight," Chet recalled with a grin. "Besides what it cost, my old lady said the kids needed a place to play, and that this baby'd take all their room up. But you can see who won. If a man can't have his own way in his own . . . well, there ain't gonna be any days like that for *this* man. I'm a mechanic, and a mechanic has tools. He's gotta have a place to put them."

Finally, after at least four futile attempts, the key got fed into the proper slot on the lock, then Chet pushed the door open. Mick whistled appreciatively at the wide assortment of hand and power tools.

"It *has* been a while. You've added to the collection. You must have a fortune in here."

"I spent enough."

"And some courtesy of Altmann, hey?"

"Hell, why not?" Chet said, shoulders thrown back, tone bragging. "They waste so much money at that place they'll never miss a little ol' tool now and then. Head guy comes around and goes something like, 'Boy, we sure been goin' through the torque wrenches lately,' and I go, 'Ain't we, though? Ain't worth shit, stuff they put out now for us to use.' "

"And they don't suspect a thing?"

"Who knows? Who cares? They can suspect all they want, but they can't do nothing but talk and complain until they got some proof. And I'm just a little too slick for them to have any proof. Anyway, we ain't out here to look at wrenches and ratchets and whatnot."

"So, show me what's so special out here."

After another faltering battle with a lock and key had been won, Chet threw open the lid to the silver-and-red metal tool chest bearing a "Snap-On" label.

Taking one step closer, Mick stared down at the contents. "Holy shit!"

"Exactly. Said it was special, didn't I, huh, man?"

"Yeah, but still . . . holy shit!"

Face beaming with pride, Chet stepped back while his

46

brother surveyed the mini-arsenal inside the tool box. Just about anything anyone would need to do battle was there. It was a small store of supplies, but a complete one. Three rifles, three or four handguns, box after box of ammunition, several knives and shivs, hand grenades, sticks of dynamite, small bomb-and-detonator setups, cans of mace, smoke bombs . . . at least one of just about anything that could be used to terrorize or control.

"Hey, man, fantastic!" Mick commented. Then, quite suddenly, the bright expression faded and the sullenness returned full force. "So, what's been the big secret up to now? If we're partners through-and-through, how come the hushed-mouth bit? You didn't trust me to know it's here, or what?"

"Trust you? Man, I'd trust you with my life. It's like you just said, Mick — we're brothers, through-and-through. Truth is, I ain't had it long. It was more like a surprise for you than a secret I was keeping from you. Each times I'd get hold of something new to put in there, I'd think, 'Is it time to surprise old Mick yet?' Then I'd think how I wanted to get just another thing or two to make it complete, you know. Lots of times I'd look in here and imagine how you'd react — like you just did when you said, 'Holy shit,' — and I'd grin to myself and wanna tell you right then. But I wanted it to be the best. And it is, right?"

Not totally convinced, Mick was nonetheless intrigued enough by the threatening display before him to want to start handling it. He reached down and lifted an M-1 rifle out of its resting place. With the motions of a man caressing a lover, he ran his hand up and down the barrel.

"Where the hell did you get all this shit?"

"Here and there. You know those *Soldier of Fortune* magazines I get?"

"You know I do. I look 'em over pretty good when I'm here."

"They pretty much tell you what you need, give you some ideas on where to get stuff. Lots of the stuff is floating around, you just got to know where to look. Survivalist groups, you get in good with them people and they'll give you some real tips."

"Yeah, well . . . you got a lot. There's some mean-looking stuff here."

"*We* got a lot," Chet corrected.

"Huh?"

"*We*. It's half yours, bro. I built it up for the both of us. Ain't much either of us can do alone. But with each other and what we got here . . ."

Mick nodded. Chet did not need to complete the sentence. They both knew exactly what he meant. Maybe there wasn't enough here for them to control the world, but they could go for one segment of it.

"So, what you got in mind?"

Chet mulled the question over.

"We're going to St. Paul's, you and me. And when we leave, Marianne's leaving with us. I don't need the law to deal with what that bitch did to me. I'll deal with her myself."

"We'll never get in with this stuff."

"Won't we? Not all of it. No need for all of it. Let's go get some food and coffee down us. We'll plan what we need."

A sandwich and a cup of coffee later, the red-haired, florid-complexioned brothers had sobered slightly.

"I don't know," Mick said. "Sounds kind of drastic."

"Drastic? Hell, yes, it's drastic. But taking my wife and kids away was pretty drastic, don't you think? They'll be getting nothing but what they deserve."

"The hospital? There's sick people there. They didn't do nothing to you."

"Someone at that friggin' hospital decided they had the right to tell me I couldn't come see my wife, said I couldn't even be told the number of the damn room she's in. If they're so worried about these sick people, then maybe they'll listen to reason when we tell 'em how it's gonna be. You in or not, Mick?"

When Mick did not reply immediately, Chet lashed out at him.

"You don't want in, then get on home to that fancy apartment and your ol' lady. *Your* world's okay . . . no reason to put

48

yourself out just because mine's come apart on me."

When Mick replied, his voice had a whining quality. "You know I won't fink out on you. Like we said, we're brothers through-and-through. But I never did anything like this before. It could be the end, man."

Chet shook his head. "We'll handle it better than that. Sure, we'll have to get out of state, start over again somewhere else, but what's the big deal? We got anything here we can't have bigger and better someplace else?"

Mick thought it over. Pam was okay, but not fantastic. Same thing with his present job. Maybe Chet was right.

"And if we don't handle it exactly right, what a way to go, huh?"

"Exactly. You're in, then?"

"I'm in."

To seal their pact, the two men clasped their hands together momentarily.

"You still hang around with that guy who has a wife that works in a hospital, Mick?"

"You mean Ken Robertson? Yeah, we get together weekends some and bum around. Why?"

"His wife's big, right?"

"Real big. I'll bet she weighs a good two hundred pounds. You gonna tell me what you're leading up to, Chet?"

"We need hospital clothes. Think you can borrow us some?"

"What kind of clothes?"

"Anything that'll help us fit in and not get noticed. White jackets. Those pajama looking things they wear. You know what I mean?"

"Scrubs," Mick said thoughtfully. "I dunno. I'll call and see. But you gotta know, Chet — I don't trust the guy all that much. And I don't trust his wife at all. They get any wind of what we're doing, they'll rat. I'll bet on that."

Chet shrugged his shoulders. "So let 'em rat. By the time they've ratted, the whole world just might know it's us anyway.

Who cares? This is our chance to make the headlines, baby brother."

"Yeah?"

"Yeah."

"Okay, so I'll call Ken, then."

The conversation that ensued on the telephone was brief and to the point. Robertson's wife was at work, but he'd get out some of her older things for them to borrow. The man did not ask why they needed the scrubs, nor did Mick volunteer a reason.

"We'll be by to pick 'em up in thirty minutes or so," Mick said. "Thanks a million. I owe you one."

Back out in the tool shed, the brothers deliberated over which of the weapons to take with them to St. Paul's. They finally decided on a handgun and a sharp knife for each of them, ammunition for the snub-nosed revolvers, and two of the small explosive devices. Once more, Mick ran his hand lovingly down the M-1.

"Maybe next time," Chet told him. "Too long to hide for this deal."

With obvious reluctance, Mick agreed and allowed the M-1 to be locked away. They placed the items they were taking with them in a dark blue nylon duffel bag.

Moments later, they left in Mick's pickup truck, so fired up with liquor, anger, and lust for action and adventure that they did not really stop to consider the odds or the consequences. Chet had said they would get away, and that was that. Later would take care of itself.

Chapter Three

"Why do I get the feeling that I might as well have arranged to spend the night at St. Paul's?" asked Dave Rasmussen.

"Maybe," replied Mary Riley, testy veteran RN, "it's because it's your third time out this evening. Or so you say."

"So I say it as it is, I'm afraid, Mary, my love. Sadly enough, it's documentable. First the appendectomy. Then the stitch job on the guy whose wife went after him with a butcher knife. Now this. I'd barely gotten back home and into my jammies. Needless to say, my sex life is a wreck."

Mary gave a loud snort of disapproval, as she always did when the subject of sex was raised. It wasn't that she was a prude or easily embarrassed. Quite the opposite. In her forty-year career as a nurse, she had proven equal to any occasion, never once displaying any squeamishness. It was just that as a no-nonsense celibate lady, she had long ago decided the entire business of sex caused a whole lot more trouble than it was worth.

Since thirty of Mary's forty years had been spent in the employment of St. Paul's, she had her choice of shifts, and her choice was, as it always had been, night shift. Over the years, she had so frequently been heard to say, "I want no part of evening shift, and even less of day shift," that it was almost her motto. "Night Shift Queen," she was laughingly called, and jokes about her reign over the dead of night were numerous. If

Mary knew of the jokes, and she probably did, being no fool, she paid them no heed. She viewed jokes as she did sex — totally unnecessary — although she would have conceded that she was more tolerant of jokes, since witticism did not produce unwanted babies or venereal diseases.

"So?" she retorted archly. "I don't think your patient is going to be having much of a sex life for the next few weeks either."

With a sigh of acceptance, Dave turned his attention back to the middle-aged man on the gurney. In a few easy strides, he was at the patient's side.

"Hanging in there, pal?"

"Barely. The shot hasn't helped much, Doc. The pain's pretty . . ."

Rasmussen patted the man's shoulder.

"It looks like we're going to have to do surgery, Bill. I'm sorry. I know you hoped to avoid that. We gave it a good try, but the conservative approach just hasn't worked."

"You can't send me home with more pills, eh?"

" 'Fraid not. Actigall has proven very effective for many. It just wasn't for you. We knew you had a gallbladder full of stones. Now, from your symptoms, I'd say you have at least one lodged in the biliary tract."

"And?"

"Nothing's getting past it, my friend. The bile is backing up. Hence the pain. You're getting a yellow look to you, you know. Not bad yet, but there is a definite icterus to the sclerae — that means the whites of your eyes are yellow — and your skin is more sallow-looking than I remember it. At any rate, we should have the lab tests and X rays back in just a few minutes. Till then, well . . . just hang in there."

"And if I don't have the surgery?"

"I think you know the answer to that as well as I do, Bill. If I thought it could wait till morning, would I be out here? I'd rather stay in my bed till a normal hour and get you on the schedule as a regular setup, but it's truly my opinion that we don't have that many hours."

"Dammit, I . . ."

"Sure, sure, I know. Look, I'll have someone get your wife in here from the waiting room, then I'll go over all the risks and expectations and alternatives — the whole bit — with both of you. Be thinking up your questions. Now is the time to ask them, okay?"

"Okay." The reply was grim and terse.

Walking away from the patient, Rasmussen took Mary Riley out of the patient's hearing range and said, "Alert Surgery for me. This one won't go till seven or eight o'clock in the morning."

"Cholecystectomy?"

Dave nodded. "Probably a complicated one. I'll need full intraoperative cholangiograms. If my guess is right, he has multiple loose stones in the biliary tract. He's badly obstructed and beginning to jaundice. There's danger of rupture of the biliary duct."

"Then I'm off and running."

"You're a great gal, Mary. Too bad I'm already married, or . . ."

The look Mary gave the surgeon would have withered a man of less ego. Rasmussen, being Rasmussen, merely laughed heartily. He enjoyed Mary, he always had. So many people were willing to kiss his ass because he wore those magic initials after his name that he found those like Mary, who refused to pay homage, refreshing — refreshing, and perhaps necessary to keep his opinion of himself in its proper perspective.

It was twenty minutes past eleven. Except for a few evening shift people who were late leaving, and a few night people who were late coming, the shift change at St. Paul's had been accomplished.

The flu and pneumonia season had not yet started up full force, and the three-hundred-and-fifty bed hospital was running a relatively low census, there currently being one hundred and twenty-three patients in-house. Also in the building were approximately forty St. Paul employees, the bare minimum needed to keep things going until the daylight hours, when all departments would be fully staffed and things, instead of humming along, would be jumping.

Outside old St. Paul's, two young, reddish-blond young men drove slowly by the front entrance in a red-and-silver four-wheel drive pickup truck.

"Look at that crazy statue," said the driver, the younger of the two men. "I never saw a statue like that. Only ones I ever saw, the people were standing up. What's he doing, anyway?"

The older brother, whose biblical knowledge was no greater than Mick's, gave a shrug. "Who knows? Some artist's idea, I guess. But who cares? Get the hell out of here and on out back. Front doors are locked after visiting hours, anyway. There's gotta be a back way, a door where employees come and go."

Mick applied his foot heavily to the accelerator, causing the powerful engine to roar lustily.

"Maybe we shouldn't be so loud, and draw attention to ourselves?"

"I thought we was here to get noticed," Mick challenged.

"That we are. But maybe we better wait till we get on the *inside,* and get a few things done."

"Like plant the bombs?"

"Egg-zactly. Like plant the bombs."

"Great, Chet, baby. But no sweat about the truck. We'll park out back, and the way we're dressed, ain't no one gonna connect us with the truck that went by the front. You wait and see."

Just a few seconds later, Mick had selected a parking place in the far corner of the back parking lot. He was proud of his four-wheeler and liked to park in remote spots, where there was less chance of getting dings and chips from other people's car doors.

"Pretty sharp looking, aren't we?" Mick asked proudly as they walked across the parking lot.

"Sharp enough," Chet agreed, still secretly pained that Mick had ended up with the white lab coat and he got stuck with the blue scrubs. Mick, the stockier of the two, filled out the jacket belonging to the heavy woman better than his more slender brother had. Although he felt like insisting on the more prestigious garment, Chet had given in, agreeing it was best to look as inconspicuous as possible. With scrubs, fit wasn't as important.

They stood and watched for a moment as a door opened at the rear of the hospital, a white-clad person walked in, and the door closed.

"That's it," Chet said. "That's our way in."

"When we go in, we divide up, or stay together, or what?"

"Together," was the firm reply. "Together until we get the bombs in place and the other stuff divided up. Then we'll take it from there. Ready?"

"As ready as I'm gonna get."

Their two heaved sighs sounded as one in the artificially lit parking lot. Duffel bag in his left hand, Chet reached for the doorknob with his right hand. A thrill of excitement ran through him. The effects of the liquor had lessened somewhat, and Chet's anger, although not greatly abated, had cooled enough that he could think about other things.

The two of them stepped forward slightly and, as the deeply treaded soles of their sneakers made audible contact with the highly polished floors, they looked at each other.

"Tell me again, brother, why are we doing this?" Mick asked.

For a fleeting second, Chet looked genuinely puzzled. He quickly recovered, however, and found some words to use.

"We're here to get even with Marianne for what she did to me — and to get even with the sons-of-bitches who say I can't see her."

Mick nodded. He had thought it was something like that. At least, that was the reason Chet was here. As for himself, he was here because his older brother expected it of him. Through thick and thin, from earliest childhood on, they had always stuck up for each other. Tonight was no exception.

For a few minutes, they walked the halls of St. Paul's. The hospital was so quiet that even their cushioned steps seemed loud to their own ears. After the first two encounters with other people, they both relaxed somewhat. No one paid any attention at all to them. St. Paul's was not a huge medical complex, not compared to the hospitals in nearby New York City. Neither was it so small that all the employees were acquainted with each other. Staff members drifted in and out all the time, so the Hamilton brothers were totally unremarkable in their hospital attire.

"Where we gonna put the bombs?" Mick whispered.

"I'm not sure yet," was the low return. "Lots and lots of hidey-holes in this joint. We just need to find a couple where no one else'll think of looking for a while."

"How about there?" Mick asked, nodding in the direction of a pimply-faced young man in a white top and white jeans coming out of a door.

"Let's check it out."

As soon as the employee had left the area, Chet and Mick went to see what was behind the door.

"Perfect," Chet pronounced, seeing that they were in a large and not very well-maintained storage room. Boxes of supplies and various pieces of equipment were scattered about the huge closet in haphazard fashion. Some things were placed untidily on the shelves. Others were strewn here and there on the floor. "No one could ever find anything in this joint."

"Look," Mick said, "Pampers. Need any Pampers?"

"Not at the moment, stupid. Yeah, all of this stuff is baby stuff. That means we're near the nursery, I bet. What more could you want?"

"What's so great about baby stuff?"

Chet grinned widely.

"Stay by the door. Let me know if you see anyone coming." He unfastened the duffel bag and took out one of the crude, but potentially very effective, bombs. "I'm gonna slip this little sweetheart right in here," he said, nodding toward an isolette that had been pushed into a corner to await repairs. As carefully and as lovingly as any mother ever tucked in a child, Chet nestled the device in the corner of the isolette, then surrounded it with cardboard cartons of disposable diapers and other supplies.

Mick complained, "You never did say what was so great about this place."

"Leverage, man. That's all. Can't you imagine the reaction when we tell them the whole nurseryful of itsy-bitsy babies is gonna blow to smithereens?"

"I get it," Mick said, returning Chet's grin, then sobering. His handsome brow was deeply furrowed when he looked at his brother. "You're not gonna kill babies, are you, Chet?"

"Hell, no," he said stoutly, sensing it wouldn't take too much for his brother to get cold feet. "Only if they force me to."

"And how could they do that?"

"By not doing what I want."

"What are you gonna tell them you want, Chet?"

"Shhh. You'll see. I'll tell you. But right now let's get the hell out of here and find a place at another end of this joint."

"Chet?"

"Yeah, what is it? But keep moving. We got things to do."

"These bombs go off, won't we be killed or hurt same as anyone else in here?"

"You worry too much, Mick. I look like I'm ready to commit suicide? No way. We're gonna hold on to the detonators, kid. I coulda used time bombs, but I think this'll be better. We can stand at one end of the building and activate the bomb we have planted at the other end. Each one'll bust up a good size area, but one by itself ain't nothin' like powerful enough to down this whole building. So relax."

"Relax?"

"Yeah, sure, why not?"

Mick shrugged. Maybe it was "why not" to Chet, but reassurance about the explosive devices not withstanding, he still did not feel in any way capable of relaxing. Leaving the second floor, where the nursery was, they took the stairs to the third floor, located an elevator, and rode down to the basement.

"Look at all this!" Chet exclaimed in delight. "So many stairwells and elevators, little rooms and closets and offices . . . we can play hide-and-seek forever in here."

"Not forever, I hope," Mick fretted. He was beginning to feel almost sorry he had come along. His courage, fueled by the many cans of beer, was waning in the face of progressive sobriety.

"You got better things to do?"

For a moment, Mick closed his eyes and thought about getting in his truck, driving to the apartment, and settling down to an evening of Pam and TV. Not exciting, but safe.

"Don't get hostile, Chet," he said with a sigh. "I'm in. I won't chicken out on you. But I do want to get out of here safe and sound. I do want a future. Anything wrong with that?"

"Nothing at all—and we will have a future. I promise you that. I ever promise you anything I didn't deliver?"

At the moment Mick wasn't able to think of anything, so he shook his head slowly.

"So there. Ease up, okay?"

After a few more gleeful trips through the hospital via the elevators and stairwells, Chet selected the site for the second bomb, in a recessed place in the wall in the boiler room. It was an area where metal boxes and wires abounded, and where one more thing, carefully placed, would attract no attention.

"Now let's find us a restroom and divide up the rest of this stuff," Chet suggested, nodding toward the duffel bag he carried. "Then we'll be ready to make our little announcement."

While the brothers were familiarizing themselves with St. Paul's and planting their explosive devices, Marianne Hamilton, the alleged reason for this escapade, was also familiarizing herself with St. Paul's, though in quite a different way.

"What you in for?" the middle-aged woman with the wild and curly hair asked Marianne.

Marianne sighed. She had wanted to be alone, but no such luck. Even though she had been assigned to a room by herself, the psychiatric ward had an "open door" policy. Some of the patients, such as this woman, went in and out of other patients' rooms without giving it a second thought.

Marianne had been sitting on the edge of the bed, tablet and pencil in hand. Normally suspicious of strangers, she had found herself drawn to Dr. Dvorak. She wanted to be able to trust him. God knew, she needed to trust *someone*. It was too soon to say about the lady doctor because she hadn't really talked to her yet, but Dvorak seemed to care. Voices and words could lie. Smiles could lie. Gestures could lie. But it was hard to get the eyes to lie. In Neil Dvorak's eyes, Marianne had seen compassion. She wanted to please him by coming up with some goals, but she had stared at the paper for ages and no goals had come to mind. They were not likely to, either, now that she had been interrupted.

"Don't want to talk about it, huh?" the woman persisted when Marianne had not answered.

"I'd rather talk about you," Marianne finally said, her voice sounding alien and small in these surroundings. "What are you here for?"

"I hear things other people don't hear," she said, her expression and manner smug. "I hear things over the TV and telephone, voices that tell me what to do. And that's not all. I got a good friend that lives two houses down from me. I can talk to her real good without the phone, and when all the doors and windows are closed and she's in her house and I'm in mine."

"That's great. How do you do that?"

The woman walked slightly closer and smiled, leaning forward as she confided, *"That's* why I'm here, for them to find out how I do it."

Marianne nodded. She was beginning to feel less crazy by the second.

"I hope they find out," she said politely. "It sounds very interesting."

"Oh, it is. I tell you, uh . . . what's your name, anyway?"

"Marianne."

"Oh, I like that. Mine is Gladys. But I never liked being called Gladys. Sounds like an old lady. When I was in school, I tried to keep my name a secret. None of the other girls had a name like that. From kindergarten on, I told 'em I was Gigi."

"I see. And do you still want to be called Gigi?"

"Beats the hell out of Gladys," the woman said, with a loud cackle.

Marianne sighed again and, reaching up, wound a strand of her hair around her finger. She wished she could find a way to get rid of this person.

"Anyway, I was going to tell you," the woman continued, "about the stuff I can do. It isn't like I try, you know. It's just there. Like a gift. And I use it. I only hear the voices one at a time, but there are four different ones. Three of them are women, but one is a man. He's a real devil, that guy. Always and forever trying to get me to do harm. But I've always resisted. Always. Say, you never did say what you were here for?"

"No, I didn't, did I? It really wasn't anything at all, Gigi. I just took a butcher knife from the kitchen and attacked my husband with it while he was sleeping."

"A voice tell you to do it?"

Marianne thought it over. Had the devil made her do it? Interesting thought.

"I don't know. I just know it happened."

For a moment, Gigi's face looked different. She looked at Marianne and, for the first time in their strange conversation, actually seemed to see her. "He hurt you, didn't he?"

"Many times and in many ways," Marianne answered softly.

Then, as quickly as it had occurred, the moment of awareness was over for Gigi. Her smile was mocking, and as empty as the smile of a jack-o'-lantern, and in reality a parody of a smile.

"Maybe someone told him to do it," she suggested.

"Maybe. Gigi, I have some work I need to do, and it's late and I'm tired. Could we talk some more tomorrow?"

"Tomorrow? What is tomorrow?"

"Just another day."

"True enough," she said, then slipped out of the room as quietly as she had entered it, and Marianne went back to staring at the pad in her hand.

In the break room, Steve Cates and Jennie Weiller dawdled over the last of their late-night snack. Jennie was in no hurry to get home, because no one was there. It was a peaceful life, and Jennie craved peace, but still, there were times when the loneliness got almost as hard to bear as discord. And Steve was in no hurry to get home, because someone *was* there. He wasn't sure if he loved Elizabeth at all anymore. Most certainly, he did not like her. He would always be grateful for her support in the past, support that had come at a very crucial and needful time in his life. However, one could not live in the past, and the present didn't seem to have much connection with the past. He was, he felt, a different person than he had been a decade ago. Maybe Elizabeth was, also.

In the third-floor Stress Center, Julie tried hard to stifle a yawn. The times she got to be alone with Neil were rare. Almost always, there were others around them and the pressure was on to get things done. At this hour, the pressure was off. The hustle and bustle of the day had subsided. The phone did not ring, and people did not run in and out of the office. It was nice. But the fact remained that her body needed sleep.

"We ought to go," Neil said, perceiving the yawn she had tried to hide. "Even as it is, I'm sure we're going to feel we just got home when we have to get up and come back."

"True," she admitted. "I guess most doctors feel that way from time to time — all too often, in fact. Your wife ever mind?"

Noting his hesitation, Julie flushed.

"I'm sorry. I shouldn't have asked that. If you'd rather not talk about it . . ."

"It isn't that. I suppose I *do* need to talk about her. I don't often have the opportunity, you see. People shy away from mentioning anything about her, so it's as if the subject is taboo,

61

when it isn't at all. There is still pain in the fact she's not here anymore. Perhaps there always will be. But there's nothing we can do about that. To answer your question . . . yes, I am sure there were many, many times when she minded. Once she said to me, jokingly, 'Here I thought I was safe in marrying a psychiatrist . . . I didn't think they got called out at night the way surgeons and obstetricians do.' But she learned, as did both our girls, that psychiatric emergencies do occur on a regular basis, that there are crises of the mind as well as of the body. Jan never really complained about my hours, though. She kept busy, had her own life. She was a very talented musician, and there was always some project going on that she was part of. I'm afraid I haven't been as good as she was . . ."

"How's that?" Julie asked softly.

"Since she left me, I've complained a lot. A whole lot. A few days after the funeral, the girls went back to their lives. I was angry at them, too, at times. Although it had always been stressed in our household that we were each individuals, as well as part of the unit, I just never expected to end up in that big house all alone. Muffin didn't handle it well, either."

"Muffin?"

"Our dog. A little shaggy ball of fuzz Janet rescued from the pound, about the time Emma went to college. Poor Muffin tried, but she wasn't very young anymore, and she was stiff and tired and her little heart was broken. One night she looked at me in that heart-rending way only a dog can. I gave her a special treat and sat with her a bit longer than usual. When I got up the next morning, I found her dead. I knew then what she'd been trying to say: 'I'd like to stay and be of help, but I'm too tired and hurt. I'm sorry.' That was only three months after Jan died."

"Have you ever thought about getting another dog?"

Neil laughed heartily, jolting himself out of the self-pity that had been threatening to engulf him.

"For a minute there, Dr. Singer, I thought you were going to ask if I'd ever thought about getting another wife." When she turned dark red, he took pity on her. "Sorry. I didn't mean to embarrass you. I know you would never say such a thing. But there are those who do. You cannot imagine how many times people have invited me here or there and I find myself seated next to an 'extra' woman. Very disconcerting."

"Sometimes it's the same with me," she confided. "Oh, not here in Bainbridge, of course. I really don't know anyone here well. But when I go back to see my parents and friends, well . . . it's as you said. I'm twenty-eight years old and don't even have anyone I date regularly. It appalls them, I think. So there is always this poor 'extra' guy planted everywhere I go."

"Disconcerting?"

She nodded. "And awkward. It's *my* life, and I do wish they'd just let me live it."

"People mean well, I suppose. Even in our supposedly enlightened society, single isn't viewed as a natural state."

"Do you think it is?" she challenged.

Laughing, he said, "You first. I'd like to hear the viewpoint of youth on this."

"I can't speak for all youth, just for myself. I'd like to marry and have children. Even from the limited experience I've had in the field of psychiatry thus far, I can see the role of the family is so important. But I am who I am, without marriage. Unlike so many women of previous generations, I think most women of my generation don't see marriage as something they *have* to do to be whole. I'm in no hurry."

"Good philosophy. If the right young man comes along, you're fine. You'll also make it if he doesn't. I call that a very healthy attitude."

Julie kept her eyes slightly downcast, half afraid Neil could read her thoughts. She did not want a young man. She wanted the man across from her. In fact, she wanted him so much she was beginning to wonder if she was obsessed. Even so, she was reluctant to let him see too much of her feelings. She had some idea how rejection by him would hurt.

"What about you—you haven't said how you feel about

the naturalness of the single state."

Neil glanced at his watch.

"You sure you have time for this? It *is* awfully late."

"I don't mind," she replied, thinking that was the understatement of the century. For the moment, this was all she dared hope for, to be with Neil like this. The hope was always there that, as he came to know her and grew used to being with her, his feelings would change, that he would come to want her in the way she wanted him. With that in mind, Julie settled back to listen to the philosophy of Dr. Neil Dvorak.

On the OB floor, Dr. Glen Fielding was in the birthing room with a sixteen-year-old ready to deliver her first. "Come on, sweetheart, push. You can do it."

"It hurts," she said between clenched teeth, tears coming to her big brown eyes.

"I know, baby, I know, but if you push you'll get it over with. The holding back only makes it go on longer and longer. Come on, now, *push!*"

As he coaxed the girl, still a child herself, the thought flitted through his mind that she should have thought of this pain and inconvenience before she decided to prove her "maturity" by having unprotected sexual relations. His thought was not an angry thought, not really even a judgmental one, just a weary thought. It never seemed to end, this parade of children having children. Even if they learned their lesson and stopped with one, he could have felt encouraged. However, all too often, they were back time and time again, girls twenty years of age with four and five pregnancies in their history.

"There," Fielding said out loud, "you're doing great, Dawn. Can you manage one more? Just one big push . . . come on, that's a sweetheart. The baby's crowning. I see the head—lots and lots of dark hair. That's it, here it comes!"

A blue-swathed pediatric nurse stood nearby as the combination of maternal pushing and physician's hands brought the baby through the perineum. She suctioned the baby's nose and mouth with a bulb syringe after the head was fully delivered.

"It's going to be a good one," she said softly. "Great color. No signs of meconium."

Nodding, he moved to free the shoulders from the birth canal. Dawn's cries of outrage continued, but no one paid her any attention for the moment. She was safe and sound, that much was apparent, so all eyes were on the new member of the human race.

"It's over, Dawnie, it's over," Fielding said, his voice almost a croon. "You have a fine little girl."

The wailing stopped, a choked sound that was a mixture of tears and laughter ensued, and then the girl broke into a full smile.

"A girl? I wanted a girl. She'll be just like a doll, only real."

Fielding and the attendant nurse exchanged a glance that said volumes. No need for words here. The scenario was all too familiar. They mentally shrugged and went back to the business at hand.

The baby was a pink and perfect seven and one-half pounder. Her Apgar scores were nine at one minute and ten at five minutes. Her cry was lusty and her tiny fists flailed the air. For a moment, Fielding was misty. It always happened, no matter what the socioeconomic situation. Where there was life, there was hope, right? Some people overcame the odds . . . and this tiny girl just might be one of them.

"She's mine," Dawn was saying, "my little baby. Mine!"

"No, Dawnie, no . . . she is under your care temporarily, but she is not yours. No human being, not even from the beginning, can belong to someone else."

Fielding's voice was very low, more as if he were talking to himself than to the patient. Maybe she heard. Maybe she didn't. It really didn't matter, for she wouldn't have believed him anyway. *My* baby."

* * *

"What is it?" the aide on the telemetry ward asked into the intercom. 337's light was on again. It seemed to her it had been on more than it was off. Maudie was having a restless night.

"I'm thirsty. I can't even think about sleeping, I'm so thirsty."

"I filled your pitcher."

"I can't reach it. I tried and some spilled." The thin voice had a whining quality.

"I'll be right there," Ruby said. "You just hold on."

"Problem?" the charge nurse asked as she passed by.

"Nothing I can't handle. Poor old Maudie is having a hard time settling down."

"Poor *old* Maudie?" the RN said, with a weary smile. "You do know how old Maudie Evans really is?"

Ruby nodded. She knew. They all knew. The patient's age was on the chart, a matter of record. To enter a hospital is to give up a great deal of privacy. Maudie Evans was younger than Ruby herself. It just didn't seem that way. Having inhaled at least two packs of cigarettes a day for over forty years, the once attractive fifty-seven-year-old patient was gaunt and haggard, gasping for every breath. Any admission could be the last for Maudie, and she knew it.

In the patient's room, Ruby skillfully maneuvered the nasal cannula out of the way to allow her to sip from the curved straw. Ruby suspected that Maudie feared to sleep, so she invented being thirsty, cold, hot, needing to go to the bathroom, and all of the other excuses, to put off the moment when sleep would claim her. Ravaged though she was, she was not ready to let go, and feared that each nap might be the one from which she would not awaken.

"I can stay a bit if you'd like," she offered. "All's quiet on this end of third shift."

"Everyone but pesky me asleep?" Maudie's voice was hoarse.

"Something like that," Ruby said, patting the patient's hand. "But a body can't always sleep just because the clock says it's time, you know."

Maudie nodded eagerly, grateful that someone appeared to

understand. Except for her smoking, Maudie had never been a rule breaker. She had enjoyed life, gone with the flow, and now it seemed it was almost over. She didn't want to die. She just didn't. . . .

Seeing the panic in the patient's eyes, Ruby made a stab at diverting her attention.

"Did I ever tell you about the little guy we had on this floor here a year or so? He was ninety if he was a day, but spry as could be, and I don't think that turkey ever slept. Never caught him at it. Why, he was up and down the halls, and in and out of other people's rooms all the livelong night. Doctors would order him put in Poseys — that's what we call the restraints we sometimes have to put on people for their own protection — but we never found any that old Houdini couldn't get out of, left alone for a few minutes. That's what we finally called him, more than we used his own name — Houdini. Once he got in bed with another patient — a female — recovering from hip surgery. Had a bad ticker, so they put her up here for a couple of days postop. Scared her almost to death, but I'm happy to say she suffered no harm — just a couple of skipped beats on the monitor."

Maudie attempted to laugh, but the sound was more like a wheeze.

"Oh, that's not the end," Ruby continued. "Houdini, he took what he wanted from the other rooms. It sometimes got busy and we always have a light crew at night, so that's when he did most of his prowling. Come one morning, three geriatric patients were missing their false teeth. You guessed it . . . my guy had 'em all."

Maudie wheezed her appreciation again. Encouraged, Ruby continued with her tale, "Then there was the night Houdini . . ."

Jennie and Stephen lingered in the cafeteria. Neil and Julie lingered in Neil's office. Marianne chewed the end of the pencil and stared at the paper. Goals? As Bill's lab reports began to come back, Rasmussen shook his head. Through telephone calls by Mary, the surgical crew was being assembled. The pediatric nurse attended to the newborn baby in the warmer, while the obstetrician repaired the child-mother's episiotomy. Midnight shift though it was, St. Paul's was not entirely silent.

And while these people, and many others within the walls of St. Paul's Hospital, carried out their activities, the older redhaired Hamilton looked at the younger one and said, "Ready?"

"Ready," Mick said, still not entirely sure what he was ready for.

"Let's see how this baby works," Chet said, heading toward a telephone located on a desk at the end of the Surgical waiting room. It was one Surgery personnel used to give information, usually to a volunteer, about the patient coming out of Surgery. "Says right here you dial 700 to page."

"You want to page someone?"

"It's more like I want to make an announcement."

"You're not going to try to see her first?"

Chet lifted one shoulder. He dialed 0, which connected him to the switchboard operator.

"I want to be put through to Marianne Hamilton's room immediately. This is her husband. It's an emergency."

"I'm sorry," said a cool voice, obviously that of a very young woman, "but that patient isn't allowed to have visitors. If you have questions, maybe you can talk to her doctor or someone else in charge in the morning."

Chet spoke a word that in recent years had lost some of its shock value, but still wasn't used in polite circles. The girl at the switchboard repeated the expletive angrily, adding, "and more, too."

But he had hung up and didn't hear. She would have been sorry to know that. She was a girl who prided herself on always having the last word, and to know it had fallen on deaf ears would have been a disappointment.

"See there, Mick?"

"I see," Mick replied soberly.

"You got your stuff?"

Mick checked. He did. The pockets of the white coat and the waistband of his white jeans held the detonator to one bomb, a knife, a snub-nosed revolver, and a box of extra ammo for the gun.

Chet nodded approvingly. He was similarly equipped. Picking up the telephone, he dialed 700.

"Hear me and hear me good, all of you," he boomed. "This hospital is now under siege. Me and my crew have planted bombs all over this hospital. We have the detonators on us. Anyone crosses us, we'll set 'em off. All entrances are to be locked tight. No matter what, no one else comes in. And no one goes out. And don't think we won't know. There's enough of us to watch. We'll see. So get it done. We'll be back with instructions."

The sleepy-eyed security guard exchanged looks with the midnight shift maintenance man, with whom he had been sharing coffee and lazy conversation.

"Is that a joke, or what?" asked the maintenance man.

"I don't think so. Somehow I just don't think so," was the grim reply.

Sleepiness evaporated, replaced by terror.

Chapter Four

In general, the first reaction was stunned disbelief. All over St. Paul's, up and down the corridors, on and off the wards, people looked at each other, scanning faces in the hope that, through the reactions of others, they might find the truth and know what to believe.

After a few seconds of silence, more noisy reactions began. An aide dropped a bedpan. A young housekeeping worker fell backward over his bucket of water. A nurse-nun grabbed at her rosary. Expressions like, "Holy shit!" were prevalent. "Call the administrator," someone said. "What's the use?" was the reply. "You heard the guy on the intercom—no one is to come in." "Still, Ms. Laramore needs to know, don't you think?" "So, call her, then."

In the Stress Center, Neil and Julie looked into each other's eyes.

"You don't suppose . . ." he began, then trailed off.

The idea was too preposterous for words. Even so, the same idea was in Julie's mind. *It won't work, you know . . . keeping Chet away from me, out of here.* Those words were too fresh in their minds not to resurface.

Only one person in St. Paul's was not surprised. Marianne Hamilton knew that voice. And that voice and its message did not shock her. She had not, of course, known exactly what to expect, but she had expected something.

"I don't understand," Gigi whined, her heavy-set form filling the doorway to Marianne's room again. "I heard that voice, only it wasn't one of my regular voices. Besides, mine don't say things that way. Did you hear it, too?"

Marianne's face was grave and impassive. "I heard it. This time's for real, Gigi. Yes, this time *is* for real."

Down on the first floor, Marcus Chapman, the maintenance worker, asked Ken Sandusky, the security guard, "What do you think? Treat it as a joke, or do what the guy says?"

"I think we better go do what the man says," was the unsmiling reply. "We can't afford to take any chances, so let's get it in gear and go lock the entrances that aren't locked already. Then we call the powers that be."

"One thing I always liked about midnight shift, no bigwigs around. Funny how your point of view changes. Right about now, I'd love to have some honcho here to tell me what to do, to take the responsibility."

"Nice thought, but the heat's on us, pal. Come on, let's go check those doors."

"What about ER?"

"The man said *all,* didn't he?"

Back up on third floor, Marianne Hamilton got up slowly from the edge of the bed, where she had been sitting. Her expression was still bland and unperturbed. She walked toward Gigi who, as she neared the door, stepped aside and let her by. Gigi may have been considered crazy by some, but she was in no way stupid, and it was plain enough to see Marianne Hamilton was a woman with a mission.

Marianne stopped at the nurses' station and looked directly at the ward secretary there.

"Is Dr. Dvorak still here?"

"I think so. I'm not sure. I—"

71

"Then find out. I have to talk to him immediately. If he isn't here, call him."

The secretary's face plainly said that she resented Marianne's demanding tone.

"You don't understand," Marianne said, reading the other woman's thoughts. "You heard the intercom?"

So that was it, mused the secretary—the patient was worried about that strange message. She herself knew it was just some weirdo playing a trick; however, the patients couldn't be expected to be that rational. If they were so rational, she reflected, they surely wouldn't have been on the unit.

Soothingly, she began, "Oh, don't worry about *that*. Someone's being cute, I guess. We've had plenty of pranks played here, although never over the intercom that I can remember, but I'm sure it's nothing to worry about."

Marianne drew in a deep breath.

"I said you didn't understand. The voice on the intercom belongs to my husband. The same husband that did this to me." Her hand reached up to touch her bruised and swollen face. "It's not a prank. And it is something to worry about. Now, are you going to find the doctor for me?"

The ward secretary, whose name was Penny, swallowed hard. Not a crank, not a joke? Then what were they supposed to do? Her hand was trembling as she reached out to push the buttons on the telephone.

"Dr. Dvorak? This is Penny, out at the desk. I'm sure glad you're still here. One of the patients says she has to see you. It's Marianne Hamilton. She says the voice on the intercom . . ."

At that point, the spurt of words stopped. Penny's bravado had run its course; her adrenaline had stopped flowing now.

"Bring her here, Penny. Right now."

"Dr. Dvorak, tell me it's a mistake, that what she says is wrong. I mean, I can't . . ."

"Penny, what will be, will be. Just see her on in, please."

With quick and awkward movements, Penny removed herself from the desk and showed Marianne to the office, where the two sober-faced psychiatrists were awaiting her.

All eyes met in turn, and questions and answers were exchanged without a spoken word.

"Chet," Neil said, no inquiry in his voice.

Marianne nodded, still unable to speak.

"Sit down, honey," Julie said softly. "Would you like something to drink, a soda or some coffee?"

"Just a glass of water," she was finally able to say.

"You're sure it's your husband on the intercom?" Julie asked.

"Positive. I was certain he'd do something. I don't pretend I knew it'd be anything like this. But I knew he wouldn't let it pass."

"Has he ever done anything like this before?"

The patient shook her head. "Not that I know about. He's never been in jail, though he did come close a few times. He's high-tempered. Always has been. Anyone crosses him, he'll go after them one way or another. When he was really young, it didn't matter who it was. Any small injustice had to be punished. Later on, he got the good-paying job and he wanted to keep it, so he knew he couldn't hassle anyone there much. Things happened he didn't like at work, he came home and . . . well, it was this sort of thing." Again, her hand went to her sore and pitiful face. "Nothing like this before, but . . ."

When she hesitated, Neil urged her on. "Go on, Marianne. Anything you can think of that might help, tell us. If this is Chet, and he's serious, we're going to need all the help we can get. There are a lot of people inside St. Paul's right now. Innocent people, some of them very ill, and none of whom have done anything at all to your husband."

"The last couple of years, Chet has gathered up a lot of . . . things. For a long time, I didn't know what kind of stuff he was bringing in and locking up in that little storage shed behind our trailer. He kept it locked and I didn't have a key. But when he got drunk, he bragged about it. He got most of it, a little at a time, from those places that sell to survivalists, and to . . . what is it you call the men who fight for pay?"

"Mercenaries?"

She nodded. "That's it. Guns, knives, land mines—he has all kinds of stuff."

"Bombs?" Julie asked.

"I assume so."

Neil began, "Marianne, I want—"

But before he could complete the sentence, the intercom blared again.

"That's great, folks." Chet Hamilton's voice scratched through the equipment. "Real great. Doors locked, just like I said. No one in, no one out. I'll be back in just a few minutes to tell you what I have in mind. Till then, be cool."

Both psychiatrists observed the involuntary chill that shook Marianne Hamilton's slight body.

"Neil," Julie said, "before she gives us more of a profile on Chet Hamilton, you think we'd better get someone else up here to listen? We aren't the only ones dealing with this. I think someone else needs to know who this is, and what Marianne has to say about him."

"Excellent idea."

Dialing 700 to page, Neil announced over the intercom, "All charge personnel to the conference room, *stat.*"

Rising, he offered his arm to the pale Marianne. "Come on, come with Dr. Singer and me to the conference room."

"I thought legally I had to be confined to the psychiatric ward," she reminded them wryly.

"Circumstances have changed. Besides, are you going to escape?"

Smiling slightly, she shook her head.

"That's what I thought . . . so come on."

74

* * *

While the hospital personnel requested to assemble did so, Stephen Cates and Jennifer Weiller walked down the long and polished corridor to the Emergency Room. They were hand-in-hand, each one as needful of moral support as the other.

Steve's expression was puzzled as he tried the double glass doors and found them unyielding. To his knowledge, those doors had never been locked. Not once.

"I thought it was a joke."

"Maybe it is," Jennie said dubiously. "But someone is treating it as if it isn't. It's safer that way."

"Let's go to the conference room and see if we can tell what's happening."

"They only paged charge personnel. We aren't in charge of anything at the moment. Officially, we aren't even here."

"True. But even if they don't want us in the room, maybe someone will be in and out who can tell us what's going on."

Neil greeted the dozen or so hospital personnel as they entered the conference room and sat down around the long and narrow table. Julie sat quietly at the upper end, pressing Marianne Hamilton's hand with her own for reassurance. When Steve and Jennie approached the door, no one objected to their presence.

"We aren't supposed to be here," Steve explained to Dvorak, "but maybe we can help. When our shift was over, we went to get something to eat in the snack bar. We got to talking and stayed too long, but . . ."

Neil nodded and did his best to smile. Although he hadn't worked with either of them often, he knew their reputations as exceptionally capable nurses.

"You worked the Emergency Room tonight, both of you?"

They concurred, and Jennie's blue eyes sought out Marianne Hamilton's face.

"She was one of the reasons we stayed over a bit," she said softly. "We felt for her so much. We wanted to see how her X-rays came out."

"I see." His eyes narrowed. "Were you on duty when her husband was brought in?"

Grimacing, Stephen nodded. "Both of us."

"Then you're in the right place at the right time. Come on in." Turning to face those assembled in the room, he announced, "Take your seats. Keep your wits about you. We have work to do. Some of you I know. Some I don't. Before this is over, we may all know each other a whole lot better. Employees of St. Paul's, the lady with Dr. Singer is Marianne Hamilton. Marianne tells us it is her husband speaking over the intercom. We have reason to believe she is correct. I'll give you a capsule version of the background, then Marianne will talk to us. I don't know that it will help, but if we know the man we're dealing with . . . well, it can't hurt."

"Son of a bitch!" Stephen whispered in an aside to Jennie. The others listened in rapt attention as Dvorak talked, but Steve and Jennie, having met Chet Hamilton, knew the background firsthand, and had a quiet conversation of their own.

"I can't believe this. It doesn't seem real. It isn't really happening."

"Oh, it's happening, darling. Got the keys to that cute little Mustang of yours?"

"Sure, they're right here in my purse. I was all clocked out and ready to go home, so . . ."

"Exactly: *so.* Try to open a door and go out to the parking lot and use those keys. That's when it'll hit you just how real this is."

When Neil had finished his "capsule version," he said he was ready to bring Marianne Hamilton into the discussion, but Kevin Donati, a dark-haired young man from Data Processing, spoke up. "We can open up the phone lines, get the police in on this conversation. Have they even been noti-fied? It seems to me they should be."

"I called Helen Laramore," Ken Sandusky said. "She told me she'd notify the authorities."

Kevin nodded approvingly.

"Then what we need to do is get both Ms. Laramore and someone in charge at the police station on the phone. We can fix it so they'll hear everything said in the room and can talk to us."

"Fantastic," Neil said. "Will it take long?"

Kevin shook his head and left the room. In less than five minutes he was back, and said he had the speakers opened up and the administrator and the Bainbridge Chief of Police connected up. When Kevin, holding a phone receiver, gave the nod that all was set up, everyone in the room exchanged nervous glances.

"Chair it," Julie said to Neil when she saw his hesitation.

"I seem to recall that this gathering was *your* idea."

"But I'm only a lowly resident! Seriously, Neil, I haven't been here long enough to know these people well. You were doing fine. Keep it up."

Resignedly, Neil stood and faced his colleagues. "Before we came down here, Marianne Hamilton informed us that her husband has been gathering up a supply of weapons for quite some time. That means we have to take his mention of bombs very, very seriously. I'm going to ask Marianne to tell us what kind of person her husband is, then I'm sure Ms. Laramore or Chief Inman will have some things to ask her."

"I don't really know where to begin," Marianne said in a low voice. "I want to help, but it's all so complicated."

"For starters," the veteran psychiatrist said, "talk up a little more, so everyone can hear you. If it will help, I'll ask ques-tions. Just don't limit your comments to answers. If you can think of anything at all, no matter how off-the-wall it seems to you, just tell us. Okay?"

"Okay," she replied, her mouth tremulous. With great effort, she controlled herself and looked expectantly at Dvorak for the first question.

"Marianne, would you say that Chet Hamilton is a violent person, one dangerous enough to activate a bomb that might hurt or kill many people he's never even met?"

In the gesture she had repeated over and over, Marianne's hand touched her face.

"I think he is more than capable of it. I don't say that just because he's hurt me. I know lots of men beat their wives or children but are too yellow to stand up against anyone else. But when Chet was younger, when he really lost his temper, he'd go after anyone. He has no control. He drinks too much, which doesn't help. And, as you've already been told, he's been buying up terrorist stuff for a couple of years now. I can't tell you anything that's proof he'll do what he says. It's just that I know him. Nothing is so dark, so warped that he—"

With that, her voice broke. Several people who had been staring at her intently let their eyes drop away in compassion.

"But, to your knowledge, you are the only one he actually harms?"

One of Marianne Hamilton's slate-colored eyes darkened—in fact they probably both did, but one was too swollen to be visible.

"The children. He's always abused them . . . in every way."

"What do you mean by 'in every way?' "

Swallowing hard, Marianne looked down at the table, careful to avoid any eye contact. She felt guilty and dirty, as if she were somehow responsible. As much as she told herself she was trapped and helpless, she still did feel responsibility. She had married Chet and brought three children into the world, two of them even after knowing what he was like. But that had its other side, too. She had conceived Alix by choice. Brie and Jacob had been the result of rape. Marianne tried to

78

think of the last time she had eagerly, willingly had sexual relations with Chet—tried, and could not recall. It was too long ago, another life ago.

"Marianne?"

At Neil's gentle prodding, Marianne snapped out of her reverie and struggled for a brief but effective answer. It was so important that this group of strangers understand what sort of person Chet was, but she felt doubtful about her ability to convey that information.

"He abuses them in every way—almost every way—you could think of. They aren't starved, and they're kept clean and have enough clothes to be like the other kids—and toys, they have toys. When they are sick, I take them to the doctor. Chet never says anything against that. But he ridicules them. He tells them they're stupid and ugly, and stuff like that. When he really wants to insult them, he tells them they're just like me. He beats them. Oh not as much as he does me and he's more careful with their faces. He doesn't want them marked. It started when Alix was only a few weeks old. When she cried too much, he would get very rough, and spank her bottom or pick her up and shake her. I was going to leave when she was four months old. I had our things packed. I don't know how he knew; maybe he guessed. We were living in an apartment then and the girl above us was a friend of mine. I had told her, so maybe that's how it happened. I can't believe she would have told Chet, but she may have told her husband, or someone else who told Chet. He broke my arm that time. The right one. And he raped me. But he did lay off the baby for awhile. I planned to try again, this time telling no one, when I had the use of my arm again. On the day I got the cast off, the doctor said I looked kind of pale and asked if I was okay. That was the day I found out I was pregnant. Chet acted happy about that. He was better for a while, so I told myself maybe he'd changed. It's been that way ever since. He's mean for a while, then he's okay for a while. And . . . I found out a few months ago he was sexually abusing our kids. All of them, even the little boy." She paused, and took a deep breath. "Maybe that isn't even the truth—maybe I knew, deep down inside, a long time ago, and just didn't know how to handle it."

Dvorak shut his eyes as if in pain—and, in a way, he was in pain. No matter how many times he heard these stories, he still felt the pain.

"You've witnessed this?"

Marianne swallowed, her gaze riveted to the tabletop.

"Not intercourse itself. But it's happened. My girls aren't babies anymore. They're eleven and nine—almost ten, Brie is, she'll have a birthday soon. When I asked, they broke down and described to me what he did. They didn't make it up. They couldn't have. What I saw, it was . . . it was . . ."

"Marianne, we're your friends. We're not here to judge you, okay?"

"I got back early from shopping. Alix was at a friend's house. Jacob had gone with me, but he got cranky and felt feverish, so I didn't go some of the places I'd told Chet I had to go. When I got home, I found him and Brie in the bathroom. He said he was helping her with her bath. She hasn't needed help with her bath for years. When I opened the door and went in there, I didn't know he was with her. He had his fingers up her. He lied and said she had told him she was sore and he was putting some cream up there to help. At the time, she backed him up. Later, when I had her and Alix together and he wasn't around, they told me the kind of things he did. Jacob has never said. I think he's too scared. And maybe also he doesn't have the words. I don't know."

"Then what makes you think he's sexually abused Jacob also?"

"Because of the girls, I watched him closely. I saw the way he played with his GI Joe dolls. When he didn't think I was paying any attention, he put the dolls in certain positions.

Once I took him to the doctor for an earache. When I was there, I lied to the doctor and asked her to check Jacob because he was constipated a lot, which he wasn't. She said the anus was scarred, and did I have any reason to suspect anyone. I lied again, because I thought she'd probably report us. If she did, no one checked. But that's how I know."

Some of those who listened to Marianne shuddered and closed their eyes. Some nearly cried. Some looked angry.

"Marianne, why did you marry Chet?"

She paused awhile, then, for the first time in several minutes, looked the doctor in the face.

"He's two people. I guess most of us are in some ways, but Chet is especially that way. I was very young and bashful. I'd never really dated before I met Chet. He was very good-looking, very nice to me, fun to be with. I felt I was the luckiest girl in the world. Some of my friends warned me, and I know my parents worried, because he came from a 'bad family' — that is, they all fought and drank a lot, and Chet's dad had been in jail a few times. He even served a prison term once. His mother had a lot of lovers. She never did leave Chet's dad, but she'd pick a guy up in a bar or someplace and go stay with him a few days, then go back home. That's just the way they grew up. It was different from what I knew, but instead of scaring me off or making me afraid of him, I just felt really sorry for him, and that threw us more together. I saw him get in plenty of fights, and I saw him lay into sales clerks when he didn't like something they said. But he never got mad at me, never laid a hand on me. And he was so good-looking that when we'd go places, other girls would just stare and act silly. When he isn't mad or drunk, Chet can be really charming. There's no other word for it.

"Sometimes he still gets that way. He'll be in a good mood and we'll all get dressed up and go out for a drive and eat out. He's still so good-looking and he makes us laugh, and I see people in the restaurants looking at us and some of them will even say, 'You're such a nice-looking family.' At times like that I find myself wondering if all of the other stuff is just a bad dream . . . if I'm truly crazy, and it isn't that way at all. But he can, and does, change in a flash."

"Thank you, Marianne. I think we all get the general picture of this man. Chief Inman, do you have any questions?"

"I was told the messages on the intercom referred to 'us' and to 'my crew.' Do you think he does have someone with him? And if so, who do you think that person or persons might be?"

"He has several friends — drinking buddies, that is. Most of them aren't the kind who care about anything. Some of them might have come in on this with him. I just don't know. Then there's his brother. Mick is a couple of years younger than Chet. Like I said, they didn't have much at home, so Chet always looked out for Mick and Mick idolized him. If Chet wanted Mick to do something, I think he could talk him into it."

"Can you give us names, addresses, places of employment? I can send officers to check them out, see if they're accounted for or not."

"Mick's full name is Michael Hamilton. He lives with a girl named Pam Gray in that new apartment house on Hemphill Avenue — apartment 212. He works for a landscaper called Greener Pastures. The guys he hangs around with most are Danny Fisher, Gil Hopmeier, and Stanley Bronofski. I can't tell you a lot about them. Danny works at the same place Chet does. I don't think Gil is working right now. I think he lives with his sister and her family over on Stone Street. Stan's married. His wife checks at Kroger's. He's a truck driver, but I don't know who he works for. Their favorite bar is one called the Hog's Breath Saloon. It's on the corner of Bishop and Franklin. I'm afraid that's about all I can tell you."

"It's great. It gives us enough to start on. We'll get someone right on it."

"Marianne?" asked Helen Laramore. Even though she could not be seen, the worry in her voice was apparent. "So far, your husband has not asked for anything, not made any demands other than that St. Paul's be sealed. Do you have any idea what it is he wants? As I understand it, he hasn't asked to see you, hasn't demanded that you be released to him. Knowing Chet, can you make a guess at what his purpose is in this?"

"I . . . I don't know. That's hard to answer. Sometimes Chet comes across dumb. I'm not saying he's brilliant, because I know he isn't. But neither is he what you'd call slow. What I'm saying is that he knows it's going to be hard to walk away from this one. If all he asked for was me and I went with him, he'd never get away. Not for long. So I'd say he has big demands in mind, now that he's gone this far. I know I don't say things really well—it's hard under the circumstances. But no one ever stood up to Chet, you see. Now they have. I did. I stood up to him, and I hurt that body he's so proud of. Then he went home and found out the state of New York had stood up to him too, and taken his kids away and refused to let him see them. Dr. Dvorak told me there was a restraining order against Chet, and that I was being kept here more or less in isolation. I guess Chet was told that, too. I'm sure he tried to see me and found out he couldn't. All of that together would be enough to push him over the edge. He can't handle frustration, can't handle being stood up to.

"But like I said, he's smart enough to know he can't get it all back again. So he wants revenge. He wants society to see what it gets when it pushes Chet Hamilton around."

"You're a very astute young woman," the administrator commented.

Marianne flushed, unused to compliments.

"You are, Marianne," Julie put in softly. "You have a lot of insight, and you express yourself very well. I'm sure all this is very helpful. Don't you think that's right, Dr. Dvorak?"

In the space of a second, Julie looked away from Marianne and at Neil, and it was long enough to have caught him looking at the patient with the strangest expression on his face. Pity, admiration, tenderness, and desire were all clearly readable to her trained and observant eye. Julie felt slightly nauseated, and bitterness welled up in her.

Was *this* what Neil wanted, this kind of woman? She was, without a doubt, highly intelligent. Yet she was uneducated, unmotivated, had allowed herself to become a victim at an early age, and had remained that way. When her face healed, if she could have the right clothes and a proper haircut, Marianne Hamilton could also be beautiful. Julie saw all that, and also sensed a combination of naïveté and sexuality in the other woman that she supposed would be appealing to a certain type of man. But *Neil?*

Julie knew she herself was bright, educated, and very attractive, yet Neil had never looked at her in the way she wanted him to, the way he had just looked at Marianne Hamilton—a woman who was not of his age group, but of her own.

"I think Marianne is very—" Neil began.

"Here I am again," burst the intercom. All action stopped in the conference room. No one stirred, whispered, or moved a chair. Almost all eyes were riveted on the intercom speaker, quite as if they expected a vision to appear as well as the voice. "We've got you pretty well surrounded. Bet none of you had counted on this. Some of you thought you were so smart, didn't you? Thought you were hot stuff. Now it's all different. You do what *I* say. I don't take any crap from the system. Know who I am? Of course you don't. I can pass you in the hall or on the steps, and you won't know I'm the one who's been talking to you. Me and my crew, we don't look any different from the rest of you. But we are. Oh, yes, we're

84

different. Because we can keep you here just as long as we want . . . or we can blow you all to smithereens any time we decide to. Think about it. I've got stuff to do now. I'll be back to talk to you after a while."

"Oh, God," groaned one of the nurses, putting her head down on the table. She looked and sounded literally ill. Looking up again, she said, "Not many of the patients are sedated enough to sleep through this. We're going to have panic, Dr. Dvorak."

He nodded and, grim-faced, replied, "I'm afraid you're right. No matter how carefully we try to handle this, some people will panic. We'd better cut this short and let you get back to your people. Kevin, can you stay close at hand to reorganize the phones after we're through here, in case we need to do something like this again?"

"Sure thing. Doesn't look like I'm going anywhere for a while, anyway."

"The rest of you," Dvorak said, his gaze sweeping over the strained-looking St. Paul employees, "go back to your departments. You've heard Mrs. Hamilton talk enough to realize the kind of person we're dealing with. Do your best to stay calm, and to keep those around you, patients and fellow employees alike, calm. We have a bad situation here, but not as bad as it can get if we have panic and dissension among ourselves. We'll use this room as a headquarters of sorts for as long as we can. Come back here periodically and we'll keep you posted."

As the others filed out, Steve and Jennie lingered behind. "We don't have official duty stations," Stephen said to Neil. "As I said, we'd both clocked out and were just late leaving. I think I speak for Jennie too when I say that as long as we're stuck, we'll help out any way we can. Just let us know where we're needed most."

Dvorak nodded, doing his best to smile to show some semblance of thanks. But inside, he was very aware of a growing sense of something inside himself that was closely akin to panic. Out of a feeling of necessity, when Marianne Hamilton had approached him he had assumed a "take-charge" attitude. He had had no reservations about doing so . . . until now. They were turning to him, all of them, deferring to him as if he were the one in charge. And, God help him, he hadn't any idea how to proceed, what it was best to do or not to do.

Anything he had ever attempted professionally, he had achieved. Even though St. Paul's was a small hospital, off the beaten path of the Big Apple scene, it received patients from far and wide, and had its pick of the best psychiatric residents. The reputation of his work in the Stress Center was growing. His methods were being emulated in far larger facilities than St. Paul's. Those who knew Dr. Neil Dvorak said he ran a tight ship, that he was always in control, and that he kept a tight rein on his patients, often managing to reach the never-before reached. He was accustomed to things going his way at St. Paul's — until now. Now the reins were in the hands of Chet Hamilton, an idea that scared him witless when he let himself dwell on it.

Finding his voice, he said, "You were both there in ER when Chet Hamilton was brought in. What was your impression?"

"From what I saw, I'd not doubt a word Marianne has said," Jennie said immediately.

From across the room, Marianne shot her a look of gratitude. She had felt a rapport with the nurse in ER, had sensed that she could trust the young woman, and now Jennie was proving that feeling had not been in error. Marianne felt she had made so many grave mistakes in her life that she almost always doubted even her most obvious reactions.

"A thoroughly bad ass," Stephen concurred, "though I won't pretend I guessed he'd go this far. I just didn't like anything about him. He doesn't like black people, does he, Marianne?"

The unbruised side of Marianne's face turned slightly red.

"Hey," Stephen said with a laugh, "don't let it bother *you*. I'm not so sensitive that I'd hold you responsible for *his* bigotry."

"He didn't used to say anything about it. But some of the people he knows now, some of them I think he's bought some of the weapons and stuff from, are white supremacists as well as survivalists. I think the people are loco. They really seem to have it in their heads that the blacks or the Jews or *somebody* are going to rise up and start a war and take over, so they're getting prepared. Now he's about like a Nazi, with all his hatred. If you aren't white, protestant, and born in the United States, then you're the enemy."

"I'm coming to the hospital," Helen Laramore said over the phone line. "I have a portable phone. I'll use it to communicate from outside. I know I can't get in, but I can't just sit here at home while St. Paul's and everyone in it are being threatened."

"Helen, there's nothing you can do here."

"I don't care, Neil," she said defiantly. "I'm coming."

"I have four men there already," Chief Inman said. "We've called an alert and are pulling more into duty. What we can do, I don't know. But we are calling up the manpower. I've also notified the FBI. This is a hostage situation, definitely in their territory. They have a couple of agents on the way from New York now."

"Anything yet on the men Mrs. Hamilton told us about?"

"They're running it down. It shouldn't be long now. Mrs. Hamilton, you've been most helpful, and I'm sure we'll have to question you again. So there's no reason you shouldn't have a turn. Is there anything at all we can do for you?"

"Oh, yes, yes, there is," she said, her voice breaking. "My children . . . I just want to know that they're okay. I want to know if they're all three together. And I want someone to tell them I love them."

"We'll get that information and get back to you soon," the chief said, his own voice none too steady.

When he had signed off, the few left in the room looked at each other uneasily.

"Dr. Dvorak, what's going to happen? I'm scared. If Chet just wants me to go with him, let's find out and I'll go. The longer we stay here, the more likely it is that innocent people are going to be hurt. This is awful . . . I . . ."

One corner of Neil's mouth turned up slightly.

"In my practice, I try to get people in the habit of thinking positively. No matter how grim the situation, I try to train them to see what possible good could come of it. Given *this* situation, that's quite a challenge. Can you meet the challenge, Marianne?"

"I don't know. I guess I don't quite understand. I can't think of anything good at the moment — I . . ."

"Can't you?"

She shook her head, a curtain of long, straight hair falling across the injured side of her face.

His voice was barely above a whisper when he spoke to her. "If you get out of this alive, if Chet fails to get to you, you'll never serve a day in any institution. No jury, no judge, no panel of psychiatrists would pronounce you either of a criminal nature or dangerously insane . . . not after having a dose of Chet Hamilton."

Marianne met his eyes for a long moment, then a choked sound escaped her. Unheedful of those around her, she sank into a chair, put her head down on the table and, pressing her brow hard against the polished surface, she sobbed. Those present watched her, wanting to heal her and knowing they could not, and yet they were all glad for the tears. Marianne Hamilton needed the release.

Like guardian angels Jennifer and Julie stood by her, one on each side. As soon as the sobbing abated somewhat and

Marianne was able to lift her head slightly, they offered tissues and hugs.

"I don't cry," she said, obviously genuinely surprised at her own outburst of emotion. "I did once, but I haven't for years. Not in so long I can't remember when, I simply don't cry . . ."

"Then it's time you did," Julie said. "We all need the release of tears from time to time."

"I suppose, but I feel so foolish."

"No need," said solemn Jennie. "Cry all you want. I intend to. I may wait till this is over, but I have a feeling I'm going to have a good one."

They offered comfort and compassion, and Marianne acknowledged that with gratitude. But it was to Neil's face that her eyes went most often, and it was there she found what she needed at the moment. He did not say a word. He did not have to. Julie watched the silent feelings flow between the doctor and his new patient. She pressed another tissue into Marianne's hand, and in doing so felt that she administered to the enemy, an enemy for whom she felt an empathy so great it was almost love. It was not a simple set of emotions she was feeling — not simple, and not pleasant.

Chapter Five

Dave Rasmussen looked over the lab reports, then slammed them down on the desktop. "Damn it to hell," he said, half under his breath. He made a cradle of his hands and, for a long moment, pressed his tired head into that cradle.

"He has to go to surgery, Mary, and right away."

"I know that," was the quiet reply. "I'm not a doctor and I'm not trying to be one, but in my time I've seen enough that I can see the signs. But . . ."

"Yeah," he said, grimacing, meeting her eyes. "My thoughts exactly."

Part of the surgical crew had responded quickly to Mary's telephone calls and made it into the building . . . and part had not. Among those caught on the outside were the anesthesiologist and Dr. Matthews, the surgeon who was going to assist him. On minor surgeries, an anesthesiologist and assistant were not required. Bill Rothman was facing very major surgery.

"Nurses?" he inquired.

"Owens and Kwan . . . they're both capable and experienced. And you know there are no better anesthetists around than Brian Lake."

"Doctors in the house?"

"Dvorak and his resident. Intern McMichael. And Glen Fielding got caught in here. I understand he was still in the middle of an episiotomy repair when the first announcement came over the intercom."

Rasmussen inhaled deeply, then exhaled.

"They're capable people," Mary Riley said. "We can make it."

For once, there was no nonsense about him. "It's illegal, Mary. If something goes wrong in surgery, we can be sued and we won't have a prayer of winning."

"And if we don't do surgery?"

Rasmussen glanced down at the slips of paper that showed the steadily rising amylase and liver enzyme levels. "He dies. And not a pleasant death."

"And you sit there thinking we have a choice?"

With a nod, Rasmussen rose. He walked slowly to the cart where the patient waited, still writhing in pain despite heavy administrations of Demerol and Valium. His wife was by his side, tears already in her eyes.

"Bill and Ruth, you heard the man on the intercom?"

With fear-filled eyes, they looked at him, then nodded mutely.

"I have to level with you. As far as we can tell, this thing is for real. Until we know just how serious he is, what he has in mind, no one can get in or out of St. Paul's. Bill, your situation is getting more grave by the minute. The numbers on your lab tests are skyrocketing. We have to get you on the operating table within the hour The problem is that part of the surgical crew can't get in, but we do have good experienced people in here. The letter of the law says that for your type of surgery we have to have a surgical assistant and an anesthesiologist. I don't think we're going to have them. Because it's better to be prudent than to be sorry, the law is often overly cautious. Even with surgery under these conditions, you stand a real good chance. Without it, . . .

Ruth Rothman sobbed and turned away.

"Do what you have to do, Dr. Rasmussen," Bill said quietly. "Doctors used to do surgery with a kerosene lantern for light and Jack Daniels for anesthesia. I reckon my chances now are better than in those days—and some of them even pulled through."

"Bill, don't be too hasty," his wife said, composing herself. "Dr. Rasmussen, can't we appeal? Surely this man isn't a total monster. If he can talk on the intercom, can't we? Tell him how sick Bill is. Tell him it will be on *his* conscience if the surgery doesn't go well."

The patient and the surgeon exchanged glances of understanding: how could they appeal to the conscience of a man who all too obviously did not have one?

"We can try," Dave Rasmussen said, "but don't get your hopes up, hon. I'm not sure what it is this guy wants, since he hasn't seen fit to tell us yet, but it's plain to see he isn't rational." Turning away from the Rothmans, he faced Mary Riley. "Anyone I should check with before I use the page system? I guess what I'm asking is if anyone is running the show."

"I don't know if you'd call it that or not, but Dr. Dvorak called a conference of charge personnel a few minutes ago. It seems that a patient under his care thinks it's her husband causing the disturbance. Since he knows human nature, maybe you'd feel better asking his opinion."

Rasmussen nodded and, within moments, had Neil Dvorak on the telephone. Rubbing his weary brow, Neil listened as Dave explained his predicament. He could hear the concern, and even an edge of panic threatening to emerge, in his colleague's voice.

"I've never met this character face-to-face, Dave," he answered slowly and carefully, "so I can't pass judgment on what he might or might not do. From what his wife has told me, I'd say there's little decency to appeal to. Still, it can't hurt to try. If he won't agree to let them in, then we're back where we started—not an enviable position, but no worse off. Keep it humble. For us, it's hard. But do it anyway. That's the one way you might get to him, if it appeals to his sense of power to grant a favor. Try the page, but dammit, don't get haughty. Grovel if need be."

"For me, that ain't gonna be easy," Dave said, just a hint of humor returning to his voice.

"How easy the coin doth turn, hey, my friend?"

"How easy. Thanks, Neil."

"For what? That may turn out to be the lousiest advice you ever had."

"I guess we'll know soon enough."

When the connection with Neil was severed, Dave swallowed hard and dialed 700. "I don't know who you are," he said clearly. "I don't even know what you want. I just know you have us frightened. Maybe more than you even thought you would. My name is Dave Rasmussen. I'm a surgeon. We have a man here who has a gallbladder with its ducts ready to burst and spill out poison. We have to operate right away. Outside the doors we have some surgical people we need to perform this operation the way it should be. I'm begging you to let us open the doors and bring them in."

The reply took a few seconds to come, because Chet and Mick had to hunt for a telephone they could use.

"No way," Chet said. "We open those doors even once, and no telling who might come in. You could say they were surgery people and they'd be a SWAT team or something. I don't trust any of you. So no way." He hung up.

"We got a SWAT team in this town?" Mick asked his brother.

Chet gave him a withering look. "Not in Bainbridge. But this might be big enough before it's over they'll get one in from New York."

"Please," Rasmussen said again. "Just think about it. Bill is a good man, an honest man. All his life he's painted houses for a living, and he's known as the best in the trade in this area. He and his wife are fine people. They have a new grandbaby on the way. All we ask is for the other surgeon, the anesthesiologist, and the radiologist to be allowed in so we can do the operation right. We'll set up any kind of check you like so you'll know their true identities. If you don't let them in, he may well die."

"Big deal. Big hairy deal." Chet's voice was as hard as nails. "He might not be the only one to die. You heard what I said. No one in, no one out. Got that?"

Rasmussen did not reply. Ruth Rothman began to cry anew, and the physician noted that it was the patient who comforted her. Neil walked into the ER.

"I thought I was properly humble," Dave said, spotting his colleague.

Neil put his hand on Dave's shoulder. "You did great. It was a long shot. No one could have done more. So what's next?"

Grim-faced and pale, Dave explained the case in detail to the psychiatrist.

On the third floor, Maudie Evans walked out of her room and into the hall, where the nurses, aides, and a few other patients were gathered at the nurses' station.

"This is a surprise," Ruby said. "You usually have us come to you."

"Tonight seems to be full of surprises," Maude countered. "Is this for real?" Again, all eyes were riveted on the intercom speaker nearest them.

"We don't know, Maudie, but we think so," said an RN. "We're just all going to have to keep calm and wait it out. Funny how we always practice for fires, earthquakes, air raids. We never did practice for this. We can't mobilize everyone and prepare to evacuate, because there's plain ol' no place to go."

"I'm going to die anyway. And soon. I've known that all along, but I've tried not to know. I've been so afraid. Suddenly I'm not afraid anymore. If I get killed, so what? Big loss. Save me some trouble and the insurance company a few bucks. But what he's doing, it makes me mad. The rest of you here, you're not in my shape, and you don't deserve this. Who *is* this guy? What's he got it in for us for?"

"We don't know for sure. The few times he's talked, he's not asked for anything specific."

"Isn't that odd?" Maudie wheezed.

"Very odd," Ruby replied.

The employees and patients of St. Paul's weren't the only ones who questioned their captor's technique.

"Hey, Chet?" Mick asked, after the conversation over the page system with the surgeon. "That guy, that doctor, he said he didn't know who you were or what you wanted. When you gonna tell them?"

"When I'm ready. I want 'em good and scared, ready to give in. When they're desperate, when they know we're for real, they'll give us what we want. Right now, some of them probably think it's a game. Soon they're gonna know better."

"How's that?"

"You'll see."

On the OB floor, Glen Fielding sat surrounded by new mothers and OB personnel. Six babies in the newborn nursery, six mommas on the ward. A light crowd, thank God! Some of the women were crying. The most copious sobs came from Dawn, the sixteen-year-old who was still in the birthing room. From where they were gathered, the others could hear her noisy protests. "Get me out of here," she railed. "I didn't go through all this just to die. When I get out of here, I'm going to sue. All the pain and mess, and now this . . . just listen and mark my words! I'll sue."

The other mothers, despite their own worry and distress, exchanged smiles.

"Exactly what is she going to sue for?" one of them asked.

Fielding laughed. "I don't know. Think she wouldn't have gotten pregnant if she'd known we were going to have a madman in the building tonight? Bad planning, I'd say. Maybe we should add that in with the risks we have to explain to patients. 'Do you understand, Gail, that we cannot guarantee there will not be men with bombs in the hospital at the time you go into labor?' "

The woman named Gail laughed through her tears. They all did. Why not? The tears certainly weren't helping.

"Dr. Fielding, it's for you," the ward secretary said, holding out the receiver. "It's Dr. Rasmussen."

Nodding, Fielding neared the desk and accepted the receiver.

"What's up?"

"Your presence in surgery is requested. And round up Vic McMichael. I have an emergency gallbladder, and you two are going to assist."

"You have to be kidding, Ras. I haven't even *watched* gallbladder surgery since my own internship."

"So now's your chance. I'm serious, Glen. The patient's bad. Obstructed and jaundicing. I have a feeling that gallbladder is going to look like an overripe tomato ready to burst open. That is, if we're lucky, and it doesn't go ahead and burst before we get him in there — or intraoperatively. And we're going to have to do it without fluoroscopy control. The radiologist is outside and no one in the building knows how to do a cholangiogram, which is bad because there definitely are stones in the duct."

"I'll do what I can, but . . ."

"I know, I know. And hopefully, you won't have to do anything but help with hemostasis and closure. It's a bad situation, and getting worse by the minute. You think I'm a glutton for punishment? You think I'd be going into OR under these circumstances if I had any other viable option?"

"Right. I'll round up Vic and be on down. Pick me out a cute gown. I'll do what I can."

"Great. See you in five."

While nurses Owens and Kwan stayed in the recovery room with the patient, giving him preoperative preparations, Dave surveyed the rest of his surgical crew, all scrubbed, gowned, and ready for work. He noted the veteran anesthetist, Brian Lake, looked a little green around the gills—a nice match for his surgical ensemble.

"What's the matter, Lake?"

"You want the truth?"

"Straight on."

"I've worked with anesthesiologists for years. Truth is, there have been times when I resented them. I figured I could do anything they could do. I've never seen why they were totally necessary, except in the most difficult of surgeries. I always figured I'd pit my experience and training against anyone's. And now . . ."

Rasmussen smiled.

". . . it's time to put my money where my mouth is. Major surgery, complicated case, and I get to be the big cheese. You know, if an anesthesiologist walked through those doors now, I'd kiss him or her . . . even if it was Doc Cleavenger."

"You can do it, Lake. I think what I hate more than anything is not having the X ray monitoring. Tricky stones in the ducts and no fluoroscopy. It's scary. But, like a lot of things, when one considers the alternatives, one digs in and tries. I'll make do with the choledochoscope."

The nurses wheeled the patient into the operating suite. He was already asleep, having received intravenous sedation in the recovery area. Gently, skillfully, Brian Lake administered the general endotracheal anesthesia. Giving a nod to the physicians, he stepped back to watch the blood pressure and cardiac monitors. The nurses did the Betadine scrub and sterile draping.

"Want to open?" Dave asked Glen Fielding.

"No, you go right ahead. You may need me more later, though I hope not. McMichael and I will stand by with the electrocautery."

Dave nodded his agreement, then made the right subcostal incision. The gallbladder, on first visual inspection, was about as he had expected . . . knobby, with multiple stones, and containing a strange dark looking area—an area almost ready to burst open. He placed it on gentle traction, then identified and traced the connecting ducts. Also as he had expected, the common duct was distended. But there was no cholangiogram to tell for sure if there were stones, or where, he reminded himself. He swiftly ligated the cystic artery, high on the gallbladder, then divided, and handed the gallbladder off to the waiting nurse to take to Pathology. While Intern McMichael assisted with copious irrigation, Dave utilized the choledochoscope to locate and retrieve the stone from where it was impacted in the distal common bile duct.

"Hand me the dilator," Dave ordered. Perspiration was dripping from his forehead. "Now the Robnell catheter."

"Oh, God," he muttered.

Seeing that the perspiration was beginning to stream and would soon obscure the surgeon's vision, Nurse Kwan reached out and patted his forehead dry.

"We're going to make it," he said between clenched teeth. "Give him a gram of glucagon. I think this is free, but there's too much spasm. I need the distal sphincter votive to

98

relax. Brian, how are the stats?"

"Steady and holding," Lake said, jubilation plain in his voice. "I assume you're almost done?"

"I certainly hope so. The catheter passed easily this time. If there were any other stones, we've pushed them out of the duct, at least. Nothing left but to insert the drain and close him up."

With the assistance of both Fielding and McMichael, the wound was irrigated with Garamycin saline, closed in layers, and the Penrose drain installed.

"That it?" Lake asked, when the last suture had secured the drain in place.

"That's it. Extubate him! We're out of here."

The doctors hugged each other and clapped each other on the back. The anesthetist and the nurses, still attending to the patient, looked on with happy smiles and the odd tear of relief.

"Let's go tell the wife," suggested the exultant Rasmussen. "I think she was a bit nervous. Can't imagine why."

"You know," Fielding said, as they walked into the recovery area, "this wasn't half bad. I may consider making a change."

"Really?" Rasmussen asked, not sure whether the ob-gyn doctor was kidding or not. He assumed he was, but this was a strange business, and one never knew.

"Why not? At least *your* patients are almost always asleep. Most of mine lie there and scream. They even call *me* names, as if I were responsible somehow. I had one just before this happened that—oh, well, forget it. Who wants to hear my problems?"

Rasmussen grinned. "It all evens out. You deliver a human being, I deliver a pelvic organ. No comparison."

"But you never have to buy Nikes for a gallbladder or send it to university," argued Fielding, who was often heard to grumble at the expense of having his twins and their younger sister all in college at the same time—although it was a grumbling edged with pride, for he had earned his education the hard way and was pleased that he could make it easier for his own brood. "You going for a specialty, Vic?" Field asked the intern.

"Dermatology," the young man answered.

"Smart choice," Rasmussen answered. "Never heard of a rash getting a guy out of bed at night to be looked at."

"Surely must be a low mortality rate in that field, too," Fielding mused. "Now, why didn't I think of that?"

But even as they shot the breeze, they knew they lied. Each had chosen his field because that was where his heart was. Sometimes they grew weary with the interruptions, demands, and stresses, but then they rested and went on.

Rasmussen stepped into the surgical waiting room and spied Ruth Rothman, looking very small and pitiful, perched on the edge of a chair. Her eyes were riveted on a magazine, although it was very obvious she wasn't really reading it.

"Ruth," he said softly. "We made it. Bill came through it just fine. He's going to be sick for a while, but it's a sickness he'll get over. It went better than I expected. There was a large stone obstructing the duct, but we got it out okay."

She dissolved into tears. He opened up his arms and she ran into them. This woman was no more than an acquaintance to him, yet the embrace seemed right and good. Over the small woman's head, Fielding and Rasmussen exchanged looks that said, "Let the twerp have his dermatology. The moments like this make the stress and strain worthwhile . . . and ease the pain of the ones we couldn't win."

"Anymore intercom messages?" Rasmussen asked Ruth when she had gained control of herself and withdrawn from his arms.

"Just one. I didn't understand it all. I've been so worried.

100

And it wasn't clear, very staticky. He just said he'd be back soon with a list of what he had to have, and to be prepared to listen or things were going to start happening. That was about it."

Rasmussen shook his head, but couldn't think of a thing to say. Neither could either of his colleagues. It was at the back of all their minds that they had just struggled to save a life, and a man they couldn't even see was hinting at taking lives. It rankled, yet they were helpless against it.

It was three in the morning and the atmosphere was brittle with tension. Some patients slept because they were sedated, or very ill and unknowing. Even a few employees dozed because they were exhausted and nothing was demanding immediate attention.

Outside St. Paul's, Helen Laramore stood helplessly and stared through the plate glass window of the ER. Despite her silver hair and the deepening crinkles at the corners of her eyes, Helen Laramore had always presented a youthful, vital appearance. Not so tonight. When called, she had grabbed up the baggy jeans and old sweatshirt she had worn during the evening, and it was only when closed up in the car on the way to the hospital that she remembered she had worn the clothes when bathing and grooming their sheepdog.

"I smell like a dog," she complained to Philip, her husband, who had insisted on making the trip to St. Paul's with her.

"Think anyone will notice?"

"Under the circumstances? No."

Now, after over two hours of just waiting, she looked every year her age, and more. Philip had remained in the car, reluctant to leave although he knew there was nothing he could do, nothing Helen could do. His presence was in no way a statement that she could not handle this herself. Instead, it was a statement of support, loyalty, concern. Long before such a thing had been discovered by the Yuppie set, their marriage had been one of quality. They had, from the first day of their relationship, tried to pull in the same direction as much as possible, and to exercise patience and tolerance when it was necessary to pull in opposite directions. St. Paul's meant so much to Helen. It was more than a job; she really seemed to love the hospital as if it were a living thing. In its way, he supposed it was. His world had always been a different world, a more clinical and technical one, and all he knew of hospital life was what Helen shared with him. St. Paul's. Philip sighed and took in the scene. From a distance, he watched Helen in an animated conversation with a policeman. He put back his head and tried to rest, but found he could not relax. He was scared. There were bad feelings inside him that he could not rationalize away.

"We just got a call back from the chief," the young officer was telling her. "Of the men that Mrs. Hamilton told us about, only Michael Hamilton can't be located. The other three, if not exactly where they ought to be, at least aren't here. We can't say for sure, but it's beginning to look like the crew is just Chet and Mick."

"You've told them inside?"

"The chief was going to do it over the phone line. Unless we get someone out here with a speaker setup, we can't talk to them on the inside."

The few people inside received the news without a great deal of jubilation.

"How come I don't feel happy there's not a whole bunch of them?" asked Ken Sandusky.

"Because," Marcus answered, "we feel too stymied to feel glad about anything."

"Have you seen anyone at all suspicious-looking?" Neil

asked the maintenance and security employees. The two men had been going over the building in an attempt to find anyone or anything out of order.

"Nothing," Marcus replied grimly. "But you have to remember, we don't know who or what to look for."

Stephen Cates spoke up and said, "Chet Hamilton is young—thirty, maybe, but could pass for less. He has light red hair—kind of a reddish-blond—that's straight and thick. Blue eyes, sharp features, with an especially pointed chin. Good-looking guy, kind of like a much younger Kirk Douglas. He has that fair, clear skin that goes with the rest of his coloring—the kind that has a ruddy look. Seen anyone like that?"

The men shook their heads.

"As for the brother, I don't know. Dr. Dvorak, you want to call Mrs. Hamilton's room and ask?"

"I don't know," he said hesitantly. "She badly needed rest. She didn't want to go, but I insisted she go at least lie down for an hour or so. But I suppose she hasn't had time to settle in anyway. Go ahead, Julie, if you don't mind."

Julie left, and returned very quickly. "Mick Hamilton is twenty-five or twenty-six. His coloring is the same as Chet's, but his hair is curlier and his chin more rounded. He's also shorter and heavier. Chet is five feet and ten inches. Mick is only about five feet six or seven inches. She says he's quite nice looking. And, at first meet, more easygoing than Chet. Got it?"

Marcus and Ken nodded, neither appearing happy at having "got it." They looked at each other, a brief, conspiratorial glance that said, "Now what?"

"Let's go look for redheads, Ken."

"Are either of you armed?" Neil wanted to know.

"Security here has never quite meant that," Ken said softly. "Until now. What little happened out of the way, it was enough to say a word, to walk up to someone and dis-

103

play the uniform and badge, to quietly suggest the police be called. We've never had anything like this."

"Never," Marcus agreed. "The worst I've ever seen was when lightning struck the west wing and it caught fire. We actually had to do a partial evacuation of the hospital until it was under control. No one was hurt, and there wasn't even a lot of major structural damage. Not like this."

"Nothing has happened yet," Julie said. "Nothing at all."

No one answered. She was right—nothing really had happened. Yet they all felt as if it had.

"Just a suggestion," Neil said to the two men. "Keep together. I know you can cover more territory if you split up, but I'd still advise you to keep together. You're both sizable fellows. They might think twice about tackling two of you where they wouldn't blink at one."

"Great idea," Ken said, though he tried to make it a joke by adding that he'd hate to think his life depended on the likes of Chapman.

When they were out in the hall, they looked at each other again in hesitation.

"Sandusky, if you were going to hide in this building, where would you go?"

"Me? I'd probably go to those old rooms up on third. You know the ones I mean? They used to be the luxury suites, the private rooms for those who really liked to pay through the nose. When it got to where the rich didn't come here anyway, the rooms got run-down, and the way things are arranged now they're not convenient, so they've never been turned into regular rooms. Only time they're used is peak season when everything else is packed full. That's where I'd go. Fact is," he added with a grin, "I have. On a few days when I couldn't handle things, I found a reason to be gone. No one ever bothered me. But I know the rooms are there. Chet and Mick Hamilton wouldn't."

"Phones still in there?"

"Probably extension ones. Patients' room phones aren't the kind you can page on, or make long distance calls on, or anything."

"And Chet is paging."

"But not often."

"No, not often enough. I tell you, the waiting is giving me the willies."

"Tell me about it. Well, let's go have a look there anyway. Then let's try the supply rooms."

Upstairs from where Ken and Marcus discussed their plans, Chet and Mick sat in silence and stared at each other. They were in the Education and Training classroom. It was a spacious room filled with projectors, video equipment, chalk boards, and all sorts of audiovisual aids, most of it very portable so it could be taken anywhere in St. Paul's and set up as need be. Only two people worked in Education and Training, both days. It wasn't exactly the sort of position that required a midnight shift.

"This is stupid, big brother," Mick said. He was sulky. To him, this was no fun at all. They had sat for hours, it seemed, and all they had done was deliver those silly messages over the page . . . and Chet had done that. "There's no action. You said there'd be action. Those people don't even know what we want, so how can they give us anything? Much more of this, they won't take us serious. They'll start doing stuff we said not to."

"Let them," Chet said grimly. "That's when we strike, and then they'll know we ain't to be fooled with."

"But why the wait? It's stupid. It's boring."

"Shut up, Mick."

"Don't go telling me to shut up, you fool. You know what I think? I think you don't know what you want, and that's why you haven't asked for anything. You know we're in a hole. You ask for Marianne and they give her back, what then? Where do we go and what do we do? You don't want to live with her or love her up, you just want to kill her. After that, what? I don't want to die, and I don't want to be locked up. You got us into this, and now you don't know how to get us out of it, and—"

Chet jumped up, fists clenched. Mick recognized the look in his brother's eye well enough to put a stop to his rhetoric. No use getting Chet crazy-mad at this point. The trouble was, Mick realized, they were both getting too sober. To pull a stunt like this, they really needed to be drunk.

"It takes time, Mick. I admit I didn't have it all thought out. But I've had time to think now. We're going to ask for Marianne, and for money. Lots of money."

"How they gonna get money in here? We said no one in and no one out."

"I'll figure that part out. But hospitals make big money. They'll just have to get some of it for us."

"How much we gonna ask for?"

"How does a million sound?"

Mick grinned. It sounded good. Really good. "But how about two million, then we can each be millionaires?"

"Hell, why not? As for my dear wife, she's going to be the mouse and we're the cats. We're going to get her and give her what she deserves . . . which is to die. But before she dies, we play with her, keep her guessing, pass her back and forth. Know what I mean?"

Mick knew what he meant. Right now, it didn't sound so bad. He was feeling horny. And he'd always had an itch for Marianne. He'd never done anything about it because Chet, after all, was his brother, and there were some things brothers didn't do to each other. But now it was that brother's idea.

* * *

In her narrow room, Marianne shuddered. The sleep Dr. Dvorak had sent her to get would not come. Somewhere in this very building, Chet lay in wait. She did not know in which room, or what he was doing, or what he had in mind. She just knew he was there waiting . . . and waiting . . . and waiting. She had seen him in the trailer. The quiet times, when he did not speak or look at her, the times when the quietness grew and grew . . . worse even than the red-faced, bellowing rages . . . *those* were the times he did the unspeakable, inflicted the scars that did not show.

She was so tired. She wished she could turn over, but between the clavicle injury and the bruised face, she was limited in the number of comfortable reclining positions.

In the conference room, Stephen said, "I'm going to go get a Coke. Anyone else want one?"

Kevin, Neil, and Julie all shook their heads. To keep awake and going, they had already all pumped enough caffeine, both hot and cold, into their systems to make them jittery and strained.

"Jennifer, come with me?" he asked.

Nodding, she arose from her chair. The joining of their hands seemed the most natural act in the world. Neither of them planned or initiated it — it just happened.

When they were out of hearing range, Julie looked at the two men and said, more for diversion than because it mattered to her, "They seem such a nice couple. He's so lively and she's so quiet. They seem to complement each other, rather than clashing. You think they have a chance?"

"You're like my wife," Kevin said with a smile. "Always trying to make a romance out of everything. I don't think it's that way with those two — but then, what do I know?"

Julie felt slightly foolish. Kevin was right. Just this evening, she and Neil had talked about how people always tried to fix them up, and here she was, trying to make an item out of two people she barely knew.

"I don't think there's a racial handicap there," Neil said kindly. "I think that's what you meant. I don't know either of them well, but from what I've observed I'd say they don't even think of a racial difference. But that wouldn't be their major handicap."

Julie raised an eyebrow at him inquiringly.

"Steve's married," Kevin explained. "Anyway, like I said, I think they were just thrown together because of this. The same way we all were."

"Maybe," Neil said, not believing it. If something had not existed between Jennifer and Stephen before, it did now. A profound something. He had seen it before, just often enough to appreciate its rarity — that quality where one reaches out without thought with the total and complete knowledge the other one is there.

He and Jan had been like that — not all the time, but in special moments. Looking at the girl beside him, and he did think of her as a girl, he smiled. She tried to smile in return, but the smile was a shaky one. It was a trying time. Since he was so scared, how much more scared must this young person, just starting out, be? He found himself wondering just how much she could stand, under stress. He did not know the answer. So many people involved in this fiasco, and he felt he did not even know how well he himself would cope.

"Attention," the voice demanded over the intercom. "I have things I need to say. Whoever is in charge, you'd better listen. I'm not kidding around. I want Marianne, I want money — lots of money — and I want me and my crew safe out of here. You hear me?"

They heard. Except for those who were in a world of drug-induced sleep, they heard.

108

Chapter Six

When it became clear that Hamilton had said all he was going to say for the moment, Neil dialed 700 to connect him to the paging system.

"Chet, we're listening. We hear. We're willing to work with you. We listened about the doors, didn't we? But we have to have more information. This way of talking . . . it's scaring innocent patients. We're going to have panic on our hands. There's another way you can talk to us: instead of going over the page, dial 4592. Someone will always be in this room to answer you, okay?"

Chet's laugh was harsh and eerie-sounding. "So, you've found out who I am. Thought you would. Well, I might call 4592. I might not. Depending on how I feel. And I told you what I want—money, Marianne, and out of here."

"Then give us details, Chet. When and where do you want Marianne? How much money, and when, and where? And how can we promise you safety out of here?"

"The amount is two million, cash. Unmarked. You work on getting that. When you do, let me know. I'll tell you then how to go about it."

"Chet—"

"That's it. No more talk. Every thirty minutes from now, I'll check back and see if you've arranged for the money."

With that, he was gone. A turn of his wrist had replaced a

receiver somewhere and cut them off. As Neil hung up the phone, he turned to face his colleagues.

"Two million dollars," he said softly.

They all gasped. It was unreal, totally unreal.

The telephone rang and Julie answered. After identifying herself and listening for a moment, she said, "I'll be right there."

Facing Neil, she explained, "That was the charge nurse on First. Several of the patients are crying, and one man is threatening to get out of here even if he has to jump out a window. She wants to know if one of us can practice some soothing mass psychology. I said I'd do it. If you want to go, fine, but I thought maybe you were more needed here."

"Go on," he said with an encouraging nod. "I need to inform Chief Inman of the demands—and see if the FBI people have arrived yet. If you need me, let me know. If what you do there works, you might drop by the other floors. Conditions have to be bad all over."

When Neil was connected with Inman, he was told that the FBI agents had just arrived at St. Paul's, and were out on the grounds with the Bainbridge officers, the administrator, the press, curious members of the public, and employees and their families, none of whom could gain entry to the building.

Neil then got hold of the administrator on the portable phone she was carrying.

"Helen, if we decide to give in to his demands, if we have no other choice, can we get that kind of money?"

"No way," she said, desperation edging her words. "St. Paul's barely operates in the black, Neil. We don't have that kind of bank account."

"Get calls in to the board and the chief-of-staff," he suggested. "See what kind of thoughts you come up with, then get back with me. We're going to have to come up with something convincing to tell this character. And by three-thirty."

"I'll call them. It's going to be a shock. At the hour this

happened, I'm sure most of them were in bed—if they knew this was going on, they'd be here. Under the circumstances, I wouldn't expect any brilliant ideas."

"I'm short on those myself. I'll settle for any serious input."

"Neil, I want to get inside. My place is in there. I can't work from out here. I have—"

"Shhh, Helen. You have no choice. I have no choice. Maybe it will all be over soon . . . with a little bit of luck. Till then, hang tight."

She sighed deeply.

"I suppose I have to. Are things truly okay in there?"

"As okay as they can be. Some tears, some threats, lots of stress and worry. The staff is being great. Ken Sandusky and Marcus Chapman have been going over the building with a fine-tooth comb. No sight of the men or any bombs yet, but they're going to keep trying. No real panic yet, and we'll do what we can to keep it down. Helen, if you think of anything else we can do . . ."

"Yes?"

"You know where we are."

"Yeah, sure, Doctor. I know where you are. And how I wish we could all be somewhere else!"

Neil walked away from the telephone setup and looked up to see Marianne Hamilton staring at him from the doorway. Her own clothes being soiled and rumpled, she had changed into green scrubs given to her by an employee in the Stress Center. In them, her face so pale and thin, her long hair so straight and flowing, she presented a very wraith-like appearance, an effect that was enhanced by the darkness around her left eye.

"Marianne."

"May I come in, Doctor?"

"You don't have to ask."

"I'm still a prisoner, almost, aren't I?"

"Not exactly," he said softly. "Remember what I said when you were down here before. Things change, Marianne.

111

Strange circumstances cause strange reactions."

Marianne stepped into the conference room. All eyes were riveted on her.

"Let me go to him," she said in a barely audible voice. "To do anything else would be foolish. In a way, a very big way, this mess is my fault. My actions brought all this about. Why postpone what has to be? Let me go to him. Find out where he is, and let me go. Perhaps that will be enough for him. Maybe I can talk him into giving himself up."

"Were you ever able to talk him into anything, or out of anything?"

She bit her lip and shook her head. "No, nothing at all."

"Anyway, right now, my dear, the choice is not mine. Chet is calling the shots. But if I have any say-so, you will not go to him like a lamb to the slaughter. What is happening is not your fault. Your actions may have been the catalyst, but we are dealing with a madman here. You did not make him that. And until we know where he is, until he says where he wants you or the money, we can't make that decision anyway. So sit down, or go back to your room."

"Can I stay?"

"Feel free." Turning then to the computer programmer, he asked, "Kevin, can you disable the paging system? No reason the patients or majority of the staff be subjected to his bullying messages. I want him forced into calling here when he has something to say. Can you do that?"

"I'm not sure. I can try. I'll go to my office and get some numbers, and call a few experts. Maybe they can tell me what to do. Then I'll get hold of Marcus and see if he can lead me to the right wires. Ready for me to do that?"

"The sooner the better," was the quick reply. "His messages are getting more menacing, and I have a feeling he's just getting warmed up. We don't need the patients subjected to this."

* * *

Down the corridor, Coke can in hand, Steve looked at his companion. "Ready to go back in there?" he asked, nodding toward the doorway of the conference room.

"I don't know. I suppose so, for the time being. But I feel I should be doing something more concrete to help."

"Me, too, but right now we seem to be stymied. Go somewhere quiet and take a nap if you can, Jennie. Could be you'll be needed more later."

Shrugging, she said, "I'm too keyed up to rest. Let's just go see if Dr. Dvorak has any new ideas."

As they walked into the room they heard Neil, on the telephone setup, discussing the case with the newly arrived FBI agents. "I can understand," he was saying, "that you're opposed to meeting ransom demands. But we have no idea how much potential danger we're dealing with here. There are approximately three hundred people involved—three hundred at the mercy of two. Since there's not a chance in the world they'd get away with it, I tend to favor promising them the money."

"And the woman?" came back an agent's voice.

Neil winced and glanced at Marianne's tortured face. "No," he said, in a voice like steel. "She has volunteered to go, says she feels she ought to go, but I can't see that. To let her go with them would ensure her death or, at the very least, extreme mistreatment. I just don't see how any of us can in good conscience sanction meeting that demand."

"But I *want* to go. It's something I have to do," she began.

Neil raised his hand to silence her, and the agent continued to talk.

"Then there isn't any real need to discuss the ransom money, Doctor. You say they aren't going to be satisfied without Mrs. Hamilton *and* the money, so it would do no good, and indeed would only serve as an irritant, to offer one and not the other."

"We could make them *think* we were giving in, just to draw them out."

"And how do you propose we do that? We could fake a bag stuffed with money. Not so easy to fake a living, breathing woman . . . especially the man's own wife."

"I don't know," Neil said, his desperation sounding in his voice. "I just know we can't let her go. I have no doubt they'll get stopped, and any money would be recovered, if they try to get away. But I'm not sure they could be stopped before harm was done to the woman, and—"

"Exactly," the agent cut in. "My suggestion is that, at contact, you tell them they can't have anything they want. Because they can't. That's only honesty."

Neil broke out in cold perspiration. "I've studied and worked with the human mind for many, many years, sir. I've reached people from time to time who had been pronounced unreachable by teams of experts. I've thought of myself as a confident and competent professional. Now all that confidence and competency seems to have left me. I don't know these men. I feel they are capable of anything, but I don't *know*. Thus far, we have babied them, let them think they are running the show—which, in truth, they are. It scares me witless to think of antagonizing them. I can't—"

"Don't you think they're going to feel antagonized when they can't page, when you've forced their hand on that issue?"

"I suppose. I just felt that for the sake of the patients and personnel—"

"Exactly, Dr. Dvorak. In a situation like this, any decision at all, no matter how well thought out, is like playing Russian roulette. It's a game where the odds are against us."

Neil gave a weary sigh that was audible over the mechanical device.

"Then tell me, from your experience with similar situations, what I should say to Chet when he contacts us again. That time, incidentally, is only ten minutes away."

For the next few minutes, Neil listened intently. As he listened, he watched Chet Hamilton's wife's face. He nodded intermittently, sickeningly aware of the knots in his stomach.

Then, when the signal for an in coming call went off, Neil told the FBI agent and switched phone lines. It was Helen Laramore.

"I've talked with several members of the board of directors. If need be, to save the lives of our patients and people, we can get the money. But not until regular banking hours. Even if bank officials went in at this hour, they couldn't get into the vaults. It's that way as a precaution against this sort of thing. It just can't be done."

"What was the general reaction?"

"What do you think, Neil? They reacted the way I'm reacting, the way I assume you're reacting. We're all scared stiff. We want our hospital back."

"We're going to get it back," he said, with a good deal more confidence than he felt.

When Neil signed off with the administrator, it was 3:25. At 3:27, Kevin Donati reentered the conference room, his dark eyes flashing with triumph, although the rest of him looked very tired.

"It's done. Not only can't Chet Hamilton use the page, no one can. Not for days. I didn't ask exact directions, so what I did may cost me my job. But I didn't see that just doing a simple disconnect would help — it would be too easily reconnected on demand. Besides, this joker is a mechanic and might find a way to do it himself. Doubtful, but possible. So now he can't. The lead-ins are all severed. Severed and torn away, so that splicing can't be done. Not readily."

Neil nodded in approval and clapped Kevin on the back. "If we're going to do it, then let's do it right. You won't be losing your job, my boy. If any heads roll after this fiasco, mine will be the first. Funny, I thought being Medical Director of St. Paul's Stress Center was my whole life, and suddenly I find I don't care if I have to walk away from it tomorrow."

It was 3:30 on the dot. The intercom was silent. The second hand on the clock on the wall seemed to have a life of its own, moving forward inexorably, no matter how much the onlookers wanted time to stand still or, preferably, go backward—back to a time prior to midnight, to a time when they had been safer and happier without realizing it.

At 3:31, the telephone rang. Chet's fury-filled voice boomed into the room. Neil paled even more, recognizing the depths of that fury, but he was still glad the patients and the bulk of the others caught inside St. Paul's did not have to hear this exchange.

"Who disconnected the frigging page system?"

"Does it matter, Chet?" Neil asked. "What's done is done. And it's totally out of commission. There's no way it can be fixed for you to use it. It will take experts . . .and remember, by your own edict, experts aren't allowed entry."

"Someone will pay for this."

"Who says, Chet?"

"*I* say. No one seems to take it serious that me and my crew are calling the shots here. I said someone will pay and they'll pay. Now, about what I want—my money and my bitch of a wife."

"Your wife says she'll willingly go with you, Chet. And the administrator and the board say they can get that much money, but not until regular banking hours. Bank officials can't get into the vaults at odd hours. That's the system they had."

"Then let 'em figure out another way. Dynamite the goddamned vaults if they have to. We ain't waiting till eight or nine o'clock. That's four or five hours or more. No way. When I call back at four, have a better answer, or you'll pay—same way you'll pay for what you did to the page system, hear?"

"No, Chet, *you* hear. Marianne says she'll go. The hospital officials say the money is possible in a few hours. But *I* say no way. You don't get Marianne and you don't get the money, and you'll get out of here alive over my dead body!"

There was a collective intake of breath as spectators heard the normally soft-spoken Dvorak get hard as nails with the heretofore humored captor of St. Paul's. For a moment, there was a stunned silence. When Chet spoke again, disbelief was evident in his voice.

"I hear you right?"

"You heard."

"You'll pay."

With that, Chet Hamilton was lost to them.

There was dead silence in the conference room. After a long, long while, Steve quipped, "Damn, Dr. Dvorak, for a minute there, I thought we had Rambo in here."

"I only wish!" the psychiatrist said dryly. "You don't happen to have his number, do you?"

"Let me see," Steve said, pretending to search his pockets. He came up with a piece of rumpled paper and said, "Ah, yes . . . here it is. But it's in L.A. and it isn't a toll-free number."

"Then forget it," Neil countered. "We have enough expense going on here, without running up long distance calls. Who needs him, anyway? He'd want all the publicity whether he really did anything or not. I don't know about you, Steve, but I want the glory out of this."

"I can buy that. I'm into glory this year. When I ran with a street gang, a life ago, I had no use for glory. But I'm older. I've settled, mellow. I've paid my debt to society and become, perish the thought, a solid citizen. So glory's okay. You ask me, that guy Rambo sucks, anyway."

"How can you two joke?" Jennie cried out, her distress very real. "We don't know what that awful person might do to our patients, to some of us, and you two stand there like a bad Abbott and Costello routine. I can't —"

She broke off, obviously near tears, and Steve took one of her hands in his and placed it against his cheek.

"Jennifer," Neil said softly, "if there was ever a time that called for the relief of comedy, this is it. All the tears and dramatic outpourings in the world won't alter a thing. We have to do the best

117

we can. If we can find something to smile at along the way, then we should grab onto it for dear life, or we'll sink in a sea of our own tears. Laughter is the liferaft, the driftwood which we can hang onto. Can you see that, my dear?"

With tears rolling down her cheeks, she nodded. "I see, but I can't do it. I just can't. I'm not like other people. I think life *is* solemn. I've so often been told I take it too seriously, but I don't know any other way to take it. Maybe I wasn't as much angry at you and Steve as envious. I can't do it. I can't be Costello while the sky is falling."

"Can't you, Jennifer, can't you? If I could give you a gift, it would be —"

But what he was going to say was lost when FBI Agent Alterauge came through on the phone.

"You did fine, Doctor."

"Fine? Then why am I shaking?"

"Same reason we all are, I guess. Look, my partner is going to come on out to the hospital grounds. I'm going to stay down here and aid the police chief."

Tucked away in a basement classroom, Chet and Mick listened to the tomb-like silence of the hospital.

"Kind of spooky, ain't it?" Chet said.

"Real spooky. But you know what? I'm hungry."

"Me, too. Let's go look for food."

"Okay. But you told the doctor we'd get even for what he did to the page system."

"And so we will. But why do it on an empty stomach, hey?"

That made sense to Mick. One of the biggest problems in the life of Michael Hamilton, although he had no inkling of it himself, was that nearly everything his older brother said *did* make sense to him.

Just around the corner from the classroom, they found a row of vending machines.

"Got any quarters?" Mick asked, staring covetously at the

array of canned sodas, candy bars, and other snacks.

Chet gave a derisive snort.

"What does it matter? You got money, save it. This place is ours. Anything here is ours for the taking."

He walked away from the vending machines, narrowed his eyes, then took a flying, feet-first, martial art style jump at the glass-fronted confectionery machine. Glass and paper-wrapped snacks flew in every direction.

"Hey, what's up?" asked Ken Sandusky, rounding the corner. He had been a security guard at St. Paul's for several years, too many years of reacting to the slightest thing out of the ordinary for that habit to be broken easily. "Holy shit," he said under his breath, when he caught sight of the two reddish-blond young men in the midst of the breakage.

"You got it, man . . . shit's about right." With that, Chet pulled the wicked-looking knife from his waistband, dived toward the blue-uniformed older man, and plunged the knife deep into his stomach, withdrawing it almost immediately. Sandusky fell to the floor, groaning. Stepping back, Chet picked up two candy bars and a bag of salted peanuts. "Get your food," he reminded his brother.

Mick obeyed numbly. He took numerous items, because the patch pockets on the labcoat were large and he could carry them easily.

At that moment Marcus Chapman, who had been in the restroom, walked onto the scene. He took in what had happened and blanched. Chet took the snub-nosed pistol from the other side of his waistband, pointed it at the pale and sweating Marcus, then, with a laugh, turned the short barrel of the gun downward.

"Get hold of that shitty-sounding doctor of yours and tell him what he caused. Consider this your lucky night—this part of it, anyway. We're going to start out slow and easy, one at a time. If need be, we'll get rougher. You gonna tell the little shit that?"

Knees shaking, Marcus nodded. The brothers took off and

Marcus immediately bent down to see to his co-worker. His pulse was weak but palpable. Swallowing hard, Marcus looked down at the dark red blood seeping from the gouged wound. Apparently Chet had twisted the blade viciously in withdrawing it so that, instead of a clean, straight stab wound, he had inflicted a tearing trauma. Marcus tried talking to his friend, but there was no response. It was probably to Ken's advantage that he had passed out from pain and shock, but the fact remained that Marcus would have given a year's pay to hear Ken speak at that moment.

"Hang on, pal," he said to the unhearing man. He spoke out of nervousness, out of the need to hear the sound of a human voice, even if it was just his own. Realizing that his knowledge of first aid was minimal and could cause more harm than good, he ran to the nearest telephone. In his excitement, he could recall no extension numbers.

"Connect me to ER," he said rapidly. *"Stat."*

The nurse on duty took the call. "Be right there," she said, "Keep him quiet. Put some pressure over the wound — gentle, direct pressure. Get something under his head to elevate it slightly — anything at all. Just keep your head, we'll be right there."

Marcus hurried the few steps back to his felled colleague, cursing his lack of knowledge and equipment. He took off his shirt and used it to cover the gaping wound, then he pressed gently in an effort to stop the flow of blood. While trying to keep pressure on the stomach with one hand, he reached around with the other and lifted Ken's head off the tile floor. Nothing else was available, and that would have to do. Until a nurse or doctor arrived, he wasn't going to leave Ken and search for a pillow or jacket. Besides, how far off could those clowns be? In his mind's eye, he saw the ugly little pistol pointed straight at him. He felt that, when he had time to think about it, he just might be sick to his stomach.

In the ER, the medic who had taken Marcus's call reached for the phone and dialed 700. "All available doctors, nurses, and medics to the ER, *Stat,*" she said.

"That go over?" she asked a nearby EMT, almost sure it hadn't.

The EMT shook her head. "Dead silence."

The nurse tried again with the same result. She immediately dialed the switchboard operator, who apprised her of the situation.

"Then connect me somewhere, fast. We've got a real emergency on our hands."

The operator connected her quickly to the conference room.

"Dr. Dvorak, this is Peggy in ER. Ken Sandusky has been stabbed in the stomach. Marcus Chapman said it looks bad. They're on the basement level, right by the vending machines. I just found out I can't page for help. Dee and I are on our way now with an emergency cart, but from the way it sounds we need a doctor there bad. He may have to go straight to surgery instead of back to the ER. Can you get me a doctor down there?"

"I'll do it. If there's anything fortunate here, it's that we have a surgeon in the building. I'll locate Dr. Rasmussen and get him there immediately."

"Please do, Doctor."

Neil looked somber as he regarded those around him.

"Jennie, Steve, you heard that. You've wanted to be of active help. I'd say now is your chance. Get on down there. I'll stay here and call around to try to locate Rasmussen. Right now I don't think I want to be reminded it was *my* idea to disable the page system."

They were gone in a flash.

"If you don't locate Dr. Rasmussen on the first call, I'll go out and run the halls—leave messages at all stations," Kevin volunteered.

"Good idea," Neil commented.

When Neil's first two calls did not make connection with the surgeon, Kevin took off. He told every person he saw to locate Rasmussen and send him to the basement-level vending machines *stat*.

By the time Dave Rasmussen reached the supine figure of the security guard, he had been given the message by at least a dozen people.

"Sweet Jesus," he muttered, more prayfully than profanely as he knelt beside Ken.

It all was such a mess. Marcus Chapman now sat to the side, tattered undershirt exposed to the world, with a stunned expression on his face. Ken was still on the floor, but there was a real pillow under his head now, and Marcus's shirt had been replaced with sterile cotton compresses.

"We wanted you to see him before we transferred him to the cart. Pulse weak and thready, down to about 40. BP low at 70/38 but it's holding steady, hasn't dropped since we got here."

"Any of the abdominal viscera involved?" Rasmussen asked.

"I don't think so, though it seems to go deep. But how can I tell? I'm no doctor," Steve said.

Dave carefully inspected the wound, which had entered the lower belly on the left.

"The *regio hypogastrica*," he muttered under his breath, "right in the center of the left inguinal area. As a surgeon, I usually cuss and fuss about the fat, but this time I'm ready to sing 'glory hallelujah' that Ken has a big gut. We'll have to get him to OR for a closer look, but it looks hopeful to me that the adipose tissue took a beating, along with some muscle layers, of course, but anything vital got missed. Steve, there's nothing more we can do here, so you help me get him on the stretcher. Peggy and Jennie, we'll take him from here to the ER. You two go locate my surgical people and get them into OR *stat*. Brian Lake's in the building, so are Owens and Kwan, the scrub nurses. If you can locate Vic McMichael and Doc Fielding, they might as well come along for the fun."

Peggy and Jennie had a quick conference, in which they

divided up the areas to cover in search of the people they needed.

"Oh, how I wish we could page," Peggy commented.

"Do you? Then Chet would have a better idea what we're doing and where people are. So would the patients, and I think they're better blissfully ignorant at this point."

"I hadn't thought of that. You're right, so off I go."

On the second floor, Jennifer located Fielding and McMichael together. She gave them the message and they were ready to take off when Rita, a frightened-looking nursery aide, called out, "Dr. Fielding, please . . . the Booker baby doesn't look so good. She's tachypneic. It just started up. Barb is with her. She said to tell you we may have to pulse ox the baby."

Glen Fielding heaved a deep sigh.

"Go on, Vic," he told the hesitant intern. "I'll come down when and if I can, but I'd better see to the baby."

By the time Fielding was in the newborn nursery, young Dawn's infant was having grunting respirations and retrosternal retractions. He had seen it often, this tachypnea of the newborn. It was fairly common, generally transient, and, as long as the baby was watched, no harm usually resulted. Still, the respiratory distress always made his heart beat a rapid tattoo. It was usually harmless and fleeting, yet there were other things it could be, most of which he had come across at one time or another. Trouble was, he usually experienced them secondhand. Once that cord was severed and the baby handed off, his responsibility to the infant ended. The mother was his patient, and the new human being became the patient of one of the pediatricians. Only there wasn't a pediatrician in the house at the moment. Respiratory alkalosis, hyaline membrane disease, congenital heart defect? Surely not—she had seemed such a perfect baby at birth, all pink and rosy. It just *had* to be simple transient tachypnea of the newborn—didn't it?

* * *

While Fielding worked with the pediatric nurse on placing the infant on a pulse oximeter and getting an IV running, the reassembled surgical crew had gathered in the operating room.

"It's like *déjà vu*," Brian Lake said, as he prepared to do the endotracheal intubation of the patient.

"Not exactly," Dave Rasmussen said dryly. "*Déjà vu* is when you've not really done it before but feel like you have. We *have* done this before."

"But not on Ken," McMichael said. His eyes, the only portion of his face visible over the surgical mask, were filled with concern.

In the few months he had worked at St. Paul's he had, as all interns do, spent many, many nights on call in the hospital. Ken Sandusky, who almost always worked the midnight shift, had been unfailingly kind and helpful. Vic had appreciated that. He was a long way from home, and the security guard had somehow reminded him of his father.

"I'm playing this one by ear, folks," Rasmussen said, when he received the nod from Lake that the patient was under the proper level of anesthesia to begin the procedure. He enlarged the area torn by the knife by making an incision at the upper edge of the wound, then at the lower one. This would allow him to enter the peritoneum far enough to assess the damage. McMichael was with him every move, keeping all bleeding points electrocoagulated.

"Just as I thought, we're going to get lucky in at least one way. There was so much adipose tissue that the knife didn't really reach the viscera. This seems to be my night for knife wounds that could have been worse. Right now I'm wishing one had been a hell of a lot worse, and we'd all been spared this."

"Call it lucky if you want," the intern said. "It looks a mess to me."

"It is a mess. But it would be a bigger mess if he'd ruptured the intestines or punctured the spleen . . . or a dozen other things I could mention.

"Owens, get your cultures. No use really trying to close this mess. McMichael, when she gets the cultures we'll do an antibiotic saline irrigation, then pack him open, put in drains, and see if he'll heal up by secondary intent. In a few days, if some of the inner mess looks like it's healing, we'll close the outer layers then. Game?"

"Game," McMichael said firmly.

When Nurse Owens had obtained the cultures, packaged and labeled them, and had them ready to submit to Pathology, Rasmussen began the irrigation and the Garamycin saline solution. It was a long and painstaking process. At frequent intervals the surgeon would glance at the anesthetist, who would give him the nod to continue, which was the signal that the patient's vital signs were still stable. When the wound appeared clean, and all the tissue fragment debris had been irrigated out, Rasmussen installed the drains, then sutured and taped them in place.

"Where's it going to end?" Neil Dvorak said, one load off his mind when he was informed that Ken Sandusky looked like he was going to make it. "We *have* to find those two. We have to get them out of St. Paul's."

Kevin nodded in agreement. He wanted the same thing, yet nobody inside or outside St. Paul's had any brilliant or infallible ideas on to how achieve that goal.

In the ambulance parking bay, an EMT took a call. Just outside of town, there had been a motor vehicle accident.

"I think I know the answer," he said to Helen Laramore, having called her portable phone, "but I just want some confirmation: what do I do with them?"

"Take them into New York," she said, biting her lip. "There's nothing we can do here."

The same thing was told to a distraught elderly man who drove his car as far into the ER parking area as allowed. When told he could not enter further, he gestured frantically at the blanket-wrapped figure in the back seat. "My wife, she's very sick. I think it's her heart."

"Take her into New York City, sir. The hospital has been seized and we can't get in. We can't help her."

"But we always come here, Dr. Mackey always sees her. I can't drive in the city. One reason we like to live in Bainbridge is St. Paul's. I—"

"I'm sorry. I truly am. But we can't get in."

Remembering the pain and confusion in the little man's cataract-clouded eyes, Helen shut her own eyes against the inward pain. *I want my hospital back.* Although she had yet to say the words out loud, they beat against her mind over and over again: *I want my hospital back.*

Inside St. Paul's, as 4:00 neared, Chet and Mick wandered the dark corners of the hospital looking for a place to strike. They had promised Dvorak action, and action was what they were going to deliver.

Chet peeked around a corner. They were on the third floor. No one was in the corridor, so he took a few steps forward, Mick right behind him. They moved stealthily until they had a fairly clear view of the nurses' station. A portion of this floor was used for patients requiring telemetry monitoring. For a moment, Chet stared in fascination at the TV screens with their green backgrounds and ever-moving white linear patterns.

"Heart monitors," Mick whispered, obviously proud of himself.

"I know what they are," Chet said angrily. But his ill humor passed quickly. He had an idea. With a smile flashed at his younger brother, he said, "I got this plan. But we have to move fast. It's almost four . . . time to communicate again."

"But it's *my* turn to turn a trick this time," Mick insisted.

"Right. You're right."

Mick smiled in delight. He tried not to think of the repercussions, for they had gone too far to turn back now. He just had to live for the moment and, if need be, go out with a bang.

Chapter Seven

"Then go to it," Chet said, his grin bestowing his blessing. "Just be careful. If we don't both get out of this alive and in one piece, then it'll all have been for nothing."

"Oh, I'll be careful, all right."

As if to prove his point, he paused just out of view of the nurses' station and took in the tableau, his blue eyes bright with interest and anticipation. Two women, a nurse in white and an aide in dark pink, were the only personnel present. The nurse looked very young, tanned and leggy with her sun-streaked hair French braided. In another setting, she could have passed for a teenager. The aide was middle-aged and frankly plain. She was watching the green screens and the nurse was doing charting. It was very, very quiet. As he watched, the two women spoke to each other only once, and then in tones so low he couldn't possibly catch the words.

He removed his knife and gun, anxious to handle them now that his older brother had used his weapons. He took a step forward. Chet placed a hand on his shoulder — not a restraint, just a warning. Mick nodded silently. Careful. That was the operational word here: careful. Moving silently on rubber-soled feet, he rounded the corner. Careful to keep his weapons out of sight, he approached the wooden divider separating him from the nurse. It struck him at mid-chest, making it easy to hide his forearms.

"How's it going?" he asked softly.

The nurse looked up, big eyes growing bigger with surprise. Softening at the sight of the good-looking young man with the million-dollar smile, she smiled back. With a shrug, she said, "It's all pretty boring. Up here at least. I guess we should be grateful for that, considering everything."

"What's that? Oh, I know what you mean. Think there's really anything to it, that one or two guys could control everyone in this place?"

"When you put it that way, it sounds weird. But it seems to be happening. One of them hurt Ken pretty bad, I hear."

Ken, Mick mused silently. That must be the hefty security guard Chet had knifed. "Yeah, nice old guy, too. Think he'll make it?"

The nurse shrugged again. "Everything we hear up here is secondhand. I hope so. You new here? I haven't seen you around before, have I?"

"I know I haven't seen *you* — *that*'s something I would have remembered. I've been here since April, but I mostly work days. What about you?"

"This shift, usually. Most people hate it, but I don't. I think I'll stay on it even when they offer me a chance to move. Who knows, maybe I'll be like Mary Riley."

"Who?"

"Oh, you know, that really outspoken old RN who's been here forever and a day."

"Guess not. But then I've been on days."

Mick had her where he wanted her, all mellowed out. Women! Give 'em a certain look, talk to 'em in a certain tone of voice, and they were like putty in his hands. From the corner of his eye he could see the older aide, while pretending not to pay any attention, was very aware of their interaction — aware and disapproving. He had permeated the atmosphere with his sensuality, and the French-braided nurse had responded. In other circumstances, he would have made a play for her. Too bad he had to pass. She was really quite nice.

He could just imagine those long, long legs . . .

"Carla," the aide said sharply, "did Mr. Moskowski get turned at two o'clock or three?"

"It was just at three, so we've got till five before we do it again."

"That's what I was hoping. Poor guy has some of the worst decubitus sores I've ever seen."

Geneva knew to the minute what time they had last turned the patient in question. Her aim had been to divert her co-workers attention from the young man who, in her opinion, spelled bad news. Good-looking and knew it, too slick by any standards. And Carla should know better, too. Married, the girl was, and definitely should not be flirting around like this.

Mick had noticed the rings. He always looked at the left hand of a potential conquest. He had run across a couple of married girls who didn't wear rings, but most of them did. Mick liked the married ones. Most of them weren't wanting to rock the boat by leaving their husbands, they were just need-ing someone to love them up a little, make them feel good.

"Carla, is that your name?" Mick asked, getting back in the conversation despite the aide's obvious disapproval. "I like that name. It suits you. Like your hair suits you. You do that yourself?"

Carla's hand flew automatically to the braid. "Yeah, sure. It's easy now, once I got the hang of it. It was hard for me when I first started."

"Turn around, let me see . . ."

"Why, you thinking of doing yours this way?" she asked teasingly. She did, however, turn around as requested.

"Oh, I might . . . I just might."

He stepped around from in front of the counter and stood directly behind the nurse. "Nice," he said softly, "so nice." He had shifted both the knife and gun to his left hand. With his right forefinger he touched the braid, then ran his fingertip along the smooth line of neck, so deliciously tanned, until it disappeared into the white collar of her uniform.

Able to ignore the situation no longer, Geneva turned in the direction of the pair. She knew Carla was her supervisor, her job superior, but she didn't see that that gave her a license to carry on like a two-bit whore. The sharp words that were on the tip of her tongue fell away when she saw what Carla's averted eyes did not see. Under the fluorescent lighting, the metal weaponry gleamed wickedly. Suddenly her anger with the girl-nurse was gone, replaced by concern and caring. She recognized her protective, maternal feelings. Carla wasn't so different from her own Sandy, and that was perhaps why she had reacted so adversely to Carla's coy manner with the young man — because Sandy had had an affair with her boss at the shirt factory, bringing grief, shame, and trouble to the whole family. She hadn't been brought up that way. She . . .

"Carla," she said, suddenly jolted out of her shock-like trance. "Carla, watch out!"

Mick laughed loudly.

"What is it, Geneva?" Carla asked, clearly patronizing. Her tone was that of the young who cannot believe the antecedent generation understood about the strong call of the glands. But her annoyed expression changed to one of terror when she had made a half turn in her chair — a half turn that brought her face-to-face with the knife and gun. "Oh, God!" she said.

Still laughing, Mick transferred the gun to his right hand and pointed it directly at the young nurse's forehead. Carla let out a low moan, the realization dawning that she had just looked lustingly into the eyes of one of St. Paul's captors.

"You," Mick said, indicating the frightened aide, "turn off the monitors."

"I can't," she blurted out.

"What do you mean, you can't? If you don't, your little nurse friend here goes bye-bye. They're just machines, there are ways of turning them on and off. So do it."

"But the patients — they have to be monitored closely. That's why they're here. There are two especially with really bad arrhythmias. We can't —"

131

"Do it," he interrupted curtly. "No sob stories, just do it, hear?"

He stuffed the knife back into his waistband, then used his free hand to grip Carla's shoulder. "Chet?" he called loudly. "Mrs. Hatchet-Face there," he said as his brother appeared, "is turning off the monitors. You take your knife and cut the cables in two, then they can't turn 'em back on. It's almost time to call that dipshit doctor. I think that'll make a nice piece of news."

While Chet cut the cables, Mick kept the pistol firmly pressed against Carla's brow. He let the other hand slip from her shoulder to her breast, which he proceeded to fondle enthusiastically. He had her top pushed away enough that he could look down inside it, down to where, at the bra line, the tanned flesh came to an end and cream flesh began. Although she was too terrified to make a sound, tears flowed freely down her smooth cheeks. Mick liked those tears. They made him feel strong and powerful — and even more turned on. By the time Chet's knife had severed the monitor cables, even the cables to those units that hadn't been in use, Mick was nearly panting with lust, his breath coming in uneven gasps.

"Let her go," Chet said. "We have to make the call."

"You made the rest, go ahead and make this one. You watch the old one. Me and this one's going to have some fun."

"No!" she protested violently, a reaction that only made him laugh.

With a sigh of resignation, Chet put up the knife and withdrew the gun, pointing it at Geneva. Mick spied the small office used by the nursing director in the daytime and pulled Carla in that direction.

Chet dialed 4592.

"Dvorak," Chet announced proudly, "we got some news for you. We're up on third floor. We put all the heart monitors out of commission. Think you're the only one that can tamper with equipment? No way. And Mick's having some action with a cute little nurse, one of those California

132

surfer-looking girls. You got news for me?"

"What kind of news, Chet?"

"About my money and my wife," was the impatient reply, "and my guaranteed way out of here."

"Chet, I can't guarantee you anything. We can't do it. Even if we could, we wouldn't. I'm sorry about the monitors. I'm sorry about the nurse. The thing is, you see, that I'm a psychiatrist. All I hear all day long, day after day, week after week, year after year, are sad stories. What's a few more?"

Chet saw red. Quite literally, red and black streaks crossed his vision. "You stupid son of a bitch, you'll pay! By four-thirty you'll hear from us again."

Chet had hung up the receiver with such a bang that Neil fancied he could still feel the vibration in his ear. He stood there, feeling all alone in the world, with beads of cold sweat on his brow.

Looking at him, Marianne Hamilton felt her heart ache, ache in a way it had not done in years. Just as she had not cried in years. Even with the cruelty to her own children ongoing, she had learned to be stony faced, to push it aside as something to be endured, pretending later that the ugliness had not occurred. This was all so different. These people were strangers, or had been, and now their lives were inextricably linked with hers.

Dr. Julie Singer entered the room, her own face pale and stricken. She had been in the doorway when Chet gave his message.

"I'll go straight up to third," she said.

"I'll come with you."

Julie shook her head. "Let me see to her. If there has been a rape, I imagine she'd rather deal with another woman anyway."

"They might still be there," he warned.

"I'll walk up with her," Kevin Donati volunteered. "I imag-

133

ine they've slunk off by now to God only knows where, but I'll see Dr. Singer safely there. You're needed here to communicate with the police and FBI, and the others on the outside."

Accepting that, Neil sat down and put his head in his hands.

On third, Chet watched as his brother came out of the little office, wearing a big grin and zipping up his white jeans. His own lust aroused, Chet thought about having a turn, but then changed his mind. The hospital was full of women. He would find a fresh one. Somehow the idea of partaking of Mick's leavings was not appealing.

"Let's get the hell out of here, Mick."

"Sure thing."

"By the way, how was it?" Chet asked, as they went down the silent corridor.

"Okay. She wasn't very lively. She just laid there and cried. It woulda been more fun if she'd put up a little fight, but I got no real complaints. I got my rocks off and I feel one hundred percent better."

As soon as they were out of sight, Geneva ran to page, then did something rare for her by uttering an obscenity when she realized the page would not work. Before she could take any other action, Julie and Kevin rounded the corner.

"We have to help Carla," Geneva said frantically, "and we need extra nursing staff up here. The monitors are all damaged, and—"

"I'll help you see to Carla," Julie said gently, "and Kevin will call to the other floors for you and see who can be spared to come up. Carla is who they raped?"

Geneva nodded, then led the psychiatrist to the door of the little office.

The woman lay there, unmoving. She was not bruised or beaten. The only marks on her were where Mick's fingers had dug into her flesh, pressure marks that would fade quickly.

134

Looking into the nurse's green eyes, however, Julie assessed the damage. Not all scars could be seen from the outside, and Julie knew all too well that sometimes they never really healed.

Kneeling, she took the young woman's hand, "Carla, I am Dr. Singer. Can you walk? Can you come with me to an examining room?"

"I want a bath," she said dully. "I want to wash every bit of him away from me."

Julie knew how that was. Rape victims often became obsessed by such washing, bathing and showering repeatedly for weeks and months after the rape, their feelings of uncleanness too deep to be reached by soap and water.

"I know, and we'll let you do that in just a little bit. But I do need you to come with me. We need slides, for more than one reason. We'll prepare some for evidence in court, and we need some to check for disease. With people like these men, it pays to be safe."

"What about being pregnant? What if . . . oh, God, I can't stand the thought."

Geneva, standing in attendance, turned away slightly as her eyes filled with tears. She felt only compassion at Carla's pain, now willing to forget her ill feelings of so few minutes ago. The girl had engaged in light flirtation. That was just something some girls did. It wasn't an invitation to a rapist.

"It isn't likely, Carla. There's something about the shock that throws the system out of kilter, and luckily so. Few conceptions take place at the time of rapes such as these. Now, come on, we'll go to the examining room. I'll find out about your cycle, see if I can put your mind at ease. But I'm sure you know it's too early to detect a pregnancy."

The nurse nodded, her eyes bright with unshed tears, and she lifted herself from the floor, rearranging her clothing.

"Come with us," the doctor said to Geneva, when she saw her hesitation. "I think Carla will feel better at having someone there she knows. Besides, I'm a psychiatrist, so this isn't my field of work. I'll need you to gather up the slides and fixatives for me. Can you do that?"

"I'll get the supplies while you get her into the room. That one's best," she said, nodding across the way.

"Do you want to call your husband or anyone?" Julie asked, while Carla positioned herself on the table. "The telephone lines still work."

"It's best not. He can't get in and I can't get out, so there's no use getting him upset. If he could get in he could hold me, but he can't. Maybe he won't even want to after this."

"Carla," Julie said sternly, "this was not in any way *your* fault. Don't start heaping guilt on yourself."

"But you don't know."

"Know what?"

Carla hesitated, hunting for words. How to explain how she had gazed into that animal's bright blue eyes, feeling excited as his gaze moved over her, letting her know he was attracted to her? Hadn't she led him on, hadn't she . . .

"Carla, say what's on your mind. Set it out now. Don't lock it away."

"When he first walked up there, the one that raped me, I had no idea who he was. He was dressed in white, a labcoat and white jeans. He started talking to me, making up to me, being very cute and flirtatious. I went right along with it. I've always been a flirt. I love Brad and I don't really want anyone else. It's just . . ."

"Shhh," Julie said, pressing Carla's hand. "I understand now. With some people, both male and female, flirting is as natural as breathing, a totally natural response. It can be quite healthy, and is no sign of any intention to be disloyal or untrue. Don't blame yourself. Don't allow anyone else, including Brad, to blame you. You were in the wrong place at the wrong time, but you did *not* cause the rape."

"Yes, ma'am," Carla said, smiling faintly through the tears that were beginning to slow. She liked this fierce young doctor.

"Great, now we can get down to the business at hand.

Geneva's back."

"Sorry it took so long, Doctor. Things are a mess. Ken Sandusky is out of surgery and doing okay now, they say, so Jennifer Weiller and Stephen Cates are on this floor now to help monitor the patients."

"I'll go back and work as soon as we're through here."

Julie shook her head. "You need a sedative and some sleep."

"No way," Carla protested. "No way. I'm a nurse, and I'm needed. So let's get this over with. Anyway, maybe the last thing I need right now is to go to bed feeling sorry for myself."

"You're probably right. And even if you're wrong, I admire your attitude. Now, come on, scoot on down. I'm going to take the slides first, then I'll clean you out and check for tears. You on any form of birth control?"

"No. That's why I was worried. I went off the pill a few months ago. We're wanting another baby. Amber's nearly four now, not exactly a baby anymore."

Julie kept her talking. Not only did she need the information, but she found that the flow of conversation was a relaxing technique, keeping Carla's mind diverted from the awful thing that had just happened to her. While they talked, Julie inspected the rugous folds, clitoris, perineum, rectum, and vaginal vault. Luckily, there was little damage. There was trauma to some of the external tissues, but no tearing to require repair. In a few days no physician, no matter how experienced, would be able to say that Carla had been raped. Julie couldn't have said it herself, had she not known. The amorous coupling of two consenting lovers could leave as much trauma as this behind.

"He wasn't too rough, and he didn't take long," Carla volunteered. "I didn't fight him. I was afraid to. I hope people don't think I didn't fight him because I wanted it. I couldn't bear—"

"Carla, what *they* might think is of no importance. You know. I know. Geneva knows. Those who love you will believe you. This is a hard thing, one of the most psychologically traumatic things that can happen to anyone. What you're feeling is standard, but that doesn't mean it's *right,* the guilt and the shame and the need to justify."

Carla nodded.

"Done?" she asked, when Julie had straightened up.

"Done," Julie announced. "You can go take your shower now. I doubt you want to put those clothes back on till they've been washed, but I'm sure Geneva can find you some scrubs to borrow."

"What about a douche?" Geneva asked. "Is that allowed? I think she'd feel better. I know I would."

"No reason why she shouldn't. I did all the tests I could do under the circumstances. I'll leave an order with one of the nurses for an antibiotic injection for prophylaxis, okay?"

Carla said it was okay, and went in search of a bathroom with both a tub and a shower.

"I'll go down to the OB floor, get a Betadine douche kit, and bring it and some clothes in to you, kid."

"Thanks, Geneva, you're great."

On the first floor, bone weary, Neil waited for reports. He felt totally frustrated. It seemed that all he was doing was waiting. He wanted to do more. Dammit, he wanted what Helen Laramore wanted—he wanted Chet and Mick out and St. Paul's restored to order. For one of the first times in his life, he felt a raging hatred. He could have killed either or both of the Hamilton brothers without giving it a second thought.

Suddenly he heard Chief Inman's voice over the phone line. "We're going to get some men on the roof on various levels and have them look for access. You need trained people in there, Doctor, people who can ferret out those two and locate where the bombs are stashed."

"Boy, do I know that! But I'm afraid for the officers, Chief. If they try to get in through windows, they're likely to run across the Hamiltons. I'm afraid they'll be killed."

"I'm afraid that very shortly people are going to be killed

anyway, Doctor. We may just have seen the very beginning."

"I know, I know. Like an ostrich with its head in the sand, I'm trying to tell myself it won't happen. The trouble is that I don't believe myself. I'm cold with fear. But there's one good piece of news: I just heard from Steve Cates. The patients on third are okay. They're fairly stable, and can be monitored without telemetry, just by personnel taking their vital signs every fifteen to thirty minutes. Steve is hoping Chet and Mick aren't familiar with hospitals and think they sabotaged ICU. I hope he's right. Our really critical cases, of course, are in ICU. They get down there and start pulling out equipment, people are going to die. No doubt about it."

"We're coming in," Chief Inman said. "One way or another, we're coming in."

Chet and Mick sat on the stairwell at a far end of the building. It was the stairwell nearest the administrative offices, an area seldom trafficked after five in the evening.

"When we gonna do a bomb?" Mick asked.

"When we're sure we're on our way out of here, that's when. Right now, we do what we can till they see reason. Something tells me that won't be long now."

"So, what's next?"

"Let's think about it a minute, little brother, then we'll go hunting."

Julie had left word on the third floor about where she could be reached if Carla wanted to talk. Upon entering the conference room, she told those there about what had occurred.

Neil sighed wearily. "It's almost time for another message, you know. We don't even get cleaned up from one thing they've done, and they're doing something else."

"When he calls next time, let me talk to him," Marianne said.

139

"No way," Neil said immediately.

"I didn't say I'd go to him, though I haven't ruled that out. I still think I should. I just said let me talk to him on the phone. He's already frustrated and totally out of control. What harm can it do?"

"I don't know. I just don't like the sound of it. As bad as it's been, no one has died yet because of them. I hate to —"

"I can't goad him any more than you're already doing. You and Agent Alterauge made the decision not to give in to him. I happen to think you're right. I've always given in to him and it's only made him worse. He needs to be stood up to. People may die if I talk to him, and they may die if I don't. We can't know. At this point, I doubt that Chet and Mick even know. But please let me talk to him."

"Let's let her try," said Agent Alterauge, who had an open phone line to the room. "As she says, we can't know that it'll hurt. Maybe he'll open up to her, let us know what's really bugging him, what he wants. The guy might not be a genius, but he's not fool enough to really believe they can collect two million dollars and just walk away."

"With me as hostage," Chet's wife said quietly.

The phone lines went quiet for a while and dead silence permeated the long room. Were the demands ridiculous? It seemed so to the civilized among them, to those who had, save a bit of errant rebellion now and then, lived their lives more or less according to the rules. But Chester and Michael Hamilton were not part of the establishment. They broke rules as a way of life, even at times when it would have to been infinitely more simple to just obey the rules.

Those with their feet solidly on the ground tended to believe that what Chet demanded could never work; yet there was at least a fragment of doubt in each and every mind that said, "Why not?"

If they performed enough atrocious acts, their demands would have be met. It was beginning to seem possible, this vision of the Hamilton brothers walking out across the parking lot of St. Paul's, a bag of money with them, and Marianne held at gunpoint. Other people went to parts unknown and set up new identities. Why not Chet and Mick? Two million dollars could buy a lot.

On the steps, Mick complained again. He was, Chet noted, beginning to do a lot of that.

"We're not going to have time to do a lot. It's four-twenty now."

Chet nodded glumly. Nothing was going the way he had wanted. Maybe he should have told Dvorak every hour—that way they'd have more time to plan their next moves. He felt rushed, crowded, and frustrated. The fact that Mick had enjoyed a bit of sexual relief while he hadn't did not help his general mood.

"Let's go looking, then," he said as nonchalantly as possible, trying to sound cool despite his building irritation.

At that moment, opening the door from the floor above them, a couple stumbled onto the stairwell. From their dazed looks and rumpled hair, it was very obvious what they had been doing—or, at the very least, were getting ready to do. She was young, pretty, and Hispanic, and he was none of those things, just one of those charismatic men who have a way with women. Joe Pollock was his name. He did not work at the hospital. Rather, he was a chaplain. But he wasn't there in an official capacity. He had been caught behind the doors of St. Paul's because he had come to see Rita, the young laboratory technician who had taken his eye.

He hadn't worried overly about being caught inside St. Paul's. He could always tell his family, his congregation, and the community at large that he had come to visit a critically ill patient. After all, administering to the sick and dying *was* his business. And the delay in getting out had merely meant to him more time for kisses, and more, in dark corners with his newest conquest.

141

Now, eyes wide, the trysting pair warily regarded the pair of brothers.

"I take that back, little brother," Chet said slowly. "We don't have to go looking at all. It's come to us." With a quick movement of the wrist and hand, he had his gun pointed at the pair.

"Just relax, folks. We're going to have a little party."

Mick chuckled happily. Ol' Chet sure could be a card at times.

A party.

Or maybe it wasn't such a joke after all. In some ways, it did seem like a party.

Chapter Eight

"What is this?" the pastor asked, his manner haughty. "What are you doing? Let us by." That manner, coupled with the black pants and shirt and white clerical collar, had gotten him out of many sticky situations . . . and into some places he wasn't really supposed to be.

Chet laughed nastily. His IQ lacked a whole lot by MENSA standards, but he sized up the situation very quickly and very accurately: the rumpled hair, the clothing somewhat awry, the eyes glazed, the mouths slightly swollen . . . it all told him the preacher hadn't stopped at reading the Twenty-third Psalm to this luscious young lady.

"He give it to you good, sweet thing?" he inquired of Rita, as he reached out and placed his hand under her chin, tilting her face toward his. Quite nice, he thought.

"Don't touch her," Pollock said, moving forward.

"You and who else are going to stop me? Really, Father, I'm shocked. Here you guys promise you won't screw, and what do you sneak around and do? I'm really shocked."

"I'm not a Catholic priest," he began, then closed his mouth, infuriated with himself that he had even considered defending his actions to this piece of trash. Besides, in truth, he knew himself to be beyond defense. He had not vowed to be celibate, but he had vowed to be true to Darlene. And he had tried to be, he had wanted to be, but so many women made it clear they were available to him, and he had such a hard time resisting. At this moment, though, he wished he was at home with his wife and kids.

"No?" Chet said, one eyebrow arching up. "No matter. There's a guy I promised some action. Until you happened along, I wasn't sure I could make the deadline. Now I think I can. Mick, you watch this turkey for me, keep him back out of the way. This black-eyed lady and I are going to have some fun."

"No!" she cried. "Please, no, just let me go. I won't tell anyone if you'll just let me go."

Chet threw back his head and roared. "You got the wrong idea, sweetcakes. I *want* people to know you saw me. Me and Mick, we're kind of playing hide-and-seek. It's a game — we leave a trail, they follow. *You* are going to be part of the trail." The laughter subsided and his expression turned serious. "Remember, Mick, keep the turkey back. *This* time, he's strictly a spectator. Who knows, Padre? You just might learn a thing or two." Reaching out, he grabbed hold of Rita and began tearing at her clothing.

Joe lunged forward to her assistance — and found himself propelled backward by the sheer force of Mick's heavily muscled arms.

Now it was Mick's turn to laugh, at the look of surprise and fear on Pollock's face.

"Chet said for you to stay put."

"What kind of animals are you?" Pollock cried out.

But Chet was too busy fondling Pollock's young lover to bother answering.

"Chet, ain't you going to go somewhere more private?" Mick asked, when he saw that his brother was fumbling with the drawstring on the pants of his scrubs. Mick had taken his own victim aside, and he was almost shocked that his brother was apparently planning on having intercourse in front of him.

This time Chet did reply. "I like it this way. I want him to watch. And I want her to know that he's watching."

"Joe, help me," Rita screamed, her dark eyes wide with terror. She was struggling with every ounce of her strength, but she was no match for Chet Hamilton. Breaking away from Mick, Joe made another lunge forward, at which point Mick withdrew his gun. Joe paled but lunged again, and Rita screamed, "No . . . no!" And between the first *no* and the second *no,* the gun went off. No one who saw the expression on the younger Hamilton's face would have doubted that the squeezing of the trigger was an accident. Eyes suddenly fixed, Joe slumped forward, his tall body a dead weight now against Chet. Rita's screams intensified. Chet placed one hand over her mouth and forced her down on the landing.

"Get to a phone," he ordered Mick. "It's just about time. Go call Dvorak. Tell him what we've done."

"The shot—they'll hear, they'll come. You better get out of here, Chet."

Chet shook his head. "Who are 'they?' I'll take my chances. I'm not done. Now go call, then meet me back here."

"What'll I say?"

"Figure something out. You're always crabbing because I get to do all the talking. Now's your chance."

Troubled, scared, more than a little sick to his stomach, Mick stumbled out of the stairwell and ducked into the first unoccupied room he saw that had a telephone.

When he had dialed and the phone was answered, he swallowed hard and said, "Dvorak, you asked for it. You were warned. Now a man is dead. And his woman is not much better off."

"You're not Chet," Dvorak said. "Mick? Is that you, Michael Hamilton?"

Suddenly Mick didn't feel so anxious to claim his own identity. He did not deny it, nor did he admit it. Ignoring the psychiatrist's words, he went on.

"You ready to give us what we want?"

"We can't. I've told you that. It isn't that we won't, we

can't. Who have you hurt? Where are they?"

"That's for you to find out. We'll be back with you in thirty minutes. That'll be five A.M."

"Mick, for God's sake . . ."

But Mick was gone, and Neil's appeal for the sake of God or humankind went unheard.

"We're going to have to find who he's talking about. And we're going to have to find *them*. Dammit, this place isn't that big. Unless they're just blowing smoke, someone needs help. And when that is done, we're going to have to organize some sort of search and flush them out."

"Careful, Dr. Dvorak," Agent Alterauge said, over the phone system that was now St. Paul's only connection to the outside world. "It's apparent these guys have decided they have nothing to lose. What they've already done is enough to put them away until they are old, old men. And I imagine they know that; on some level, they have to know it. That means they don't have a whole lot to lose, so they'll probably stop at nothing to get their way. In your searches, be extremely careful. I'd rather you held off completely. We should have some men in there shortly."

"And they can do exactly what, sir? I mean no disrespect. But those who know St. Paul's haven't been able to locate these two men, let alone get them in a vulnerable position. I don't see what your men, who know nothing about the building, can hope to do. Helen, do you have any ideas on where to look?"

After a long pause, the administrator said, "Neil, I'd like to be encouraging, but in all honesty I can't be. St. Paul's is old. They don't build structures this way anymore. The hospital is almost castle-like in its complexity of structure. Even if it is a relatively small hospital, there are myriads of storage places and little rooms and crannies. In addition to it being the dead of night *and* a relatively low census period, I'd say that two people who aren't wanting to be found could float around from unused area to unused area indefinitely. It's a gamble.

146

They could step out at any given time and be face to face with a group of men hunting for them — or the concealment could last as long as they want it to. Like the man says: use caution."

"I'll do what I have to do," he said, his tone as curt as it ever got. Turning to Julie Singer, he said, "You take the messages for a while, please. Kevin is going with me to hunt for these people. We'll collect others as we go . . . whoever can be spared until we locate the injured." And the dead, he added silently.

Julie was not pleased at the order, although she gave a brief nod of agreement to do as she was asked. She wanted to go where she could be of hands-on help . . . and also, she wanted to be with Neil. But as displeased as she was with the arrangement, she could not argue with its logic. Someone had to stay here to receive the messages, and she could not argue that Kevin would be of more physical help and protection to Neil than she would.

Having delivered his message, Mick returned to where Chet waited for him. When he first reentered the stairwell, Mick avoided eye contact with his brother, and that avoidance caused him, in the narrow area, to look straight at the face of the man he had killed. The eyes were still open wide, frightened-looking though unseeing, their expression frozen in the last emotion Joe Pollock had felt in his time upon the earth. Mick felt nauseated and sweaty. Not only hadn't he killed before, he had never seen a dead person.

"You get through to Dvorak?" Chet asked.

Mick pulled his gaze away from Pollock's still form, which he found surprisingly hard to do. The dead man's horror-stricken face was like a magnet that pulled him in its direction.

"I did. He still says it can't be done. Chet, I didn't aim to kill that guy. He knocked into me and the gun went off. I —" At that, he stopped. Catching sight of the still form of Rita Queterez, his nausea intensified and he felt vomitus rise from his stomach up to his esophagus. What he had meant to say was lost. "Chet, what did you do to her?"

The young woman was alive. Her dark eyes were accusing and pain-filled. Mick remembered seeing eyes like that once when he was a little boy. While visiting a friend who lived in the country, he had found a raccoon caught in a trap. Its eyes had been like Rita's, and its small body had trembled in much the same way.

"She's okay," Chet said in an offhand way. "She's just making a big deal out of it. She put up a fight, Mick. I hadn't had it that way in a long time. Marianne, she quit fighting years ago. I used to like her for the fire, and then there was no fire."

"But she's . . ."

There were no words. The brothers stared down at Rita's still form, one in satisfaction, the other in horror. She was completely naked, making it easy to see the multitude of scratches, abrasions, and bruises. One arm lay at a strange angle, and her inner thighs were smeared with blood. She whimpered again, like a small animal, low and soft.

"So I gave it to her good, Mick. So what? What's she to us, to you?"

Mick didn't know how to answer that. She was a stranger, just as her illicit lover had been. It was hard to say what Chet wanted to hear. They weren't family or friends, so he guessed they were nothing to him. But what had they done to deserve this? They hadn't locked Marianne away from Chet, nor had they caused his children to be taken away.

"Don't be so self-righteous," Chet sneered, when Mick did not offer an answer. "You got it on with the blonde upstairs, so where's the big difference?"

Again, Mick was at a loss. He'd never raped a girl before. Probably he shouldn't have raped this one. But he hadn't been overly rough with her, and he hadn't injured her physically. To his confused mind, it seemed different. Perhaps it wasn't. Chet had always been the one to know these things. Taller, older, more aggressive, Chet had always been his leader.

"Let's get," Chet told his numb, silent brother. "We'll find a place to sit a minute, then decide what's next."

Mick nodded and they moved out from the stairwell. Just before opening the door and entering the corridor, Mick looked back once more at the corpse. And as he made his exit, his eyes met those of Rita, and a violent shudder shook his body. Stepping into the hall, he retched and the candy bars he had recently consumed were vomited onto the shining tile floor.

Chet laughed. "Shit, man! You okay?"

Mick nodded.

"Then let's get. You know, I really wanted that turkey alive. At least for a while. I wanted him to see me get it on with his girl. But never mind. Like you said, it was an accident. Let's duck in this room here for a minute. I want you to tell me, word for word, exactly what Dvorak had to say."

Mick did as he was told. It was too late to turn back now. He had killed a man, and he had a feeling no one would listen or care when he said he hadn't meant to.

Near where the brothers had come from, Kevin Donati and Neil Dvorak combed the passageways. Kevin was the first to spot the heap of vomitus on the floor in front of the door to the stairs.

"It's not dried up. It happened in the last few minutes. Someone's been down this way."

Face set grimly, Neil nodded and grasped the door handle. "Oh, lord!" he exclaimed, and rushed up the steps, Kevin right on his heels. Neil knelt beside the young woman. His keen eyes made an initial gross assessment. She was hurt, but not critically so. Her physical wounds would heal, most likely without visible scars of any sort. Where the emotions were concerned, only time would tell. He didn't feel the prognosis was good. Her eyes . . . oh, God, those eyes! The look in them would haunt him till the end of his days.

149

"It's too late for this one," Kevin told him.

Dvorak nodded. "Mick said a man was dead. Somehow I didn't think he lied." Turning his full attention to the injured woman, he said, "I'm Dr. Dvorak. We'll get help for you."

She averted her eyes slightly. Even in the present circumstances, she felt embarrassment. She knew he was Dr. Dvorak, but how could she expect him to recognize her, naked and beaten, sprawled on the concrete steps?

Looking about, Neil observed the white garments that had been stripped from her slender form.

"You work here?"

She nodded the best she could, the movement almost imperceptible.

"The lab," he said, his memory coming to his rescue. "You're Rita, from the lab."

Again, she nodded.

"Kevin," Neil said, "get me a blanket . . . or anything at all I can cover her with. Then hunt up some of the other people. Tell them where we are, and that we need a stretcher for Rita. We need to get her to an examining room. Alert Glen Fielding so he can take a look at her. I think she's badly torn."

Kevin went on his way, none too sure he wouldn't have to stop and throw up, just as someone else had done. He wondered about that. It was beginning to look like this act of violence had sickened even those who had perpetrated it.

Minutes later, Rita was in an examining room, her wounds cleaned and dressed, and her fractured arm splinted as a temporary measure until X rays could be obtained and properly assessed. With a nurse and surgical assistant helping him, Glen Fielding made his examination. What he found angered him, the sense of anger rendered impotent by the situation in which they had all been placed. His voice deliberately quiet, he asked for the Vicryl suture material and began very meticulously to repair the tears to the vaginal mucosa, the labia,

150

and the perineum. "You'll be okay," he told Rita when it was over. He hoped his words sounded surer than he felt.

Two rapes within an hour. He didn't even want to think about the probable damage to the psyches of these two young women.

"Who was the man on the stairs with you?" he asked her gently.

Tears filled her eyes, this time tears not of pain but of a strange combination of grief and shame.

"His name was Joseph Pollock," she said dully.

"Okay," he said, patting her hand. "Just take it easy. I'll order something to help you sleep and someone will take you to a regular room. Either Dr. Singer or Dr. Dvorak will come talk to you after a bit, if you want. We'll also get some antibiosis started."

In the hallway, Fielding informed Dvorak of what he had found, and what he had done in the way of treatment and repair. "She said the man was Joseph Pollock," he added. "I didn't ask her anything else. She was visibly upset."

Neil nodded. "I recognized him, he's a minister. I've met him in the Stress Center a few times, when he's been there to visit patients. I can't remember now if he's Episcopal or Lutheran, but he isn't a Catholic priest. Wasn't, I should say."

"But he must be at least twenty years older than that girl."

"True. And he was sporting a wide gold band on his finger. But what do we know? Maybe it wasn't the way it looks on the surface."

"True. There must be thousands of reasons why they'd be in dark corners together — and why he'd even be here at such an hour to get caught up in this mess."

"Are you shocked?" Neil asked. "I'm beyond that, with all the things I hear and see. I'm not so hard that I'm not saddened, but I've learned to be accepting. Human nature is human nature. I don't fight it anymore."

"You think man is innately good or bad?"

Neil laughed. "Weighty question for the hour and circumstances."

"And if I don't ask your opinion now, when will I ever have the chance again, or the courage, or even the inclination? Our paths don't cross much."

Neil nodded. "Glen, the answer, in my opinion, is both. Mankind can fight its demons, or it can accept them. And we don't all have the same powers with which to resist. Until now, I thought I'd seen it all. I admit I'm stymied here. I'm used to getting my way. Even if, by some miracle, I can get through to Chet and Mick and talk them into quitting now, I will have failed. Look at the harm already done! The preacher dead, Ken wounded, two women brutalized—and all of us terrified."

"There may be another victim," Glen said quietly. "The baby I was delivering when this started up . . . the little thing isn't doing well. And no pediatrician in the house. I've talked to Schultheis by phone and he's walking me through her care, but I don't mind admitting I'm scared. Even with the oxygen, she has some grunting respirations and remains just a tiny bit cyanotic. I don't like the look of it. I want her shipped out to somewhere where they have a real newborn ICU, but instead I have to—"

As his voice broke, Dvorak patted his colleague on the shoulder, his own sense of frustration and rage steadily on the increase.

"Schultheis is a good doctor. So are you. Between the two of you, you'll save the child if she can be saved. This world we live in is such a strange place."

"Strange? Yeah. I know you can best me on stories, Neil, because dealing with the deviant is your business. You asked if I was shocked that a lovely, bright, and educated young woman and a middle-aged, married man of the cloth would have an affair. Not quite. OB isn't all fairy-tale work. When one is young, one thinks it might be that way. When I was still a medical student, I had this image of myself presenting an infant to its loving parents. Sometimes it's that way. But I've delivered babies to mothers who wanted no part of them—and tried to show them to fathers who were indifferent or angry. I've delivered infants damaged because their mothers smoke, drank, or used drugs during the pregnancy. More times than you'd think possible, I've seen the mother cry because the baby wasn't the sex she wanted. Lots and lots of babies with no daddy in the picture. And a few times when there were two daddies."

"Pardon?"

Glen laughed. "I've been trying to tell you that all the bizarre behavior isn't confined to your unit. Just a few months ago, we had two young men in the birthing room. One was the husband and the other was her lover. There seemed to be some question as to who fathered the baby, so they decided they should both be there. And a while before that, I delivered a baby for this married couple, both as pale as milk . . . but the baby was half black. *They* didn't seem surprised or upset, but it threw me for a loop. They told me about it then, rather matter-of-factly. They were having some marriage problems, so she fooled around hoping to ease her depression, then she and the husband decided to get back together. He was very supportive, even accepting the blame, saying he'd pushed her off the deep end and into the arms of another man. I guess he went down on the birth certificate as the father of that child. Can't remember now how we handled that one. But the strangest one I can recall was the one with the two boyfriends there and a preacher in the waiting room. Somehow the girl had managed to apply for marriage licenses with both of the boyfriends. As soon as they all decided who the baby belonged to, the preacher was going to marry them."

Neil grinned. "And I guess the other one would be best man."

"Something like that. They got it decided, though how the hell they did it I'll never know. They didn't ask for a blood test, and all newborn babies look more or less alike. I don't know."

"Exactly. Who does know? Well, I'd better get back to the conference room, see what's developing there. I guess we'll be hearing from Chet or Mick soon. Frankly, I'm scared."

"Yeah. Like I said, I know the feeling. I'd better get back up and see how my baby's doing. They were to call me here if she worsened, so in this case no news was good news."

It was almost five A.M. when Neil reentered the conference room. As he delivered the news of what had happened, the room grew even more still. He watched Marianne Hamilton's face when he informed them of what had taken place.

So one of them is now a murderer, she thought. It was an ache in her soul that she, too, had almost been one . . . and it was also a regret that she had not succeeded. If she had done what she had intended, none of this would be taking place.

"We have two men in now," Agent Alterauge told them, "and we're trying for two more. We don't know that it'll do any good. But you *are* short on men in there, and you have no one at all with training and weapons. Things are bad, anyway, so we feel we have to try this."

"Sure," Dvorak said. "I understand. And I'm grateful. But I want to tell you what you told me: be careful. And explain to me, is the way they got in a way we can get anyone out?"

The answer came quickly. "Unlikely, Doctor. They climbed to the roof and entered, via hooks and ropes, through upper-story windows. Not exactly a safe route for your average patient."

"That's what I figured, but I thought I'd ask. It's almost five o'clock, you know."

"Most likely they've already done what they mean to do for this interval. But maybe we can prevent the next incident. We're sure as hell going to try."

At 5:01 the signal went off. Neil stared at the telephone unit with loathing, as if it were somehow a fault of the plastic and wire system that all this was happening.

154

"Hello, Dvorak . . . like what I did to the little Chicano girl?"

"Not much, Chet. She's badly hurt. Only an animal would hurt an innocent girl like that."

"Innocent? Hell, she had just been balling the parson before they ran into us."

"That's not what I mean by innocent, Chet. Whatever else she did or didn't do, she was innocent in this situation. She had never done anything to you and Mick. Neither had Joe Pollock. Which one of you sons of bitches killed that man, Chet?"

"Chet, Chet, Chet. How come you call me Chet and I have to call you Dvorak, huh?"

"No one said you had to. My name is Neil."

Chet's laughter was harsh and rude.

"Neil? What a pansy-assed name. You a pansy, Neil?"

"Not by my standards, no."

Again, the laughter. "By *my* standards, I'll bet you're a real pansy. Probably even got pink lace on your undershorts. Huh, Neil?"

"Whatever you say, Chet. Whatever you say."

"What I said was I wanted my woman, the money, and a guaranteed out."

"Can't do it, Chet. FBI is here and they won't let me. Hospital administrator is here and she won't let me. Trouble is, you got stuck talking to me, but I have no real authority over this sort of thing. I can't say, 'Pay him the money now and send the woman to him.' Just can't do it. No one listens."

"Maybe they'll listen when they've found my next message."

"What is that message?"

"Oh, you'll find out . . . and soon, I hope, because five-thirty will roll around soon. We're getting tired, me and my crew. We need out of here. If we have to get really rough to get you to listen, we will."

"You've been rough enough, Chet. It's just that my hands are tied. The way I figure it, you might as well give up. Because I can't, and the others won't. You think you're the only one to whom other people's lives don't matter? Don't kid yourself. There are plenty of others around who don't give a shit who dies and who doesn't. We know the 'crew' is just you and Mick. We know you haven't had any sleep, just like we haven't. Sooner or later you'll slip up, walk around a corner at just the wrong moment, and then it'll be your turn. It's what they're all hoping for, so they're not about to meet your demands. No way."

"They'll be sorry, Neil. And know something else? I don't believe a word you say. I think you're a lying cocksucker. You carry some weight in this joint, and don't think I don't know that. What you advise counts. If your hands are tied, it's because you want them to be."

"All I can do is deliver your message, Chet," Neil said, knowing his coolness was infuriating Chester Hamilton. If Chet had only known how faked that coolness was, how hard to sustain, he would have been delighted. Neil wiped away the beads of perspiration that had formed on his forehead.

"Then deliver it, you prick. The message hasn't changed. You know what we have to have."

With that, he severed the connection.

"What do you think, Doctor?" Police Chief Inman asked over the wires, when it was clear Chet was no longer on the line. "With your knowledge of human nature, can you tell from his voice if there is any strain, any breaking?"

"I can perceive some," Neil said. "It's my guess that he's becoming increasingly fatigued and frustrated. But that's dangerous for all of us. They've committed it all now: kidnaping, assault, rape, murder. It would take a miracle for them to walk away from it. Possibly they know that. If so, they might try making their own miracle. What has happened is bad, but that doesn't mean it can't get worse. Something else has already happened . . . we just have to find out what. It's a game to them."

"They haven't mentioned the bombs lately," the FBI agent

156

commented. "I'd like to think there aren't really any bombs in there."

"And I'd like to believe in Santa Claus and the tooth fairy," Neil said quickly, "but there's not much evidence in that direction."

"We'll play it conservatively, Doctor. Very conservatively."

At that moment the telephone rang again, with another inside call.

"The lab," the excited voice said. "Dr. Dvorak, they've wrecked the lab!"

"Calm down, okay? Just tell me about it."

The caller took two very audible deep breaths. "This is Danette Carlson. I'm an aide on third. I was just running an errand for the charge nurse, bringing a patient's blood sample down. It's been . . . well, it's awful."

"Is anyone hurt, Danette? Do you see anyone there at all?"

"No, no sign of anyone. But it's all ruined. You can't imagine."

"Thanks for calling. Some of us will be on down. But, Danette?"

"Yes, sir?"

"Don't go out alone again. If you're asked to do something, ask for a companion to go with you, okay?"

"Okay. That's one thing you don't have to say twice."

Again, Julie stayed behind with Marianne while Neil and Kevin went to survey the damage. The two women were too tired and emotionally beaten to chat much, but their silence was not an uncomfortable one. When they did talk, it was with a complete understanding. Except for the fact that she had married Chet Hamilton, Marianne was no fool.

"It isn't your fault, you know," Julie reassured her once.

"Isn't it?" Quite suddenly, she felt the need to voice her thoughts. "If I had killed him as I intended to do, this wouldn't be happening."

157

Julie found herself smiling at that, and then wondering just how tired she was, since a smile of any sort didn't seem appropriate. "You see murder as an answer?"

Marianne returned her smile, though very weakly. "Not really. But it would have saved a hassle."

"I can't argue with that."

The two men found the lab, as the aide had warned them, a mess. Expensive and sophisticated equipment had been smashed and broken into little pieces. Jars of acids and chemicals had been located, opened, and poured over every available surface. Papers were soaked and ruined, the floor stained, the walls splattered. Boxes of supplies had been emptied out and thrown about. Little, if anything, was salvageable.

Even with the chaos before him, Neil found himself heaving a sigh of relief. At least no one had been hurt, not this time. What had happened to the machinery was regrettable, but it could be replaced, walls and floor restored.

As they turned to leave, they found themselves looking into the faces of two strange men.

"McDaniels here," one said, "and my partner Jacoby."

"The policemen?" Kevin asked.

When they acknowledged that, Neil glanced at his young colleague and saw his own relief mirrored in the worried face. Most likely these men had never been in a situation like this either, but that didn't seem to matter. They were strong, and armed, and on the side of St. Paul's.

"They can't hide from all of us forever," Neil said softly. "You walked up right behind Kevin and me before we knew it. Soon someone is going to walk up right behind them."

"It'll happen," the one called Jacoby said. "It'll happen. And we hope it's soon."

He sounded almost happy, and clearly very excited. Neil sighed again. Jacoby was very young. At his age, perhaps he too would have felt the thrill of being challenged.

There was no thrill for him now. He was pushing fifty, his Jan was gone, and now the reputation he had worked to build was in danger of being irreparably damaged. It was enough to make a man cry. Or go get drunk. But they were locked in St. Paul's and there wasn't a drop in the house, so he supposed he'd just have to remain sober. As he would have anyway. He knew that, but quite often in his lifetime he had wondered how it would be to just give up and give in, as so many of his patients did. He had wondered and wondered, never more than now, but he also knew it wasn't going to happen. Not to him.

"We'll keep on the lookout," one of the policemen told them.

"See that you do," Neil said, then he and Kevin went back to the conference room. Upon entering, he took in the scene. Julie sat alone at the long, long table. A mug of coffee was untouched in front of her. No one else was in the room.

"Where's Marianne?" he asked quickly.

"I don't know. I honestly don't know. I guess I finally got so exhausted I dozed off, just sitting here like this. When I opened my eyes, she was gone. I thought she had probably just gone to the restroom, but no one is in there."

"How long has she been gone?"

"I'd guess less than ten minutes. I couldn't have slept over five. When I first saw she was gone, it was five-fifteen. It's five-twenty-one now. Do you think she may have gone to find him?"

"I think it's very likely she's done just that. But she'd have no idea *where* to find him, no more idea than we do."

"Any signs of the Hamilton woman yet?" asked Agent Alterauge.

"I told them," Julie mouthed at Neil.

"Not yet. I'm afraid . . ."

"I know, Doctor, I know—it's what we're all afraid of. But if she made that decision, she's on her own now. There's little or nothing we can do."

"Seems to be our theme song."

"Get some rest, Doctor."

"How can I do that?"

"Let someone else man the phone."

It was reasonable enough, but Neil knew he wouldn't do it. He'd stay awake as long as he could, until he dropped from exhaustion—a state that threatened them all.

Neil stared into the hallway. There had to be a way. There just *had* to be.

Chapter Nine

The pediatric nurse paled, hung up the telephone, and turned to face Dr. Glen Fielding, who was awaiting the latest blood gas readings on the newborn infant.

"Well?" he asked, his manner impatient. It was not the customary attitude for this soft-spoken, easy-going man, but strain was taking its toll. He was suffering from lack of sleep coupled with the burden of dealing with the distressed neonate, a situation that was not his milieu. Even in a small hospital environment, this was the era of specialization, and it was Glen's custom to separate the child from the mother, then pass it on to someone else's care. Only now, there was no one to be the receiver.

"There is no lab. It's been destroyed."

"What?"

The nurse stood helpless, a stricken look on her face.

"The men . . . they completely demolished all the equipment in the laboratory, and dumped out lots of reagents and stuff. Besides, the only lab tech in the hospital has now been admitted. She was raped and beaten, and one of her arms was fractured. So, there's no way to run the tests, and no one to do it anyway. The best we can do is draw and label the samples till something can be done. Even if we could get the samples out and transported to another facility, the results could be phoned in, but they say nothing in and nothing out."

All color faded from Fielding's face. He went quickly to the baby girl's Isolette. Such a tiny scrap of humanity, and so dependent on all the tubing running into her body. She needed out of here. She needed experts taking care of her. What was a new situation here was routine in a Neonatal Intensive Care Center. For the moment, she seemed stabilized. Even without the close laboratory monitoring, he could see on gross assessment that her color was pinking up, that her respirations were less labored, and that capillary reperfusion was improved.

"Little one," he murmured, "I sure wish your life wasn't in my hands." There was an actual physical aching in his heart. With a child such as this, a few moments of fulminating anoxia could occur—an event that could result in sufficient cerebral damage to render her mentally defective for the rest of her life. He checked the readings on the oximeter. She was okay for now.

"I'm going to the conference room to talk to Dr. Dvorak," he told the scant pediatric night crew. "Call me there if there are any changes."

In the surgeons' lounge, Dave Rasmussen lay sprawled on the sofa, still dressed in the wrinkled scrub suit. He was not as young as he once had been and, at this moment, was feeling every one of his years. He had received the news about the laboratory situation and his imagination, though tired, was running rampant. His mind was filled with an obsessive succession of "what ifs." What if someone else required surgery? What if someone who had had surgery started hemorrhaging? Conditions under which they could operate were getting more and more primitive. No anesthesiologist, no radiographic monitoring, and no laboratory control available. He had also been told the acute care cardiac telemetry monitoring was disabled, and that was a service frequently used for postsurgical patients. Telemetry service was still intact in ICU, but it was hard to say how long it would last. He could only hope their captors did not realize they had not ruined every unit. Rasmussen shuddered at the thought of Chet and Mick entering the Intensive Care Unit, with all its sophisticated and temperamental equipment—most of it currently being employed to prolong the lives of critically ill patients.

A knock on the door came timidly. Rasmussen sighed. He was resigned. Too tense to sleep, even with the profound fatigue, he decided he might as well interact.

"Come in."

"I hate to bother you, Doctor . . ."

"But you decided you would anyway, hey, Jennie?"

Jennifer Weiller smiled. Dr. Rasmussen was being himself. She found that bit of normality, comforting. People were changing under her very eyes, worry, fright, and grief making them behave as they normally did not.

"I guess that's exactly what I decided, Dr. Rasmussen. You see, there's this patient . . ."

"And I was hoping this was a personal visit. No such luck, hey? Wishful thinking of a semi-dirty old man. Or maybe that should be dirty semi-old man?"

"I don't know . . . I mean, I don't think you're either. I—"

Jennie floundered, red faced. She had never known how to respond to levity. By the time she realized the other person was joking it was usually too late, and she had already made some inane remark that showed her ignorance.

"It's okay, Jennie," he said kindly. "Now, what is it I can do for you?"

"Maudie Evans . . . she's a cancer patient, probably end-stage. She has an epidural catheter for narcotic/analgesics and it slipped out. I'm not sure how, except that she has been moving around more than she usually does. I checked with the intern but he says he hasn't replaced it yet, doesn't feel comfortable with it. So we were wondering if you . . ."

He nodded. "Lead the way."

"Great. We'd really appreciate it. I know you're tired, but . . ."

"Exactly: *but*. We're all tired, aren't we, Jennie? We're ready for this to be over."

Jennie thought of the little house she rented, a quiet place that she seldom had the opportunity to share with anyone. Except, lately, that scraggly-looking cat who had been hanging around. She had fed him, too soft-hearted to watch him starve. She had considered calling the pound to have him picked up, but her heart had not allowed it, knowing that would seal his fate. In his present condition, he wasn't the sort of cat most people would select as a pet. She hadn't wanted him, yet there he was. When she looked into his yellow eyes, she was aware of looking at *someone*. There was an eerie sense of understanding between them, a feeling that was so strong she knew she could never again regard animals as almost inanimate objects, creatures far removed from humanity. She had left plenty of food and water in the place he had come to expect, so she knew he would not go hungry for a while yet.

Suddenly Jennie wanted to be home, the very home she had been trying to avoid when she agreed to stay and have coffee with Stephen. She hadn't wanted the quiet of home. She hadn't wanted the cat. And now she ached for them both. God, she prayed silently, if I get out of this, I'll clean up that cat, and take him to the vet for shots and neutering, and I'll never, ever complain again about the quietness, because the quietness was of my choosing.

"Jennie?"

"I'm sorry," she said, giving a shake of her head. "You said we were ready for this to be over, and I started thinking about home and hearth. I wanted to be there so badly."

"I know, Jennie, I know."

Seeing the tears well up in the young woman's eyes, Dave reached out and put an arm around her as they walked down the hall. It was getting to them all, this terrible, terrible mental and physical strain.

"We have to hang together. We have to keep our heads."

"I know. But it isn't easy."

"Yeah, but we're tough, we can do it. So lead me to this errant epidural. Hmmm. *The Errant Epidural.* Good title for a book or movie, you think?"

Jennie felt a giggle rise in her throat, not at the corny joke itself but at the realization that she had recognized the attempt at levity.

"You're just like Steve."

"Who's Steve, your husband?"

"Oh, no . . . I'm not married. He's one of the nurses I work with in ER."

"Oh, yeah, Steve Cates. Good nurse."

"I know. You can always count on him to work and be professional, but you can also always count on him to make jokes, no matter what the situation. That's what I meant — you're like him."

"There are worse qualities, my dear."

"Believe me, I know that. I wasn't being critical — maybe envious, but not critical. Anyway, let's see to that shunt. Have you ever met Maudie?"

"Not that I can recall."

"Then you're in for a treat."

As they walked and talked, they felt somehow revived, nurse and doctor drawing a strength from each they could not attain singly.

Outside St. Paul's, word had spread quickly. The hospital parking lot had become so jammed with hospital personnel, relatives of those inside, police, members of the media, and, of course, the merely curious, that crowd control was becoming a problem.

"We're going to have to radio the chief for extra cars," one young officer said wearily, "so that we can blockade the entrance. We have to get some of these people out of here, and keep others from coming in. It's —"

Before he could complete the sentence, a red Escort that

had seen better days squealed into the parking lot. The driver slammed on the brakes right in the middle of the area where Helen Laramore and two of the hospital board members sat and waited. The policeman walked over to the car and began saying the same thing he felt he had said so many times that the words weren't real, just poured out automatically. "We'll have to ask you to move on. If you have a medical emergency, then we suggest you start for the nearest hospital of your choice immediately. We have a crisis situation here and we cannot—"

A very young man, not much out of boyhood, jumped out of the little car. At first glance, he appeared very excited, and close inspection revealed that excitement to be due to fright more than anger.

"I can't move on. There isn't time. My girlfriend is having a baby."

The officer talked with exaggerated patience. "Then she'll have to have it elsewhere. Like I said, we have a crisis here."

At that moment the girl in the car, her hair as red as an autumn bonfire, let out a screech that any banshee would have envied. "Wesley, help me, I can't . . ."

"Oh, Jesus," the boy moaned. "Baby, hold on, we're going to get you a doctor." He jumped up on the hood of the car and began shouting, "I need a doctor over here, right now. Erika's having our baby, and she can't make it nowhere else."

"You mean it?" the policeman asked, his eyes growing bigger.

Erika let out another screech, this one very prolonged, which gave credence to young Wesley's proclamation. The policeman threw open the car door on the passenger side to find the girl, who looked about fourteen, writhing in pain, doing her best to recline in a bucket seat that didn't readily accommodate the position. The policeman said a few swear words, told the girl to hold on, turned around, and bellowed, "I need a doctor or a nurse—or both—*now!*" But Erika's baby was in no mood to be held back.

166

"It's coming now," she yelled at the top of her lungs, then gasped a few words that rivalled the officer's for pithiness. She turned sideways, threw herself backward until the middle of her back was pressed against the console dividing the bucket seats, and began clawing at the waistband of her elastic-topped stretch pants. Not knowing what else to do, the officer helped the girl pull the pants down to her ankles . . . and found himself staring at two clumps of dark hair, the mother's pubic hair and her new baby's head. With trembling hands, he cradled the infant's head and said what he felt he ought to say, words picked up from episodes of "Marcus Welby" and "Trapper John." "Push. Come on, push." And push she did, freeing her child's shoulders, allowing the rest of him — and it was definitely a boy — to slide into the policeman's hands.

Suddenly, help arrived.

"I'm Dr. Yates. I'll take it from here . . . but you've done the big job, young man."

The officer agreed with that wholeheartedly. This was the first time, and he hoped the last, that he had been caught in such a situation. He relinquished the wet, slick infant into the physician's hands and backed away. His eyes had a glazed look as he took in the situation, saw the sobbing red-haired girl with stained stretch pants gathered around her ankles and the now lustily crying infant the doctor held. A few more steps backward . . . and then he ran toward the edge of the parking lot, where he soiled a grassy knoll with his vomitus.

He was just wiping his mouth when the kid named Wesley walked up to him. "Great job," he said, extending his hand. "We appreciate it. I guess we still have to drive to the city so Erika and the kid can get checked out, but you're the one that got him here."

The policeman still felt dazed. What had he done? That baby was going to be born if he had to land on the floor of the car, no two ways about it. "No problem," he mumbled.

"Uh, what's your name?" Wesley wanted to know.

"Petrowski."

"I mean your first name."

"Malcolm."

"Oh," Wesley said, looking crestfallen.

"Something wrong?"

"I guess not. I just thought we might name the kid after you, only . . ."

"Yeah, I know," said Malcolm Petrowski, his skin color beginning to return to a more natural hue. "Give the kid a break. Name him John, or Jim, or something. Life's hard enough, without having to carry around a name like Malcolm. But good luck to the two of you. Uh, it's none of my business, but you think you might get married?"

"Sure thing. We wanted to, but Erika couldn't talk her mom into signing for her. Maybe now that the baby's here, she'll change her mind. Might as well — she'll have a birthday first of the year anyway."

At a signal from Dr. Yates, Wesley returned to the Escort. "Drive carefully," the doctor cautioned. "No need to rush, now. Just keep the baby wrapped warmly, and make sure Erika stays as quiet as possible till you get to a hospital. Both are fine, in great shape."

With a nod, Wesley hopped in the car. Just before the parking lot exit Wesley stopped the car, stuck his head out the window, and yelled back, "Paul Malcolm is his name — Paul Malcolm Hinckly, after the hospital, the cop, and me!" Then the car rounded the corner and disappeared.

Their exit was made to a burst of applause from onlookers. Even the stoic Helen Laramore was caught wiping away a tear.

"Babies will come," she said softly. "No matter what, the babies will come."

Her words carried over the system that connected her portable telephone to the setup in the conference room.

"Maybe that's life's way of telling us something, teaching us a lesson," Neil said. "No matter how much bad happens, no matter how grave and awful a situation seems, life has a way of

168

reaffirming itself, of reminding us it's ready to try again in some new form, some new way."

Julie wiped away the tears that had gathered in her own eyes. "I don't have much of a green thumb, but when I first moved out of the dorm and into my apartment when I was in college, a friend gave me a shamrock plant as a house-warming gift. I guess it didn't like making the move or something, and it got all funny looking. The leaves all turned yellow and crumpled up. Basically, I was left with this pot of dirt. Only I hated to throw it out, because I saw a little tiny green speck. So I set the pot in the window where the sun comes in, and watered the soil a couple of times a week. Sure enough, a little green thing had been there. And it grew and it multiplied, and after a while my shamrock was back, more beautiful than when Becky had given it to me. And it's just like you said, I learned from that not to give up. To keep nurturing and hoping."

By the time she finished her tale, the tears were flowing freely.

Neil looked at her and burst into laughter, and she soon joined in, laughing through the tears.

"I think we're all cracking up," Julie said, when she was at last able to talk. "At least it's a fact that *I* am. If the circumstances were different, I'd suggest I see a psychiatrist."

"So, you're in luck. There are two right here. Don't be embarrassed, Julie. The story may have come out a little hokey, but the philosophy is sound: as long as there is a sign of life, there is hope."

"Hope. Neil?"

"Yes?"

"We have to find Marianne. I doubt that I talked her out of feeling guilty and responsible about all this. I think she's walked out there in a mood to sacrifice herself."

"I think so, too. The question is, where do we start?"

"Nowhere," barked Chief Inman over the telephone setup. "We have two men in there and, hopefully, they'll be joined by two more shortly. What we don't need is doctors and nurses and other hospital staff trying to be policemen. People messing around when they don't know what they're doing, well, it's a good way to get people hurt."

Julie and Neil exchanged looks that said the chief was probably right, but they weren't going to obey him anyway.

Neil tried to think of someone who might be of assistance, and his mind flashed to Stephen Cates. The male RN had impressed him as someone who did not hesitate to take action. He quickly dialed the number that put him through to the telemetry ward, where Stephen and Jennifer were working.

"All under control at the moment," Stephen told him.

"Then if they can spare you, come on down to the conference room. We have a problem."

In record time, Stephen appeared at the door, Jennie with him.

"Marianne is gone. She disappeared just after the last call, about the wreckage in the lab. I think it's time to organize a bigger search. Even if this hadn't happened, we'd have needed to do something. I'm tired of waiting."

"Anything you say," Stephen said. "I'm game."

"Somehow I knew you would be."

"Dvorak," Agent Alterauge shouted over the system, "you stay put. You heard what Chief Inman said. It's too dangerous out there for amateurs. Besides, Chet will be making his call soon. He'll expect to talk to you. It might infuriate him more if he can't."

Neil glanced at the clock. The next call was a mere seven minutes off, so he was willing to concede that much. "I'll stay for this call and see what the little shit has to say. After that, I make no promises. And we aren't exactly amateurs, gentlemen. We don't pretend to be trained in law enforcement, but we do know St. Paul's."

"We'll go on out," Julie said, placing a hand lightly on Neil's. "The three of us will try to locate the officers who are in here,

170

and we'll set up a division of territory to cover, then we'll come back and collect you."

Neil nodded. His head was aching. Seven minutes. He knew already it was going to seem like an eternity.

Chet and Mick sat in the third-floor linen room munching on snacks from the busted vending machine. Most of Mick's nausea had subsided, but he was quiet. To be really rowdy, Mick Hamilton needed a bit of liquor in his bloodstream. The blood-alcohol count that had spurred him to agree to all this had now all but dissipated. He took the last bite of the Snickers, then made a face. It was his third candy bar in the last hour, and suddenly he had lost his taste for chocolate.

"We need something to eat, Chet," he decided. "Not more junk, but some real food. A hamburger and fries, or a plate of bacon and eggs."

"What do you suggest we do, dummy? Go to the cafeteria and order out? When we get out of here, we'll have lots of money. We can eat then."

If Chet was unsure, he did not betray it, but Mick was definitely suffering from a multitude of doubts.

"Chet, can't we just break our way out of here, and forget the money? They'll never give it to us. Even if they did, what the hell would we do? Anywhere we'd show up and start spending that kind of money there'd be questions asked. We're in a corner, you know."

Chet glanced at his watch.

"Almost time."

Mick thought again of what had transpired in the stairwell, and his blood turned cold. He was tired. Chet had set up the phone calls for every thirty minutes, and that simply was not enough time to plan something, get from one place to another, and carry out the action. Especially not if Chet was going to take as much time as he had with the Hispanic girl on the steps. Forcing himself into the body of the doe-eyed nurse—

well, that had been okay. He had been careful not to get rough with her, and she was certainly no virgin. And wrecking that lab had been a real gas. After it was over, he had felt somehow calmed, his frustrations spent in the wreckage and spillage. But the dead preacher and the girl Chet had . . . well, it didn't bear thinking about. Mick closed his eyes. How he wished it would all just go away! Suddenly he was shaken out of the lethargy that possessed him, when he saw that Chet was running his fingers along the black detonator.

"Maybe it's time, time to show 'em we really mean business."

"Not yet," Mick said, his sickness returning full force. "Not the nursery, Chet."

Chet shrugged. "Why not? Someone came and got my kids, took 'em away, and said I can't even see them unless I make an appointment and get it arranged—and even then I can't be alone with 'em. Think that's right and fair? They took *my* kids, and for all the good they'll ever be to me now they might as well be dead. Think it would bother me to kill someone else's kids? No way, man. It's no big deal. They're just babies. They never even been home yet."

Mick broke out in a sweat. He didn't have any babies, not that he was sure of. Back when he was still in high school, Melanie Rawlings had said she was pregnant by him. He'd given her the cold shoulder, saying how could she know, she'd balled so many—which was true. Later, though, he'd heard the kid looked just like him, but he'd never tried to see it or Melanie. What was the point? Still, he couldn't see killing newborn babies. What had they done to them, or to anyone?

"Chet, don't do this. Maybe you'll get yours back. After they've investigated, and everything."

Chet shook his head. He knew, and Mick didn't, just what the authorities would find when they examined and interviewed Alix, Brie, and Jacob. No, his own were as lost to him as if they had never been.

But not Marianne. Not yet. They were inside the same

172

building, and there was a chance he could claim her, teach her a lesson, punish her.

"Please, Chet, just do something else this time. Something milder. Then if Dvorak doesn't listen, we can set off one of the bombs. But hint at it, remind him of it."

"What do *you* suggest we do, baby brother? Time is running out."

"Let's go out in the hall. First person we find, we'll take. Depending on who it is, we'll go on from there."

Chet shrugged again. It didn't really matter, anyway. Why not humor the kid and let him have his way this time?

They stepped out of the linen room, into the hall — and straight into the path of two officers, who had just made entry through a window. Both the officers were caught off guard, preoccupied as they were with brushing dust and debris from their uniforms and hair.

Chet and Mick both immediately had their pistols out and pointed at the policemen.

"I said no one in and no one out," Chet said coldly. "Some people seem to have a real listening problem." With that, he fired a slug straight into the chest of the younger man. He then whipped the .38 around and fired another bullet into the right arm of the second man. "Go find yourself a doctor and tell him about your buddy here. Tell 'em that's my message."

He glanced down at his watch, and grinned.

"Great timing. We still have a couple of minutes to find a phone and call Dvorak."

This message was short and sweet. He dialed the number. "Dvorak?"

"That's me," Neil said, glad he had heeded the words of Inman and Alterauge. He wasn't sure exactly how it had come about that he was Chet Hamilton's arch enemy, but that relationship did seem to exist in Hamilton's mind. Perhaps it did in his own. More times than he could count, Neil had lectured that any human being was reachable, redeemable — one just had to find the right key, or combination of keys. But in the

173

space of a few hours, he had come to doubt his own basic philosophy, for he could see no way to reach Chester Hamilton, much less redeem him. To him, the Hamilton brothers were evil personified, or at least close enough to it that he didn't ever want to encounter the real thing.

"One part of the message is finding its way to you. The other part of the message is that I want Marianne, the money, and a guaranteed way out of here. I'll be watching that statue out front. When you're ready to deal, have someone throw a cover over the statue. If that don't happen, thirty minutes from now it'll be 'Rock-a-Bye-Baby-boom,' you hear?"

"I heard. I don't see how it can be done, but I do hear you."

But Neil had a feeling he hadn't been heard, that Chet had already severed the connection before he spoke.

"What's that supposed to mean?" Alterauge asked immediately. 'Rock-a-Bye-Baby-boom'?"

"My first guess would be that it's a threat to set off a bomb in or near the nursery," Inman said.

"Oh, God, I hope not," Dvorak cried out. But he had no delusions about Chet's limits. With all of his being, he believed Chet had no limits. Not at this point. "But he did initially mention bombs, and I agree that seems the most logical interpretation."

"Get someone out there, that Cates fellow, or someone, and have him hunt up my men," Inman said. "There should be at least four in the hospital by now. Tell them to drop everything else and go to the nursery area, search it with a fine-tooth comb. And tell 'em to get those damned walkie-talkies operative. We need some communication."

Anything else he meant to say was lost when Dave Rasmussen came on the line.

"An Officer Horstmeier just walked up to the third floor desk a bit worse for wear, with a .38 slug in his right arm, fired at close range. He says they killed his partner, a Pat Jameson. They're taking Horstmeier downstairs now, getting ready to prep him for surgery. We need to get the bullet out and repair any damage we can. Just thought you guys might need to know."

Inman let out a moan. "No wonder I hadn't heard from them. God*damn* it! Jameson was just a kid."

"And so we have the other part of our message," Dvorak said. Turning to Kevin Donati, he said, "Man the equipment, please. Get someone else in here to help you if you can. I'm going to go see what I can find."

"Dvorak," Alterauge bellowed.

"You can't stop me. You're out there and I'm in here, and you simply cannot stop me."

"I can tell that. All I was going to say was get the revolvers off the two downed men for Cates and yourself. I hope to God you don't have to use them, but I'm sure you'll agree you'll be better help to everyone if you're armed."

There was a long pause, then Neil said, "Thanks, guys."

Just outside, he located Stephen, Julie, and Jennie, who were on their way back to him. Before they could report what they had done, Neil gave them the news about the two latest policemen to enter the building. Within moments, they were on the third floor rounding up the revolvers. Shuddering, Neil took the one that had belonged to the dead man. He looked at it with loathing. To carry such a thing, even under the guise of protecting himself and others, went against everything he had believed in all of his adult life. He was a healer. He had chosen that his healing be applied to the mind rather than to the body, but it was healing all the same. The ugly black police revolver was the antithesis of healing.

"It won't bite, Doctor," Stephen said, smiling at the psychiatrist's expression.

"Won't it? I'm not so sure. But I must say you look rather at home with yours."

"Remind me to tell you the story of my life sometime, sir. When we're sitting around sipping tea or something. I'm such a solid citizen now that one would never suspect that once I —. well, we don't have time for that now. Where do we go from here?"

"You and Jennie cover here and second. Julie and I will check out first and the basement. Just be damned careful. And remember that our goal is to get Marianne back to safety. We're going to have to leave the Hamiltons and the bombs to the experts. Agreed?"

"Agreed," they all said solemnly.

When the other pair had gone and Julie and Neil were alone, she looked up and down the corridor. They walked in silence for a while, then she said, "It's eerie. And very frightening. This isn't a big hospital, not compared to the city ones, but it's big when you're hunting for just one small person. I get the feeling we could walk for hours and our paths could never meet."

"Well, at least it should be easier than hunting for Chet and Mick. They're ducking into closets and crawl spaces and hiding out. She's out in the open, I'd guess, in search of signs of them."

Julie sighed dispiritedly, and Neil tried to reassure her.

"We'll find her. We have to."

But she heard the desperation in his voice, and digested it in silence as they walked up and down one shining hall after another.

It was fully ten minutes later that she faltered in her steps, looked at him, and said, "She means something to you, doesn't she?"

After a long hesitation, he replied, "I'm not sure how you mean that, Julie. I scarcely know her. But beneath what she has endured, despite the passivity until now, I sense a keen intelligence, a valiant spirit. As a patient, she intrigues me."

"I see."

It was not quite that simple, and they both knew it. In some strange way, Marianne Hamilton had come to mean a great deal to him, in a way that wasn't totally professional. But he

176

didn't know how to define it, and he didn't know what to do about it, so, considering the circumstances, denial seemed the safest approach.

Having covered the third floor as well as they felt they could, and seeing no trace of Marianne, they located a stairwell and descended to the second floor.

Just as they rounded a corner, Neil felt a hard object thrust into the small of his back. A moment later, Julie was jerked backward, her step no longer in line with his.

Chapter Ten

"Julie!" Neil called out.

"Just take it easy there," said a voice Neil had come to know well, although it was clearer now that it wasn't muffled by the intercom or telephone system. "Turn around, but take it slow and easy. In case you haven't figured it out, that's a gun that's pointed at your back."

"I gathered as much," he said, his sense of wryness not leaving him even under such circumstances.

"And another pointed at your girlfriend."

"She's not my girlfriend," Neil said as he turned around — turned very carefully, as he had been instructed. "That's Dr. Singer. She's a resident working with me for a year. Don't hurt her, boys. She's young and brilliant and has a great career ahead of her. Leave her alone . . . and just keep remembering that *I'm* the one you hate."

Chet laughed out loud. "Sounds like she's your girlfriend to me. Touching how you're trying to save her. But *you* just keep remembering that I'll do what I want. How smart she is means nothing to me."

Neil stared deeply into Chet Hamilton's gray-blue eyes. He saw there only a cold, cold hatred. It was not too dramatic, he thought, to consider those eyes demonic.

"What a big one we've bagged here, Mick," said Chet, laughing out loud again. "Know who this is? Can't you tell by the snooty voice?"

"Dvorak?" Mick said slowly, his eyes, so like his brother's, taking in the tired-looking, but still dapper, middle-aged man before him. "Why, it's the dipshit on the intercom and phone."

"Right, little brother. Never can tell what you'll bag in the halls."

For a moment, Neil cursed his own stupidity. Taken by surprise, he had jumped to the conclusion that Chet and Mick had nailed them on purpose. Now he could see it wasn't that way; the brothers had been out to find trouble and they were the first ones to happen by. To Chet and Mick, he had been only a voice at the other end of the line, and Julie less than that. Until now, they had had no idea what he looked like. But with a weary sigh, he absolved himself of guilt. He had given nothing away that they would not have discovered for themselves once they heard him talk.

"Get my message, Dvorak?"

"About the policemen you killed and injured? Yes. Chet, this is all so uncalled for."

"Don't lecture me, dipshit. You keep getting high-handed, keep forgetting who's in charge here. Mick and me are calling the shots."

"I haven't forgotten that. It's just that I have to try . . . try to keep you from hurting more innocent people. That cop you shot, he was twenty years old, Chet. *Twenty*. And what had he done to you?"

"He came in the building when I had ordered no one was to come in."

"But that wasn't his choice. He was just following orders. You know that, don't you? He would have rather been at home, or anyplace else at all."

While Chet and Neil talked, Mick stared in fascination at the dark-haired young woman at whom his gun was pointed. Her face was drained of all color and her brown eyes were wide with fright. She didn't look like any doctor he had ever seen . . . so young, so pretty, so timid.

179

"What are you going to do to us?" Julie asked in a low whisper. "Are you going to kill us, like you did those two men?" She did not ask about the rapes, could not bring herself to even say the word. Even as she stood there in terror, she wondered at herself, wondered why death seemed preferable to rape. Then her mind flitted to the two victims she had helped tend and, especially at the thought of Rita, her eyes closed momentarily in pain.

Mick shrugged. How could he answer her? He didn't know what they were going to do. He was getting pretty ticked off at Chet. The guy was berserk—no game plan, no rules. Just go down the hall and do something to the first person you see—okay, it had been Mick's idea, but Chet could have come up with something else. He was supposed to be in charge, but first he had said they would set off the bomb next to the nursery, and the next thing he knew, here they were with two shrinks at gunpoint. Not that Mick wanted to waste the babies—far from it—but he sure did long for a game plan.

"Well, babe," Chet said, turning his face away from Neil for a moment to answer Julie's question when his brother could not, "we're not entirely sure. You're just a couple of little bonuses that happened along. But rest easy. We're not going to kill you . . . not just yet. I figure there's some bargaining power with you two, so we'll just keep you on ice till we see how she blows. Oh, speaking of blowing, you figure out that message?"

"We think we did," Neil said slowly. "You guys do know, if you do something that reprehensible you'll never get away? Every law enforcement agency in the world will be trailing you."

Chet's reaction was to laugh again, but Mick's was to turn pale. Through it all, however, they kept their .38s trained on the doctors.

"Let's go find a place to store our bounty," Chet suggested. "Just move on down the hall, folks. We're walking right behind."

While the Hamiltons hunted for a place to hide Julie and Neil, everyone on the OB ward was in a flurry of activity. Once informed of the veiled threat, Glen Fielding was single-handedly running an evacuation of the ward.

Since the hospital wasn't anything like full, it was no problem to transfer the few new mothers to rooms in other areas. There was more of a problem with the babies, but except for the one on IVs and the pulse oximeter, Fielding and the nurses found a room on the first floor with enough outlets for the warmers to be plugged in. Somberly and with brisk efficiency, the nursing staff moved their records and what they needed most in the way of equipment. Fielding worried and fretted over the newest addition to the nursery, Dawn's tachypneic little girl, and decided that all-in-all she was doing better.

The two remaining uniformed men inside the building received the message from their chief, and temporarily abandoned their search for the Hamiltons to scour the nursery area for the bomb. Along with their instructions, they had received word of what had happened to their colleagues. Each bore his grief in a different way. As they went about their task, the taller one's face often crumpled, tears filling his eyes, and the shorter, more stocky one wore a look of deep and abiding anger.

In the parking lot, the mood grew even more solemn when the replacements for the two fallen men arrived. Both of them looked young, vulnerable, and scared, but despite that, they let the harnesses be fastened around them and prepared to scale the red brick walls of St. Paul's.

"Don't hesitate to shoot to kill," had been their chief's instructions. "To tell the truth, I'm not curious enough about how their warped minds work to want to bring them to trial and sentencing. Bring them alive if you can, but only if there's no risk, no risk at all."

Thus informed, they went up to, and in through, the window. After they had disappeared from sight, Helen Laramore returned to the car where Philip waited. His eyes were closed, but he opened them easily as soon as she walked up to him and before she had said a word.

"Want to go home for a bit and get some rest, freshen up?" he asked, knowing the answer even as he spoke.

She shook her head. "I have to be here. It's my responsibility. But go on home yourself. You have your job to see to. Perhaps bring me back a thermos of coffee and a sandwich, but then what about . . ." Her gaze took in the many people milling about.

"Yes," Philip said, "what about them? I'll tell you what I'll do: I'll round up a couple of volunteers, and we'll go see what's open in town. We'll bring back what we can. Even a few dozen doughnuts and a couple of urns of coffee would help. As for working tomorrow, or today, rather, considering all this, I think I won't have any trouble getting the day off. But don't wear yourself out, Helen. That won't help anyone or anything."

"I know. When you get back, perhaps I'll lie down in the back seat of the car for a few minutes. And Phil . . ."

"Hmmm?"

"Thanks for being here with me."

"No problem. If the shoe were on the other foot, you'd be there for me." He squeezed her hand warmly and went in search of volunteers to help him round up the refreshments.

On the second floor, Chet and Mick ushered Julie and Neil into a supply room.

"Damn!" Chet declared. "I need the rope and stuff out of the duffle bag."

"We left it in that room with the VCRs and stuff. You want

182

to go get it, I'll stay here and see these two don't go no place."

With a shake of his head, Chet rejected that action. "We need to stick together, so we'll just make do." He located two big rolls of autoclave tape, then ordered Julie and Neil to put their hands behind their backs. He used one roll of tape to bind Neil's hands together, while Mick did the same to Julie with the other. Since there were no chairs in the room, he ordered them to sit on the floor, their backs up against the corners of some metal shelves that ran from floor to ceiling.

"Wish we'd waited to tape their wrists till we had 'em down . . . but no matter, we'll think of something."

"Straddle them."

"Huh?"

"Have 'em each put a leg on each side of a post. Tape one leg of each one to a post, then tape their other legs together. See what I mean?" None-too-gently, Mick shoved Neil along the hard, tile-covered floor, awkwardly arranging it so that one of his legs was on each side of one of the shelf posts. Getting the idea, Chet arranged Julie in a similar position at the next post. Mick looked inordinately pleased at having thought of the idea. When four ankles were taped to their satisfaction, the brothers decided to tape the mouths of the doctors. However, they had barely started when Chet looked at his watch.

"Leave it," he commanded Mick. "That's good enough. They won't be going anywhere. We have to go find a phone."

In the OR, Dave Rasmussen looked at the gray faces of his crew, knowing their fatigue was mirrored on his own face. He worried about how much longer they could hold out. This one was going to be okay. Not that the bullet hadn't done a lot of damage, for it had, shattering the radius, severing the abductor pollicis longus, and sending shards of bone, as well as cloth from the uniform sleeve, into the layers of tissue. It was a fairly messy job on first inspection, yet it cleaned up well and the surgeon ran into no problems with excess bleeding or debris so deeply embedded it would not flush out with the saline irrigations. After the layer closure of the wounds and the insertion of the drain, Rasmussen hung around until Brian Lake had the patient extubated and partially aroused from the anesthesia. Not that he didn't trust Lake, but he had noticed how exhausted and stressed the anesthetist looked during the procedure.

"Crawl off somewhere, all of you," Rasmussen said gruffly to the crew, "and try to get some sleep. That's what I'm going to do. If they bring us one more surgical case, we'll never make it through a procedure, no matter how minor, the way we feel now. It's not a choice, it's something we have to do as professionals, if we hope to provide service. I need to have some rest before I can do anything else. I think the rest of you do, too, judging from the way you look. But bless you for all you've done. You've been terrific."

They nodded grimly, knowing he offered good advice, yet wondering how they could heed it. Who could rest under the circumstances? But Rasmussen was right . . . they had to try.

On the third floor, Maudie Evans had returned to her room. Things were temporarily quiet at the nurses' station and the personnel had seemed so weary, so subdued, that she felt perhaps she was in the way. She sat in the room alone, perched on the edge of the hospital bed, and lit a cigarette. She looked at the slender white tube without joy. When she was young, no one had been able to tell her anything. Now she wasn't so very young, although nor was she so very old, but she had never seemed to learn. Not about some things, anyway. She thought of those she was leaving behind, of the grandchildren she would never see grown. As she pondered these things, tears of self-pity filled her eyes. From time to time she puffed on the cigarette, but the nicotine brought her no joy, no relief.

Reaching back behind her, she touched the bit of plastic

tubing the surgeon had reinstalled for her. This was what it had come to; this bit of plastic through which morphine or Demerol could be injected was the most she could hope for. No cure at this stage. What was the funny word the oncologist kept using on her? Oh, yes—*palliative*. What they were doing at this point was palliative therapy. No matter how anyone defined the word, it meant one thing as far as Maudie was concerned: no hope.

Then, for no reason she could think of, Maudie's mind strayed to other things, to the events of this night that had caused her to quit pushing the bell for service every fifteen minutes and to venture out into the corridors. Maybe she didn't know all the details. Chances were, she didn't. Informing patients was not, she was sure, a priority. Still, she knew about most of it, had been in on the talk at the nurses' station.

The security guard wounded, two women raped, one of them badly injured as well, two men dead, and the surgeon who had replaced her epidural catheter had been called away to patch up another of the wounded. Cigarette in hand, Maudie got off the bed and wandered to the window. She looked down at the section of St. Paul's grounds visible from this viewpoint. People were milling about down there. One would have thought there was a picnic on the grounds. Except that the sun wasn't up yet, and everything was gray, except where the rays from the artificial lights sent out fuzzy paths of yellow.

For a long, long time, she stood there and looked, then she retreated back to the narrow bed. Tears were no longer a problem. A worried-looking Ruby came in to check on her, finding her sitting bolt upright in bed with a cigarette and a magazine.

"Maudie? I got worried. We hadn't heard from you for a while. Don't you need some more morphine? It's been long enough."

Maudie shook her head.

"You mean you're not having pain?"

"Oh, yes, darlin'," she answered in her raspy voice, "the pain is very much with me. But no morphine. Not right now. You see, I figured out that as long as I feel the pain, I know I'm alive. Most of you here, you got it worse than me. I brought it on myself, this cancer. I admit it now. You guys, you didn't ask for this mess. There was nothing you could have done to prevent it. Maybe I can be of some help. And even if I can't, I want to see how it comes out. You hear what I'm saying?"

Ruby's eyes were damp when she nodded her head. "I hear, Maudie. It's a big event. You want to stay till the end."

"Right," the patient barked. "And if I'm so wiped out on morphine that I don't know what's going on, it's like I'm already dead. One way or another, I'd miss the ending. So I'm going to sit right here and stand it just as long as I can."

"You do that, Maudie. And I'll come check on you from time to time. Funny—it's almost breakfast time, and there won't be any breakfast cooked. The kitchen crew can't get in. Wonder if anybody thought of that."

"You just did. So go do something about it. Me, I'm okay. Sick people gotta eat, though. Bet there's stuff in the kitchen don't take much cooking. Cereal and juice, and fruit, and toast and stuff."

Ruby nodded. "I'm sure you're right. So I'll go see what the others want to do. You take it easy."

"What else is there to do?"

"Careful there, you get too sassy and we're likely to put you to cooking breakfast."

"Know something? I wouldn't mind."

When Ruby was gone, Maudie lay back against the pillow and took a puff of the cigarette. She knew she wouldn't be helping with breakfast, or with much of anything else. She was so weak that she could not tie the belt to her robe. Pulmonary cancer did that to you. Along with the pain, one dealt with the terrible, terrible weakness. But no matter: she was determined to see the outcome of this crisis, so determined that she would not close her eyes even to rest them, fearing that she might fall asleep . . . asleep or something more final.

Out in the hallway on the second floor, Mick Hamilton looked at his older brother. "Chet, when we find a phone, what are you going to say? We didn't do anything yet."

Chet grinned and scratched his head. "You're getting tired, little brother. Real tired. Did we just nab us a couple of doctors, one of them the honcho that's been doin' all the talking, or what?"

Mick thought it over, then returned Chet's grin. "Yeah, I guess that is something, after all. I guess I was just thinking we didn't really *do* anything to them, know what I mean?"

"I know. And maybe that'll come later. But we need to do some bargaining."

Around the corner, only a few yards away, Steve and Jennie walked hand-in-hand, their gait slow, their expressions wary.

"Something is behind us, Stephen," Jennie whispered. "I can feel it."

"Then let's turn around, slowly."

They did so, their movements as perfectly synchronized as if they had been rehearsed. They found themselves face-to-face with Marianne Hamilton. At the sight of them, her good eye widened perceptibly and she became poised to run, like a deer on the edge of the road.

"Don't," Jennifer said softly. "Please don't run. We're out looking for you, you know. You can't make a deal with him, Marianne. It would be the same as committing suicide, and it wouldn't help the rest of us at all."

"Maybe not. But I feel so responsible."

At least, each of the nurses thought, she had not bolted on them yet. Walking very slowly, they drew nearer to her, and she did not seem to mind.

187

"Come with us somewhere, and we'll sit down and talk it over," Stephen suggested.

"Anyway, we couldn't make you do something you don't want to do, so it can't hurt to talk about it," Jennie said. As soon as the words were out, she recalled the police revolver Steve had hidden under his loose-fitting smock top. No, she thought, *no*. It was unthinkable to point a gun at this frail woman who was both timid and brave. Closing her mind against the thought, she continued, "When this is over, Marianne, if you just hang in there, there's a good chance you'll walk away from it. If they do anything at all, it will just be to place you on probation for a while. You heard what Dr. Dvorak said—no judge or jury would ever convict you of anything, not after what they've seen from your husband. That means you'll get your children back, and you know they're going to need you in their lives after this. So for their sakes, don't throw your life away."

"I don't know. I wish it was easier to tell right from wrong, but it isn't. How can you do the best thing or the right thing, if you have no idea what it is?"

"That's stuff we need to talk about," Steve said. "Come on, go with us."

"I suppose it wouldn't hurt. Not for just a few minutes. Not that I'm promising I'll change my mind, but I am willing to listen to someone else's ideas. We have to stop them. You know that. We just *have* to."

During the exchange, the three of them had just stood there. Now then turned and walked, three in a row, in silence down the hall. They turned the corner to the right . . . and found themselves only a few feet away from Chet and Mick. It would have been hard to say which set of people was the most surprised. Everybody gasped.

Chet, after the initial surprise, only had eyes for Marianne.

"There you are, bitch. Are they bringing you to me? About time. Where's the money? Did you bring the money, too?"

"She's not coming to you, Chet," Steve said tensely, "and

there is no money."

With a harsh laugh, Chet pulled out his gun once more, then motioned Marianne to come to him. When she started to obey him, something snapped inside Stephen. Swiftly he pulled out the injured policeman's revolver and said, "Marianne, get back here."

Marianne, however, thinking she was going to save the situation somehow, made a lunge forward instead of doing as Steve commanded. Chet reached out, grabbed her by the arm, and pulled her to him. Red flashed through Steve's brain. He pointed the revolver at Chet, squeezed the trigger, and felt his own arm jolt with the force of the firing. The bullet struck Chet in the left shoulder. His eyes widened and protruded and he let out a yelp, at the same time releasing Marianne.

Jennie ran forward and got hold of Marianne's arm. The Hamilton woman seemed to be in a trance-like state, and allowed herself to be manipulated. From the corner of his eye, Stephen saw Mick pull out a .38 that matched his brother's. In a flash, he turned in Mick's direction and fired. This time it was not a flesh wound, but a hit dead center in the chest.

"What have you done? Jesus Christ! What have you done?" Chet screamed. They all stood in horror, listening to the gurgling sound in Mick's chest as he fell to the floor.

"We'll help him. We're nurses," Stephen said. "RNs. But before we'll take one step toward him to do anything at all, throw your gun to the floor and kick it this way."

Chet looked down at his fallen brother, looked across at the two women and the tall black man with the gun, then down at his own gun. The pain in his shoulder was unreal. Not even he knew what he was going to do until he did it. He fired a shot blindly in the direction of his three adversaries, then turned and ran in the opposite direction. Stephen started to run after him but found he could not, a searing pain letting him know that Chet's errant bullet had landed in his left ankle. Not serious, he felt, but it hurt like hell, and his white sock was quickly turning red. He made one more lurch forward, trying in vain to get his wounded extremity to cooperate. Jennie reached out and put a restraining hand on his arm. "You can't catch him, Steve. Not the way you are now. But he's wounded, too, and now he's alone. It won't be long till he gives up or till someone tracks him down. Now sit down, let me look at the ankle."

"Better see to him first," Steve said, pointing at the man he had shot. A flow of red was still pumping from Mick's chest, accompanied by the nauseating gurgling sound.

"Go for help, Marianne," Jennie said. "Go to the nurses' station, tell them we need nurses and any interns or doctors available, right now."

Some color had returned to Marianne's face, making her seem less ethereal and frail. She turned and ran as fast as her long, thin legs would carry her.

"I'll make my own tourniquet," Steve said between clenched teeth, "until help comes. Just go see to him."

"I'm not sure I want to help him, Steve."

"Yeah, well, I know how you feel. But we'll do it all the same, right?"

"Right," she said, walking forward, then dropping down on one knee beside Mick Hamilton.

Slowly, and with a great deal of distress, Stephen maneuvered himself into a sitting position on the tile floor. He slipped his left shoe off and grimaced to see how much blood was inside it. Putting it aside, he stripped off the bloody sock, then removed the shoe and sock from his good foot. He took the clean, dry sock and tied it around the ankle over and above the wound as a combination bandage and tourniquet.

While he did that, Jennie did what she could for Mick Hamilton, as distasteful as she found it. The bleeding was steady but not profuse. In truth, she did not feel there was much chance of saving him, but she knew she had to try — and try her best, since it was something she didn't want to do. Gently, carefully, she placed his head in the proper position and bent to do mouth-to-mouth resuscitation. His pulse was extremely shallow and thready, and his respirations were very harsh and labored.

Within moments, they were surrounded by colleagues.

"Looks like we get to do more surgery, Dave," Glen Fielding announced to his colleague.

"Hmmm," Rasmussen said, his sense of humor temporarily falling by the wayside. What had happened to the brief naps he and his crew were to have?

"Mine's no big deal," Steve said staunchly. "Just bandage and splint me up, and let the bullet wait till this is over."

Rasmussen eyed the ankle skeptically. The second white sock had turned red. "Let me be the judge of that, young man."

"This one looks and sounds like a goner anyway," the intern said from where he knelt over Mick Hamilton's still form.

"Wish we could be so lucky that he'd give his final gasp here and now," Glen Fielding said coldly. "It's a shame that we have to even try to patch up scum like this. But I know we can't make these decisions. We have to treat the patient, not the personality. Anyway, get this one on a gurney and take him to OR. Steve here can make do with a ride in the wheelchair — just keep the injured leg well elevated. I'm going by to check on my baby, Dave, then I'll be along to OR to help where I can."

"Thanks, Glen. We're going to need all the help we can get. I'm about ready to drop, and I'm sure the rest of the crew is too. Oh, lord, I just thought of something: has the nursery area been completely evacuated?"

"Completely. Not just the nursery, the entire OB wing of the second floor. Maybe we should evacuate all that floor completely. I don't know. It's hard to know what we're fighting. We don't know if there really is a bomb, or what kind it is and what kind of range it would affect if set off."

"The reason I asked is, it just came to me. That maniac is wounded. We've as good as killed his brother. What does he have to lose? I'm afraid he will set it off."

Fielding nodded. "I'll go by the conference room and talk it over with Neil Dvorak. He's heading things up in there. I can see what idea he has on it."

"Dr. Dvorak isn't in the conference room," Stephen volunteered. "That is, unless he's gone back in just the last few minutes. Marianne Hamilton took off about an hour ago. Some of us got worried about her and went looking. Jennie and I were searching on the lower floors when this happened. Dr. Singer and Dr. Dvorak were covering the second and third."

"Then they don't even know this happened?"

"I don't know. Probably not."

"I'll go look for them," Marianne said, stepping out of the shadows. Everyone, including Jennie and Steve, had forgotten she was present, so unobtrusively did she retreat into the background having brought help.

"No," Fielding said, taking her by the arm, "let's just go see who's there and talk it over, *then* I'll go see about the baby."

Some version of what had happened to Mick Hamilton and Stephen Cates had already filtered down to the few tired people in the conference room. When Glen and Marianne appeared there, they found that Neil and Julie had not returned.

"It's past six o'clock," Kevin Donati observed, "and we haven't heard from Chet. Think he's seriously wounded?"

"From what I was told I'd say it hurts, of course, but I doubt it's mortal. So much the worse for us."

From his post at the Bainbridge police station, Chief Inman swiftly issued an order to his officers on the grounds of St. Paul's. "Get on the walkie-talkie and get word to the four men searching for the bomb to get out of there. I have a feeling—and I don't think I'm alone—that Chet Hamilton just might be outraged enough to let 'er blow. And get someone down to get the detonator off Mick."

One of the officers asked, "What are the chances on getting word to that pair of psychiatrists to clear out of the OB and nursery area?"

"Nil. No walkie-talkies. The intercom's disabled. No way at all of communicating. I told those fools not to go off, but they did. Now they haven't been heard from for over thirty minutes. It's not a good sign. I told them to check in frequently. But at least we know Chet and Mick didn't have them."

"We don't know that at all, chief. Apparently they didn't have the doctors with them when the other bunch ran across them, but that doesn't mean they hadn't disposed of them first."

There was a long pause. "You're a great comfort."

"I try to be."

Outside the surgical suite, the four officers stared down at the small arsenal removed from Mick Hamilton—the knife, the snub-nosed revolver, and the detonator.

"How I wish we knew," one said, his forehead furrowed with worry, "if this is the only one, or if they both carried one, or whether this would set off only one specific bomb or all of the ones they may have hidden."

"One way to find out," another said, playfully reaching his thumb toward the device.

"Oh, shit, Roy, don't even kid around with that. Let's just go somewhere where we've got light and elbow room, and de-activate the thing."

"You know how? I mean, you ever done anything like this?"

"Hell, no. But there's always a first. And we got all of Bainbridge's finest, plus the FBI, plus a few recruits from the Big Apple itself out there. Surely someone can tell us what to do and how to do it."

"We can hope."

While these two went off with the detonator, the other two officers went to meet two more who had been sent to gain entry to St. Paul's through the top-story window.

"What I want to know," one of the new ones complained as he undid his harness, "is why the third floor? It looks like it would have been just as easy, and no harder to hide from this guy, if we came in through a lower-level window."

"Maybe so," was the reply, "but the powers that be said we'd do it this way, so we did. I think the reasoning was that Chet wouldn't be expecting it. And you gotta admit, it wasn't easy."

After a bit more in the way of mild grumbling and griping, they settled down, divided up, and went in pairs in search of a worn and bleeding Chet Hamilton.

In an empty room, the two policemen stared in fascination at the detonator.

"Find the way into the casing," came the slowly and clearly stated instructions through the walkie-talkie. "Find where it fits together, then as carefully as you ever did anything, pry it apart at that area to get inside. Got it?"

"Got it."

With the thinnest blade on his pocket knife, the lanky man manipulated the crease that seemed to join the two black sides of the tubular device together. "It's off," he said, when the metal casing yielded to the gentle pressure of the knife blade. "There's no wires. I expected wires. How can I take it apart with no wires?"

There was silence at the other end of the walkie-talkie for a moment, but somehow the other man's exasperation managed to make itself known even before he spoke, "Officer Seabaugh, the wires are in the bomb itself. This thing you have is like a remote control device to a TV set or garage door. Mostly we see two kinds. The simplest kind has some buttons or pegs that can be depressed. The other is most like a garage door-opening device. You'd have a certain code to press in to activate it. Which kind does this look like?"

"Just a couple of buttons on top of a dull black box—kind of a flat box. I don't see any way into it. I guess it has seams somewhere, but I can't see them."

"I see. Then go put it someplace it can't be touched. Find someone in the business office or someplace who can open the safe where patients' belongings are stored. Put it in there, lock the safe, and label the door in letters about a mile high that no one is to get in there. I'd like to see the thing put out of action, but I'm afraid we're going to fool around and set it off, and that's the last thing we need. You made a valiant try, guys, but I don't think it's the kind we can mess with. Better concentrate on finding the bombs themselves. *Them* we can disable."

"Speak for yourself," Seabaugh said, the sweat dripping from his brow. "When this is over, I may see if I can find a job in a shoe factory or something."

The FBI man chuckled. "Where's your spirit of adventure? A man needs a challenge now and then to remind him he's alive."

"Could be I'll agree with that later. Right now I'm so scared I'm about ready to mess my drawers, so if you'll excuse me for a minute . . . I have to run."

"Meet you down by the conference room and we'll find out where the business office is," his partner said. "I'll see if I can get this thing put safely to bed. You know what, Seabaugh?"

"What's that, McElheney?"

"Broke as I am, I'd give a year's salary to know if this is the only detonator, or if good ol' Chet is still carrying one."

"Yeah, me too. But I wouldn't bet on it being the only one. The one the nurse shot had a .38, a knife, and this thing. We know the other one has a .38 and a knife, so . . ."

"Yeah, you're probably right."

Seabaugh grimaced and said, "See you in a few minutes," then he rushed to the nearest restroom.

In the parking lot, a member of the press from New York gratefully accepted a grilled cheese sandwich and a cup of coffee. Shivering, he pulled his jacket closer around him. "Anything else?" he asked the now gray-faced administrator of St. Paul's.

"Nothing," she said with a shake of her head. "Mick Hamilton is in OR now. As soon as they can, they'll let us know about his condition. As for the nurse, Stephen Cates, he's stable. They said they'll keep his leg elevated, get him on antibiotics, and see if he can wait till we can get a fresh surgical crew in there. Dr. Rasmussen says he needs an orthopedic surgeon."

"Any word from Dr. Dvorak? He was the spokesman, now he seems to have disappeared."

Helen Laramore felt her blood run cold. "He and his resident went out in the halls to see if they could help. It really hasn't been long, it just seems that way. Please, sir, I'm tired. As soon as we have an announcement, we'll make it."

"Yes, ma'am."

On first floor, a cursing Chet Hamilton staggered into the stairwell at the far end of the hall. It was seldom used, for it led only to the fringe areas of the hospital used by engineering employees — and even they rarely had need of it. With a great deal of awkwardness, he extricated himself from his shirt. Cursing with renewed fervor, he looked down at the wound made by the police revolver. Although it was still jetting a small amount of blood, he saw that the force of the stream was slowing and that there was some dried blood around the edges of the wound, a good sign that his blood had begun its clotting process.

He felt a greater anger than he had never known. He had always been an angry person, yet this was different. This was an anger tinged with despair. Mick had been right all along. There was no way out. His initial rage had led him into this when he had no real plan for escape, nothing even to escape *to* that he could count on. Still, when Mick had been there with him, he had wanted to believe that there was hope, that the two of them together could do something to show the world.

Now Mick was gone, killed by that smart-alecky black bastard he'd taken a dislike to in the Emergency Room. Or he assumed Mick was dead. No way a guy could live for long with a slug like that in the chest. For just a moment there, Chet had tasted victory. The two nurses had been at gunpoint, and his hands were on Marianne. What happened after that was a blur. Where did the other gun come from? Nurses didn't carry guns. Or not till this time.

Chet thought of the two psychiatrists bound up in the storage area a floor above him. With that, his anger intensified to the point of white heat. He wanted Neil Dvorak dead. But before that, he wanted him to suffer. Chet Hamilton might be down, but he wasn't out. He knew now he'd never walk away from this. And, in a way, that was okay. But he was going to see that he took as many with him as he could.

He pulled the detonator out of his waistband and touched its controls lovingly. All alone in the stairwell, he grinned the grin of a demon. He tried to remember which he held, the one to the bomb in the nursery supply closet, or that to the bomb in with the engineering department's gear. He found he did not know. He tried to think if he had ever known, and simply could not recall. All he knew was that he had handed one to Mick — poor ol' Mick — and kept the other for himself.

Well, he had no idea how much damage the explosion would do, but he supposed he was just about to find out . . . him and everybody else. His mind filled with vengeance, he pressed the button, then sat back to listen.

Chapter Eleven

The sound, and the impact, was like nothing anyone inside or outside St. Paul's had ever heard. In the wake of the explosion, the old building shuddered. Brick, mortar, and plaster began flying . . . and the windows on the west wing of the third floor burst and shattered, glass and wood remnants raining down on both the ground outside and the tile floor inside.

Gigi had wandered into the corridor. Her voices had told her to. No matter that the nurses had given strict orders for all of them to remain in their rooms. When the voices spoke, how could she heed what mere mortals had to say? "Someone wants to keep something from you, Gigi," one of the voices had said, the male one that was always trying to get her into mischief. "Don't let them keep you out of anything. You have your rights, you know."

And so it was that Gigi wandered where she wasn't supposed to be. And while the irrational side of her did the bidding of the voice, the rational side of her longed to run into that nice thin girl with the long brown hair and bruised-up face. What was her name? She couldn't recall. Perhaps she hadn't said. But Gigi had liked her. She seemed a safe and kind person, with nothing menacing about her. Sometimes some of the voices warned her about certain people, but they had been quiet about Marianne.

198

Then *it* had happened—the terrible noise and the shaking of the building. An earthquake? Were they supposed to happen here? Gigi thought that was mainly a problem on the other coast. And that was the last lucid thought she had. A very large piece of plaster fell from the ceiling and struck her on the back of the head. With a moan she fell to the floor, where she lay very, very still.

In the psychiatric unit, once the initial shock was over, the three hospital personnel on duty dusted themselves off and did a quick head count. There was hysteria, which was only to be expected, but all the patients were present but one.

It was the somewhat timid ward secretary who found Gigi, buried at the far end of the hall beneath a pile of broken plaster. Penny was a secretary, not a nurse, but she knew dead when she saw it. She cried out at the sight of the limp form, so very still. From the waist down, the woman was clearly visible, but Penny had to peer closely into the rubble to find a trace of Gigi's trademark, the dyed red hair tortured into an afro-style hairdo.

"Martha, Rosa," she called, "come here. I've found her, but I'm sure she's dead."

They ran down the hall and Martha, the RN, cleared away enough of the plaster to allow her to feel Gigi's skull. There was a soft, depressed area on the posterior occiput, the sure sign of a depressed fracture.

"At least it was quick," she said softly, her tears flowing. "She couldn't have known what hit her. And she'll never have to hear those awful voices again."

Rosa nodded solemnly, cried a few tears, and then, being a practical woman, said she'd go make a call, see how wide the damage was, and see what kind of help they could get in taking their surviving patients to an unharmed area.

In the east wing of the third floor, the trembling was fierce but the damage minimal—a little plaster here and there, a few shattered windows, but the brick walls remained intact.

As calmly and efficiently as possible, given their fatigued states, the staff of St. Paul's helped those being ushered out of the destroyed wing. Except for Gigi, no one was seriously injured. A few lumps, bruises, and scrapes, but, on gross assessment, nothing that qualified as severe, not even a fracture or a laceration that required repair.

Earlier, in the surgical suite, David Rasmussen and his weary crew labored over the thorax of Michael Hamilton. They did not talk to each other except as was necessary to perform the task at hand. They all hated what they were doing. It was not something they talked about, but all thoughts ran along the same lines: This was a man to be abhorred, this was a man who had brought violent death, injury, and destruction to peaceful little St. Paul's. It was right that he should die, yet they could not make that decision . . . and knew they could not.

It was soon clearly evident that, as they had first suspected, theirs was a futile task. Not even a bigger and better team of experts in a much large facility could have repaired the damage laid before them.

The bullet Stephen Cates had fired had entered the thorax, turned through the pleura of the left lung, taking a goodly section of the right lower lobe as it went, then proceeded to pierce the right ventricle of the heart.

When the mediastinal incision was complete and the thorax open, Rasmussen gave a low whistle of dismay. "No wonder he looks and sounds bad. I'm out of my league here, folks. I'm a general surgeon, not a thoracic one. We're not just talking muscle and tissue damage here . . . we're talking about parenchymal damage to two vital organs. I can't—" At that point, his voice cracked. Glen Fielding, who was once more serving, albeit reluctantly, as surgical first assistant, stepped forward. In Rasmussen, he recognized the signs of a man at his breaking point.

"Do what you can, Ras. No one can ask more. If we could get word to Chet that his brother needs to be taken out by helicopter to a bigger hospital, maybe he'd listen to reason. But under the current system, the only way we could get a plea in to him would be if he called us first. He hasn't done that in the last while. Repair what damage you can, secure the hemostasis, then we'll just have to put in some drains and let nature take it from there. He's a young and healthy specimen, but somehow I don't think that's going to be enough at this point."

"Glen, I—"

Glen placed his hand on Dave's wrist. "You're a talented man, Ras. A blessed man. You're just worn out and under tremendous pressure. Like all of us. Just take it one step at a time. Whatever happens, no one will blame you. We all know the shape this guy is in. Now, can you retrieve the bullet?"

Rasmussen took a deep breath, looked into the eyes of his colleague—funny how you never paid any attention to a person's eyes until the eyes were all you could see, as they were in OR when the mask and cap covered the rest of the face and head—and gave a slow resigned smile.

"I think I can. I really think I can. So let's do that first—let's go for the slug. You and Vic stand by with the cautery, okay?"

"Okay."

Within moments, Rasmussen had the .45-caliber bullet grasped with the small forceps. Smiling, he deposited the slug on the specimen tray, listening wish some satisfaction to the metallic ringing sound as it hit.

But his moment of pleasure, though sweet, was brief. One look back into the damaged chest and he felt as inadequate as he could ever remember feeling. There wasn't a darn thing he could do, not a darn thing. With the aid of Fielding and McMichael, all visible bleeding points were cauterized. He then began a slow and careful irrigation with an antibiotic-laced saline solution, then re-cauterized after that. Through it all, he knew they were fighting a losing battle.

"Pulse?" the surgeon asked Brian Lake.

"Twenty and falling. BP 40/12."

"Shit."

"Exactly."

Making use of a variety of plastic catheters, shunts, and drains, Rasmussen did his best to compensate, with a variety of suture ligature, for the missing tissue.

"It's amazing," he mumbled, "that we haven't had a pneumothorax here."

"It's coming, I can almost promise you," Lake said.

"And then what?"

"You know the answer to that."

Rasmussen did. They all did. It didn't take a degree, just a certain amount of experience, to recognize what constituted a dead man.

One of the nurses mopped Rasmussen's profusely sweating brow, then he continued his work. Suddenly, they were aware of a powerful, though muffled, noise, and a sensation of trembling ensued. The lights flickered, some of the equipment took on a different sound, then things were quickly returned to normal.

"Oh, lord," Rasmussen said, "not something else. I simply cannot handle one more thing. One of you who has a free hand, go call someone, see what that was."

The intern, currently not needed in the operative field,

went to the phone on the wall. As he walked back to the operating table, his eyes had a dazed look.

"It was a bomb," he said in a hushed voice. "Chet set off a bomb. They said a good portion of third floor was badly damaged."

"How many people are going to need surgery?" Dave asked. "We can't. We just can't go on. It isn't physically possible."

"No head count yet, sir. It just happened. She said they'd call us back when they knew more."

With that, they again devoted their full attention to Mick Hamilton, all of them waiting for the patient to breathe his last. But the labored, sonorous respirations continued, and the pulse and blood pressure, though awesomely low, did not drop further.

On the second floor, in the supply room, Neil Dvorak had just managed to chew through the tape that covered his mouth. He gave a small sigh of relief when he felt the break in the tape. He felt inordinately grateful that Chet had been in too much of a hurry to tape their mouths as thoroughly as their ankles and wrists had been taped.

"I'm ungagged," he said.

"Hmmm," Julie said, indicating that she was not.

Laboriously, Neil bit and chewed away as much of the tape as he could until he was able to talk unimpaired. He then inclined his head toward Julie's and began using his teeth to tear at the tape still covering her mouth. Within a few seconds, enough tape had been removed that she, too, could talk.

"Sorry, kid, but I damaged you some," he said. "There's a couple of drops of blood on your lower lip. The tape held a bit too tight there."

With a nod, Julie ran her tongue over her swollen lower

lip. "Oh, Neil, where will it end? How are we going to get out of here? What does he have in mind for us?"

"I don't have the answer to any of those questions, and you know I don't. But at least we can scream now. Think anyone will hear?"

Julie's dark gaze took in the heavy walls and steel rafters, and the thick double doors. She shook her head. "We'll try, of course. But the doors are so thick, and we're so far away from them. Maybe if someone just happens to be right outside . . . we can only hope."

For the next few minutes, they both yelled at the top of their lungs, then, throats raw and aching, they eased off. Neil gave a slight smile. "I feel somewhat foolish."

"That makes two of us. We'll have to rest a bit. Or at least I will. My throat hasn't felt this way since I cheered at a really exciting football game in my junior year of high school."

"Did you win that one?"

"We won. And, who knows, maybe we'll win this one."

"You were a cheerleader?"

"Oh, yes. For years and years. From seventh grade all the way through my senior year. There were times when I felt my life hinged on whether or not I made the squad. There were tryouts each year, very grueling things."

"I know," he said with a laugh. "Emma was a cheerleader and, as you said, her very being seemed to hinge on that. Abigail, on the other hand, thought it all rather silly. She wanted no part of that side of school. Two girls raised in the same home, and so different."

"Still different?"

"Very. But both very level headed and seemingly well adjusted. I just wish they were closer—but they had to follow their own stars, not live where I chose to follow mine. Emma is a CPA and Abbie—my God, what's happening?"

Eyes wide, they sat helplessly and listened to the rumble

that seemed to split the earth apart. Following the initial rumble, they heard the falling of brick and plaster, the shattering of glass.

"The bomb," Julie said softly. "They set off a bomb. I'll bet anything that's what it is."

"I wouldn't bet against you. Oh, boy, do we need out of here. Can you imagine how many people might be hurt out there?"

"I can imagine. I just don't want to."

They tried another yelling session that brought what they expected: no results. With all that mayhem outside, they felt there was little chance their own noise would be noticed.

"Julie, I'm constantly rubbing my hands and wrists, as much as I can, up and down against the post. Think you can do the same, or are you bound too tightly?"

"It's pretty tight, but there's a little play. I'll do what I can."

"Great. If one of us can wear through the tape at the wrists, then we can probably get out of this and get out there where we can be of help."

"*This* was supposed to have been help," Julie reminded him wryly. "We were going to locate Marianne and bring her back to the fold. When, and if, we get out of this, you know what the police chief and FBI agents are going to say, don't you?"

" 'Told you so, told you so,' " he said, in the mocking tones of a child out to be spiteful.

"Neil?"

"Yeah?"

"If it doesn't hurt your throat too much, talk to me."

"About what?"

"Anything. Everything."

" 'Of shoes — and ships — and sealing-wax — of cabbages — and kings — And why the sea is boiling hot . . .' "

" '. . . and whether pigs have wings,' " she finished for him.

"Or words to that effect. I'm scared. Can't you tell that?"

"Under the circumstances, I'd wonder at the sanity of anyone who wasn't scared."

"More than being afraid of Chet and Mick, more than being afraid of what's happening to St. Paul's and its people, I'm scared of what it's doing to me inside. Neil, I don't think I have the emotional stamina to be a psychiatrist. I can't handle things well. Not this, not my personal life, not anything. I can't see why or how I have any business trying to straighten out the psyches of others, when my own is such a mess."

"I see. May I ask why you decided to be a psychiatrist in the first place?"

"My mother."

"She wanted you to be one?"

"Not quite. She died when I was sixteen. She committed suicide while in a mental institution. From the time I was four years old, she was in the hospital more than she was out. I grew to hate it when she was home because she wasn't normal even then, not like my friends' mothers. When she was in the hospital, at least I had Daddy to myself. When she was home, she seemed to take most of the attention. She was schizophrenic. Nothing they did ever helped, not for any length of time. I used to want her dead. I wanted it so very much. Then, when it happened, I had all this guilt, as if I had somehow caused it. When my father saw how I was hurting, he got me into therapy. He also gave me a box of her things I had never seen before. There were pictures of my mother as a child, teenager, and young woman. There were clippings she had saved, and a few poems she had written. I look just like her. I could see that so clearly. And, more than that, the little things she had saved were the kind of things that always appealed to me. It seemed so awful, so sad, such a waste."

"And so you wanted to be a psychiatrist to see if you

could help people like your mother?"

"That—and, to be honest, to help myself. You see, I feared I had inherited the same disorder. Daddy assured me that I had not, that my mother had had a dark side even as a child. But I still worried."

"You put that in the past tense . . . is the worry really in the past tense for you, Julie?"

"I don't know. I think so. From what I've learned about her, from what I remember about her, I know I'm not like that. Not yet. But I feel so confused."

"Just about your professional future, or is there something else?"

"You'd never believe it."

"Try me."

"I'm in love with you."

For a moment, Neil was stunned, almost more surprised by Julie's announcement than he had been by the shaking of the building.

"Yeah, well, I said you'd never believe it."

"I think you must be putting me on. I would have been able to tell. Surely I would . . ."

Neil looked into his young colleague's pleading eyes, then swallowed hard. The signs had been there. In retrospect, he could think of a myriad of ways in which she had tried to communicate her feelings, but he had steadfastly ignored them all.

"I guess I've had a bad case of tunnel vision," he said slowly. "Julie, I'm sorry. If I've done or said anything to hurt you, it was unintentional. I had no idea how you felt."

She did her best to smile. "Funny, when you were chewing the tape off my lips, I kept thinking how long I had dreamed of that . . . and there we were, mouths pressed together frantically, and it was anything but an erotic event. Until the last few hours, I truly believed you'd look up one day and really see me, discover you felt something for me.

207

Night after night, I've gone home alone and fantasized about that. It's been lonely here in Bainbridge. I know no one except for a few people here at the hospital. I know it's my own fault—I've let the work consume me, that and my stupid passion for you, so I haven't made friends. I haven't been out on a date in months. Work and you—that was my life. Only the work was real. You were never a possibility for me. The last few hours have taught me that.

He gave a slow, sad smile. "Mind telling me what the last few hours have had to do with it?"

Julie was wishing very much that she had not confessed.

"Maybe we should just scream some more and let this drop. I'm feeling rather embarrassed."

"This is an exceptional time. There's no room for embarrassment. Yet perhaps we should make some noise, and do keep working those hands against the post. But after that I would like to hear, unless you mind terribly, what you mean."

Again, the yelling brought no one to the door. Neil found himself thinking the worst had happened, that perhaps everyone out there was dead or out of commission, that perhaps he and Julie were trapped in a little isolated section of St. Paul's that had not crumbled and collapsed. It was not likely, but he felt so isolated, so frustrated, that the idea kept recurring. Still constantly moving his hands as much as he could against the post, he turned to Julie. He looked once more into her eyes and felt a bevy of emotions, beginning with a strange sense of loss. She was truly such a special person, yet he knew she would never be *his* special person. For him, the spark simply was not there. Maybe it was because, even though reason said he should be over most of his grieving, he still felt he was in mourning. When he thought of wife or lover, he thought of Jan, and he did not seem to be able to train his thoughts otherwise.

"You going to finish talking to me?"

"Why not? I've blown my guilty, and rather stupid, secret anyway. I'm still in the beginning stages of this profession, Neil. I fully realize that. But I'm learning to read people. I exist for you as a doctor, a colleague, a student, a nice person, someone like one of your daughters' friends, but not as a woman. I told myself over and over that you didn't see anyone that way, that you still weren't over your wife's death."

"That much is true, my dear."

"But you reacted to Marianne Hamilton as a woman, and she's no older than I am." The words came tumbling out with a will and force of their own. Julie looked taken aback that she had spoken in such a way. Where was her reticence, where was her pride? But now that it was out, she could not withdraw the words.

Neil looked almost as if he had been slapped. Since Julie was being totally honest, he did not feel he could lie to her, not even with the intention of sparing her feelings. He gave a small laugh. "I'm going to have to see if I can do something about developing a poker face. I had no idea I could be read so clearly. It isn't something I can define, the pull I felt toward that young woman. Maybe it was just a chemical reaction."

"And you feel sorry for her."

His smile twisted to one side and his voice was wry. "I feel sorry for the entire human race, Dr. Singer. Including you and me. I deal with patients day in and day out, and I feel their sorrow as my own. But I've encountered few of them I wanted to go to bed with."

Julie's cheeks flamed at Neil's frank admission. She had half expected him to deny her allegation, and more than half wanted him to.

Smiling at her discomfiture, Neil went on, "But I'm *not* going to bed with her. She needs years and years of therapy, of help. I rather suspect that out of bed we'd not have a lot to talk about after a while. Considering everything, I truly believe she'll serve no jail time, but I wouldn't be surprised if the court made counseling mandatory, as well it should. She has three young children who have probably been more damaged than she has and will undoubtedly all require extensive help, also. I'm half a century old. I lack the stamina to take on three children to rear — even if they were normal, healthy, well-adjusted children. It is possible that, at some point in the near future, a lusty, kind, and supportive lover might be just what our Marianne needs, that such a relationship could help her self-esteem. But that lover can't be me. Such a relationship would be much, much too complicated. For both of us."

"Oh, I agree with all that. But I'm still jealous of that chemistry. I so wanted the current to run both ways for us, but on and on it went, with me being the only one to feel anything."

"It's for the best. Tell yourself that. Just as I don't have the stamina to take Marianne Hamilton and her children into my life, I don't have the stamina for someone like you, either. You're quite young enough to be my daughter. And most likely you want children some day, when I have that all behind me, very content to know I'll be a doting grandfather soon. I don't want to start over. I want . . ."

"What is it, Neil?" she asked quietly, seeing the pain that suddenly filled his eyes.

"I want it to be the way it used to be. And it never can be. Never again. Anything I do from now on *is* starting over. That got thrust on me when I lost Jan. I may want to go back, but I can't. *God!* Aren't people amazing creatures?"

"Very amazing. Neil, I think my hands are getting looser. I think the tape is wearing away."

"Splendid! Just keep going. *He*'ll be back soon. I don't know what he has in mind, but he'll be back."

So on and on they worked, anxious to free the hands of at

least one of them as soon as possible.

In his office, Chief Inman made his decision. "We're going in," he called to his staff. "There's nothing to lose at this point. Too many lives are being lost anyway. He's wounded and alone. We got one detonator off Mick, and Chet just made use of the one he had. We're going to assume those are the only two that exist—and pray that the assumption is correct. Get them to unlock the Emergency Room door, and keep a couple of guards posted there. Law enforcement people can go in, and hospital personnel. No one else. Keep 'em back, even if you have to get a little rough."

"Police brutality?" someone teased him.

"Hey, I'm all for it if it's in a good cause," he returned.

From what he felt was a safe vantage point, Chet surveyed the damage the bomb had done. He felt a deep and abiding sense of disappointment. Although he had never set off such a device before, nor had he seen anyone else set one off, he had expected more spectacular results. Some people he thought, might assess the damage as considerable. He felt otherwise. Seeing one wing of the third floor crumble and fall was not the same as seeing the entire structure leveled, with everyone in it. Chet continued to stare, but he no longer saw the structural damage. Instead, he saw Mick lying on the floor, the thick red blood oozing copiously from his chest. Damn it, Mick deserved better than this, better than the pathetic damage that had been inflicted on the hospital. If he had succeeded in blowing St. Paul's to smithereens, he might have gone down in history for it. How was he going to be remembered now? A few weeks or months and the damaged wing would be restored, and where would he be? The same as poor Mick, perhaps.

The seething anger built, as the reality of his brother's demise registered in his mind. *There has to be a way,* he kept saying to himself, . . . *there has to be a way.*

In the ER, just as anesthetist Brian Lake extubated the patient, just as Rasmussen was ready to leave the surgical suite, Brian was heard to say, "Oh, shit."

All of the surgical crew, practically cross-eyed with exhaustion, turned as one person.

"The pneumothorax," Brian said, "it just happened."

"Get me a number thirty-two French chest tube, and get it in here fast," Dave said to one of the nurses.

They moved almost as automatons, feeling wooden and unreal. Within five minutes Rasmussen had rescrubbed, regloved, and had inserted the chest tube. He watched to see that the lung was reexpanding, then made another attempt at escaping from the OR. This time, he got away.

Maudie Evans sat in her bed and played at smoking. Ruby had come to tell her about the latest events, including the explosion and the loss of the poor, unfortunate psychiatric patient.

Glen Fielding checked on Dawn's baby and on the other transferred OB and nursery patients. All was well thus far. He gently touched the baby's clenched fist and, as his highly trained ears took in the sounds of improved breathing, at a rate that was both slower and smoother, tears rolled down his cheeks. Although some of the staff undoubtedly saw that he was crying, he made no move to wipe away the evidence and pretend otherwise. If he felt like crying, then, dammit, he was going to cry. It was just that kind of night . . . but, he realized, it was morning. He looked out the window and saw that the darkness was beginning to lift, to make way for the day.

"Steve, how is it, really?" Jennifer Weiller asked.

"It's not that bad, Jennie, it really isn't. I'm sure the worst is yet to come as far as pain is concerned. A lot of injuries are like that—it's like you're numb, or something, and the reality hits a few hours later. It's a bit inhibiting, but I'll find a way to overcome it. Say, did you ever hear about the one-legged man who—"

"Stop it!" she cried, cutting him off. "It's not a joke. None of this is a joke. It's the worst thing I've ever been through. And I won't stay here and listen to you crack bad jokes. I won't!"

Tears welled up in her blue eyes and she started to turn away. Stephen caught her hand and held it, and she slowly turned back to face him, responding to the pressure of his touch.

"I'm sorry," she said softly. "Your way *is* right. I know that. But all this is so hard, and I know how you must be suffering."

"No so much, sweetheart. The hardest thing is being helpless, being unable to help with this mess."

Unsmiling, she looked into his face. "I could get used to this. So make a joke about that, please."

"Get used to what?"

"You know. To hearing you call me sweetheart, to feeling your hand on mine. I'm a lonesome person. I think it's dangerous for you to be too nice to me."

He smiled crookedly, already in more discomfort that he was prepared to let her see. "Being nice to you comes natural. Too natural, I'm afraid. Considering the circumstances."

Biting her lip, she nodded.

"Do you love her, Steve? And does she love you?"

"Love? That's a word that's hard to define. I think it can mean so many things to so many people. I was a real rounder as a kid. I grew up in a bad part of New York, and instead of fighting it, I joined it. I ran with a gang and we got in some bad trouble. I ended up with a light prison sentence—light because I had no previous convictions and wasn't armed, so it looked like I had just tagged along for something to do. I looked around at what I saw in prison and it scared the hell out of me. So I became a model prisoner. I started my schooling in there. The warden told this church group about me, and they agreed to sponsor me when I came out—give me a job and a place to live while I finished the work for my degree. A woman called Elizabeth Jackson was in that church. Quite a lady. A few years older than me, never married, daughter of one of the deacons, well-respected, not a blemish on her name. She made it clear she didn't mind being seen in public with me, sitting by me at church. Somehow we ended up married. It was fine at first. Sometimes I think she liked it better when I was an underdog, but that's been behind me for several years. She resents what she calls my 'over-dedication to my job.' She resents it because we don't have kids. Her plumbing is out of alignment or something, and she won't hear of adoption, but somehow she translates it into being my fault. She complains an awful lot—so much that I don't like to go home. And I suppose that has as much to do with the overtime I work as my so-called 'dedication' does. Well, all this is because you asked about love. I don't know, Jennie. I owe her a lot. I wish her the best. But love? Not by my definition, I guess."

"She's probably worried about you tonight, though, don't you suppose?"

"Of course. She isn't an evil person, just an unhappy one. I'd worry if she were in a dangerous situation. That isn't the same . . ."

"I know," she said softly, then her practiced eyes caught a wince he could not hide. "Listen, like it or not, I'm giving you a shot of Demerol. The doctor ordered it, and there's no point in your being noble."

Within moments, she had given him the drug IM. He flashed her a smile of gratitude. Bending, she kissed his cheek.

"How I wish things could be different. So many things."

"Me, too, sweetheart."

She would have liked to stay and hold his hand until he drifted into oblivion, but there was too much out there that needed to be done.

Soon it was seven A.M. and the sunrise was complete.

The door to the Emergency Room was slid wide open, and relief poured in. Members of the press tried for entry, but were held at bay.

Nurse Kwan stood and watched as Michael Hamilton continued to breathe. He had not moved or spoken a single word since Stephen Cates had fired the slug into his chest.

A surge of hope possessed Julie Singer as she felt the progressive loosening of the tape on her wrists. "I think I can break it through soon," she said to Neil, whispering, though she wasn't sure why.

And Chester Hamilton, still at large, not knowing that his brother was still alive and struggling with every breath, was digging at his mind for ideas. Now he had more to avenge than ever. The bastards had killed Mick and for that, they would pay. Until now, it had been child's play. "They ain't seen nothing yet," he vowed silently.

Chapter Twelve

Crazed with rage and fatigue, Chet Hamilton stood in a seldom-used hospital room and stared out of the window at the flurry of activity in the parking lot. Although his view was limited, he could see enough to know that his edict was no longer being obeyed. People were entering St. Paul's. He closed his eyes for a moment, his memory an unfolding cascade of images—the way it had been when he and Mick were growing up, how he had first met Marianne and how sweet she had been, how he had wanted her so much for his very own, how proud they had both been when Alix was born. Even after things had gone so sour, even then, there had been moments . . . there had been times. . . . Tears formed in his eyes but he willed them back. Crying was not acceptable. He could not weaken now, could not be soft.

Never again would he and Mick go hell-raising on a Saturday night. Never again would he lie in bed next to Marianne, touch her soft hair, smell the clean and soapy scent of her skin. Never again would he see his kids lined up, their hair brushed to a high shine and with clean outfits on, at McDonald's trying to decide between the hamburger and the McNuggets.

They had done that, the bastards—they had destroyed it all. *They* thought he was powerless now because Mick was down, because he had the bullet in his shoulder, and because the only bomb he could control had been set off. It was obvious that *they* were counting him out, which only increased his rage.

Chet took the snub-nosed revolver from his waistband, aimed down at the crowd below, and was about to pull the trigger, when the one shred of common sense he had left surfaced. No way, Jose, he said to himself. It was doubtful that the slugs from the .38 would carry far enough to inflict any serious harm. Even if they did, his position would be known. Apparently quite a few police were inside the hospital now, and once his general location was pinpointed, it would be all too easy to get him cornered.

Dvorak, he thought. That doctor was his ticket out. He had to find his way back to that supply closet where he had Dvorak and his pretty sidekick trussed up like a pair of Thanksgiving turkeys. But he had to be careful . . . very careful. One slip and they'd have him where they wanted him instead of the other way around. If he could just get back to that pair of shrinks, he would have some bargaining power—more than he had had before, even. He could not imagine anyone turning down his demands when they saw he had a gun to one shrink's head and a knife to the other's throat.

Both wary and filled with emotion, those men and women who were allowed in entered the hallways of St. Paul's and mingled with those who had been trapped inside. The influx had been limited to fresh medical personnel and law enforcement officers, a policy that left concerned family members and friends still cut off from their loved-ones inside St. Paul's.

Helen Laramore was one of the first in. She was not at all sure what she could do, if anything, and she had no idea where to start. But at the moment, all that did not seem to matter. Tears rained down her cheeks as she surveyed the interior of the old, and very beloved, building. Dave Rasmussen came up to her and took her in his arms.

"My, God," he exclaimed, "you look bad, Helen. What's the problem? I've never seen you look this way before."

Laughing through the tears, she said, "And you, you old goat, how good do you think *you* look? When did you last shave? And your skin looks positively gray."

He held her at arm's length and smiled into her eyes. "Let me tell you about it sometime, lady. I have done surgery under circumstances you don't even want to know about."

"True. But I do know. We were told what was going on. Is Michael Hamilton still alive, Dr. Rasmussen?"

" 'Dr. Rasmussen,' " he repeated in a mocking, mincing way. "Haven't I told you a hundred thousand times to call me Dave?"

"Possibly. And I've told you just as many times that it's against my policy."

"You can call me an old goat but you can't call me by my first name? Some policy."

"It's *my* policy," she said sweetly. "Now, answer the question."

Rasmussen gave a deep sigh. "The boy is alive. Just barely. I don't know how he's held on this long."

"I wonder if Chet knows how bad he is."

"That's something else we don't know. Stephen Cates said Chet took off when Mick fell to the floor. We don't know if that means he assumed he was dead, or just that he was trying to get the hell out and save his own hide. I just checked in the conference room. There haven't been any more phone calls from Chet. No word from him since the bomb went off.

"And no one but the one woman was hurt?"

Mary Riley approached them, gave the administrator a hug, and said, "I can answer that one. I just came from there. Outside of a few bumps and abrasions from falling plaster and whatnot, they're all okay, personnel and patients alike. Of course, you can imagine the emotional chaos, with all this happening to people who weren't stable anyway, but they seem to be coping better than one might expect. In fact I think that's true, from what I see, of the entire hospital. Considering everything, we've coped quite well. There hasn't been the panic one would fear. The one unfortunate lady up there was killed instantly, they say. The patients had been advised to stay in their rooms *and* to stay with a group, or at least a buddy. She didn't do that. Maybe it wouldn't have made any difference."

Little by little, St. Paul employees entered the building and found their way to their departments, where they were greeted with tears and hugs from those they were relieving. Uniformed policemen, most of the Bainbridge Police Department and numerous others recruited from nearby towns and cities, almost seemed to outnumber employees. There were so many of them . . . and yet Chet Hamilton remained at large.

"I wish I knew this was the right move," Chief Inman said, now on the scene himself and watching closely the open doors of the Emergency Room.

"There comes a time," Alterauge told him, "when a person has to more or less say, 'Let's do something, even if it's wrong.' We can't *know*. We just have to use a combination of knowledge, experience, and pure old gut instinct, and hope for the best."

Jennie Weiller, face drawn and pale, walked up to where Helen Laramore, Mary Riley and Dave Rasmussen were talking.

"Dr. Rasmussen, I hate to interrupt, but . . ."

"But you're going to do it anyway, right?"

"Right," she agreed, trying to smile at him and not quite

making it. "It's Mick Hamilton. Vic McMichael sent me to tell you he woke up for just a few moments and was very combative. Incoherent, and combative. He didn't say anything that made any sense, but he dislodged his chest tube. They sent me to tell you. They need help."

"Girl, can't you see the man is dead on his feet?" Mary barked—then immediately, at the sight of the young nurse's crumpled face, softened her tone and added, "But then, aren't we all in the same shape? Dr. Samuelsen is in the building now. Go hunt him down, then get along home, or at least get some sleep."

Jennie nodded. "I'll do that."

"I'll go with you, Jennifer, my dear," Dave Rasmussen offered.

"Now, you listen here," Mary began, reverting to her usual sternness. "You're in no shape to be doing one more thing."

Dave smiled wearily. "One more is about the best I can do. But no more surgery till I've slept for about three days. And that's a promise. I just figure I owe it to Samuelsen to fill him in on the case, *then* I'm going somewhere and have my own private little breakdown. Okay by you, my sweet Mary?"

To show her disapproval of his blarney, she sniffed loudly.

Rasmussen laughed. "Take your own advice, Mary, and get some rest. Let someone else run things for a while."

Jennie and Dave left, Mary glaring at their backs as they went down the hall.

"He's right, you know, Mary," Helen said gently. "You've worked so hard, been up so long. Go on home. Relief is here."

"Helen Laramore, you may be the administrator, and I won't argue one bit that you're more important than I am in the scheme of things and that you have more than enough power to fire me and everyone like me, but the fact remains that I've worked at St. Paul's longer than just about anybody left standing, and I have more than a passing interest in this place. I may take a nap if I can. I'm not saying I won't. But what I am saying is that I'm *not* leaving this building until that wretched man is out of here and everything is safe and sound. Can you understand that?"

"I can understand it. And I can respect it. I know how you feel. I just spent six hours out on the parking lot, barred from even coming in the door. It just about killed me inside not to be able to come in. And I'm sure the little I did out there made no difference, but I had to be there. It was my place to be as close as I could get. So I do know how you feel. I appreciate your spirit. But do find a room where you can freshen up and rest. If you pass out from exhaustion, well . . . that's no help."

"And you?"

"I'm going to collect my patient husband, retreat to my office, and take it from there. We could both use a nap, too. But . . ."

"Exactly," Mary said grimly. "And that's quite a large 'but.' It's hard to curl up and relax and take a snooze, no matter how badly it's needed, when Chet Hamilton is still on the loose."

"Precisely. But it's a situation that can't last for long. The police have too many people in here now for him to escape for long." But although she made her tone firm to give credence to her words, inside she wasn't all that sure.

A few short hours ago, she wouldn't have believed two men could take things this far, wreak this much havoc. Three people dead, Mick near death, others so badly hurt, the laboratory totally wrecked, all of the telemetry monitors on third floor disabled, and a large section of the other end of third floor turned to rubble—it just didn't seem possible.

She and Mary said a few words in parting, then Helen went to rescue Philip from the car and escort him through the barrier set up by the police and into the hospital. Technically he did not belong, but she didn't mind exerting her authority under the circumstances. She needed him . . . oh, how she did need him. Tears threatened to break through, and she fiercely fought them back. Crying was a luxury she could not afford at this point. She somehow felt that once she let go, she would have difficulty regaining her composure. In time, she would allow herself a good cry, but that time wasn't now.

In the recovery room, where Dr. Kelvin Samuelsen was scrubbing for surgery, Dave stood by his side and explained what he had done on Michael Hamilton and why. "But he's a goner, Sammy. Only the hand of God could save that man now . . . and somehow I don't think God's going to be intervening to that extent. By everything I know, he can't even be alive now. It's almost medically impossible."

Samuelsen nodded, his ugly little face grave with concern. "We have to do what we have to do, Dave."

Their understanding was complete. Not only did they loathe the patient and everything he stood for, they knew they were fighting a losing battle — yet they could not give up. Legally and ethically, they could do nothing but continue to try to save the man's life.

Rasmussen turned to leave, then found he could not. He had to know how it turned out. Quickly he scrubbed and gowned and then, standing well to the side, he observed the procedure being performed by his colleague with a fresh crew.

"What is the oxygen saturation running?"

"It dropped to 91 percent with supplemental O2. And we have the pneumothorax confirmed radiographically."

Rasmussen smiled to himself as he listened. How good it would have been to have X ray monitoring during some of his emergency cases! But he had made it without it . . . just barely, maybe, but he had made it.

After the chest was once more prepped and draped,

Samuelsen made an incision in the interspace just under the site of the previously placed chest tube, then entered the chest bluntly. A large gush of air escaped, its whooshing sound audible all the way across the room. Samuelsen then selected a number 28 French chest tube and secured it with three nylon sutures.

"Take his picture," he ordered, as soon as the antibiotic ointment and sterile dressings were in place.

In just moments, the post-procedure chest X ray confirmed proper placement of the chest tube and reexpansion of the lung. The breathing was less sonorous, vital signs improved slightly, but Mick showed no signs of regaining consciousness.

"What are the stats now?" he asked the technician.

"Up to 95 percent already. This turkey may die, but he's going to do it in his own sweet time."

Kelvin Samuelsen nodded, looking down at the young man's face. Under other circumstances, one might even have appreciated his male beauty, his almost Adonis-type features. So young, so attractive . . . and so doomed. What was keeping him alive? Surely not willpower, for he was not even rousable. As far as could be ascertained, he had not had a single lucid moment since the bullet had entered his body. The surgeon sighed, took his weary colleague by the arm, and said, "Come on, Dave, we're getting you out of here. If I didn't tell you how bad you look, I should have."

"Death warmed over, eh?"

"Worse."

"What can look worse than death warmed over?"

"At this moment, *you.*"

David Rasmussen did not debate the point. He only knew that if he looked the way he felt, then his looks were undoubtedly beyond description. He didn't care. However he looked, he was alive. This ordeal had made him realize just how badly he wanted to stay that way. With all its imperfections, he felt life was worth sustaining.

"Are we going to 'copter him out?" Samuelsen asked, giving a nod toward Mick's silent form.

Dave shook his head. "I'm in no shape to make that decision. I doubt that it would do any good. He can't live—not for long. On the other hand, to get him out of here before he dies would get some of the responsibility off our shoulders. Also, if you can get word to Chet that his brother is still alive, it might give us some bargaining power. I don't know. Look . . ." He reeled forward slightly, and the other surgeon reached out to steady him.

"Dave, get out of here."

"I'm going. I'm going. Don't be so pushy about it, hey?"

He meant to shower. He meant to call his wife. He meant to do a lot of things. However, the couch looked so tempting. Quite suddenly, it was as if his knees had turned to jelly. Just for a few minutes, he told himself. He would just lie down for a few minutes, then he'd get up, call Edie, shower, get something to eat. But once he was supine, he sank into oblivion, and an anxious wife and a smelly body no longer mattered to him.

In a limited way, St. Paul's was being restored to normalcy. Hospital personnel moved about the halls and their respective work areas, doing so with fear—an ever-present emotion, and one they were not allowed to forget. The strange men, uniformed and plain-clothed, with whom they now mingled made it impossible to forget that Chet Hamilton, unseen and unheard, was still within the walls of the hospital.

"Maybe he's dead," one policeman suggested, not trying to hide his hopefulness.

His partner shook his head. "Doubtful. Not from the way the witnesses say the bullet hit. Besides, we haven't found a body. If he was dead, we'd find the body. I think he's on the move, creeping around, staying low till he's ready to do something else. Maybe he's trying to find out what's up with his brother. Who can say? But I don't think he's dead. Call me crazy, but I feel it in my bones that's he out there somewhere, waiting for us."

"I won't call you crazy," was the wistful reply, "but I sure do wish I could call you wrong. Trouble is, I have the same kind of feelings. So, where now?"

"Same beat. Back and forth. Like I said, he's on the move. Just because he wasn't there the last time doesn't mean he won't be this time. Stick to the beat and stick to each other — those are the orders. If we think something else needs to be covered, we get on the walkie-talkie."

"Being with his partner didn't help Jameson a whole lot."

"No, but it might have helped the other guy. All they had to do was dig a bullet out of him. Two or three weeks, and he'll be good as new. Which is a hell of a lot better than being dead."

In the kitchens, preparations were under way for a proper noon meal to be fixed. By order of the administrator, kitchen staff were to fix enough for all employees and all law enforcement officers to eat, without charge. The two laboratory technicians who had come in cringed at the sight of their workplace. It was going to be a while, and would require many thousands of dollars to be spent, until they were back to business as usual. For the present time, they salvaged what they could and made their rounds, drawing samples from patients for tests that had been ordered before Chet and Mick had struck. They could not run the tests, of course, but slides and samples could be taken by courier to a reference laboratory in New York City, with results available in just a few hours.

"You still have to send my baby out?" Dawn asked.

226

Whatever her deficiencies, she had expressed true worry and concern over the distress of her newborn child.

"I don't think so, babe," Glen Fielding said softly. "A pediatrician is on his way here, and I want him to check the baby out before we decide for sure, but I think she's out of the woods now. She's been breathing on her own without oxygen for the past hour and doing great."

"What was it, Dr. Fielding? Is she going to be a sick baby?"

In his mind, Fielding prepared the answer. Although she did not have the vocabulary to say exactly what she meant, he understood. Dawn wanted to know if her child had a chronic disease, something she would struggle with throughout her childhood, or perhaps her entire life. The trouble was, a doctor could not always say, and a doctor could not make promises. No matter how sure he felt, how much he wanted to remove any worry from this young woman's mind, he knew all too well there was a chance for error. If wrong, he could be sued — and he could lose the case. It hadn't happened to him yet, but it had to several of his colleagues. "Cover yourself first" had become the first commandment among physicians. It was sad that such a commandment had to be obeyed, even at the cost of worrying a patient unnecessarily, yet such was the case. He had delivered Dawn's baby. According to the laws that now existed, until that little girl was twenty-two years of age, he could be sued if Dawn got it in her head that he had done something wrong during delivery, or prior to delivery in the antenatal period. It was not a comforting thought.

"I don't think she'll be a sick baby at all, Dawn. A lot of babies have problems like this, then go on to lead perfectly normal lives afterward. Maybe due to the immaturity of the lungs, some have a harder time adjusting to the atmosphere outside the womb. By the way, do you have a name for this child?"

"Michelle. She has to be Michelle. I planned on that ever

so long. But I want to call her Michelle Glenna, if it's okay with you. You've done so much for her. I —" At that point, her voice broke and she could not continue.

"I'm very honored, and very touched. I'd be proud to have her named after me. I feel that she and I have been through a lot together. But back to what you wanted to know . . . I foresee no more problems, but we have to do some more tests to be sure. We've obtained specimens for a sepsis workup, and that's under way. We need to rule out hyaline membrane disease and cystic fibrosis. Understand that I don't think she really has these things, but we have to make sure before we can give her a clean bill of health. As things stand now, if she remains stable over the next couple of days, and if the other doctors agree, I see no reason why you can't take Michelle Glenna home and put all this behind you."

Dawn seemed pleased with his answer, and not overly concerned about the diagnoses that had to be ruled out. Glen doubted that she even really understood. But it hardly mattered; he had done his part.

In the first floor surgical ward, Dr. Samuelsen studied the X rays of Stephen's ankle, then interviewed and examined him.

"You want it out now, or you want to wait till we're more back to normal?"

"I want it out if the schedule will allow. *I* need to get back to normal. There's so much to be done."

The surgeon put a hand on the younger man's shoulder. "The regular surgery schedule has been postponed, of course. There's no reason why we can't do you. But don't get it in your head that there's going to be instant recovery because it isn't going to be that way. The bullet did a fair bit of damage, even sheared off some bone. It's all going to take time to heal. You won't be running the halls for a bit. Is that clear?"

"Abundantly," he said, the pain suddenly sharper. "Dr. Sam, you heard anything lately about how Ken Sandusky is doing?"

"I didn't just hear, I saw for myself. As usual, Ras did a terrific job. Of course, it's going to take him a while to re-cover—a hole like that in the gut—but I can't see where he should have any big problems. When I went in to see him, Marcus Chapman was there checking on him. I'd say poor Marcus is almost in worse shape. You know how some people are with guilt. If he hadn't gone to take a leak, Ken wouldn't have been alone and this probably wouldn't have happened. After all, they had been advised to stay together. He says those things over and over. But Ken doesn't hold him responsible. Of course, no one holds him responsible."

"Except himself."

"Right."

Steve sighed deeply. "I'm carrying a load around myself, you know. I was pretty much of a hoodlum in my younger days, but I'd never killed anyone till now. I know, I know . . . you can go on and on about how rotten Mick Hamil-ton was, how many people he had killed and hurt, how many more he might have been prepared to damage. But it all boils down to the fact that I took a life."

"Listen, Cates, I know shit when I see it—and hear it, for that matter. I don't have to get my nose stuck in it to recog-nize it. Just let someone who deserves to feel guilty carry it around. I'm sure you have more important things to do. If you hadn't fired, no telling how many of you the two of them would have taken down. It wasn't even just self-de-fense. You had Jennie and the Hamilton woman there to consider. And besides, he's not dead yet. Just a few minutes ago, I put a new chest tube in him. He's alive."

"Isn't 'alive' an over-optimistic word to use, considering everything?"

Samuelsen gave a crooked smile. "You said you killed a

229

man, Cates. Technically, Mick's alive. Thus, technically, you did not kill him. But you're also right: I'm splitting hairs. The man is a medical miracle. He can't be alive, but he is — a state that can't last long, of course. Look, I gotta run. Don't eat or drink anything else. We'll get that bullet out in the next few hours, just as soon as we see what's what."

In the parking lot, Elizabeth Jackson Cates had just arrived and was making her presence known.

"What do you mean, I can't go in?"

"Exactly what I said, ma'am: you can't go in."

"But people *are* going in. I've seen them."

The officer on guard silently counted to ten. How many times did he have to go through this? If the general public and the press had their way, the halls of St. Paul's would be so crowded one couldn't walk through them.

"Those you see going in, ma'am, are hospital employees and *our* people."

"But my husband is in there. He's been wounded. Stephen Cates is his name. I just learned about this a few minutes ago. He works nights, so I had gone to bed. When I woke up this morning and he still wasn't there, I called and found out about this. I *have* to see him."

"I'm sorry, Mrs. Cates. I know how you feel. If you go talk to the gentleman over there — see where I'm pointing? — he'll see that a phone call or message to your husband gets put through. But you won't be going in. Not until things are calmer, until the situation is resolved."

Elizabeth accepted that and turned away. She clearly did not like it, but she did accept it. Walking slowly toward where the officer had specified, she joined the line of people waiting to get their messages through. A girl with long hair, jeans, and a none-too-clean looking jacket walked up to her and said, "Who you got in there?"

"My husband. He's a nurse. One of these crazy men shot him in the ankle. They've not been able to do surgery to take it out yet."

"Cates? That's great. Well, I mean . . . you'll see what I mean." Turning around, she called, "Over here," and Elizabeth soon found herself face to face with a video camera.

"We have here," the girl said, talking into a microphone, "the wife of Stephen Cates, the courageous nurse who shot Mick Hamilton a few hours ago, and was himself wounded by a bullet fired by Chet Hamilton. Tell me, Mrs. Cates, what are your thoughts at this time?"

"Right now," Elizabeth said in her clipped way, "my thoughts are that you are disgusting, bothering people at a stressful time like this and looking so unkempt to boot. When was the last time you washed your jacket—or your hair? You don't present a professional image, I can tell you that. Now, both of you, get that thing out of my face."

They both did as they were told. Only temporarily daunted, however, they moved on up in the line. They figured, by the law of averages, that someone would be happy to talk, to tell how they were feeling.

Even though she was supposed to be in custody of some sort, no one was paying much attention to Marianne Hamilton. The members of the news media would have loved to get hold of her, but they were still barred from entry. Marianne sat on a hard chair in the hall outside the Emergency Room and watched the guarded doors, those who entered, and the many who remained outside. She felt slightly dazed. It all seemed so unreal. But, then, no matter how unreal the present seemed, the past seemed more so. She tried to remember back to a pleasant time, to a time when she hadn't felt like this. The early days with Chet, prior to the first pregnancy? Maybe, but anything connected with Chet had gone sour and didn't bear thinking about. Childhood — she would think of some of the nice things that had happened when she was a little girl. Not that her childhood had been perfect, far from it, but it had been a simpler time . . . a time when the joy of the rainbow more than compensated for the rain. She hadn't seen a rainbow recently. Not for a long, long time. Maybe they had been there and she hadn't had a chance, or had just forgotten, to look.

In her office, Helen Laramore had not had a chance to get the rest she had wanted. Too many things were happening, too many decisions had to be made. Two of the hospital board members were with her, both male, both hot-headed, and very much at odds with each other. Each was wanting Helen to side with him and break the deadlock that existed.

"We have to evacuate," argued McKeown, the one who looked like a bulldog. "We have to think of the patient, not the census. And if thinking of the patient doesn't pull any weight, then think of all the lawsuits we're going to be facing if we could have gotten patients out of here, didn't, and something catastrophic happened."

"Now, now, McKeown," said Birdsell, a man who bore more than a passing resemblance to Herman Munster. "It seems to me the most catastrophic things have already happened. The police and FBI say it's almost certain Chet set off the only bomb he *can* set off. We got out of that bombing with only one fatality. Not that I'm saying the loss of that poor lady's life isn't tragic, because I'm sure we all feel that it is, but it could have been a damned sight worse. We're just going to create more panic and confusion by evacuating patients at this point. They've survived the worst. The rest of it should be a downhill course."

"Yes, it should be, but things don't always go as they should. The guy's a madman and still very much at large. At any given moment, he could pop around a corner and start blasting away. Or grab a patient and put a knife to his or her throat. I tell you, Mont, we *have* to get them out of

232

here, while we still can. Helen, can't you talk some sense into this man?"

Helen smiled weakly. She wasn't sure she was in favor of evacuation, not at this point. "Maybe we should get the opinion of an expert. Let's get Dr. Dvorak and Dr. Singer in here. They can give us educated opinions on the mood of the patients in general, and their guesses as to what Chet Hamilton might be thinking by now. I haven't seen Dr. Dvorak since we were let in. Let me see if I can locate him." She reached for the telephone and did some dialing around. When she replaced the receiver after the fourth call, her expression was definitely perplexed.

"What is it, Helen?" Birdsell asked.

"It's been at least an hour since anyone seems to have seen either one of the psychiatrists. They went out looking for Marianne Hamilton, who has since been returned by Steve Cates and Jennie Weiller, and no one can recall seeing them since. As you both well know, Dr. Dvorak was the one doing the talking to Chet and Mick over the intercom and then the phone system. Everyone thought he'd go back to the conference room, but he isn't there. On third, they say neither of the doctors have been by to check on the patients after the explosion. Frankly, I'm worried. I've known Neil Dvorak a long, long time, and that wing is very dear to him. He's such a caring and conscientious man that I know he would definitely check on his patients if he could. Something has happened to them. I'd bet on it."

"What could it be? Hamilton had been big on letting us know when he does something atrocious, and we haven't heard from him lately. If he'd really done anything to them, wouldn't he have found a way to let us know, to brag about it?"

The other two thought about that for a while.

"Unless he's saving it," Helen said, her voice low.

Her eyes met those of the board members, neither of whom had to ask what she meant.

Chapter Thirteen

"I'm free!" Julie exclaimed, holding up hands from which the tape hung in ragged strips.

Neil grinned broadly. "I knew you could do it. Can you reach mine to finish freeing them, then we can each do our own feet?"

By twisting her body into an awkward position, Julie was able to reach Neil's wrists. "You were almost through the tape, so this won't take long," she said, as her still-numb fingers began working with the frayed tape.

Once he had his hands back around in front of him, Neil wriggled his fingers in an attempt to get some of the feeling back. He then began picking at the shreds of tape stuck to his wrists, an act that made him wince with discomfort because the tape had adhered to the hair on his wrists and forearms.

"Dvorak," Julie barked, "just leave that mess on your wrists. We can get that off later. Right now, we need to get our legs and feet freed up. He's likely to be back any minute. In fact, it's a miracle he's stayed away this long."

Nodding in agreement, Neil nonetheless ripped off one more piece of tape, grimaced, and then bent to touch his mouth against the drops of blood that stood out on his wrist.

"Something tells me," he said as they labored away on the

many layers of tape binding their ankles, "that he's been awfully busy out there. Otherwise, he never would have left us this long. I'm sure that was some kind of explosion we heard. He had threatened us with bombs, so . . ."

Julie nodded, not looking up, but continuing to work fiercely with the tape.

"Don't think about it now, Dvorak. Don't dwell on it. We can't do anything about it. We just have to concentrate on getting loose."

Despite all he felt, Neil had to grin. "You sound different all of a sudden. So very authoritative. What has wrought this wondrous change?"

"Distress," she retorted from between clenched teeth. "Aches, pains, agony—both mental and physical. And I've heard all my life that confession is good for the soul. Well I don't know about that, but I do know that once you've made an ass of yourself, there is very little to lose in dignity, so I guess you go for broke. Or something like that."

"Julie, don't do it . . ."

"Do what?" she asked, still not looking up.

Neil took a deep breath and sat back for a moment to flex his fingers and rest from the tedious work. "Don't feel embarrassed—or any other adverse emotion—because you said what you did to me. In thinking it over, I'm glad you told me. I feel quite flattered, a man of my age with a young and beautiful woman saying she's in love with him. Even with all this going on, I feel a decade younger."

"But there's still no change in the way you feel, right?" For just a moment, she dared to look away from the tape and at his face.

"If anyone knows a person can't help the kind of feelings he has, you do. We can govern our actions, but not our emotions. I'm still not ready to be in love with anyone, Julie. I'm sure most experts would say it's time, past time, I snapped out of mourning. With grieving patients, I've always encouraged them to take an interest in other activities as soon as possible—including new relationships. But I've not been so good at taking that advice myself. I still feel so bruised inside. It's as if part of me is missing. In truth, it isn't 'as if,' for part of me really *is*. We married, Janet and I, before I was even out of school—long before. She helped see me through all that, working day and night, even when she was pregnant. From the time I was twenty-one years old, she was part of me. Maybe the best part. Her conscience was so big that, when mine failed me, as it tended to in my young and hungry years, she had enough to see us both through the temptations. I'm not canonizing her just because she is gone. We had our differences. But she was such a good person, and I do miss her so. I think I always will."

"I guess it's that way with some people, those who feel things deeply. The grief never goes away, but you get more used to carrying it around." Flinching, Julie moved her ankles slightly. "Look, only a few layers left. I'll be peeled out of this mess soon. How about you?"

"About the same. I keep wanting to tear it away, but it's high-filament stuff and just won't tear. What I wouldn't give now for some scissors!"

"Or a nice sharp scalpel."

"That, too, would suffice. Anyway, back to what we were saying . . ."

"Do we have to go back to that?"

"You have nearly half your residency with me left, Julie. I can't have you feeling uncomfortable and embarrassed all those months."

"So by telling me you're not ready, you think it's an easy letdown. So much easier for me, for both of us, than if you just said I wasn't your type."

"Defensive, huh? Look, if I even have a type, I don't know what it is. I'm a strange duck by some male standards. I've found many women attractive from time to time . . . a few very much so, enough so it troubled me. But I was never aware of any of them being a 'type.' I just hap-

236

pened to be a monogamous man. I think that is the wise, practical, safe, and ethical way to live. But I admit I wasn't that way for any of those noble reasons. I had what I wanted, and I was too complacent to take any risks. I don't particularly like living like a monk. But I have this hang-up—pardon me if it sounds weird—about going to bed with someone, or even taking someone out several times with no sex involved. I just feel a relationship entails a commitment, and that's what I can't make at this point, an emotional commitment, not to anyone."

"Dvorak?"

"Yeah?"

"Anyone ever tell you that you talk too much?"

He gave a snort. "Come to think of it, no. I suspect, over the years, that many have wanted to, but I also suspect I intimidate people to a degree. Like my residents. Until now, they've always been so respectful."

"Well after we get out of this, I may go back to that."

"Don't."

"Huh?"

"You heard what I said: don't. It's more interesting this way. Hey, look, Julie, I'm down to two more layers. Just a few seconds and I'll be walking. That is, if my legs remember how."

At just about the same time, Julie and Neil unwound the last strands of tape that bound their ankles together.

"I'm going to stand up," Julie said, "just to see if I can, before I try to get any more tape off. I'm free, and that's what counts. If I have to wear tape for a few more hours, so be it."

"My feelings exactly," he said, rising to his feet. Getting upright was no problem, but staying that way definitely was. Laughing and crying at the same time, they latched on to each other and held tight.

"Kiss me," she ordered.

"Now, look, Julie . . ."

"Just do as I say. It doesn't have to be spectacular. Just a reassuring kiss. Then we'll get on about our business, okay? Don't blow your chance, Dvorak. I'll never be able to ask again."

She was light in his arms, a thin slip of a girl, though her height was close to his own, making bending to find her mouth unnecessary. He kissed her briefly, then pulled away. Troubled by her sweetness and proximity, he took refuge in levity and said, "Better no more. We both have so much tape and adhesive on us that we'll stick together permanently."

"Well, would you believe that was my plan?" she asked, with a wry smile. "Look, one more thing, then we'll try our legs and get out of here. Maybe in your opinion I'm not right for you. I can accept that. But as doctor, student, and friend, I feel like I have to say to you: It's okay to get involved with someone. You can't replace Jan with anyone else on earth, because there was only one of her. But there's no need to feel disloyal if you ever want to find a different person to help you fight the loneliness, fill the voids. You say she was a good person, and I believe you, so you know a good person would not resent it when someone they love needs companionship they can no longer provide. Right?"

Neil's bleary eyes misted over, and he reached out to press Julie's hand. As she said, maybe she wasn't the right one. For him, the chemistry just wasn't there, or not yet, and he knew he couldn't will it to be. Still, she was a very special person. Until now, he had seen her as an extremely bright and competent doctor, nothing more, nothing less. Now she had started letting her guard down, revealing her personality, her inner self, and he liked what he was seeing. How long was it since anyone had talked to him like that? He honestly could not recall the last time. Even Jan had been "guilty" of not lecturing on his feelings. Because he was a psychiatrist, everyone seemed to believe he was exempt from the feelings most people had. Nothing was further from the truth. Lust, envy, greed, pride, anger—and whatever the other two deadly sins described by St. Thomas Aquinas were—he had felt them all at one time or another. Nor was he exempt from guilt, and feelings of isolation. To know that something existed, to see it in others, to advise them on it . . . that was so different from what a person was inside. It was difficult to be one's own psychotherapist, and another person with insight, kindness, and courage was welcome.

"Thanks," he said softly. "I needed that. Now, come on, let's walk."

For each of them, the first two steps felt awkward, then circulation began to return.

"Hold my hand, Julie, and let's go toward the door. I don't think he could lock it from the outside, so we should be able to get out. Chances are, he won't be out there at the point we open the door, but be prepared to run. Are your legs strong enough yet for that? I'm sure it won't take as long to get the blood flowing for you as it will for me."

"I think I can run. Maybe not enough to worry Florence Joyner, but I can do it. But I'm going nowhere without you."

"I know that. Why do you think I asked you to hold my hand?"

"Neil, think maybe there's something we could find in here to take with us to use as a weapon?"

In short order, they located two sharp instruments designed for slitting open cardboard cartons and boxes. Careful to keep the guards on them, they pocketed their finds, then walked slowly toward the door.

"You in there, Dvorak, and your Miss Long-Legs," came Hamilton's voice from the other side. "Did you think I'd forgotten you? Never! I've been busy. I'll tell you all about it."

"Run and hide," Dvorak hissed at Julie. "Anywhere. Behind something. Just stay out of sight. I'll make him think you got out."

"No, I won't leave your side. I'm going to stick with you, no matter what."

"Use your head, girl. He'll be through that door in a minute. We would never both get away with hiding. But if he has me to distract him, I can probably convince him you're gone. If he comes in and sees us both, he'll just do what he did before all over again . . . or worse. You've got that knife-thing. Be careful what you do, but if I get him distracted enough, you just may be able to sneak up behind him and cut his ugly throat. Think you could do that?"

"At this point, I think I could do it and laugh about it. Maybe even lap up some of his blood. Those two bring out the ghoul in me."

"Then get. I'll go back to where we were tied up. He'll look there first. You go in the opposite direction."

Neil had barely gotten back down on the floor when he saw a ray of light where Chet was pushing the door open. The light disappeared as Chet closed the door. Neil said a prayer, as he heard Hamilton fumbling for the light switch, that Julie had been able to secrete herself before he flooded the room with light.

Squinting, Chet walked toward Neil. "Where's the girl?" he asked immediately.

"Gone. She got out of her tape. And she's gone."

Chet's eyes, their pale blueness now watery and weak, narrowed. "You're lying," he hissed.

"How could I lie about something like that? Do you see her, Chet?"

"If she could get out, you'd have gotten out. Why would you have stayed behind?"

Neil's voice was a whisper. "A couple more seconds, Chet, and you would have missed me, too. Dr. Singer got free first and I insisted she get on out, that I'd be along as soon as I got my ankles free. She was reluctant to leave me, but she saw the wisdom in it . . . no point in both of us lingering longer than we had to, right?"

"You're a lying son of a bitch, Dvorak . . . now tell me where she's hiding. I saw her making those calf's eyes at you—she'd never have gone off and left you bound up."

Even under the extreme stress of the moment, Neil was able to feel chagrin that Chet Hamilton, with his quite low mental ability, had been astute enough to see what he had missed: Julie's obvious adoration of him. In looking back, he could see the signs, signs he had missed completely while they were going on. But that was irrelevant now.

"I told you the way it was. There's nothing you can do about it."

"No? Then have another think."

In a flash, before any of Neil's reflexes could defend him, Chet had struck out, the edge of his hand hitting hard against Neil's jaw, so hard that he went reeling backward. If it had not been for the metal post behind him, he would have gone all the way to the floor. As it was, his shoulder blade came sharply in contact with the metal, and the pain there was more intense than in his jaw. In time, he was sure he would feel the pain where Chet had struck him, but just now he was aware only of numbness. He rubbed his hand against his jaw gingerly, hoping to restore some feeling. For just a second, he worried that some of his teeth may have loosened, then instantly decided it did not matter. There was nothing like staring death in the face to make one forget about the little vanities and inconveniences that seem to loom so large when they are the only problem.

Chet was immediately on Neil, using the strength of his right arm to keep Neil pinned against the steel support post. "You dipshit!" Chet hissed. "I hate you, you know that? I truly hate you. Nothing would make me happier than to take out my knife and start peeling your skin away, little by little, and hear you scream like a rabbit in a trap."

"But you won't do that, will you?"

"What makes you think I won't, you oily bastard?"

"Because you need me alive too badly. The process you're

referring to would surely result in death, would it not?"

"One of the things I hate most about you is the highbrow way you talk, know it? Like you're looking down. Like you think you're better than everybody else."

Neil was able to make a quick assessment of Chet Hamilton. Emotionally and physically, he had about had it . . . a factor that could swing either for or against them.

Keeping his voice calm and level, Neil said, "I don't think I'm better than everybody else, Chet. I just think I'm better than you. I don't talk like this to my patients and colleagues. Just you. Because, you know something? I hate your guts, also. Isn't that nice? We have something in common, this hatred of each other. However, that's neither here nor there. As I was saying, you *do* need me alive."

"Yeah, sure. Because I figure if I walk out of here with you in front of me, and with a gun pointed at your head, I got a ticket out of here. That what you mean?"

"That and your shoulder. You're in pain. I can tell. And you're oozing fresh blood. I can help, if you'll let me."

"You don't touch me, Dvorak. No way you get near me with a knife or anything. You'd turn on me and cut my throat in a minute."

"It's a thought. How'd you get that bullet, Chet? And where's your brother? I thought you two were inseparable."

"Oh, you don't know? Of course, the dipshit doesn't know. He's been tied up. By the way, how'd you like being tied up, Dvorak? Bother you any, being that close to your girlfriend and not being able to touch her?"

"I think I've told you before—if not, I'm telling you now—Dr. Singer is not my girlfriend. She works and studies with me, that's all. You have a problem, Chet, know that? You seem to think that any time a man and woman come in contact, no matter how businesslike or how casual, there has to be sex going on. It's just not the case. Sometimes, maybe, but not all the time. I guess your obsession with who's screwing whom is just another little thing about

242

you I don't like."

"Listen, dipshit . . ."

Neil stared at the doubled right fist just a couple of centimeters away from his nose. He remembered the impact of that hand against face, remembered it so keenly that it took every shred of willpower he possessed to keep from flinching. He did not mind that he was antagonizing Chet, for such was his intention. The storage room was very large, and filled with all kinds of cartons and boxes. He felt that the only hope for keeping Julie out of this was to keep Chet so agitated he didn't know what he was doing, infuriate him so that he would forget about looking for her for a while. Please, God, he prayed silently . . . don't let that girl be stupid enough to try to be brave and come to my rescue.

With his injured shoulder, one hostage would be all Chet could handle. Therefore, Neil did not believe it would bother Hamilton at all to kill one of them, not if it took his fancy.

"Go ahead, Chet. Do what you want. You think I really care?"

"Why shouldn't you care? Don't you want to live?"

"Not so very much."

"Huh?"

"Surprised? You work with hurt people as long as I have, Chet, you put death in perspective. Sometimes it seems downright peaceful, this thought of death. I lost my wife. Together over a quarter of century, then she just dies. And I'm still here. It's been hard to get used to. Fact is, I'm not used to it yet. And I'm not sure I even care enough to get used to it. So do what you want, you ugly bastard, and just see where it will get you."

To Neil's surprise, Chet loosened his grip. A half-smile formed on his face, and he gave a low sound that may or may not have been a chuckle.

"Well, you may get your wish, Dipshit Dvorak. But only when I'm good and ready. Like I was saying, while you was

243

tied up in here, that nigger shot us both, me and Mick. Can you believe that? Tall black guy, acting like a nurse, all cocky in the Emergency Room, looking down on me. Like you do. I could see it in his eyes, that he was looking down on me. I wanted to take him by his thick black neck and choke him till his eyeballs bugged out. Wish now I had. But I got in a shot, too. Just his leg, but I got him. A wing isn't as good as a kill, but it's better than landing no punches at all, don't you think?"

"Whatever you say . . . but where's Mick? How badly was he hurt?"

For a moment, Chet's face was in danger of betraying his grief, but the moment passed quickly and his face resumed the sneering mask of rage.

"He's dead, asshole. That's what I'm trying to tell you. The nigger killed him, right in front of me. Poor ol' Mick fell to the floor, and the blood was pouring out of his chest and he was kind of gurgling, like. Shit! My little brother, and right before my eyes. They'll pay. They'll all pay."

"Who are 'they?' "

"Everyone. You. Marianne. The black guy. The people who took my kids away. The people who said I couldn't see my own wife. Who do they think they are? A man's wife and kids, they're *his,* don't you see? No one else has the right to take them away. Dipshit that you are, you can see that, can't you?"

"I understand how you feel, Chet. Lots of people feel that way about their families. I suppose it's a natural way to feel. But life isn't that way. We can't own people — not our mates, not our children. They have rights of their own. And if for any reason they can't assert their rights, there are people legally empowered to do that for them."

Chet's anger flared again visibly, and Neil felt a moment of nervousness as he saw Chet's fingers toy with the knife at his waistband. However, Neil's words, unlike others he had spoken recently, had been soft and low, instructive but not argumentative or authoritative. Chet, after a bit of hesitation, responded to that.

"I get mixed up sometimes," Chet said. It was the first doubt he had expressed openly since the onset of his reign of terror.

"Seems like they ought to be *mine*—my family, that is. I always felt that was the way it should be. But I never meant to hurt them. I just wanted them to do what I said. If they didn't, I had to show them. Know what I mean? If they didn't know who was boss, didn't respect that, then they'd get away from me. Know what I mean?"

Dvorak nodded. The slight motion made the top of his head pound. Apparently some of the numbness was wearing away now.

"I know. No matter how careful we try to be, sometimes those we care about get hurt. . . . Chet?"

"Yeah?"

"Give it up. Give it up now, before anyone else gets hurt, including yourself. I'll see to it your wound gets cleaned up and you get some pain medicine. I'll check on Mick for you. You don't really know that he's dead, do you? You saw him fall, saw the blood, but he could be alive. You don't know for sure. Let's find out. I can't promise you that you'll walk away from all this, because you won't. But I can recommend that doctors examine you. If you'll put that knife and gun away and walk out of here side-by-side with me, I promise I'll do what I can for you."

Chet's eyes narrowed with suspicion. "Why would you do anything for me? You already said you hate my guts."

"It's called a bargain. I hate what you've done to St. Paul's and the people in it. I don't want to hate, but things have gone far enough that hatred is what I feel. But helping you is a small price to pay if I can see that no one else gets hurt."

For a second, Chet looked almost tempted. He was very tired, and the tiredness showed. For the space of that second, Neil felt a surge of hope—a hope that dissipated quickly when Chet shook his head.

"No way. No more fancy talk. You're making my head hurt. Like I said, you're my ticket out of here. But I want the woman, too."

So he hadn't forgotten. Neil's sigh of disappointment was audible. But at least, he thought, he had purchased a little bit of time—time in which he hoped Julie had hidden herself well out of reach.

"You'll have to forget her, Chet. She's out of here, out of reach. Listen, before you do whatever it is you're wanting to do, there's one thing I want to ask you . . . if I may?"

Actually, there was a lot he wanted to know about this man—such as, how can you sexually assault your own kids, then turn around and say you didn't mean to hurt them? And how can you hurt and endanger so many innocent people, people you don't even know, just because your own life got out of control? But this wasn't the time and the place . . . and Chet couldn't have supplied the answers anyway.

"Shoot, then enough talk. Ask your one thing, and then you and me are out of here. One way or another, we're out of here."

"It's a simple question. When Dr. Singer and I were still bound up, we heard an explosion. What did you blow up, Chet?"

Chet's grin was obscene.

"Your place."

"Pardon?"

"You know, the place you work . . . the wing where they keep the nuts. It's smashed to smithereens. Personally, I thought blowing up the nursery would have been a good touch, but Mick didn't like the idea. A bit soft, that boy always was. Mind, he could be as mean as me when the circumstances was right. But soft as a woman over little kids and puppy dogs, and stuff like that. He was after me not to bomb the nursery, all those little babies, he said. Truth is, I forgot which detonator I carried and which Mick had.

Guess they must have took his off him. Funny feeling, when I pushed that button I didn't know which place would blow."

Neil closed his eyes, mentally listing the patients on the ward as well as the few employees who had been caught in the fray. Had any of them survived? He shuddered, knowing that the loss of *his* people was in reality no worse than the loss of anyone else, but in his heart he was not feeling as if that was true.

His voice was very quiet. "How many died?"

Chet laughed. "You had your question. No more. Time for some action. Truth is, though, Dr. Dipshit, I don't know. I quit calling. You weren't there to talk to, and the fun went out of it. Maybe a bunch was killed, maybe no one at all. Like I said, I don't know for sure. Just like you say I don't know Mick is dead. Only he is. I saw how he looked, how he sounded. He was a dead man by the time he hit the floor. It was always the two of us against the world. Now it's just me, so *you* been elected to help, hear?"

Chet looked around, his eye catching a wall telephone. Neil could see the wheels turning in Chet's mind. Under the best of circumstances, thinking was not Hamilton's best point. Due to duress and fatigue, his thinking had slowed to a quite visible process.

"Call that number," he ordered. "There's still someone there, ain't there?"

"As far as I know. Don't forget, Chet, I've been confined. What's happened out there the past hour or two . . . well, it's just something I don't know about."

"Try it. Call 'em. Tell them they didn't listen to me, they've opened the doors and let people in. Now they'll pay. No, no . . . that's not what I want you to say. Tell them you and me are walking out of here and they're going to help. They're gonna open a door and stand back and let us pass. And if they don't, it's goodbye Dvorak because I'm going to have my gun right at your head. Anyone makes one move toward me and you're dead. So you call them and tell them that."

Wearily, Neil walked toward the phone and dialed the 4592 extension.

"Kevin?" he asked, hearing the familiar voice. "Neil Dvorak here."

"Thank God! Boy, have we been worried about you!"

"I've been a bit worried myself, Kevin. As a matter of fact, I still am. Chet and Mick taped Dr. Singer and me all up and left us in the main supply room on the second floor. Julie got free and got out just in time. I wasn't so lucky. Just as I got the last of the tape off and was ready to leave, Chet walked in. We've been having a nice little chat. Now he says it's time for action. He says he and I are going to walk out of here, and I'm going to have a gun pointed at my head to ensure his safe exit."

Neil wasn't sure if he actually heard, or just imagined, the sharp intake of breath at the other end.

Inman suddenly came on the line. "Put Hamilton on, let me talk to him."

But when Neil tried to do so, Chet shook his head.

"I only got my good arm. I'm not going to try to hang onto you, a gun, and a telephone receiver. So you just tell 'em the way it is. You and me, Dvorak, we're going to the front entrance. Somebody is going to be there to have it unlocked for us. And they're going to hand me ten thousand bucks—the safe in this joint surely has that much—and they're going to let me and you walk out, all free and clear. When I think I'm better off without you, I'll let you go. That is, unless I decide to waste you."

"If you're going to kill me either way," Neil said, calmly and evenly, "there isn't any point in us doing what you want. Just do it now, and get it over with. You kill me, they kill you. Then it's all over but the shouting."

"Dr. Dvorak," Inman hollered from his end of the line, "you still there?"

"Still here. Chet and I were just having another little

chat. Some things have to be ironed out, that's all."

"There's nothing to work out," Chet cried in frustration. "Okay, I won't kill you. I'll let you go as soon as I can . . . like I said, as soon as I think I'm better off without you. That'll be the deal—they don't come after me till they have you back."

Neil delivered the message.

"Ten thousand dollars? I suppose it can be arranged. I'll check with Ms. Laramore. That's quite a drop from the original request," Alterauge said.

"Chet's tired. He wants out. He's broken up over Mick's death. He—"

"Mick isn't dead," Alterauge said. "Does Chet think that? He's wrong."

"Say it again, Agent Alterauge. I'll hold the receiver where Chet can hear."

"Hamilton," Alterauge boomed, "your brother isn't dead. Not yet. I see where you'd get that idea, the way he took the bullet in the chest. He's in serious condition, but he is still alive. He needs to be transferred out to a bigger hospital. You know who's standing in the way of that, don't you?"

"You're lying . . . Mick *can't* be alive, not after what I saw."

"Things have gone too far for lies, Hamilton. Your brother lives. That's a simple statement of fact. The same surgeon that saw you in the Emergency Room, Dr. Rasmussen, did a bang-up job of operating on his chest—took the bullet out, put some patches over the damaged areas, put in lots of drains and tubes. Not very long ago a lung collapsed, and one of the doctors that just came in went back and put a chest tube in to reexpand the lung. He's not walking and talking and dancing in the hallways, but he is still alive."

"Then I'm going to see him. Get him and put him where I can see him."

Dvorak said, "Chet, be reasonable. If Mick has to have

that many tubes in him, if he can't breathe properly on his own yet, they can't be rolling him out to the front door to wave goodbye to you."

"I need to think. Hang up, Dvorak. Tell 'em we'll call back in five minutes, then hang up."

Neil did as he was told. He felt he was back to square one with Chet. But at least Julie was safe. He had always been big on telling his patients to count their blessings, run a tally of their assets. Right now, he felt pretty low on blessings, but the fact that Julie was out of sight counted as one.

Neil watched Chet closely. As he had previously observed, Hamilton's thought processes were sluggish. His own must be, too, he was sure. The whole scenario seemed in slow motion. Chet opened his mouth to speak—and before the words came forth, there was the sound of a muffled sneeze. Chet's eyes widened, his mouth snapped shut. Neil closed his eyes as if in pain. So much for counting that particular blessing.

Chapter Fourteen

"You lying son of a bitch," Chet said. The surge of anger caused the blood to rush to his face, suffusing the skin with a florid coloration.

While Neil struggled to come up with some plausible reason for the sneezing sound, knowing his mental task was hopeless, another muffled sneeze occurred. Julie, *Julie*, he thought. She was probably crouched down near a lot of dust and lint.

"You lied," Chet practically screamed. "You lied to me, you dipshit."

"And I'd do it again if there was a chance of saving a life. Why shouldn't I lie to you? Answer me that. I owe you nothing, Hamilton, nothing at all. Now forget about the girl. Let's call the authorities and we'll walk out like you planned. You can't handle two hostages anyway, especially not with that bad shoulder."

"I want to see her first. I want her out here with you and me. Then I make my decision about which one of you goes with me. Clear?"

Leave her out of it, Chet. I didn't think I could ever beg, but I'm begging now. Come on, let's just get out of here, before things get any more complicated. Can't we do that?"

Nearly apoplectic with anger, Chet jerked the .38 out of his waistband and pressed it against Neil's forehead, right in the area of the temporal arteries.

From a few feet away, Julie's voice came loud and strong. "Here I am, Chet. What was it you wanted with me?"

Surprised, Chet turned in an effort to locate the owner of the voice, and the action caused his grip on Neil to loosen. Taking advantage of the slight loosening, Neil made a grab at the wrist that held the gun—but Chet was too quick and was able to maintain, and strengthen, his hold on both the gun and Dvorak.

"I'm going to blow your friggin' brains out, right here and now. Just to show you I can. You talk too much. And you lie. And I can hunt down your little cunt of a shrink and use her like I was going to use you. Only it'll be more fun with her."

"Here I am, Chet," Julie said, springing forward.

Neil's heart lurched at the sight of her, cheeks smudged, suit and blouse torn and dirty, holding onto the sharp carton-opener they had found before she attempted to hide. She wasn't very far away, and her nearness seemed to confuse Chet as well as infuriate him.

"Julie," Neil found himself yelling at the top of his lungs, "what are you doing? He has a gun. You can't—"

"He was going to find me anyway. We both know that. This way, at least one of us has a chance."

"You sure about that?" Chet asked. The laugh accompanying his words was the most evil sound either doctor had ever heard. "I can pick you both off, and don't think I can't."

"And then you're back to no hostage," Neil reminded him.

"Shut up, old man. When I want you to talk, I'll ask you to talk. Till then, just keep your suggestions to yourself."

"It's not that easy, Chet," Neil said, keeping his voice steady. "You know it and I know it. It's just not that easy."

"Huh? What are you talking about?"

For a second, Neil dared himself to hope. Perhaps the distracting maneuvers were going to work. He wanted Chet's attention on him, not on Julie.

"Can't you figure it out, Chet? . . . A big strong guy like you can't figure it out?"

"Listen, I—"

Chet was frustrated enough to let go of Neil slightly. Quick to see that, Julie lunged forward with the box-cutter. She caught Chet by surprise and was able to cut his left forearm before he could react. Letting go of Neil completely, Chet looked toward Julie, his face showing all the classic signs of apoplexy—the skin so red it was nearly purple and the veins sticking out at the temples like ropes . . . pulsating ropes. He fired the gun. Neil's scream was as loud as the shot, for he knew that at such close range, there was no way he could miss Julie, no way he could not inflict great harm. Julie's dark eyes met Neil's in mute urgency. "Run," she was saying to him, "for God's sake, run."

For an endless moment they were like a still photo, and they seemed to be outside of themselves, watching their own scenario. Then Julie slumped forward, and Chet stood there letting his frame support the inert weight of her. Neil glanced toward the door, then bolted toward it. In a flash, he shoved the door open and was out in the hallway . . . out, but still a far cry from feeling safe. With a speed he did not know he possessed, he rounded a corner, feeling it gave him a minor degree of safety, since the path of a fired bullet is straight. Indeed, he heard the sound of the gun being fired again, and quite literally cringed. He stood for a moment, cowering against the wall, gripped by terror, lucid thoughts unable to form. Then, as reason gradually returned, his senses registered that he was not being pursued. There were no footsteps, no additional repeated gunfire, no shadows. Moisture stung his eyes and, reaching deep down inside himself, he realized with a shock that he had *wanted* to die, he had wanted Chet to be after him, not only for a chance of saving Julie Singer but to put himself away from it all, to distance himself from the fray. Death would be a

253

great excuse for not trying any more, a great distancer.

But there was no time for that. Like it or not, he was alive, and to be alive carried with it a responsibility.

He tore down the hall, down the nearest steps, and, still running, fell through the doorway of the first-floor conference room.

"Oh, God!" Kevin Donati said.

"Not quite," Neil was able to say. "Just me. Get on the phones and get us some help. Chet Hamilton and Dr. Singer are in the big second floor storeroom. She's been shot. For all I know, she's dead. But we need to know for sure. If there's a chance she's alive, we have to get back in there."

A stocky man unknown to Neil stepped forward and took him by the arm.

"Have a seat, Dr. Dvorak. You look shocky. Kevin's provided invaluable help. He'll get a crew there. Think Hamilton will let us in?"

Unable to relax enough to sit, Neil said, his voice scratchy and raw, "I have no idea. He wanted to hold us, one or both of us, hostage—bargain with our lives to get himself out of here. But he's hurt or killed her, and I'm out of his reach. He took a bullet in the shoulder. I'd say it's hurting him a great deal. My guess is that he's abandoned her and gone somewhere to think it out. But that's just a guess." Warily, he looked at the man to whom he was talking. "Alterauge?"

"In the flesh. How did you guess?"

"The voice. What else?"

"They're on the way there," Donati interrupted, "a police team and medical team both. Someone will call back as soon as they get a chance, to let us know how she is."

"I have a pretty good idea how she is," Neil said, his voice low and shaky. As soon as the words were said, he was aware of a trembling throughout his body, a totally involuntary trembling. He steeled himself but found, despite all the relaxation techniques he knew, that he could not stop the shaking.

"Sit down," someone said, and he was aware of a firm grip on his arm. Voices were directed at him, seeming to float above him. He was unable to differentiate one person from another. He was in a chair, but the grip on his arm did not lessen. Was it Chet still holding him, or was it someone else? He tried to look, but it was like looking through a cloud. He didn't want it to be Chet, and the voices were so kind, but Chet's face was all he could see in his mind. He knew it wasn't really the flesh and bone he saw, but the memory . . . wasn't it?

"Get him water," someone said.

"Get his feet up . . . take his shoes off," someone else said.

Were they talking about him? He wasn't thirsty, so why should he drink water? And he couldn't take his shoes off, he had to go help Julie. Didn't they understand that? Then his racing thoughts stopped for a moment. *Why* did he have to go help Julie? What was the problem? It was in his mind that she needed help, but he couldn't quite remember why.

It was then that the tears started—tears that flowed in copious amounts, the force and volume enough to make his already trembling frame begin to shake quite violently . . . and yet no sound issued from him. He found it hurt to cry like that. The shaking started on the inside, creating pressure on the thorax, causing all the muscles in his chest and back to tense and ache. As he cried and shook, he tried to analyze the makeup of the pain, and just how the lacrimal ducts could be tied into the musculoskeletal system. As long as he concentrated on the physiology, he did not have to think about why he cried, why he hurt, why he was so weary.

The hands that held him pushed up his sleeve. He tried to protest, but the silent sobs that shook his body would not let the words past his gullet. Perhaps they were killing him. He saw the glint of the needle and syringe. Did it really matter? Through a blur of tears, he was aware of eyes watching him . . . kind eyes. He saw compassion there. If this was death, perhaps it was okay. Someone cared. He could see that.

"Put him to bed so he can rest," a voice said, a voice kind enough to match the compassion he had seen in the eyes.

Yes, Neil thought, this must be death. God the Father would be like that. "You are tired, my son. Come and rest."

As Kevin Donati watched the psychiatrist being wheeled off, he felt tears form in his own eyes. "Will he be okay?" he found himself asking no one in particular. He was considerably younger than Dvorak and had not, over the past few hours, been under quite as much physical and emotional duress, yet he, too, felt close to the breaking point. He was concerned for the man he respected, and worried about himself and the others around him.

"That's a strong man there," Agent Alterauge said, nodding in the direction of the quickly disappearing gurney. "I predict he'll sleep off the sedative and bounce back to help clear up this mess. Whatever has happened to the young woman has pushed him over the edge—that and the exhaustion—but he'll be back."

"I sure hope so."

"He will be, son. Believe me, he will be."

And Kevin believed the FBI agent, not because he felt the man had any extrasensory powers to let him see the outcome, but because he *had* to believe. At the moment, anything else would have been unbearable.

Marianne Hamilton was in the hall when the stretcher

went by. For a moment she did not recognize the sleeping patient. Then, with a jolt to her system, the pattern of his features registered in her memory. Dr. Dvorak, despite the silver of his hair, had been so vital, so alive, so aware, so on top of everything, seeming to know her thoughts before they were clear in her own mind. And now? He was so pale, so still, as they wheeled him by.

She called after the white-clad nurses who maneuvered the stretcher down the hall, but her reaction had come too late. They either did not hear, or pretended they did not. She felt she had to know what had happened to him — if Chet had done this also, or if he had not. Turning, she walked in the direction of the conference room. No one watched her. No one kept tabs on her. Odd, she thought. More than odd. She was possessed by a feeling of eeriness as she moved: A few hours ago, and it really had been just a few hours, it had been deemed important to keep watch over her. They had started out in teams to look for her when she had "escaped" their watchful eyes. As a result, Dr. Dvorak and Dr. Singer had been captured, Steve Cates had been wounded, Mick was as good as dead, and Chet, too, had been wounded, and was now roaming the halls of St. Paul's, alone, in pain, undoubtedly feeling cornered and betrayed, ready to strike out against anyone who crossed his path.

She tried to find compassion for her husband, the father of her children, and she tried to find sorrow for the loss of her brother-in-law. With Chet, she had no success at all. She wanted him caught, she wanted him dead. She wanted him where he could never hurt anyone again, not even with the brutality of words, and the only way she could think of that would render him incapable of inflicting harm would be for him to be dead. So as she walked, hearing the tap of her worn soles against the tile floors, she prayed for his death as fervently, perhaps more so, as she prayed for the recovery of

257

those he had harmed. And Mick? He had never really harmed her or the children, and probably wasn't truly aware of the extent to which Chet had, for he was always careful not to be seen, to cover that darkest side of himself from all but the four of them—Alix, Brie, Jacob, and herself. Mick, in his own random and immature way, had been kind to them, doing little things, buying little toys for the kids. In his eyes she had seen fondness, perhaps even a touch of desire, and she had been glad for that. With Chet, it had been all too easy to forget she was a person and to feel like an object, so much so that she felt wooden. It was easier that way, though, to feel wooden, to feel incapable of defending the kids, to feel incapable of loving and being loved by an ordinary man. Yes, she could feel a bit of sorrow for Mick. He was, she felt, almost a victim in this . . . almost, but not quite. He had had the chance to say "no" to Chet—something the rest of them hadn't had—but years of habit, of following his older brother's bidding had been too much. He had followed merely because he had been asked to do so. Marianne was sure of that. But however she felt, it was over.

She approached the door of the conference room, pushed her long, lank hair out of the way, and stared dully at the few people assembled there. The people in there looked no brighter than she felt. She ached inside for them, wanting it to end so they could get some rest. She cleared her throat in an attempt to be noticed.

"Dr. Dvorak," she said hesitantly. "I saw him on the stretcher. Has he been hurt, or . . ."

Kevin shook his head. "They gave him a sedative, that's all. He's worn out, and he started shaking and crying. That's all. He'll be okay after he rests. No, it's Dr. Singer. We—"

"Who is this?" Agent Alterauge asked, thinking that he already knew.

258

Kevin drew in his breath sharply. Of course, they did not know. They had not seen the woman, but talked to her over the system when they were still obeying Chet's orders not to enter St. Paul's.

"I'm sorry. This is Marianne Hamilton, Chet's wife. Marianne, this is Mr. Alterauge. He's with the FBI."

Marianne raised her eyes to meet the face of the stranger. He was trained not to show his reactions, and so although she wanted to gauge how he felt about her, she could not.

"I'm sorry for all this," she said simply.

For a second, the mask cracked and there was a small twitch at the corner of his mouth—a twitch that might under other circumstances have been allowed to develop into a smile.

"Come on in and have a seat," he said. "We'll explain all this to you, what we know of it. But no apologies necessary. It's not your fault."

She searched for words to explain why it was, but when they came flooding over her mind, she held them back. Undoubtedly he knew the story almost as well as she did. He was merely being kind, that was all.

They supplied her with a cup of coffee. She hadn't asked for it. She didn't want it. She had never learned to like coffee, especially hating the acrid aftertaste of it. Yet she sipped at it, feeling it impolite to do otherwise. She was surprised to find the warmth a comfort.

"Also," Alterauge said, "I want you to help me get inside that man's head. You know this side of him as no one else does. I want to ask for your help in finding a way to reach him, get him to surrender . . . or to trick him into a mistake so he'll be caught. Can you do that?"

Marianne looked at this man who sat across from her. He was by no means good-looking, but middle-aged, plain, slightly overweight even for his stocky frame. She found she liked the ordinariness of the way he looked. She had fallen once, way back when she was no more than a child, for the charm good looks and a confident manner can create. Never again could she trust the easy smile, the wink, the features like one sees on magazine covers.

"I'll do what I can," she said. Her face must be healing, she felt, because she could see better now; the left eye was focusing more clearly, the swelling less pronounced around it. "And I also want to know about my children. Where they are, if they are together, if they know about this."

"We checked on that for you, then you disappeared before we had the information assembled, so we can take care of that before we get down to the rest of it. The children are together. They are in the home of a middle-aged couple whose own children are grown, so they got into foster care. They were hesitant about the boy, thinking he might be too much for them, but in the end agreed because they knew the harm it might do to separate them. They are safe, well-fed, warm, and physically secure. As far as knowing about this, I doubt that it could be kept from them. The girls, as I am sure you realize, are old enough to piece things together, to search for the why of things."

Marianne nodded. It was the most she could hope for. In truth, it was more than she had *dared* hope for. It was not enough, but it was what they had to deal with. No more, no less.

"I'm grateful someone took the time to find out. I'd like to send them a message soon, if I'm allowed. Right now, though, tell me about Dr. Singer." Sitting on the very edge of her chair, she listened intently . . . and as she listened, her hatred deepened, which she hadn't felt possible.

"What are you feeling?" he asked gently, seeing the change come over her previously bland expression.

"Hatred. I want him dead. And I want him to suffer before he dies. The hatred is so strong it nearly eats me up, so I try to push it down—but I can't do that anymore. I have

260

to say it's there. All those years I pushed it down, then I exploded. I can't afford to do that now. If there's a hope I'll get my children back, can try to build a life with them, then I have to recognize my emotions and deal with them when they happen. And I have to make plans. I know it isn't for you to say—I'm just asking because I think I can tell you're an honest man: do you think there is a chance they'll give my babies back to me?"

"There is a chance. A good chance. Sadly enough, the chance is because of all this. Now people will have no reason to doubt you when you tell how bad he was, how you were goaded past human endurance. Without *this,* I doubt that you would have had a chance."

Her reply was barely audible. *"He* told me that. He said if there was any good to come out of this, it would be that—that my violence would be excused and my kids returned to me. He also taught me the other things I said . . . to recognize my emotions and not push them down, and to make plans. No matter how bad things get, make plans. Then you have something to work toward, instead of feeling helpless. So little time we were together . . . and he taught me so much."

"That's what they always say about time: it's quality that counts, not quantity. I assume you're talking about Dr. Dvorak. He's a unique man, I think."

Marianne nodded, then raised her eyes to his once more. She nodded, almost imperceptibly, as a signal that she was ready to do what he wanted, that she would answer any questions about Chet and her relationship with him that he wanted to ask.

He nodded back, their understanding complete. Chet Hamilton was still at large, and they had work to do.

A few rooms away, on the same floor, Stephen Cates was

261

conscious again, his foot swathed in bandages. Due to the anesthesia and analgesia, he felt no pain, just a floating sensation. His eyes focused on the bandaged foot, and it all came back to him. His mouth felt dry, but he willed himself to speak, and was grateful when he heard the sound of his own voice. "Well, I see they didn't have to amputate." Squeaky though his voice sounded to his ears, at least he knew it was functional.

He heard a small laugh, an almost strangled sort of sound, then turned his head toward it. Jennifer Weiller stood by his bed. Apparently she considered herself off-duty, because her hair now flowed to her shoulders, a curtain of pale wheat. Even through the fuzziness, he could see that her face was pale and wan, even seeming thinner, though rationally he knew the ordeal had not gone on long enough for anyone to lose weight.

"On the other hand, perhaps I didn't survive and went straight to Heaven, seeing that I'm looking at an angel." He sounded drunk, he thought: The words came, but he was not able to control their speed or volume. Talking was like working with a radio or stereo whose controls had gone bad.

"I'm not saying you won't get into Heaven, Stephen Cates, for I won't be the one to judge that. But you know full well you aren't there yet."

He smiled, even his lips feeling loose and out of control. "It's close enough. I'm in St. Paul's, and you are here. Come and hold my hand. Just for a second."

She did as she was asked without hesitation, for no other reason than that she had been aching to touch him. Indeed, while sitting there and waiting for him to return to consciousness, she had tentatively reached out and touched his face and hand, ever so lightly, not enough to make him react. Of course he hadn't known about it. This . . . *this* was better, because he knew, he could respond to her touch.

Sitting on the edge of his hospital bed, she looked down at his face, the strong features, the kind eyes that were still somewhat faraway looking. As she did so, she struggled with her own conflicting emotions.

"Your wife is outside the hospital," she said softly. "They won't let her in. No one gets in but police and medical people who can help. They haven't caught Chet, so danger still exists in here. When I heard she was angry over not getting in, I sent word that I'd check and let her know how you are. Do you have a message you want me to take to her?"

Stephen shook his head to clear the fog, then looked down at the small white hand encased by his own larger one.

"I've fallen in love with you, Jennie," he said.

"I know," came her own shaky reply. "That isn't the problem. The problem is that I think *I'm* falling in love, too. We can't permit it, Steve."

Smiling, he attempted to kiss her hand. His position and coordination being what they were, he fell quite short and he grimaced slightly when his lips came in contact with the crisp white linens on his bed.

"Tell me about it. I'm grateful to her, Jennie. And I feel sorry for her. But I don't feel for her what I do for you. I never did. I say I could never willfully hurt her, that I could never walk out on her, that a divorce would have to be her idea, and then I think . . ."

"Yes?"

"It's so clear in my mind, but when I try to say it, it sounds like I'm trying to make excuses for myself."

"Just go ahead and blurt it out. If I don't understand, I'll say so."

"I gathered as much. A straight-shooter, that's my Jennie. What I was thinking was . . . maybe I'm hurting her as much or more by staying with her, living a lie, pretending I

263

feel a way I don't feel. In the long run, maybe that's more cruel than the truth." When, after a lapse of time, she had not replied, he looked at her. "Well?"

"I can't answer that. You know her. I don't. Some people prefer to live the pretenses, the little lies. They dread confrontations and changes, and they'd rather live with their heads in the sand than deal with reality. Others, like me, would rather face the truth and get it over with, no matter how much it hurts. I know I don't know you well. And I've been so afraid of commitment. I haven't hidden from it because I ever had such a bad experience personally. It's just that so many people close to me did. It's like I never saw any really good marriages. Or even good dating relationships. It was like my friends were two people . . . the one I knew, and the one who was obsessed with pleasing some guy, impressing him. Time after time, I saw a seemingly normal person turn into some kind of a monster—"

"Monster?"

"That may be an exaggeration—but not much of one. All of a sudden, this girl lives according to what Mark or Tim or Brad likes or might think. I was never comfortable with that, never wanted it for myself. But I always thought that is, if I did find someone—and I do know I don't know you well, even though somehow I feel as if I do—that I would just *know* if he felt the same way. I'm saying this badly, aren't I?"

"Not really. You're saying that, even though we didn't say a word until just a couple of minutes ago, you knew I cared about you. And that you think you'd know if I ever stopped caring, that pretending would never be enough, and that I wouldn't have to tell you things had changed, you'd already know they had."

"You're amazing."

"And don't you forget it. For what it's worth, I share your opinion. Which is why I knew what it was so easily.

But that doesn't lessen the dilemma."

"I know. Because your wife does not feel the same way. That is what you are saying, isn't it?"

"Probably. It's something I have to think about. Long before I got interested in you, I got so frustrated and unhappy at times that I'd make up scenes in my mind. I'd rehearse telling her I wanted out of the marriage. And no matter how many times I went over it in my mind, I never got it right, could never imagine her response being anything other that total hurt. You see, appearances mean so much to her. It wouldn't just be losing me, it would be becoming a divorcee, worrying about what her parents and the people in the church would think. As miserable as she might be now, I think she'd prefer the status quo to divorce."

"Personally, I'm not too keen on divorce myself. I always wanted to be so sure, because if I married I wanted it to be till death do us part. If it's to be that way, then one has to be very sure that one is doing the right thing in marrying."

Looking down at Steve, Jennie saw a spasm pass across his face. Although he tried to pretend it was nothing, she saw that the analgesia was wearing off and the pain returning.

"I'll go get you something. I'm sure the doctor ordered something for you."

"Leave it for a bit, Jennie. It's not bad. Anything I take will put me out, I think. I want to stay awake a while yet. Ironic, isn't it?"

"Ironic? What do you mean?"

"We sit here and talk as if my marriage is the only obstacle we face . . ."

"Well, it is a rather large obstacle," she deadpanned.

Despite his wooziness and pain, Stephen laughed. "I am so pleased, so very pleased. Oh, you're great."

Her cheeks reddened slightly, and Steve's heart nearly broke at how young and pretty she looked, sitting there.

She was nearly thirty and he knew that, yet she seemed so much younger, in many ways still a child. He had grown up so wild, so free, and she, he would guess, had been sheltered and protected, really too much so.

"You make too much of things," she protested.

"Who me? Never. But you made a joke . . . all on your own, and under the most trying of circumstances. You do *know* you made a joke?"

She nodded and, looking quite prim, said, "I meant to. It wasn't an accident. But it wasn't *that* much of a joke."

"Not from anyone else, but from you it was terrific."

"It's also true," she said, in mock sternness.

He heaved a deep sigh. "Oh, yes. But what I started to say was that we don't talk about the racial thing."

"There are a couple of reasons for that. The first is that I don't think it matters much to us. And the second is that it doesn't matter anyway, because even if we were suddenly the same color, you'd still be married to Elizabeth."

She looked so sad. So young, so pretty, so vulnerable, and so distressed. Had he caused that, created pain and turmoil in her heart? He had sought her out, he had teased her, noticed her, made sure that he had time to talk to her. Even in the beginning, he hadn't been sure why he did what he did. He had liked her, admired her work, and she had evoked a tenderness in him . . . and he had so wanted to make her laugh. Now she seemed ready to cry. And he wondered if he could allow *himself* the luxury of healing tears. If he had just left her alone; if he just had been totally professional, and left her alone . . .

"I'm sorry, Jennie."

"Nothing to be sorry about. These things happen. Look, I'm going to go see what's ordered for you, then see that you get it. Then I'm going to go do what I promised and see that your wife gets a message."

Within five minutes, Jennie had administered the Demerol and was seeing that the bed was in the proper position for Steve's proposed nap.

"Any particular message you want me to give your wife?" she asked very softly.

Stephen found himself looking directly into Jennie's eyes and knowing her pain was mirrored in his own. "Just tell her that I'll be fine, not to worry about me."

"I'll tell her that you said you loved her."

"But I didn't say that. I can't ask you to deliver a message like that. And I'm not so sure that it's true. It depends on the definition of love."

"If she seems to need to hear it, I'll say it. These are trying times, Steve."

"I know, sweetheart, I know. You're going home soon? There are replacements here now, you know."

"Oh, I know. And I'm too beat to function well unless it's a have-to case. But if I can find a corner to crawl into for a nap, I'd like to see St. Paul's safe before I go home. I *will* go home, when all is clear. And you know what I'm going to do when I get home?"

"I have a feeling you're going to tell me."

"I'm going to make a commitment. One of the first in my adult life. I'm going to quit pretending that stray cat I've been feeding is going to go away, or that I'm going to call the pound to pick him up. I'm going to take him to a vet and get his shots and give him a name . . . the whole works."

"Way to go. I'm a dog person myself, but cats are okay. I can tolerate them."

"Yes," she said archly, "but can they tolerate you?"

"You made another joke! Again, not much of one. But not bad for a beginner at this smart-alecky business."

"I'm going now. I'll be back to look in on you before I do go home."

"I don't suppose you'd consider kissing me? It's not as if I could take advantage of you, trussed up and sedated as I am."

Bending, she touched her lips to his, just for a few seconds and very gently. Nonetheless, the impact was terrific.

"You do know that's the end as well as the beginning?"

He nodded. "I know it all too well. I knew it before I even asked. You be careful."

"I will. And you sleep well."

As much as Steve wanted to stay awake, to be a part of what was going on, the narcotic had its way and he was soon asleep.

Jennie turned and walked out of the hospital room and into the corridor. Head held high, she received a pass from the guard at the Emergency Room door to go and to reenter. She had meant just to send a message out by phone, but now it was suddenly very important to her to deliver it in person. She searched the crowd until her eyes found a tall woman in her late thirties, a distraught and discontented looking woman with very high cheekbones and café-au-lait skin. Walking toward her, she asked, "Elizabeth Cates?"

Fear was in the other woman's eyes when she acknowledged her identity.

"My name is Jennifer Weiller. I just saw your husband, Mrs. Cates. He's okay. The surgeon took the bullet out of his ankle and everything is okay. He is still woozy from the anesthesia, and also having some pain. I gave him an injection and settled him for a nap. He said to tell you to go home and rest, not to worry, that he's okay."

Her previous hunch had been right. Those words were not enough. She had realized that if she loved a man, the words would not have been enough for her.

"He sends his love," she said, not feeling that she lied. In a curious way, he had done just that.

"Thank you, Ms. Weiller. I appreciate you taking the

time to come out here and give me the message. I have been awfully worried. A lot of this is his own fault, but . . ."

Jennie felt as if her blood stopped flowing, suddenly too cold to make it through the veins properly. "How is that?"

"They say the Hamiltons weren't in St. Paul's till around midnight. If Steve had come on home like he was supposed to, he wouldn't still be in there."

"I suppose one could look at it that way," she said coolly. "That is, if one were so inclined. But Stephen stayed because there was a patient he was concerned about. He wanted to know how she was before he left. As it turned out, the patient who touched him . . . *us* . . . was Hamilton's wife."

She saw the puzzled look on Stephen's wife's face and realized she wasn't making a whole lot of sense. She was so tired, so grimy, so confused.

"Sorry, Mrs. Cates. I guess I'm just trying to say that good nurses can't always work by the clock. And your husband is one of the best nurses I've ever worked with. Be proud of him for that, if you can."

That said, she walked off. She wanted no part of this woman — a woman who was attractive enough as far as features and form went, but unappealing because of attitude. But maybe that was just how she *wanted* to see things. Somehow, she felt winning would be ever so much harder if she liked her rival.

Jennie's gaze swept the parking lot. She saw a man in a trench coat headed toward her, microphone in hand. Moving quickly, she avoided him. She did not want to be asked about St. Paul's. She did not want to be asked about anything. All she wanted to do was find a quiet corner where she could sleep . . . perhaps after crying a bit, first.

Chapter Fifteen

Chet Hamilton stared down at the still form of the slender woman in the rumpled navy suit. Although she had fallen onto her back, he could not see her face because her hair had fallen like a curtain over it. His rage had reached its peak when he found that Dvorak had lied and hidden her from him. Now the situation was worse, the cunning side of him realized, and he was quickly losing ground. Dvorak had escaped from him, and the woman was, if not dead, dying. He had felt they were his ticket out, his only hope for escape. Now he had to find another way. For the first time since the onset of his escapade, he felt a sense of doom, of total futility. The rage that had fueled him was gone. All the reasons for his hatred, and more, existed; nothing had been remedied, and Mick had been taken from him — and still, he could not summon the rage. Like everything else, it had deserted him. No emotion can be sustained indefinitely, and his anger, with a will of its own, declared itself at least temporarily spent.

Chet bent down and reached out tentatively to touch the young psychiatrist. There was a pulse. He was not trained or experienced to know if it was a weak pulse or a normal one. All he knew was that he could feel the steady beating. But she looked so pale and still and, when he brushed her hair back, he could detect no fluttering of her eyelids. She would be no help to him as a hostage. To carry her, with his wounded shoulder, would be impossible. In her present state, she would be a dead weight for him to bear.

For a moment, his thoughts turned to Mick. Had they told him the truth? He suspected they had, though he knew they would lie if it were to their advantage. Chet believed them only because their words had had the ring of truth, and because they had not told him a fairy tale about a mere flesh wound and said that Mick was certain to be okay. Maybe Mick was like this girl, caught in some netherworld while unseen hands decided the outcome, a world where death might be preferable but took its time appearing.

They would come soon, he thought. Dvorak would see to that. Damn, how he hated that man! But Chet found that even dwelling on Neil Dvorak produced no change in his emotions. It was as if he was numb. He could see what was happening, remember what he was supposed to feel, and kept expecting the return of those feelings, yet nothing happened.

Although he did not think of it in exactly these terms, his position had somehow become reversed. Once he had held the reins, and now they had slipped away from him. He was on the defensive more than he was the offensive. If the others trapped inside St. Paul's had felt hunted and helpless, now so did he.

He moved toward the door through which Dvorak had escaped him just moments before. When he stuck his head out, he saw and heard nothing. He crept furtively into the corridor. Its emptiness caused him to breathe a sigh of relief. In his mind, he kept hearing poor Mick saying, "Well what's the game plan, Chet? We gotta have a game plan." For all the good it was going to do him now, Chet admitted that his little brother had been right: a game plan just might have saved the situation.

The pain in his shoulder was becoming unreal. Chet ducked into a stairwell, knowing the sanctuary was very temporary. The police were thick now inside St. Paul's. He was going to have to be very clever about finding a hiding place, and he hurt so much it was hard to be clever. If only he had something for the pain. Looking at the walls that surrounded him within the stairwell, he felt a moment of bitterness so deep he could taste it like gall in his mouth. He was in a hospital, a place filled with medications of all kinds, and he had no way of even getting to a few aspirin tablets to help dull the ache in his shoulder.

Stealthily, Chet mounted the stairs, then opened the door that took him to the third floor. For the first time, he saw at close range the damage the bomb had inflicted. Again, he was struck that it was not as much as he might have wanted—yet despite everything, he felt a small glow of satisfaction. *He,* and he alone, had done this. No matter what happened, it would be remembered by some for years to come that Chet Hamilton had captured and held St. Paul's, had blown part of it to bits.

No one was around, so he crept into the area of the rubble. It seemed so deserted, so eerily quiet. Apparently all the patients had been taken out. Maybe it was what he needed—just for a while. Moving quietly, he wandered about the ruin of the psychiatric unit until he found a few things to his liking.

In the refrigerator near the crushed nurses' station, he found nourishing food—not a meal exactly, but individual containers of juice, milk, Jell-O, and ice cream. He loaded an assortment of such foods onto a plastic tray, then returned to an area he had found where the wall had collapsed in such a way as to make a slanting partition between what had once been a patient room and the exterior. He could not stand upright in the space, but he was tired of standing upright, in any event. Entering in a crouched position, he neared the bed. The stamped ID affixed to the end of it said WILLIAM MORROW, M46, DR. N. DVORAK, and then a long string of numbers, and the date 9/15/90. Chet placed the tray on the floor and, with his good arm and hand, brushed away the majority of the debris from the surface of the bed. That done, he collapsed upon it, after retrieving his tray of purloined food from the floor.

He had no idea how long he could stay hidden here. Perhaps it was not even safe. The remaining supports, the jutting angles, all looked as if they could collapse at any given moment. But it was a chance, a respite. His mind and body were both in such a state that he could not go on without some relief. He devoured the soft food and several servings of milk while sitting cross-legged on the bed. Getting up, he walked to the corner, removed his weapons, undid the drawstring of his pants, and relieved himself there on the floor. Back at the bed, he put both the knife and the gun under the pillow, then positioned himself in such a way that the weapons were at his fingertips. Sleep claimed him quickly. Whatever happened would have to happen; his body had spoken and said it was time for sleep.

In her office, Helen Laramore received news of the latest happenings with a combination of dismay and sad acceptance. For a moment, she placed her head upon the desk. Philip watched from across the room and longed to comfort her, to take her in his arms and tell her everything was going to be okay, but he knew he could not do it. The opposing board members were still present, and Helen was a professional. This was *her* arena. Here, he could not shelter her. All he could provide was solid and silent moral support. He ached inside for her, knowing how much St. Paul's meant to her. Now he felt there was a very real possibility that, when the smoke had cleared, she would be removed from the helm — not because she had done anything to cause the situation, or even to make it worse, but because someone, somewhere would find a need to affix the blame, and she was the one supposedly in charge. There seemed no way out.

There were those who favored evacuation of remaining patients, but the staff were so limited in what they could do. There were critical care patients whose conditions would suffer if they were moved. There was also a possibility that any mass exodus would be noticed by the gunman, who could open fire, find a way to set off another bomb, or doing something else equally dreadful. To date, he really hadn't gone after the patients. Except for the poor lady in the Stress Center, no patient had been harmed. There had been no mass panic among the patients. Those aware of what was going on were bearing up amazingly well. Some almost seemed to be enjoying it.

So, evacuation could bring safety . . . but it could also bring great harm. A safely effected evacuation could bring Helen praise, a disastrous one would label her rash and foolhardy. But in making the decision *not* to evacuate, Helen would be taking the course surest to bring criticism down on her head. Even if the rest of the patients remained unharmed, there were those who would argue later that they *could* have been gotten out, that she had taken unnecessary chances with their well-being.

"Gentlemen," she said at last, her gaze clear and steady, "we are *not* evacuating. I have thought it over very carefully, prayed a good deal, and talked with our personnel manning the floors. Considering everything, morale is phenomenal. It can only be a matter of a very short time until Chet Hamilton is apprehended. He's hurt, he's alone, and, although we haven't located the other bomb, we think it's out of his control."

"You 'think,' Helen," said the now furious board member

274

who favored evacuation, "but you do not *know*, and you are taking a dangerous chance."

"Anything is dangerous, Frank. At this point—indeed, from the onset of this—there are no certainties. My decision stands."

"I'll have your job for this."

"Do what you feel you have to do. That's exactly what I'm doing. Now, if you'll excuse me, I'm going to go see if I can find out what they've done with Dr. Singer." She turned to her husband. "Philip, do you want to come with me or wait here? If you're tired, it's okay to go on home."

"I'm not going home until you can go with me. But if I just sit anymore, I'll fall asleep, so I'll tag along while you check on your young doctor."

She reached to take his hand as he walked toward her. It was a gesture he could not offer, but one he could accept. Hand-in-hand, ignoring the anger of those they walked out on, they went to see what had occurred with St. Paul's psychiatric resident.

In the supply room, the medical team had located Dr. Julie Singer. Dr. Samuelsen's heart leaped, but then his spirits plummeted at what he saw. He bent and, willing his hands not to tremble, attempted to unbutton the white blouse and get the silk fabric away from the bullet wound. Someone had shot Mick in the chest, so Chet, in turn had shot the doctor in the chest. Planned retribution? Samuelsen doubted that. This shot had been fired at close range. He could only guess at the circumstances, but doubted that anything very scientifically planned had occurred here. He looked toward a nurse who had come with him and, without a word being spoken, she took her bandage scissors and cut the expensive blouse, peeling away shreds of fabric from the area of the wound.

"Some of the threads are embedded in the wound. We'll work on that when we get her downstairs," he said softly.

"Is there a chance for her?" the nurse asked, her words so slow they might have been wrung from her against her will, fearing the answer as she did.

"I'll be okay," Julie said, her voice hoarse and somewhat muted, yet clearly understandable.

"Julie," Samuelsen said, "can you really hear us?"

"He shot me in the chest, Sam, not the head. Tell me, is my wound dramatic?"

The surgeon was weeping. "Dramatic enough. We've made a hash of your nice blouse, I'm afraid. It's amazing . . . but it almost seems the bullet has missed anything vital. If your lungs had been pierced, you wouldn't be breathing like you are. If your trachea had been nipped, you wouldn't talk this well. I'd say it's missed any parenchymal mass, and just gone through soft tissue. There's quite a hole, but I think we can mend it. Donna, give her an injection of—"

"Not now," Julie whispered. "Please, Sam, let me stay conscious as long as you can. I don't want to go out. I fear going out. I might never come back."

"Julie, you're young and strong, and apparently you want to live. You'll make it. But if you don't want any sedation till we're downstairs and ready to probe, that's okay with me."

"Well, I *don't* want it."

"Good enough."

He turned to the others and said, "Take her down, prep her, and set her up. Keep the vitals monitored closely. I'll be along right away."

"First," she said, "tell me about Neil. Did he get away? I was still conscious when he left. I pretended I was as near dead as possible until Chet was gone. Chet didn't catch up with him, did he?"

Samuelsen quickly reassured her. "Dvorak is the one who told us where to find you. Chet didn't get him. On the other hand, we haven't gotten Chet yet, either. Mick is still with us, just barely. That's all the news I know. Now, just concentrate on yourself, young lady."

As soon as the others had Julie loaded on the stretcher, Samuelsen used the wall telephone to call and deliver a couple of messages about Dr. Singer's condition. How, he wondered, had Ras stood so many hours of this? *He* was already feeling stressed out, and Julie's surgery would only be the third that he had done.

While he scrubbed for surgery, he tried to remember the last time this many bullets had been removed in the surgical suite in such a short period of time. This was probably a record.

Although the radiograph had warned Kelvin Samuelsen of the extensive bone damage that foreran any underlying musculoligamentous damage, and possibly nerve damage, he was not really prepared for what lay before him after he had performed the cruciate incision to create an entrance into the region to the right of the sternum.

"Thank God for the clavicle," he was heard to say, for the bullet had struck it first, letting that bar of bone bear the full brunt of the impact. The sturdy bone and its supporting cartilage had shattered into what seemed like a million shards, the little sharp splinters scattering here and there throughout the thoracic cavity, and upward. The situation cried for an orthopedic surgeon, but none was available, and it was not felt Dr. Singer could wait the hours it would take for one to get to Bainbridge. The bullet had to be retrieved if possible and any problems underlying the bone damage had to be assessed and repaired. "I'm going to need help," Samuelsen murmured. "No offense, Fred," he said to the GP who had agreed to scrub with him and assist as needed.

"None taken," Dr. Frederick Czewski said evenly. "This isn't my field. Isn't Dave Rasmussen still in the building?"

"I imagine so. But he's spent."

"He's had a few hours, Sam." Nodding toward a surgical aide, he said, "Give him a page. I'll talk to him."

"We can't page," said the young man in a tense voice, "but I'll see if I can locate him by phone."

Samuelsen and Czewski exchanged glances over their masks. Not a word was spoken because they did not want to do anything to further break down the already low morale in the OR, yet their tacit agreement was complete. They had never imagined operating under such circumstances. Some doctors did routinely, and they were aware of that — those physicians who elected to do their work in underdeveloped and underprivileged areas. Both doctors had heard many stories from their missionary colleagues about amputations, appendectomies, and Caesareans done under the most primitive of conditions.

It wasn't *that* bad here. They had anesthesia. They had radiography available. They had a reasonably fresh surgical crew, and sterile conditions under which to operate. Still, at this particular point in time, they felt acutely what was lacking. Neither had ever taken a patient to surgery with so little laboratory testing. Using the simplest of instruments salvaged from the wreckage of the laboratory, they had obtained a hemoglobin count and a urinalysis. Other samples had been drawn and sent by courier to another facility, but they did not feel they had the time to wait until the results were phoned back in.

"Try to think, and be very careful with your answers," they had cautioned Julie in her pre-anesthesia state, "if there have been any indications at all of bleeding disorders

278

in yourself or any close family members."

"I won't sue. Want me to put that in writing?" she had said, attempting to tease.

"Just answer the question," had been the stern reply.

"There is no easy bruising. I underwent a T&A when I was six or seven with no problems. I remember my father having gallbladder surgery when I was a teenager, and he said it was a breeze. My mother died when I was young and I know nothing of her surgical history . . . if, indeed there was any. I have no brothers and sisters. I don't think there is a coagulation problem. As I said, I don't bruise more than normal, and when I've had minor cuts I don't seem to bleed any undue amounts. So you have no excuses. Just begin."

"I'd feel a whole lot better with a couple of blood-clotting studies on the chart," Czewski had grumbled.

"And I'd feel a whole lot better with an orthopedist in the room," Samuelsen had returned, "but you make do with what you have, right?"

No argument there.

Kelvin Samuelsen had first placed steel to skin with much trepidation, and could have wept with relief when the gush and flow of blood was normal and quite easily controlled. He could have wept, but didn't, because a surgeon cannot afford obscuring tears.

Both the physicians bent over the still form, now dubbed "the patient." Until the procedure was over, she could have no personality, no identity, she could not be Dr. Julie Singer. Objectivity had to exist, and that could best be accomplished when the patient was just that: "the patient." Bit by bit, they picked away the fragments of bone.

"We'll have to enlarge the incision," Samuelsen observed. "I can see splinters of bone all the way up in the sterno-cleidomastoid region, but I can't reach up there with the instruments. And, oh, how I wish we could irrigate some of this bone out of the way, but I don't think that's possible.

279

The little sharp ends have dug in and buried themselves here and there, and have to be grasped and pulled out."

"If we get some of these larger pieces out of the way, we can try."

When the upper chest was relatively free of bone fragments, they did irrigate the area, obtaining small amounts of bone and tissue fragments. Using a rongeur, Samuelsen tidied the remaining ends of the clavicle, then enlarged the upper right arm of the cruciate incision upward in a linear fashion, until the pierced sternocleidomastoid muscle was accessible. He removed the few shards of bone, then irrigated the area well.

With most of the shattered bone out of the way, he now felt he could explore the depths of the wound.

"The stars were on our side—*her* side," he said softly as he heard the metallic click of his probe hitting the bullet. "It isn't all that deep. A slightly different angle and it could have tried to make its exit through the cervical area . . . and that would have been instant paralysis."

No one reminded him—they didn't have to—that instant paralysis could still occur, so close was he working to the cervical end of the spinal cord.

After hemostasis had been achieved in the torn area with electrocautery, the surgeon exchanged the probe for the bullet forceps. In less time than he would have estimated possible, he grasped the metal slug and had it out of the patient's chest. He shuddered with relief when he heard the metallic ping as it hit the specimen tray.

"I don't think there is any nerve damage," he said with a catch in his throat. "None visible, anyway. I'd venture a guess that anything in that direction will be minimal. It's hard to consider yourself lucky under these circumstances, but some luck is on our side."

"A lot of it," the surgical nurse murmured, glancing at the monitors and charted vital signs.

280

Czewski nodded. The patient was young, healthy, and vital, which was all in her favor. Considering the extent of the surgical incisions, some scarring was inevitable, but they could not foresee any other significant residuals. And, after a period of adequate healing, plastic surgery could probably revise the scars if the patient so desired.

"There is some ligamentous injury in the articular capsule, but nothing extensive. I think we can reunite and hope for the best. But I'm stymied when it comes to the clavicle itself, and we have to do something before we close. A good two inches of bone is totally gone. We can't leave that big a hole, and there's not enough to work with to fill it with methyl methacrylate for adherence. I mean, we are totally out of bone."

The door opened and Dave Rasmussen entered. As he scrubbed, the others watched in silence.

"Thanks loads, Ras," Samuelsen said. "I owe you one."

Rasmussen shook his head. "It's not a game of keeping even. Even if it were, I recall a few I owe you."

While Rasmussen gazed into the open wound, Samuelsen filled him in on what had transpired thus far.

"Steel," Dave said without hesitation. "We'll get a piece of steel in here and we'll rongeur it to the bone. Lacking an orthopedic surgeon, that's all we can do. But I think it'll work nicely. When she's healed, we'll have an orthopedist look at it. If it doesn't suit at that point, the repair can easily be done over. Go ahead and finish with the tissues. I'll call and get my parts in here, then I'll take over if you want."

There was no cockiness in his manner, and Samuelsen knew that. Rasmussen was the master general surgeon, and few had ever resented that acknowledged fact. In his field, the man was a genius and the rest of them learned from him. If nothing else, he gave them a standard to which they could aspire.

Moments later, Rasmussen and Samuelsen had exchanged places. Using the pin of stainless steel as an obturator, Dave began the process of attaching it to the ends of bone, starting at the clavicular end. It took some smoothing with the rongeur, but in the end he had a perfect fit.

"See, who needs bone?" he said in triumph.

"Not us, obviously. Somehow I can't see them having to do this over. I think she'll hold and work just like new."

"Know something, I think you're right. You want to do the closure?"

"Go ahead. I'll assist. That is, unless you're tired."

Above the mask, Dave's eyes twinkled, denoting a smile that otherwise remained hidden. "Tired? Why should I be tired? I got to sleep two hours. I even called my wife."

"I'll bet she was relieved."

Dave chuckled. "Not exactly. Would you believe my Edith didn't know about any of this? That's what I get for staying such long hours at the hospital so often through the years. She didn't even think anything of my absence. And Edie has never been an early riser. No one had thought to call her yet, so for a minute there, I was in trouble for waking her up."

"And now?"

He chuckled again. "First, she cried. Second, she got mad. Third, she said she'd be right down to help, and hung up."

"Help? What's she going to do?"

"I don't know. When she said that, I'm sure she didn't know. But my wife is a doer, an organizer. She'll come to St. Paul's and take over *something*—you can bet your life on that."

Even as this light exchange of words took place the surgeons worked, layering sutures all the way up, then beginning on the skin closure.

To size up the situation, Rasmussen held a thorough

consultation with the nurses, anesthetist, and anesthesiologist regarding the patient's vital signs and general condition.

"You think, then, that the patient can safely stay under anesthesia another hour without problems?"

"If things remain as they have throughout the rest of the procedure, I see no contraindication to that," was the reply.

"Then I'm going to do a plastic repair closure," he said decisively. "I'm no plastic surgeon, but I think I can effect something better than a rudimentary closure. Sam?"

"I think you can, too."

"That wasn't exactly what I meant."

"I know. I'm with you, okay?"

"Great . . . now *that's* what I meant."

Over the next hour or so, with painstaking, careful movements and assisted by Samuelsen and Czewski, Rasmussen carried out the tongue-and-groove preparation of the incision edges, stitched the tongues and grooves together, then tied the ends of thread over rolls of adhesive plaster.

"What happens," Czewski queried, "if someone does decide to open her up again?"

"I'll kill them with my bare hands," Dave replied coolly.

"That's what I suspected. A reasonable approach, I'd say."

When the last stitch had been taken, they stood back to admire their handiwork. The patient might still have scars, but they would be fine-line and barely visible. Barring infection, there would be no deep valleys or ridges of keloid formation to mar the fair skin of her chest and neck.

"Reverse her," Samuelsen said, with a nod toward the anesthesiologist and anesthetist team.

In the recovery room, "the patient" became Julie Singer once more. Someone held her head as she threw up. Someone soothed her brow with a cold, wet cloth, until the worst of the post-anesthesia nausea subsided.

Her first words, when she was fully awake, were, "Are you sure Dr. Dvorak's okay?"

"He's fine," the RN reassured her. "They insisted he go to bed. When he's awake, I'm sure he'll be by to check on you. Worry about yourself right now."

Julie did worry about herself, but it wasn't so easy to shut the others out, not when Chet Hamilton was still on the loose inside St. Paul's.

Chet, at last wakening in his strange sanctuary, felt somewhat calmer. He had to get out, although nothing came to mind as to how he might accomplish a safe escape. He was still suffering from what Mick had called "no game plan." But the fact remained that he was determined to get out. He crept carefully to the nearest telephone and was surprised to find it still worked. Consulting the directory taped to a piece of remaining wall, he called the extension number he found listed for ICU. "Dave Rasmussen here," he said in a muffled voice. "What's the status on Mick Hamilton?"

"He's still with us, sir. Not a lot of changes in his vital signs. The pneumothorax hasn't recurred. His breathing is shallow and raspy, and he's never regained consciousness. He's alive — barely. And that's about it."

"Thanks," Chet said. "I'll be by to check on him when I can."

With that, he hung up the receiver, placed his head in his hands, and cried. They hadn't lied to him. Not about that. All those hours he had assumed Mick was dead when he wasn't. But the words of the ICU nurse still had a chilling effect. *He's alive — barely.* It seemed as if there was little hope for Mick. Chet sniffed back the tears and tried to develop a viable game plan.

* * *

No sooner had the phone connection with ICU been severed than Dave Rasmussen, still in his rumpled surgical blues, walked into the area.

"How's the chest tube on the Hamilton boy holding up?" he wanted to know.

The nurse who had answered the telephone stared at him in disbelief.

"What's the problem, Carrie? You look like you've seen a ghost."

"Not quite. But did you just call down here, or have someone call for you, to check on Hamilton?"

"Of course not. I came in person. As you can plainly see."

"That's what I thought."

"And?"

"I just talked to someone claiming to be you, checking on Mick Hamilton."

Dave shook his head. "I'd bet on big brother Chet."

"I wouldn't bet against you. Know what?"

"What?"

"I have this funny feeling something is going to happen soon."

"Know something, Carrie? I have this funny feeling you are right."

Chapter Sixteen

It was eight-thirty in the morning on Friday, September 22nd, and the rain had become a downpour. On the parking lots and grounds of St. Paul's, all but the hardiest of souls had taken shelter in cars or under the two large awning-like structures on poles that had been thrown up to serve as temporary shelters.

Edith Rasmussen had arrived and, as her husband had predicted, was in the midst of things, trying to organize all the stragglers and onlookers into a group with unity. Few resisted her efforts. Being tired and puzzled, they were all too willing to let someone else try to make sense of the shambles.

The artificial lights that had burned all night continued to glow, casting a garish gleam across all they touched. The sun was too obscured by clouds and rain to lend much light, despite the time of day.

The brick sides of St. Paul's gleamed with wetness, giving the building a newer and more vital look than it had when dry. Wet, the red brick was darker and richer-appearing. Out front, St. Paul groped his way down the strip of concrete that was apparently supposed to be Bainbridge's version of the road to Damascus.

A weary journalist eyed the statue. Maybe, he thought, he had been looking at it all wrong. From the first time he had seen the statue, he had thought it dumb—or, at the very best, depressing. Shouldn't St. Paul have been depicted in his glory, shown *after* his eyes were fully seeing, and he was out converting and writing and all that? Now he saw it a little differently. Since this was a hospital, maybe it was fitting that St. Paul be depicted in his humbled state. Those who entered St. Paul's had been, if not struck blind, then ill and infirm in some other way, and needed healing. He had seen many strong men, very macho in their day-to-day affairs, turn weak-kneed and pale inside the walls of a hospital. It was as if, once one submitted to being a patient, one was no longer in control.

Anyway, what did it matter? He wanted to go home. He had been up all night and was tired of cold sandwiches, greasy donuts, and too much coffee. But his editor had offered to send a replacement and he had declined the offer, so his discomfort was his own responsibility. If nothing happened by noon, maybe he'd give it up. But not yet. He could surely stand it a few more hours. After all the time he had invested in it, he didn't want to turn the story over to someone else, not even in collaboration.

In her efforts to organize the crowd, Edith Rasmussen met her first real resistance in the form of Elizabeth Cates.

"Lady, you're crazy," Elizabeth said tiredly. "No one wants to play your games."

"It isn't a game," Edith retorted. "We have to keep morale up. We have to have a sense of purpose and unity. It's not asking a lot that you do your part."

"And *you're* deciding what my part is? I'll tell you what I think my part is: my part is to be inside with my husband. He was wounded in all this and had to have surgery, and they tell me I can't go inside for even two minutes to see with my own eyes that he's okay."

"And?"

Both women narrowed their eyes as they engaged in a

stare-down, one that Edie won without a whole lot of difficulty. This was her milieu.

"Look," Edie said, placing a hand on the thinner woman's shoulder, "I know how you feel. My husband is in there, too. He operated off and on all night long, and now I hear he's back at it again, even though he told me he was dead on his feet. I'd like him to come out so I could take him home and take care of him, but he won't hear of it, because he might be needed in there. Given that, I'd like to go in and, as you said, see with my own two eyes what's taking place. But I can't. So I'm not going to sit around and pout and be mad. There's too much that needs to be done. Now, are you going to pass the sandwiches and coffee around, or are you not?"

Elizabeth had met her match. Recognizing that, and yielding to the force, she smiled slightly and held out her arms for the white boxes containing sandwiches that had just been delivered, donated by a deli downtown.

From time to time, Helen Laramore appeared in the door of the Emergency Room and issued a statement to those on the outside eagerly awaiting news. There wasn't a lot to tell. Things were slow . . . and that scared Helen. In fact, it scared them all.

Looking down at the crowd from the window of her hospital room, Maudie Evans was possessed by a strange feeling. For the moment, her pain was bearable. Not gone, but bearable. She did her best to ignore the weakness that had invaded her, generally making her not care. A while back, she had asked to call her family, but had been told it would not be permitted. Only the most emergent of calls were being placed, leaving the phone lines free for urgent matters. Maudie thought it was urgent that she talk to her family, considering that she was in a terminal state, but she didn't argue. She knew what they meant, and accepted it.

She knew anything could happen. It could all be over in a flash, or many more could be hurt and killed. Maudie felt herself to be in between the two dangers—the failure of her body, and any havoc Chet Hamilton might yet wreak. Maybe she would never see her family again.

Walking away from the window, leaving the milling crowd unwatched, she sat down in the chair by her bed, took a piece of paper and a pencil, and began her message to her family and friends.

> *I love you all,* she wrote, *and I don't want to leave you, but we all know that's the way it will be. I just want to say I'm sorry for all the smart-alecky things I said when different ones of you tried to talk me out of smoking. I wanted to smoke. I always said it was my only vice. I see now it wasn't. Stupidity and stubbornness are worse vices. But, you see, I didn't think it could happen to me. Lung cancer happened to other people, not to yours truly. I was afraid of dying, scared all the time, till these Hamilton guys took the hospital over. Then, I don't know why, but somewhere along the line I lost my fear. I know I'm going to die. Even if Chet doesn't get me, the cancer will. And that's okay now. It wasn't what I wanted, but it's what I got. I don't look on it as punishment. It's just the way things are. I gambled and, for a lot of years, I won. Now I've lost. And, like I said, that's okay. That's the main thing I wanted to say, besides I love you, and I'm sorry that you knew me as a panicky old hen. I just thought maybe it would make you all feel better to know I went with peace in my heart.*

She signed it simply "Maudie," because she meant it for all she knew and loved, both relatives and friends.

Ken Sandusky lay in his hospital bed and stared up at the

IV bags and tubing. He felt a lot of things: bitter, helpless, guilty, scared . . . and he felt pain. They gave him the Demerol every two hours and, from that, he estimated he got maybe twenty minutes of complete relief. The rest of the time, the pain in his belly ranged anywhere from a gnawing ache to something so bad he felt he was being torn apart. Everyone had been so great to him. Nearly every employee in the building had either come by or sent a message with someone else. Poor Marcus had been the most loyal, feeling he was carrying a burden of guilt. It was useless to tell him that one of them would probably have been plugged, even if Marcus hadn't gone to the john and they had been stuck like glue to each other. There had been no reason for the shooting. It was just something the Hamiltons had felt in the mood to do. But Ken felt his own guilt. At a time when he and Marcus had been the only two in the building to protect the others, he had gotten careless and been put out of commission. He cried when they told him what had happened after he had been shot, all the death and destruction that had happened inside St. Paul's. It didn't matter who saw him cry. It just wasn't a time to care about that sort of thing. He longed for his wife, but remained shut away from her. Nancy was a heavy and homely woman, and since Ken was quite handsome in a rugged sort of way, there were those who had looked at the pair with curiosity, for anyone who knew Ken knew he walked the straight and narrow where fidelity was concerned. The answer to the success of the relationship was simply love and respect. No one could understand, he thought, just what Nancy meant to him, the nurturing and kindness of her spirit. She was always there to count on, and that was so important. And how he wished he could talk to her now! Just to hear her say, "Why, Kenneth, what's this all about? Let me fix you a mug of tea and we'll talk about it, okay?"

290

Rita Queterez was in pain, both inwardly and outwardly. She was almost glad when the pain of the broken arm, or of her generalized muscle aching, was intense enough that she could momentarily forget the rest of it. It was too much to bear. Joe was dead. She had seen him die. Rita waited for the tears to come, and they would not. Had she loved him? She had thought so. Strange, in looking back, how someone like herself, raised in a strict Catholic home, and never rebelling to the extent of rejecting the traditional beliefs, had let herself become involved with a married Protestant minister. Again, the question came: had she loved him? And she knew the answer was *no*. He had been charming, exciting, an ego trip, such a different sort of man from the young men of her neighborhood who pursued her from time to time. He had been a good lover, a deft and experienced one, and she had gotten caught up in that, so caught up in the need that she was willing not to think about the rest of it . . . the wrongness, the unsuitability. Lately, her head had hurt a lot, and she attributed that to guilt — a guilt that had intensified since she had accidentally run into Joe's wife and one of their children in the hospital gift shop. They were nice, bright, cheerful, and not what she had expected. She had wanted to believe them hateful, but after that day, she could no longer believe it. She had wanted to break with Joe, but he still held that sexual power over her, a power so strong that she had given herself up to him, as she had this night, in places that could have ended her job if they had been discovered.

She had wanted the affair over. But she hadn't wanted him dead. She thought of the members of his family she had seen, and shuddered. A nurse had entered the room and saw the shudder.

"You need more MS? I think it's time."

Rita shook her head. It wasn't that she didn't feel pain, it was more like she felt she deserved the pain. And had she deserved the rape? She shuddered again at the memory of those cruel hands tearing at her body, of the degrading intrusion when he had thrust away inside her.

"Are you sure?" the nurse asked. "You don't look very comfortable to me."

"I guess I'll take it," the injured laboratory technician said, in a very little voice. Perhaps she did not deserve the respite from pain, but she was going to take it, for the memory of the rape, when it pressed itself upon her, was more than her fragile emotional state could bear.

Not too far away from where Rita lay in turmoil, Carla sat at the nurses' station doing her charting.

"Go home," one of the others said, looking at her with pitying eyes.

"And do what, Beverly? Stare at the walls and think of that animal on top of me? Brad went on to work. I told him to. I want to see how this comes out. When I shut my eyes and try to sleep, I see *his* face. So let me work. I'm okay."

"We can use your help. I guess it's just that I don't see how you can keep going, considering everything."

"Know something? I don't know how, either. But I just found out the world doesn't end because something bad happened to me. It just keeps right on going."

In the recovery room, Dr. Julie Singer, with the worst of her nausea subsided, pondered her situation. She had poured out her heart to Neil Dvorak, and her psyche had survived that. She had been shot at close range by Chet Hamilton, and apparently her body had survived that. To her, the question was: what next?

Over the last few hours she had worried that she wasn't

suited to be a psychiatrist, that she had been mistaken in choosing that field for herself. She probably already understood her mother as much as she ever would. And what was done, was done. There was no help for her poor mother — or for the hurt and puzzled child that had been herself. She could work with schizophrenics and try to help them, but it was too late for her own family situation. Irrational though it sounded, she realized that her goal had really been to rectify the past. That was an impossible goal. And who would really care if she changed her specialty at this point? It would take a bit of time and trouble and money to switch, but no real hassle. She would lose face with no one. Those who knew and loved her best would say, "Well, Julie, I never did know why you wanted to do that in the first place." So the decision was hers. It always had been. There was no pressure on her at all to remain in psychiatry. . . . Or was there? The pressure came from inside herself, and Julie knew she had to decide within the next few months if that was something she was going to yield to or resist.

Jennifer Weiller was taking a nap in the nurses' locker room on the first floor. She was very near a window and, even as she slept, she was aware of the cadence of the rain against the ground and the sides of the building. Soon she would go home and see to the cat, the cat that was to be her very own cat. Stephen Cates was a dream . . . a laughing, kind, and handsome man, perfect in every way — except for the gold band he wore on his finger. In her sleep, Jennie pushed a strand of hair away and smiled. He couldn't be hers, but what they shared hadn't been a total loss. She had made a joke — two of them really — and had caused him to laugh. That was no small feat, considering her track record.

* * *

Steve stared at the white bulkiness that was his foot—at least so they told him. He sighed. Like his fellow St. Paul employee, Ken Sandusky, he longed to be out there in the mainstream. He wanted to be hunting down Chet Hamilton. It wasn't enough that he had taken Mick out of commission, although that had certainly been a pivot point. With Mick down, the police had dared to disobey Chet's orders . . . that is, Mick's downfall coupled with the spent bomb. Steve felt a flash of gratitude that the bomb had claimed only one life, then he felt a stab of guilt that the life of poor, crazy Gigi was so easily dismissed. It wasn't meant that way. Any loss of life was, of course, a tragedy, but it could have been so much worse. All the patients and personnel in the Stress Center could have died or been badly hurt. But the guilt wouldn't go away. Surely Gigi had mattered to *someone*. Surely there would be someone to mourn. That is, when they knew. Or would all the world just say, "Gee, I'm glad it was only Gigi?"

Steve dismissed his weird thoughts, the uncharacteristic guilt, putting it all down to the stress of the situation, the fatigue, the pain. He ached for the feel of the police revolver in his hand. His own lust to hunt and kill was something he found appalling, and another thing to feed his already overworked sense of guilt. What he would do was lie here in bed and recuperate. He could not do what he longed to do, so that was that. And then there was Jennie, another burden of guilt. Strangely, he felt no guilt at wanting her. She was so very special, how could he help but love her? He felt no guilt about what Elizabeth would think of as betrayal, for, in her own way, Elizabeth had betrayed him. She had changed, and her changes had not been compatible with his, and he *did* feel betrayed by that. No, what he felt guilty about was the hurt he had possibly inflicted on sweet Jennie.

He had teased her, picked on her, sought her out, all with

294

no evil intent. But they had found themselves in love, something that could not be. How much better it would have been if he had just left her alone, just been professional, nothing more, nothing less.

But it was too late for that. Guilt could eat away at you from the inside until nothing was left, if you let it. And that was the key. He was not going to let it happen. So he willed it away, and was right back to feeling useless. It was time, he thought, to go home. But he could not. In more ways than one, he was trapped in this bed. Maybe, Steve mused, it was a good thing, this ankle wound. He thought he had put the thug in him to rest a long, long time ago . . . he had thought so until he handled the revolver and fired it. The injury had made the choice for him. He *had* to be civilized whether he wanted to be or not. At that moment, Stephen Cates, RN, vowed to keep a rein on himself. What he had done had been forced upon him, but the enjoyment had been his own. Never again, that was his silent promise.

In the conference room, Marianne Hamilton took a deep breath, then let herself relax. She took a sip of the unwanted coffee that had long been cold. The acrid taste of it made her grimace. For the moment, her grilling by the FBI agent was over. Never had she encountered anyone with more questions. She realized his purpose and was more than willing to cooperate, but he did cause a mind and body to become weary . . . more weary than usual, that is.

"I'll be the bait, if you can think of a way it will help," she had volunteered. "I set out on my own to do just that, but I didn't find him in time. I'd like to try again."

Alterauge narrowed his eyes as he regarded her. All the potential for being a pretty woman was there. When the bruises healed, the swelling subsided, and she could afford a decent haircut — and when she had enough self-esteem to hold her head high—she would, he was sure, fulfill the promise he could see in her.

"It wouldn't be safe. My superiors would be down on my head in a flash if I tried something like that. We'll think of a way without using you as a sacrifice."

"Don't think of it that way. Think of me as a volunteer. It's something I want to do."

"We'll see. I have some thinking to do. Just take it easy for a while. Drink your coffee. Get something to eat if you want."

But despite his words to the contrary, Alterauge had not entirely ruled out Marianne's plan. If he could think of a way to use her safely as bait, he really was not particularly adverse to doing so . . . but *safely* was the key word. Damn! Hamilton had to screw up and surface soon. There had to be a way they could find him. Dogs? It was a thought. With a smile that looked more like an expression of pain than good cheer, Alterauge plodded off to ask Chief Inman about the availability of dogs.

In the cafeteria, Helen and Philip Laramore sat eating a hearty breakfast prepared by the kitchen crew. On this occasion, cholesterol was just another word, and they both ate freely of the bacon and eggs without a trace of concern or guilt.

"McKeown said he'd have my job," she said wryly, blue eyes sparkling.

"And how do you feel about that?"

"It's a funny thing, but I suddenly decided I don't care. Believe me?"

He nodded. "If I couldn't see your face, I might not be able to believe the words. I didn't think I'd ever hear them. But I can see that glint in your eye. Why the change of heart?"

"I'm not sure I can explain it, Philip. But I've given a lot of myself to St. Paul's, and I'm not being Pollyanna Sunshine when I say I've gotten back more than I've given. The thing is, nothing goes on forever. Maybe it's time for a change anyway. I'd gotten too comfortable here, too possessive. When the children grew up, we had to let go of them. Sometimes that becomes true of a job. But I'll not be *fired* while there is any fight left in me. I've done no wrong. If the powers that be decide to hang me for it, so be it. I'll survive."

With a smile, he covered her hand with his and squeezed. "I hope your theory about having to let go doesn't apply to me. After all these years, I still rather like having you around, you know."

"Glad to hear it. Because you are the one thing I have no intention of giving up. My ultimate addiction: Philip Laramore. Philip?"

"Yes, love?"

"It's too quiet. It's been so long since we heard from Chet Hamilton — much, much too long. The lull frightens me."

Philip looked around at the walls of the cafeteria, then at the people seated around them at various tables. If an onlooker didn't know it, he could not have guessed this was a crisis situation.

"I know what you mean," he said softly. "I know exactly what you mean. It's an eerie feeling, this waiting game."

"I'm glad you're here. Selfish of me. It would be safer for you on the outside."

He shrugged. "One never knows what lurks on the outside. I'm just glad to be here, and glad that you're glad I'm here. Enough gladness?"

"Sufficient."

In the darkened room in which he had been tucked away

297

to rest, Neil Dvorak began to stir from the sedative-induced sleep. He hadn't actually slept very long, but his system was too keyed up for even the drug to keep him sedated for any length of time. For a moment, he felt vaguely disoriented. It occurred to him that this was how confused and troubled patients must so often feel. At least he knew who he was, so he wasn't *that* badly off. But he did admit that it took a few moments for it to really register just where he was, and what circumstances had placed him in a hospital bed. Suddenly, he felt a surge of anger—anger at himself for the moment of weakness in the conference room, anger at those who had decided he be sedated, anger at Chet Hamilton for creating all this havoc, and even angry at fate, which had caused someone like Chet Hamilton to ever be born.

He sat bolt upright and swung his legs off the bed. The sudden movements caused his head to spin, and he had no choice but to lie back for a moment, his head pressed against the pillow until his vertigo subsided. When the worst of it had passed, he tried again, this time more slowly. He felt pleased when his feet hit the floor and he was able to push himself to an erect position. He felt top-heavy, and due to the drug that had been injected into him, he suspected he would feel that way for a while. Very carefully, like a child just beginning to learn how to walk, he placed one foot in front of the other. It worked. He wasn't moving fast, but he was staying upright. As he took another step or two, the top-heavy feeling increased and he felt himself pitching forward—felt it, but his reflexes were too slow for him to do anything about it.

Just at the time when his fall became unavoidable, a nurse in crisp white entered the room. Being a hefty, heavy-bosomed sort of person, she was able to break his fall, clasping him against her and holding him there until he was able to right himself.

"Damn, Norma," he said, his speech quite slurred, "what

will people say seeing us like this?"

"Lucky for us both, we'll never find out. Because you're going back to bed before anyone has a chance to see us, like this or any other way."

"No."

"What did you say?"

"You heard me. I'm not going back to bed. I have things to do."

"Dr. Dvorak, you're in no state to be doing anything. Surely you realize that. You were given one hundred mls of Vistaril less than two hours ago. You're done in. Now, get back in bed. Or else."

"Or else, what?" He tried to stare her down in his doctorly, intimidating way, but his eyes couldn't seem to focus and he was well aware, fuzzy as he was, that Norma did not seem in the least intimidated by him. Had they put him in a hospital gown and taken away his underwear, or something? Reaching back, he was pleased to feel that his undershorts were still in place.

"Come on, sir. Back to bed."

"Shameless, the way you're trying to get me to bed. I'm going to scream for help if you don't unhand me this minute."

Norma breathed a deep sigh of exasperation. The doctor was floating in and out of a lucid state. At one moment, he was quite himself, the next he was totally inane.

"Then scream if you will," she said firmly. "I have my orders."

Neil blinked, steadied himself, and floated, though probably temporarily, back into a fully aware state.

"Norma," he said, quite sensibly, "I know I can't wander the halls and hunt down Chet Hamilton. But neither can I go back to bed and shut my eyes and sleep until I know about Dr. Singer. Can't you understand that? The silly woman tried to save my life." After telling me that she was

299

in love with me, he added to himself. He felt he owed that young woman a debt he could never fully repay. How could he? A heart is such a precious thing to give.

"Isn't it enough that I tell you she's getting along fine? No bull. On my word as a former girl scout—many, many years ago—I promise you I'm telling the truth. The bullet went high, missing any organs. A shattered clavicle and lots of tissue damage, but she's in the recovery room now doing just great."

"Fine. I believe you. It's not your honesty I'm questioning. But I want to see her, face to face. There's something I have to tell her. Let me go there. You have my word I'll come back and go to bed until this drug wears off . . . and you also have my word that I'll find the guy who ordered the damned Vistaril and see that he gets a slug himself."

Norma chuckled. "Good luck. But you're no more capable of getting to the recovery room in the shape that you're in than I'm capable of getting into Jane Fonda's clothes. So let's take a little ride. How does that sound?"

Neil's initial reaction was to resent the suggestion. Then, letting go of the bed railing he had been grasping, he tried walking again. It was work, too much work. If he wanted to see Julie, it was going to have to be Norma's way.

"Get the damned wheelchair," he said with reluctant resignation. "You win. I'll ride."

"Good boy," she said, her tone so hearty and approving that Neil felt he had to glare at her to keep her from patting him on the head. God, how he hated being infirm!

After Norma saw that he was securely seated in the wheelchair, she starting propelling him down the hall and toward the elevator. Neil began singing a rather unmelodious version of "The Yellow Rose of Texas." Hospital personnel, recognizing him, chuckled and shook their heads in disbelief. An intern laughed out loud, causing the doctor to glare at him.

"Who on earth is doing that God-awful singing, Norma?" Neil asked. "This is a hospital. People can't be singing that loud and having other people laugh at them. See what you can do about it."

"I can tape your mouth shut if you'd like."

"That was *me?*"

"Yes, sir. In the flesh."

He sighed in dismay. "I think I need two glasses of water—one to drink and one to splash on my face."

"I'll volunteer to splash for you, sir."

"You would, wouldn't you? You do know that I find all of this extremely embarrassing?"

She had assumed as much. Never had she, or anyone else, ever seen the reserved, silver-haired Dr. Dvorak be anything but staid and proper.

"If it's any comfort, you didn't sing anything dirty. Some of them do."

Neil sighed again. All his years of experience and expertise, and one bout of weakness had reduced him to "some of them," nothing more than a sorry medical specimen. Deciding to make the most of it, he began to hum, and quite loudly, the beginning of a ditty known far and wide for its raunchiness.

"Dr. Dvorak," Norma said, shaking him by the shoulder. "You're doing it again."

In response, he shot her a triumphant leer.

Norma shook her head and, more to herself than to her recalcitrant patient, said, "I'll sure be glad when things get back to normal. And for more than one reason. People who used to be silly are glum, and others who used to act respectable are cutting up. It's enough to drive a person clean out of her mind."

Neil tried to chuckle, but the floating sensation took over and he lost track of things for a while. When he drifted back to consciousness, he found he was already in the recovery

301

room. Willing his eyes to focus, he sought out the bed that bore the form of Julie Singer.

"It's me," he said, feeling a little foolish.

"So I see. Since I can't see myself, I can't be sure, but from the way you look, I'd say it's very possible you look worse than I do."

"No argument there. We can't all have your youth and beauty."

"You know what I mean."

"Precisely. They've drugged me, you know."

"They? Pray tell, who are 'they?' "

"That's what I'm trying to find out. This close-mouthed nurse won't help. But when I find out, the fur will fly. In the meantime, how are you, my dear?"

"Sore. Woozy. Nauseated. Scared. Disgusted. Angry. Mixed up. Give me a little time and I'll think up some more adjectives. And my jaw aches where Chet cracked it."

"Never mind. I get the general idea. Truly, Julie, are you okay?"

"Except for the things I mentioned, I'm fine."

"You were foolishly brave in there."

"Was I? I felt anything but brave. I was all out of choices. At least that's the way it seemed to me. Once the dust got up my nose and I sneezed, it was too late to keep pretending I wasn't there. So don't pin any medals on me."

"I'll do what I please."

For a long moment, they stared at each other. It was almost as if it was the first time they had met. In a way, it was. The nearly nine hours they had been at the mercy of Chet Hamilton had wrought many changes in them. Both had discovered strengths and weaknesses in themselves that had been a surprise.

Norma stood watching the two of them. Quite a pair, she thought. They were both at about the same level of awareness. At times, their eyes and minds focused, and at other times, they did not.

"Time to go back," she said. "You promised me, Dr. Dvorak."

"And so I did. Besides, this young woman needs to rest. I'll be back, though, when I've worn this stupid drug off."

"I should hope. Neil?"

"Yes, ma'am?"

"Do you think it's possible he's dead? I mean, it's been so long . . ."

She didn't have to use Chet's name for Neil to know exactly what she meant.

"I don't know. I doubt it. He didn't seem that gravely hurt. He was in pain, but not critically wounded."

"I know. It's just that it's been so quiet. I found myself hoping maybe the wound had broken open and he'd started hemorrhaging. Wicked of me?"

He shook his head. "Just practical of you. I'd say, using the overworked term 'quality of life,' that Chet's quality, dead or alive, is over with. He can't hope to escape, though he seems to be telling himself otherwise. He doesn't admit defeat easily . . . and that's regrettable for us."

"Dvorak . . ."

"I'm ready, Norma. Julie, would you believe this respectable-looking woman is constantly trying to get me into bed?"

Julie giggled. "I'd believe it. She has my sympathy. Take it from me, Norma, he's not easy."

With a shake of her head, Norma turned the wheelchair around. What, she kept thinking, was the world coming to?

In his haven in the wrecked wing of the third floor, Chet was getting himself ready. He had rummaged through the wreckage near the nurses' station and come up with several packets of Tylenol. He had taken four at once, washing

303

them down with a carton of milk, then had pocketed the rest. He loaded the snub-nosed handgun to full capacity, then placed extra rounds of ammunition in his pocket, along with the Tylenol. For no reason other than that he liked the way it felt, he withdrew the knife from his waistband and ran his finger along the blade. He found the sharpness pleasing. Replacing the two weapons in the waistband, he got up and went in search of a safe way down.

One way or another, he was on his way out. But he was going to see Mick first. After his nap, he had resolved to do that. With his own eyes, he was going to see his little brother.

Chapter Seventeen

John Kitchen, RN, charge nurse in ICU, was in the process of making his own personal check of each of the eight patients currently on the unit. The ideal ratio for critical care patients was one to one. Unfortunately, staffing problems did not often permit that ratio to exist. Today, a ratio even close to that was impossible. He was on duty with only two other nurses in the ICU, and one was not really an RN, not technically. Until she received the results of her state board examinations, she was officially dubbed Graduate Nurse. But John felt he would trust Becky far more than he would Patricia, the other nurse. Patricia was flighty. Becky had both feet on the ground.

No longer young, John had seen his share of nurses and fancied he could spot the ones who had what it took. He had been a nurse himself a long, long time, beginning back when male nurses were a rarity and quite subject to suspicion. John Kitchen was not gay, nor was he soft. He had simply been what he still was: a man who knew what he wanted in life, and was not easily dissuaded from that course.

The patients on the unit today were varied, as they always were. Three heart-attack victims — they always had some of those. One with an acute CVA in evolution. A teenager who had been in a motor vehicle accident. A laborer who had a flailed chest from where heavy equipment had rolled onto him. A young woman who had mixed alcohol and sleeping

305

pills — whether accidentally or on purpose was yet to be ascertained — and who remained in a comatose state. And the eighth ICU patient was Michael Hamilton.

With painstaking attention to detail, John checked Mick's IVs to see that they were running properly. Except for the steady rise and fall of the young man's chest, there was no indication that he was alive. After checking the vital signs, the white-haired RN tried various stimuli on the patient: heat, cold, pinprick, a sharp pinch, the calling of his name. Nothing evoked a reaction. However, the monitors showed no adverse changes. Both the brain waves and the heart beat were hanging in there, with no undue flattening on either graph.

John stared down at the still and handsome face and thought, for the thousandth time since he had shown up to relieve the harried night crew, what a shame it was for a man to have come to this. It would save them all a lot of hassle if Mick's body were to give up the battle. But the body didn't know that, and didn't care, so it kept right on doing its work. A good-looking young guy, thought John. He was reminded of his own son, a boy about the age of this one. If it had been Gary lying there, if Gary had done what this young man had done, would he still have wanted him to die? Somewhere along the line, Michael Hamilton had had a chance . . . and had blown it. He shook his head and retreated back to the desk to chart his findings.

John Kitchen was not the only one who watched Mick Hamilton. From a distance, Chet had spotted his brother. Standing well back from the ward doors, willing himself to be as invisible as possible, Chet stared at the silent form hooked up to oxygen and IV fluids, with tubes running from his body in all directions. For security, he touched the weapons secreted under the loose, pajama-like top. In his pocket, along with the spare bullets and the analgesic tablets, he discovered another weapon: his Bic lighter. One flick of his Bic, and this oxygen-filled place would go up in flames. It was a thought . . . a good thought. Maybe even better as a threat than the bombs had been. Those bombs had been a real disappointment. He had favored setting off the one in the nursery and, when Mick went down, it had been lost to him. And he had so looked forward to seeing all those incubators and bassinets go flying through the air, their occupants with them. He had been disappointed with the one he had set off. Having just surveyed the damage to that wing first-hand, he felt extremely let down. It had made a mess, sure. It was going to take a lot of time and money to get that wing back like it should be. But it still wasn't as dramatic as he had wanted it to be.

But maybe it wasn't too late for dramatics.

He took two steps forward. No one paid any real attention. He was a young man in a scrub suit, nothing more, nothing less, to those around him who were too busy or too preoccupied to really look.

Chet felt the sweat break out on his forehead, but he did not feel hot. Quite the contrary; he felt cold and clammy. But he had to do what he had to do. At this point in time, he was all out of choices.

Walking rapidly, he entered the ward and moved closer to the patient rooms. Rooms on ICU were different than on the regular wards. No doors. Just large cubicles with the fronts wide open. Looking down the row, he could see all eight of the occupied beds. On occasion, curtains could be drawn around the beds for privacy or modesty. But no doors. Lots and lots of wide-open space — and lots and lots of oxygen running. A few more long strides, and he was at the foot of Mick's bed. He stood and stared down at the face so like his own. Funny, he had no real sense of it being Mick there. The monitors said Mick was alive, but he felt the monitors lied. The brother he had watched grow up no longer was.

John looked up from his charting, and blinked. The guy in Hamilton's room — it didn't look like anyone he knew. It was certainly no employee authorized to be that close to a critical-care patient. Then it hit him . . . that golden-red hair. He felt as if his own heart was behaving erratically. John made his living keeping watch over monitors, and at that moment he would have hated to be watching a rhythm strip of his own heartbeat. It might have led him to think his own demise was in the near future, if not from Chet Hamilton, then from his own betraying body.

These thoughts played across his mind, then were pushed aside. It was no time to think of himself. As always, patient care came first.

Chet saw that he had been spotted and so moved from near Mick's bed to the one in the next open-fronted cubicle. He doubted that anyone in St. Paul's gave a damn if they had to hurt Mick even more to get to him, but they might think twice about getting aggressive if an innocent patient lay between them.

John, in the minimal time allowed him, decided to act as if he did not recognize Hamilton. He realized he was in no position for a real confrontation—unarmed, surrounded by critically ill patients, and very short-staffed. Any fool could size up the situation in ICU and be able to tell there was no real danger from John and company.

"You from the lab?" he called. "I don't think anything is ordered on those two patients. It's best to come on away from them. They need their rest."

"Looks to me like they're getting it," Chet called back. "Never saw such a dead-looking crew. You sure these people are still alive?"

The other employees gathered around the desk became aware of the exchange, picking up that something was amiss. John's gaze swept over the four people near him, then he silently selected Becky. She was seated in such a way that it would have been impossible for Chet to spot her yet. Moreover she was small-statured, and, as he had been thinking just a few moments ago, she was steady.

On a tablet that lay on the desk in front of him, he scribbled: THAT'S CHET HAMILTON. GO FOR HELP. KEEP DOWN, AND CRAWL ON THE FLOOR TILL YOU'RE OUT THE DOOR. He held the pad up so that she could read it. And even as he did so, he kept the conversation going. "The people in here are very ill. That's why I'm having to ask you to leave."

"Guy in there's my brother. That surprise you?"

John tried not to watch as Becky slid off her chair and started on hands and knees toward the door. He swallowed. Funny how his throat was so full of lumps. Just a few minutes ago, it had felt fine. "Surprise me? I guess I hadn't thought about it. Come to think of it, you have the same color hair. You work here?"

Even over the distance that separated them, John could make out the strange expression on Chet's face. It was clear that he was trying to decide if John was for real or not. Maybe it was possible someone was that dumb . . . he could not tell for sure.

"This here's Mick Hamilton in the bed. Looks to me like he's just about a goner. And if he's Mick Hamilton, who does that make me?"

Swallowing again, John decided to give it one more try. Becky was out of sight now. Surely it wouldn't be long until help arrived, although he had not dared ask himself exactly what he thought help was going to be able to do if Chet decided, as he feared he had, to plant a patient between himself and everyone else.

"Look, you said you were his brother. That's okay with me. But I'm still going to have to ask you to leave. I just came on duty. I don't know this guy's relatives. I guess he was just brought in today, is that right?"

Chet gave a short laugh. "You're putting me on, right?"

John felt only a millimeter away from collapse. His knees felt like jelly, and he wondered how long they would continue to support him. Patricia was at his side, and he watched her from the corner of his eye—watched and worried. He was more aware of the funny little strangled sounds she was making than of his own none-too-stable state. In her own way, Patricia was as dangerous as Chet. With all his heart, he believed the woman foolish enough to do something stupid that would set off Hamilton.

STAY CALM AND KEEP QUIET! he wrote in big block letters on the tablet. He shoved it in her direction.

She nodded. But somehow he was not reassured, even though she seemed to understand.

As John continued the verbal parrying and stalling with Chet, Becky Luna eased her way through the swinging door that closed ICU off from the outside corridors. Tears streaming down her face, she pulled herself upright and took off running. The first people she encountered were Dr. Dvorak and her fellow nurse, Norma Mitchell.

"Becky, what is it?"

"Chet Hamilton — the one who took the hospital hostage — he's in ICU right now. John Kitchen is talking to him, trying to get him confused. But he's right by the bed of Peter Chandler, that kid who was in the MVA. I'm hunting for some police to tell now."

"Go on," Neil said, his voice as hard as nails, and suddenly very clear. "They're all over the place, so you should run into some right away. Just find them and tell them all you know about the situation, okay?"

Becky sniffed. She was crying because she couldn't help it. She *always* cried when she got excited. But that didn't mean she had lost her head. Laid-back Luna, that's what her colleagues in ICU called her. She was a good person to have around in a crisis, and she knew it.

As Becky took off, the rubber soles of her shoes making quiet thuds against the tile floors, Norma gripped the bar at the back of the wheelchair and tried to start moving her patient away. She encountered great resistance. The chair would not roll forward at all. "What the—" she started, then looked down. Her patient, the esteemed Dr. Dvorak, had his feet firmly planted on the floor, creating too much friction for the wheels to overcome.

"Give it up, Dvorak," she ordered.

310

"No way. I'm going that way."

She didn't have to see his nod in the direction from which Becky Luna had come to know what he meant.

"What do you think you can do in there, man? You're woozy. Half the time, you don't know if you're going or coming. You could do more harm in there than good."

"I'm okay now," he said gently. "That was the jolt I needed to get my adrenaline flowing enough to overcome all the garbage you pumped into my system—"

"On orders."

"Be that as it may, I'm okay now. And I'm going to ICU. Go help Becky . . . go tell every policeman or FBI agent you see that we have a Code Blue in ICU. Go on, I'm okay."

"I won't allow . . ."

At that, he was out of the wheelchair. He was not a very tall man, and his eyes were nearly on a level with hers. In those eyes, Norma saw purpose and determination. Whether he was right or wrong, she knew there was no stopping him. The giddy stranger was gone and the dignified doctor had returned in his place. The fact that he was unshaven, wearing a hospital gown, and with uncombed hair somehow did not diminish his dignity. Perhaps, in a curious way, it even intensified it.

Neil walked toward ICU without looking back. He could not afford to wait. Once the policemen appeared on the scene and crowded around, he could be stopped. He did not kid himself about that. He was unarmed, and physically fit policemen could restrain him and put him where they wanted him. And he was relatively sure that where they wanted him at the moment was not in ICU.

Like Chet and Mick, he had no game plan. Chet had started a wild game in which the rules were ever-changing. Neil had never fancied himself a superstitious man, not even back in his youth before he had become professional, a physician with so much knowledge at his disposal. However, from the beginning of this, before he had ever laid eyes on Chet

311

Hamilton, he had been possessed by an eerie feeling, a feeling he had not been able to shake. It was nothing that made any sense. He could not have explained it to anyone in a way that had any rhyme or reason. The fact was, he regarded this as *his* mission. He and Chet Hamilton were bound together in some unholy war, and all Neil knew was that it had to be a fight to the finish between the two of them.

Neil pushed open the door to the Intensive Care Unit. Advancing a few steps, he saw the sturdy, broad back of John Kitchen . . . and he also saw, though from a distance, the visage of Chet Hamilton. As he moved closer, he saw that the signs of strain he had observed in the supply room had greatly intensified. The young man looked old, was crumbling before their very eyes. Yet it was not to be reasonably hoped that he would crumble quite soon enough.

"Hey, Nursie-boy, look here," Chet called in a sing-song voice. He withdrew the Bic lighter from his pocket and gestured with it in the direction of the nearby oxygen tank. "I still got my gun and my knife, but it seems to me this might work the best."

"Depends on what you're trying to accomplish," John answered evenly.

"What I'm trying to accomplish? You should be able to figure that one out, Nursie. What I want is *out* of this friggin' place. I want a fair amount of money, and no one on my tail."

John turned up his hands in the classic gesture of helplessness. "You surely know *I* can't ensure that."

"But you can get the word to someone who can, right? The Feds know what I want. I got word to them a while back. In a minute, I'm going to let you renew that little demand for me. But first—"

Neil had opened his mouth to speak, to call attention to his presence and divert Chet away from the male nurse, a man who was exhibiting unbelievable calm and bravery. However, before he could voice the words he had planned, he heard the clear voice of Marianne Hamilton.

"You say you want money and to be allowed to leave, Chet. Is that all? Does that mean you've totally changed your mind about taking me with you?"

Wheeling around, Neil found he was close enough to her to reach out and touch her thin frame. But touch he did not. There was something very commanding about her presence — commanding, and very off-putting. To reach out and touch would have been an invasion of some sort.

"Marianne," he did manage to say softly, "get the hell out of here, while you still can."

His words did not reach her. She had eyes only for her husband and tormentor.

As dim and bleary as Chet's pale blue eyes were, they did light up somewhat. The look he gave his wife was a perfect caricature of a leer — a ghastly jack-o'-lantern grin. "Come back to me, have you? I knew you couldn't stay away. All those fancy words and fits and threats, but you always deep down inside knew where you belonged, didn't you? You always were mine, Marianne, and you always will be."

"Wrong, Chet. I was never *yours*. Neither were the kids. Not the way you mean. You treated us like things, but that only works for so long, because we aren't things. But I'll go with you. I'll do it to save these people in here. No one in this hospital has done anything but try to help. I'll come with you if you'll walk away now, and leave everyone else alone."

His laugh was harsh and unpleasant. "Maybe I changed my mind about wanting you. A woman takes a knife to her husband . . . well, what can she expect?"

"You didn't want me because you were taking me back, now did you? You wanted to punish me. So that's what I'm offering. I'll go, and take whatever punishment you want to deal out. You wanted a hostage. I'll be your hostage."

She took a step toward where Chet stood. Coming to life, Neil reached out and took her by the arm. His grip, he knew, was firm enough to hurt, should she decide to resist. She turned and looked at him, face puzzled, as if she could not

313

quite focus on who he was and what he wanted. Her eyes were filled with Chet, and there was no room for anything else.

Chet's voice rang out. "Let her go, Dvorak. Get your damned hands off her."

Neil heard approaching footsteps, sounding against the tile like the thundering of an entire herd of horses. It can't, he thought, be that loud. Due to his fear, and possibly the effect of the drug, he felt, some of his senses were intensified. He only knew that any action he wanted to take had to be immediate.

"Marianne," he said, his urgency communicating itself so that she looked at him, her awareness increasing, despite the softness of his voice. "Let me handle him. This is something I have to do."

"That's the way I feel, too. Can't you understand that? You've dealt with him only a few hours, and me . . . well, there are times I can't even remember what it was like before he entered my life."

"Cut it out," Chet called. "Shut up and speak where I can hear, you got it?" He had replaced the knife in his waistband and was brandishing the gun in one hand, the cheap lighter in the other.

Showing a surprising amount of strength, Marianne broke away from Neil and stepped forward. He lunged forward to grab her in a last-ditch effort to keep her away from Chet.

"Die, bitch!" The harsh words were followed by a sound so loud it nearly split his eardrums. Neil's hand met Marianne's and he closed his fingers tightly. Her hand was frail, so very frail—small-boned, and covered in skin unpadded by any adipose tissue. He grasped that fragile hand and, for a few seconds, felt the answering pressure of her fingers. She then slumped to the floor, and the hand encased by Neil's was still. He knew that if he let go, it would fade away and fall to her side, a dead weight.

With the roar of a wounded beast, Neil lunged forward again. The man he was facing was armed while he was not,

314

but that seemed to have no meaning. With what little reason he had left at that moment, he knew Chet could not use both hands effectively. His left shoulder was too severely injured for that arm to be of real use to him.

"I'm in this, too. And, by the way, the oxygen isn't on in that room. The kid doesn't require any."

Neil was vaguely aware of the voice that followed him, but when the sturdy, white-clad form of John Kitchen hurled itself toward Chet Hamilton, the vagueness vanished. The solid bulk of his ally was sweet reality.

Their eyes met, and they nodded. With movements unused since their high school days, they each crouched forward and, bent low, went after the knees of Chet Hamilton.

Chet hadn't believed they would do it. He had thought his gun, and the fact that he had used it on his wife, would be enough deterrent to such action — or, if not, there was the fear of an oxygen fire ignited by the Bic. As they grabbed his knees he fell to the floor, but was able to retain his grip on the weapons. Before they could knock the gun out of his hand — and he had not doubted that at two against one they could do so — he fired. He aimed at neither of them in particular; it was just a random shot. The impact of the second shot made his wrist tingle. He heard a cry and a thud, and knew he had found a target. Then a strong hand reached out, and the fingers grasped his right wrist and wrenched it. The twisting made him cry out in pain, and the small revolver dropped from his grip. Through eyes that no longer felt like his own, he saw his gun fall to the floor and another hand reach out and retrieve it.

Chet tried to get it back and was surprised to find he was free. Still on all fours, he kept moving toward the gun.

"Quit moving, or you're a dead man," he heard the voice of his arch enemy saying.

But like this arch enemy, Chet was beyond caring. He knew he was on his way out, but he was not about to make it easy for them. He crawled rapidly for a few feet, then turned slightly, still on his knees, and looked up into the face of Neil Dvorak. With all the strength he possessed, Chet headed toward the bed. His smile was strange, somehow curiously innocent, as he looked at Neil and said, "I'm gonna flick my Bic and I'm gonna take this patient out with me."

Neil nodded. With part of his mind, he was trying to remember what he knew of oxygen fires—how volatile they were, how rapidly they spread. In this weird game he had one bluff left, and he put all he had into using it.

In a voice as hard as nails, he said, "Then flick it, Chet, baby. You got mixed up and crawled in the wrong direction. The patient you're threatening to take with you as you die is your own brother. You think we care if he dies? It would have saved a lot of us a great deal of trouble if he'd died a few hours back."

A look of disbelief crossed Chet's tired face. "No way," he said. "You're bullshitting me." He placed his good hand on the edge of the bed, then pulled himself upward. A guttural sound issued from his throat when he saw that the face was not Mick's. Instead, it was the freckled face of a young woman, so deep in a drug-induced coma that she was oblivious to all that was happening around her. For a moment, the tiredness lifted and he felt alight with triumph. Facing Dvorak, he said, "You lied."

"Not about everything," Neil said, and then he fired. His bullet hit its mark, and the cigarette lighter shattered.

Chet stared down at his empty hand.

Neil turned and faced the bevy of policemen who had entered ICU and witnessed his battle with Hamilton. He handed the gun over to the uniformed person nearest him and, nodding toward Chet, said, "He's all yours. I'd like to kill him, so I'd better get rid of this." Turning to the other side, Neil joined the portly uniformed policeman kneeling beside John Kitchen.

"He's gone," the policeman said, in response to Neil's unspoken question. "Bullet got him in the neck."

Neil could see that now, could see the gaping hole where the bullet, at close range, had shattered the jugular vein. "Thanks, friend," he said softly, hoping that somehow, on some plane, John would hear him and know the gratitude came from his aching heart.

He became aware of a flurry of activity. He looked up to see two policemen rush forward and grab Chet Hamilton, but from where Neil stood it appeared that they did so more to steady him than to apprehend him. *The knife,* he thought immediately . . . and his eyes went to Chet's chest where, sure enough, bright red blood was soaking the surgical smock. Chet had finished what Marianne started. With a sharp upward thrust, he had entered the left ventricle. For him, it was over.

The nurse Patricia finally stopped screaming. Until she did, Neil had been unaware that she was doing so. Only the sudden silence spoke to him. Without her steady screeching, he could hear sobbing sounds in several octaves, sobbing by patients and by staff. Turning slightly from side to side, Neil took it all in. An elderly patient, rendered mute by his recent CVA, cried without sound. Fear was in his eyes. Despite his many infirmities, the will to live existed there. Patricia sobbed quietly. An aide had thrown a glass of water in her face to stop her screaming. She mopped at it angrily, still unwilling to admit she had been out of control.

"Mick's monitor," he heard another aide say, "it's stopped. Should I call a code zero?"

When it registered on Neil that she was speaking to him, that no other physician was present, he said, "No. No code zero. He's gone. Let him stay gone. No matter what we do, there's no way he can survive much longer. Let it be."

Walking slowly away, he passed the silent form of Marianne Hamilton. More than anything else, her death hurt him. Maybe Dr. Singer had been right. Maybe he was more in love, inexplicably so, than he had known. Or maybe he had merely recognized in her a strong spirit, a keen intelligence, and a human being who just needed a chance to fulfill her own potential. He had hoped for her . . . God, how he had hoped for her! And Chet had taken it away from him, from them both.

No matter how civilized we believe ourselves to be, he thought, we revert to the behavior of jungle animals at times. He had once thought himself an exception. Now he knew he was not an exception.

Somewhere out there were three kids who needed to be seen to. He had felt a tie to Marianne, an obligation to her. Now that tie had been passed to the next generation. Before he went home, he wanted to go explain it to Julie.

Somehow he felt that she would understand, that she would say, "I know. I'll go with you. I'm going to help if you'll let me."

And he would let her. Hell, maybe he would even see if he could bring her home for a while to recuperate. He was not invincible, and no longer wanted to stand alone.

He looked at the clock. Ten A.M. Who would have thought so much could happen to St. Paul's in just ten hours?

"Where are you going, Dr. Dvorak?" someone said.

"Home," he said firmly, "but I have a stop to make first. I'd stay, but I'm too far gone at the moment to be of help. I'm sure other help is on its way. Carry on, all of you. I'm sure you'll do well. You see, it's over now. It's all over."

He said these words on his way out, but he did not believe his own pronouncement. In some ways, it had just begun.